The Sta

Judith Glover

CORONET BOOKS
Hodder and Stoughton

Copyright © 1982 by Judith Glover

First published in Great Britain 1982
by Hodder & Stoughton Ltd

Coronet edition 1984

British Library C.I.P.

Glover, Judith
    The stallion man.
    I. Title
    823'.914[F]   PR6057.L64

    ISBN 0-340-35473-9

Printed and bound in Great Britain for
Hodder and Stoughton Paperbacks, a
division of Hodder and Stoughton Ltd.,
Mill Road, Dunton Green, Sevenoaks,
Kent (Editorial Office: 47 Bedford
Square, London, WC1 3DP) by
Cox & Wyman Ltd., Reading

"For the wages of sin is death."

Romans VI : 23

1

In the churchyard someone was laughing.

Rachael glanced down through one of the high arched windows illuminating the gallery of All Souls Church and saw a dark-haired man, playfully pulling a woman behind him along the overgrown path. For a moment she watched them, then remembered herself and gave her attention once more to the Reverend Esmond Bates, delivering the morning sermon from the pulpit.

The clear March light through the stained glass irradiated the curate's handsome features as he addressed himself to the back of the congregation, and from her solitary place in the gallery above Rachael wryly observed an expression almost of rapture on the faces of several of the female parishioners as they followed his dramatic oration.

Two years ago, she, too, had sat among the pews in the nave gazing up at that tall, slim figure in cassock and pleated surplice, secretly wondering how great a sin it was to nurture such carnal thoughts about Mr Bates when her mind should be turned to the service and worship of God. Now, as she looked at him standing so nobly in the pulpit, she no longer entertained dreams and secret fantasies. The magic of his voice had lost its power even to hold her attention from a stranger's laughter in the churchyard.

She glanced away again, out through the window beside her. As recently as the end of the 1840s the church had undergone repairs, but funds had run low by the time it came to reglaze the gallery windows. In place of the leaded lights they had had to make do with panes of clear glass, affording those who sat there a view of the old part of All Souls burial ground.

The graves here were mostly Georgian, imposing

monuments to the many prosperous families already estab-
lished in Lewes a century ago: massive flat-topped table
tombs surrounded by iron railings and inscribed with the
names of generations of Sussex yeomen and merchants. For
some years this part had been neglected in favour of the
new cemetery, regarded as more fashionably suited to the
new Victorian era; and grass now grew rankly between un-
pruned bushes, railings were broken down or missing
altogether, and many of the tombs were overgrown with lichen
and ivy, their proud inscriptions obliterated and forgotten.

The man whose laughter had distracted Rachael's
attention was still in sight. He had moved away from the path
and was now standing close to his companion, a young
woman partly hidden by the sweeping branches of an ever-
green. He was looking towards the church, smiling, teeth
gleaming under heavy moustaches, eyes beneath level black
brows half-closed in pleasure. Rachael had never seen him
before. He was dressed in the hard-wearing clothing of a farm
worker, and would be in his early thirties.

She watched him catch the young woman by the waist and
press her to him, kissing her eagerly on the mouth while his
hand moved to the back of her uncovered head and released
her hair from the confines of its pins, freeing it about her
shoulders. The woman attempted to pull away, moving her
head this way and that to escape his kisses, but he held her
fast in his arms, the black curly head bent into the curve of
her neck.

Rachael felt the colour flooding into her cheeks. Quickly,
embarrassed lest someone should catch her watching, she
turned towards the pulpit, and realised that the preacher had
come to the end of his sermon. His head, too, was bent, but
silently in prayer. She collected herself and picked up her
hymn book from the rail in front of her.

Esmond Bates cleared his throat.

"Now let us sing together hymn number 545: 'Glorious
things of thee are spoken, Zion, city of our God'."

The congregation rose shuffling and coughing to its
feet as the old organ wheezed into the opening bars of
music.

8

Rachael sang with them; but after a while she found herself unable to resist the temptation to glance down into the churchyard again. The couple were still there, she saw, but they had moved a little way off into the overgrowth of bushes, the woman leaning up against a flat-topped tomb. Her companion was pressed against her, his hands on either side of her hips gripping the slab so that she was imprisoned within his arms. She was no longer struggling. He seemed to be whispering in her ear; and in a while her own arms came slowly up about his waist and held him to her.

A small pulse began to throb in Rachael's throat as she stared, fascinated, unable to tear her gaze from what was taking place.

The black-haired man lifted the woman backwards so that she lay across the lid of the old tomb, half-screened by bushes. There was a glimpse of the pale flesh of her thigh as he raised the long skirts and pushed them up around her waist, and after a moment he leaned himself forward so that the upper part of his muscular body covered hers.

She stretched her arms out above her, languorously almost; and then her head began to twist from side to side, the loose hair catching amongst the tendrils of ivy, her mouth opening on a soundless cry.

Rachael's eyes burned. She had witnessed other couples openly making love, but never like this. Those others had been poor undernourished creatures, befuddled men and wanton women reeling out of public houses in the lower parts of the hilly town. But this pair were young and vigorous, their appetites fired not by drink but by a healthy pleasure of the senses. In her dreams Rachael had once dared to hope that this would be how she and her husband might be together, passionate and uninhibited; and for the first few months of their marriage she had tried, artlessly, to draw response from him to her own half-awakened needs.

He had not reacted as her innocent fantasies had led her to imagine any husband would; and not at all in the same way as the man out in the churchyard. It puzzled and distressed her. She knew that she was attractive, and she would have

9

thought desirable. Her husband was older than she, but he was little more than forty and she had heard of men well into their sixties who had fathered children.

But she had never tried to discuss the subject. He disliked any talk of intimate matters.

Rachael realised suddenly that the hands holding her hymn book were trembling and her throat had gone so dry that she could scarcely find voice for the amen. The congregation rustled to its knees for prayer. Replacing the book on the rail as she got down, she became aware that the minister was watching her from below, and even from this distance she caught something of the censure in his pale eyes.

She drew a deep, uneven breath and forced herself to smile down at him. It would not do for her to seem distracted from her husband's service.

The Reverend Esmond Bates saw his wife's smile before her face was hidden by the black bonnet as she bent her head. He had noticed her gazing through the window, obviously caught up by whatever it was she watched out there instead of attending to the solemnity of worship. A small frown marked the high, white forehead as he began to read the prayer for the Queen's Majesty.

"O Lord our heavenly father, high and mighty, King of kings, Lord of lords, the only ruler of princes, who dost from thy throne behold all the dwellers upon earth; most heartily we beseech thee with thy favour to behold our most gracious sovereign lady, Queen Victoria; and so replenish her with the grace of thy Holy Spirit that she may always incline to thy will and walk in thy way . . ."

When the service was over, Rachael came down from the gallery to wait for her husband at the rear of the nave, exchanging greetings with the congregation as they filed out into the porch. Her youth prohibited some of the older people from paying her more than brief acknowledgment; and two or three of the women scarcely more than glanced at her as they went by. She suspected that their unfriendliness stemmed from resentment that she, of all the spinsters

10

in All Souls parish, had been chosen by the curate for his wife.

But there were many more who stopped to exchange a word or two with the quiet, gravely beautiful girl before leaving the church. Rachael had a soft, slightly husky voice that was warm and sympathetic and a natural manner that made each person she spoke to feel that they had been especially singled out for her attention; and her caring attitude was much appreciated by the infirm and needy of the parish. The vicar's wife, Mrs Bethway, came a very poor second in their esteem, a woman whose curt tone and severe expression reflected all too faithfully her nature.

Rachael turned as her husband approached. He made a distinguished figure, as well as handsome, the black of the frock-coat and trousers contrasting with the fairness of his smooth hair; but he did not return her smile.

"The service went well, Esmond." She took his arm. "I think your sermon was much appreciated."

Esmond Bates glanced about him. There was no one left inside the church now, apart from one of the sidesmen, an assistant churchwarden, at the other end; and he did not bother to lower his voice as he answered, "It is the more to be regretted, then, that you yourself should find it less than absorbing."

Her cheeks coloured at the rebuke and her hand fell back. "But I did."

"Really? A great pity we could not afford the stained glass. Those clear windows are so conducive to distraction. Perhaps it would help your concentration if in future you sat among the congregation here below."

"But Mrs Bethway sits in the gallery. Why shouldn't I, in her absence?"

"You know the vicar's wife keeps a register of parishioners attending. Since it would not do for her to be seen counting them out at the door like so many sheep, she does it discreetly from above. She does not choose to seat herself there in order to be diverted at moments of tedium by anything down in the churchyard. What was it, by the way?"

Rachael bit her lip. He would be horrified if she told him.

"Forgive me, Esmond. I didn't realise. If I've offended you, I'm truly sorry for it."

Her husband placed a hand lightly on her shoulder, a gesture of conciliation. "Very well. Now if you wish to walk on a little, I will catch up with you along the path. There is something I still have to attend to before I leave."

She nodded and moved away.

Once beyond the church porch she paused, though, enjoying the clean freshness of the air after the stuffy smell of old stone and wood. The warmth of early spring sunlight was pleasant on her shoulders through the black woollen shawl. She tilted back her head and closed her eyes; but the scene she had witnessed was still so vivid in her mind that after a moment curiosity overcame her, and looking around to find herself alone, she left the path and walked quickly over to the corner of the tower where a wicket gate led into the old churchyard.

The place seemed deserted. The dark-haired man and his companion must have seen the people coming out of church, and gone.

Just as she was turning away again, Rachael's attention was arrested by something moving on the far side of a tangle of sweetbriar. She hesitated; and a figure slowly came into view. It was the young woman. Rachael's eyes widened as she recognised Charlotte Smith, who had only recently taken up work as nursery minder at the dame school in Frog Lane.

She came on at a leisurely pace across the rough grass, her head bent, her hands up to fasten back her hair, a straw bonnet swinging by its ribbon from her wrist. The hem of her skirts was heavy with damp and the dark material was marked in places with golden smears of lichen.

"Oh!"

She looked up, startled to find someone there. Then, seeing only the curate's wife, she gave a little laugh. "It's you, Mrs Bates."

Rachael returned the greeting and waited for her to pass

through the gate. Already in those few moments of surprise she had decided to say nothing of what she had seen during the service. It was too private a thing to be spoken of; it would only cause embarrassment.

The two fell into step and moved on a little way together.

"You've been walking in the long grass?" Rachael asked lightly. "Your skirts are quite damp."

"Oh—why, so they are." Charlotte's eyes flickered downwards to the tell-tale stains. "I hadn't noticed." She paused, casting her mind round for some excuse, then went on hurriedly, "It was so close inside the church . . . I come out halfway through the service to get some air. The walk freshened me. I wanted to be by myself, and nobody goes into that part nowadays, do they?"

"None who should. But I believe undesirable men sometimes get in. Do take care, Miss Smith. It's rather lonely there and if you came to harm you might not be able to make anyone hear."

Charlotte smiled. She adjusted her bonnet and said, "Thank you, ma'am. I must remember that in future." Then, seeing the Reverend Bates emerging from the porch, she turned away and began to walk rapidly along the path.

By the time the curate and his wife had reached the lychgate at the further end she was already out of sight.

2

The shadow of the black stallion fell across the mouth of the barn, touching the face of the young woman concealed just within. She shivered suddenly and drew herself further back among the bales of straw, where dusty shafts of sunlight pierced the dimness and glinted on the red of her hair.

Dinah Flynn had no words to explain what it was about the great horse that filled her with such primitive awe; but his closeness and the rank smell of his sweat sent a prickle of fear through her, heightened by the sense of his excitement as he caught the warm in-season odour of the mare being led in across the yard.

"Easy now, Regent . . . slow, boy."

The man leading the stallion spoke softly. Hearing him, the woman edged cautiously forward again, her long skirts dragging in the straw underfoot, moving almost furtively to the barn door where she stood half-hidden in shadow, following his confident handling of the restless black Shire. Her eyes rarely left his face.

She had watched the pair of them before, in other yards on other farms, and each time had been struck by the physical likeness of the leader to his stallion. The same deep-chested muscular body, the same swarthiness, the same impression of compact strength. Not only the physical likeness, either. There was also the shared resentment of any kind of restraint; and the potent, impatient attraction to the opposite sex.

The stallion whinnied harshly and began to plunge against the restraining halter to reach the mare on the other side of the barrier—the trying bar—set across the middle of the yard. Alarmed by the sounds and the pungent smell, she tried to pull free of the two farm men at her head, the whites of her eyes glistening as the stallion was finally led round behind her.

It was a noisy business. In a while he rose up into the air, forelegs curving, and after several attempts came down heavily on her back. The woman watching from the shadows marvelled, as she always did, that any creature could carry his thrusting weight on her hindquarters without being forced to the ground.

In one swift, practised movement the stallion leader guided the shaft towards the mare. It was necessary when time was short and there were others still waiting to be covered by the Shire. He watched dispassionately for a time, dark eyes narrowed under strong brows; then he grinned at the two men steadying the mare's head. They grinned back, but there was respect in their expression as well.

"Is the water ready?" he asked. "We'll be needing it in a minute."

Above him, the stallion grunted twice, then reared up away from his mate, forehooves striking noisily against the cobbles as he came down.

"Quick, now—seal her off!"

Avoiding the spent stallion, the more agile of the two handlers snatched up the pail of water set ready by the yard wall and dashed the contents over the mare's swollen share, the sudden cold douche causing her to clamp her muscles and effectively, if crudely, sealing in the stallion seed.

"There. That's done."

The leader wiped the palms of his hands across the front of his corduroy breeches and pushed back a curling strand of dark hair from his eyes. He motioned to one of the men.

"You can lead him off now. Don't look so blasted nervous, man! He's as tame as a chick afterwards." He tossed the halter rein over. "Here. Let him rest quiet for a bit. He's earned it."

The sharp air sounded to the heavy breathing of the horses and the scrape of hooves as they were led from the yard; then the noises died away and there was a silence, broken only by the buzz of flies around the midden and the distant clucking of hens. The stallion leader pushed himself casually away from the trying bar and went over towards the barn, smiling to himself.

"Dinah?" he called.

There was a swift movement and the red-haired woman came from behind the door and into his arms.

"Silly girl," he murmured against her hair. "Hiding yourself away. One of these days I shan't be able to find you."

"Mebbe one o' these days you won't be looking for me, Frank." She flung back her head and stared up into his amused face. "You're late coming this month. I've waited near a week. What kept you?"

It was almost an accusation.

Instead of replying, he kissed her hard on the mouth. He had discovered long ago that kisses answered women better than any words, however tenderly spoken. After a moment or two he released her and said, "Well now, beauty, what's the news in Weatherfield? Anything happening while I've not been here?"

When she did not answer at once he looked at her. Her eyes were lowered.

"What is it, Dinah?"

"Don't be angry wi' me. I—I'm breeding again."

His smiled slipped to a grimace as he looked down at her body. Slowly he said, "Aye. So I see. When?"

"End o' May, I reckon. Frank . . ." She faltered, but found fresh courage and began again. "Frank, why won't you marry me? I'll be in real trouble this time if you don't. They say there's a new parson coming to the village. What if he reckons to send me to Heathbury workhouse? I could never bear that, you know I couldn't."

He took her hands and held them firmly within his own. "Nobody's going to send you to the workhouse. Why should they? You don't cost the parish nothing."

"Mebbe not. But who's to know what might become o' me wi' this new man here? Mebbe he won't be the kind to look the other way, not like old Yardley. He's only got to call me out in church for loose living and the parish overseer would have me out o' Weatherfield faster'n I could run."

Frank Morgan shook his head, but she persisted.

"There was a girl only the other week over at Shatterford. They church-named her a wanton and whore when her second chance-born come. And d'you know what they did beside? They took both her babies off her and gi' them to the foundling home . . ."

Her voice broke suddenly and she put a hand to her mouth.

". . . poor creature . . . they put her in the workhouse . . . so she killed herself. Took a bit o' broken glass and she cut her own throat. Oh God, I don't want anything like that happening to me. Frank—Frank, you *must* marry me now. Please,

16

you've got to do it. I don't want to lose my babies . . . Not the workhouse, not that place. Anything but that."

The stallion leader released the hands clinging desperately to his shoulders and pushed her gently from him, holding her there while he spoke, his tone as soft as when he had soothed his horse.

"Now, Dinah, let's have no more talk like that. You needn't fear, it'll never happen. It's only those without means to support themselves who get sent off to the workhouse. And I'll always see you're all right for money, you know that. They can't touch you so long as you're not a charge on the parish. As for us marrying—now you know it'd be no life for you as a wife. It's the truth, and you needn't look at me like that. How many times have we had this over? You've said it yourself. It'd be no life at all for a woman to be following the stallion circuit, going from one farm to another year in, year out. Besides,"—he glanced at her body—"babies need a roof above 'em, a home to grow in. You be thankful you have one here with your mother."

Dinah lowered her head and examined her ringless fingers, twisting them fretfully. "Aye, lucky my mam was never wed neither, I suppose, else I'd have been without a place to turn to when little Frankie come. Even so, Frank, that's no reason for you to use me so ill—"

She caught her lips between her teeth. Then, suddenly, flung herself away from him.

"You don't care for me, Frank Morgan—you never did! It was all words, words, till you got what you wanted from me You're so free wi' your money, aren't you—yet you won't even pay out three farthings for the scrap o' paper the marriage licence is on!" She clenched her fist against her swelling belly. "So how many does this 'un make, then? How many other women give you the same news this season?"

Frank Morgan stared into her flushed, angry face, the eyes bright with unshed tears; but he made no reply. Could not. Until he had travelled back through the villages on last season's stallion round he would not know the answer. Instead, he reached out and drew her wordlessly towards him, pressing her head into his shoulder and feeling the shudder of her weeping.

Not that Morgan had fathered many bastards. He had always taken care, using a trick learned years ago from a stallion leader up in the Midlands, and could generally take his pleasure without causing mischief. Which was just as well, since most of his partners, in common with their more respectable sisters, were woefully ignorant of any means whereby pregnancy could be avoided.

His profession seemed to make him irresistible to the ladies. It was the thrill of the danger, he supposed, coupled with the sheer animal attraction of the trade. Wherever he went in the country, leading his great black stallion from yard to yard to cover the mares for prime young stock, he could be sure of a welcoming bed.

He liked the married kind of female best. Experience had taught him that they were less demanding, less ready to lose their hearts; and, more to his advantage, provided ready-made families for the swarthy little cuckoos he might chance to leave in their nests—all boys (he prided himself that he had never once sired a daughter) and so healthy and vigorous that the proxy fathers, even if they suspected anything, seemed content to allow practicality and pride to stifle their misgivings.

Frank Morgan had started working with stud horses when he was just ten years of age (it was the year George the Fourth died) and that was over twenty summers ago. He had had a lot of women in that time, but never one he had cared for as much as he did Dinah Flynn. Dinah, she was different. She had been his one failing. Several times, usually when he was away in some other part of the country, lonely for her and in his cups, he had thought of marrying her. But he had inherited a strong sense of independence along with his mother's gipsy blood and tended to laugh at himself for such sentimentality once the drink wore off.

In any case, it had not been the same since their son, little Frankie, was born. Dinah had started to cling too much, as women do when they love and fear they are not loved enough in return; wanting to follow him about the countryside on the

18 .

stallion round, questioning him about where he had been, complaining when he stayed away too long, demanding his attention and affection. He was beginning to tire of her.

He gave a half-sigh of regret and held her closer against him, pitying her in spite of his thoughts.

"I am sorry," he said, discomforted by her tears. "But you know the way it is. I could no more stay true to you than—well, than Regent could to that mare just now. It isn't in my nature. So what kind of a marriage would that be for us, eh?"

She raised her tear-streaked face. "I know, Frank . . . I know how it has to be wi' you . . . but I do love you."

"Hush, there now. I'll be back soon, you'll see. And I'll not leave you short of money for little Frankie and the new baby."

Her voice was low. "Just so long as you do come back."

He pinched her cheek and grinned. "Don't I always?"

All the fighting spirit seemed suddenly to have drained from her. In barely more than a whisper she said, "I have to get back. They'll be starting the evening milking and I'll be missed."

"George Bashford won't mind, surely? He's a fair master."

Dinah shrugged and turned away. And without another word or a backward glance she went quickly from him across the yard and out through the gate leading on to the hill path.

Morgan watched her go. A fly buzzed around the sweat streaking his brow and he brushed at it impatiently, his eyes never leaving the woman as long as he could see her. There was something about the proud set of the head, the strong back, the sway of the hips that reminded him of a girl he had had in Lewes this last month. The memory brought a smile to the firm mouth beneath the black moustache. What was her name? He thought for a moment. No, he couldn't remember. Not that it mattered. They were all so many women to him, so many soft compliant bodies and warm lips for him to enjoy.

That girl in Lewes had been like the rest. He had met her in the market square while they were watching a muzzled old bear dance at the end of a chain. They had started to talk; he suggested some refreshment. Later, as they walked together along a lane, she had laughed and taken his arm.

"You are the most beautiful woman I have ever seen in my life," he said. They always liked to hear that.

Afterwards, when they had finished their lovemaking in some nearby churchyard, he had promised to meet her again the following day, swearing that the hours would drag unbearably until he could be with her again. But when the appointed time came, he had been well away along the road to Buckfield, idly wondering whether she would be standing there, waiting for him in the churchyard. She was a fool if she was, to trust a man so.

Frank Morgan had no conscience about the women he had used and abandoned in this fashion. He reckoned he owed them nothing. There had never been one yet who had found him less than the most skilful and satisfying of lovers. He prided himself on a virility to match his stallion's; but he was no brutal ravisher, interested only in his own enjoyment. He knew that by giving a woman as much pleasure as he took from her, he would always be fondly remembered. He had yet to meet one who could resist his advances for long. The day that happened, he told himself sometimes, would be the day they could shovel him into the cold earth, where men and women stayed quiet in their own beds.

It had been the same with his father, Seth Morgan. Seth had been one of the finest stallion leaders of his time; also one of the best barefist boxers, remembered throughout the country as readily when men talked of prize fighting as when they did of horses.

He had been a rare one for the ladies; until he fought a match with Gipsy Jack Lee. He had lost that fight and lost his heart as well, to Lee's sister, a black-haired, black-eyed beauty who had ignored all his overtures and made his existence a hell, so that he finally made the greatest sacrifice a footloose ladies' man could make, and married her.

Frank Morgan had only the haziest recollection of his father. He had been little more than three years old when Seth had taken a bad punch in a fight. He had lingered on for a week without ever regaining consciousness. His gipsy wife had grieved for a while; but she was a woman who could not sleep long in an empty bed, and after a time Frank found himself with a stepfather.

They hated each other from the start, more so as the boy grew older and better able to stand up for himself. Finally, when he was ten, his mother had sent him away into the care of one of Seth's old partners and he had learned to work with horses like his father, and grew to be a stallion man himself.

The only real security and affection he had known in his young life was during this period, in country stables and inn yards, from rough, coarse-mouthed horsemen; and his later attitude towards the weaker sex was strongly coloured by the experience of these formative years. There was no scope to respond to feelings he had never had the chance to discover: tenderness, gentleness, love. His compassion was reserved for the horses in his charge, and as he grew older he came to believe that these were the only living creatures a man might rely on never to betray him.

The hovering fly settled on Frank Morgan's cheek. He slapped at it absentmindedly, his thought turning to what Dinah had said just now, about a new man moving into the rectory at Weatherfield.

Where there were clergymen there were generally wives, and very often daughters. Plain and pious and prim most of them were, too, as though the embracing of religious belief poisoned their natures to all other forms of embrace; but from time to time he had known the pulpit to produce a Jezebel from among its Susannas. Morgan was no respecter of class and held no man his superior, especially members of the clergy, a profession he had little time for. If there was a pretty face up at the rectory it might be amusing to find out whether it knew how to smile at a man.

The fly alighted on him for the last time. The smack of his rough palm scarcely stung his cheek, but it crushed the insect. He looked at its squashed remains, wiped his hand on his thigh, and strolled off, whistling, to the stables.

3

"It *is* settled, then?" Rachael repeated incredulously. "We really are going?"

Esmond Bates nodded. Following a vestry meeting with the vicar, Mr Bethway, he was able to confirm that the Bishop had agreed to his being appointed to the living of Weatherfield, a small rural parish on the edge of the Ashdown Forest.

It would be his first experience of a farming community. Esmond had entered the Church comparatively late, having spent the earlier years of his life as a schoolmaster at St Albans. Hitherto he had worked only in urban parishes. His first curacy had been served in a town in Staffordshire, his second here at All Souls in Lewes. The appointment to rector was a step up the ecclesiastical ladder; but more than that, Rachael's first thought had been, a chance to make for them both a better domestic life.

"At last! Oh, Esmond—a home of our own at last!"

She was like a child again in her excitement. She had never felt happy or at ease in these rented rooms in Lewes, accommodation considered by her husband's superiors well suited to a curate, but cheerless, with an atmosphere unsettled by too many short-term tenants. Perhaps it was that that was responsible for the difficulty which had so far blighted their relationship.

"When do we leave? Soon?"

Esmond saw the happiness shining in her face and was loath to spoil it.

"Do you know?" she persisted. "Do tell me. When is it to be?"

"Easter."

"Easter? But that's not for another month!"

"These things cannot be rushed. No one has yet been appointed to fill my position here, and Mr Bethway cannot be expected to manage the parish singlehanded because his curate has an impatient wife."

"Impatient! Esmond, I've had to endure almost two years of these miserable rooms. Two years of trying to make this garret into some kind of a home for us. Look at it still—almost as gloomy and depressing as the day Mrs Bethway first brought me to see it. And you call me impatient. I tell you, once we're out of this place I never want to see it again."

Rachael looked around her, at the shabbiness of it all. She had been eighteen years old when she and Esmond Bates first met, and nineteen when they married. She had sold the linen shop inherited from the elderly aunt who had raised her, and with the money they were able to buy the few necessary items to make a home, with a little left over for saving.

Though Esmond was twice her age he had never cared for material things, putting his love of scholarship first, sacrificing comfort for books, preferring to make do with threadbare belongings instead of spending his limited income on what he considered the superfluous luxuries of domestication. A bachelor's spartan lodgings had always been enough for his needs. A bachelor's life, too, although he had not realised it.

He did what instinct told him was right. He put his arms about his wife's slender body and drew her to him, resting his cheek against the softness of her hair.

"Easter will not be long coming, dearest. A few weeks, and then a new start. A new life—a better life—for us both."

She clung to him, her eyes closed, feeling the gentle pressure of his embrace and yearning for his arms to hold her tighter. As tightly and possessively as the unknown man had held his woman in the churchyard. She turned her head so that her mouth was against his; but the kiss he gave was no more than a light caress, and then he released her, his arms falling to his side.

"Esmond . . ."

"My dear?"

She stood in the middle of the ill-lit room, her eyes full of an unrequited hunger which her lips were forbidden to name. Although she could not shape it into words, something of her quickening desire communicated itself to her husband. His expression altered, hardened, and he turned away from her.

"I must prepare myself for Evensong."

She watched him go, his footsteps sounding hollow on the bare staircase beyond the door. The breath she drew was almost a sob as she clenched her hands together, pressing them hard against her breast, willing herself back into self-control.

But her body betrayed her. Sightlessly, she continued to stare towards the doorway while fantasy insidiously filled her mind with the image of a black-haired man lowering himself upon a woman snared in ivy.

Unbuttoning his black frock-coat, Esmond Bates went slowly over to the low sash window lighting the cramped space that made do for a bedroom, bending his head to avoid the bulge of warped ceiling rafters. For a while he stood looking out across the neighbouring rooftops at the setting sun where it hung cherry-red on the rim of a gable, balanced like a conjuror's ball above the irregular shadows of chimney stacks striping the bareness of slates and tiles.

The coat now hung limply by its collar from his hand. Imperceptibly, the dying rays crept from the corner of the window across his motionless figure, pitilessly picking out the darning on the elbow of his shirt, the frayed tabs securing the clerical stock, the shine of wear on the collar encircling his throat.

There was no expression of pleasure on his face. Rather, it was drawn down, for Esmond had no wish to go to Weatherfield. Were it possible to remain here in Lewes in other, better accommodation, he would have grasped at the chance and thanked God for it. He was an urban creature, urban by habit, inclination and custom, and the thought of

24

moving away into the isolation of a country parish filled him with bleak misgiving.

What did he know of rural life? Nothing. He had asked; of course he had asked, made enquiries about what differences he would find, what difficulties he would meet with, ministering to men and women who, by the very nature of their lives, were unlettered, unsophisticated, governed by superstition, incurious of the changes coming about so rapidly in the towns.

He enjoyed Lewes immensely. It was an ideal place for a man of his leaning and temperament: a centre of progress, advancing firmly and confidently into the second half of the nineteenth century. Its trade was prospering, its industry flourished, its slums were being swept away, its people given the advantages of modern institutions to encourage their education, health and moral welfare.

In particular he valued the libraries, the literary societies and debating clubs; and his most fulfilling work was the supervision of adult classes at which those thirsting for a knowledge of the Lord met together to study the Scriptures and their teaching.

What scope would there be for such rewarding ministry now? To go from all this to some rural confinement—to be miles from anywhere buried among fields and woodland, in a parish unaffected by the movement of the times but following still a way of life virtually unchanged since the Middle Ages—it would be akin to removing himself to the dark side of the moon.

But go he must. The change had to be made, however reluctantly, for Rachael's sake, for the sake of her happiness and the salvation of their marriage. For his own salvation, too. He must not, he told himself grimly, allow himself to become too content. Never that. He was a man who did not permit the pleasure of self-satisfaction, believing that the sins of the past could only be expiated by suffering and sacrifice in the present.

The red sunset had died now, the warmth of its light replaced within the tiny garret room by the cold shadows of early evening. The whole house was silent. From the street far below came the clip of horse hooves and the rumble of iron cart-tyres; and somewhere in the neighbourhood the strains of a barrel organ drifted up in faint, tinkling echoes.

A sudden feeling of desolation came over Esmond and he turned from the window to the deal-wood washstand in the corner.

On the shelf behind stood several of Rachael's pots: Rowland's Kalydor lotion, eau de quinine for her hair, a toothpaste made of areca nut and ground cuttlefish bone which she insisted on applying every day, contrary to his advice. Once a week was ample enough if one used the paste in conjunction with the softened end of a wooden probe.

He lifted the chipped ewer and poured himself half a bowl of water. It was cold and the piece of coal-tar soap refused to lather. He was about to call down to his wife to have more heated up on the kitchen range when his glance was arrested by the mirror on the wall above. In the half-light the image was distorted by shadows, and for a moment it was as though it were his father's face that stared back at him.

Esmond Bates had been born in 1810 in St Albans in Hertfordshire, the only child of a schoolmaster whose profession he was later briefly to follow.

From his earliest years the only emotions he experienced towards this man were ones of fear and hatred. Reared in accordance with his father's rigidly strict Fundamentalist beliefs, the happiness of a normal childhood was denied him. There was no laughter in the house: laughter was a wickedness. There was no affection: affection was the first step to sensualism. There was no freedom, no time when young Esmond might put aside his books and go out to join his friends. He had no friends. He had no leisure. Every waking moment must be spent in obedience to his father's will; and if he ever dared to act contrary to that will he was stripped and bound across the table in the study and flogged with a cane until the blood ran down his naked legs.

Flogging was his father's chief appetite, next to praying. He flogged his pupils for the slightest misdemeanour, he flogged his servants for the good of their souls; he flogged his wife on occasion, reasoning that like horses and dogs, women were all the better for their master's beating.

For the first eight years of this miserable childhood, Esmond's one source of refuge and consolation was his mother. Like her husband, Jerusha Bates directed her life within the rules laid down by Fundamentalist teaching; but in her case those rules were softened by natural maternal instinct. Though never allowing herself physical contact with the boy—kisses and caresses were Satan's sign of a lustful nature—yet she smiled at him often and spoke gently, and would sometimes weep with him over the pain of his father's chastisement.

But Jerusha died; and from the age of nine Esmond lived alone with servants in his father's house, cut off from any source of tenderness.

It was about this time the seeds of hatred first began to bear fruit, though in small ways. Paltry thefts from the desks of fellow pupils, exaggerations that could scarcely be called lies, a window broken, a box of pencils deliberately mislaid. All went unremarked; and as he matured into early manhood he remained outwardly a faithful reflection of the elder Bates.

But those seeds continued to flourish in the private darkness of his thoughts and from the age of seventeen his rebellion showed itself more openly. He began seeking out the poorer quarters of St Albans, the narrow, medieval alleys and closes whose crumbling tenements harboured the detritus of the town.

When his days of schooling were completed, Esmond became an assistant teacher to his father; and no one seeing them together, so alike it seemed in heart and body and mind, could ever have suspected that when the younger man went up to his room at night it was not to scour his soul for its sinful shortcomings and pray for forgiveness and enlightenment to the wrathful God of the Old Testament; not to contemplate upon his knees, but to clamber out through the casement window and spend the hours of darkness pursuing physical enlightenment in the arms of the town's whores.

He proved an apt pupil, and a greedy one. Having been raised to believe the body a wicked, filthy thing, he now flung himself headlong into debauchery and revelled in the pleasures of the flesh, equalling in appetite the tastes of his companions in vice. It was noted that his activities were confined solely to physical lust: Esmond Bates never gambled, never drank, and never flouted the law.

When his mode of life at length began to leave its telltale marks on his appearance, his father attributed the tiredness, the sunken lacklustre eyes and pallid complexion to mortification of the body in pursuit of spiritual purity; and rejoiced accordingly.

Then, in the autumn of 1833, he received an unsigned letter which informed him otherwise. At first he refused to believe its scurrilous accusations. But the suspicion had been planted; and it grew.

One night he had waited unseen at the end of the back lane, and witnessed his son leave the house by a rear window. He followed him into the warren of alleys, even then assuring himself that Esmond had come to this desolation of Satan solely in order to bring the fear of Hell to its inhabitants, that he entered the slime-pits of Siddim to cleanse them, to put them to the torch so that they should become as the valley of Ben-hinnom.

Again, he waited. And when his son failed to re-emerge from the stinking tenement, went in after him.

Esmond Bates never returned to his father's house. He left St Albans at first light and travelled into London; and for a time was lost to the knowledge of decent men.

The clock chimes of All Souls church broke suddenly into his thoughts, warning him that time was running on and he would be late for Evensong.

He looked away from the washstand mirror, from that accusing face, half in shadow just as his life had been, and washed himself hurriedly, drying his hands on the thin, sour-smelling piece of towelling on the rail beside the stand.

Then put on his coat once more and went quickly out, down the steep, gloomy stairs in search of his wife.

4

The view rose suddenly as the carrier's waggon lurched into a deep rut on the bend, throwing Rachael sideways against her husband and bringing a crash of crockery from inside the wicker hamper lashed to one of the trunks on the bed of the waggon.

"I wish I'd thought to wrap the plates inside the clothing," she said, vexed. "At this rate there'll be nothing left for us to eat off by the time we reach Weatherfield."

Esmond Bates sat stiffly upright on the bench seat. For the past hour he had felt quite ill with a sick headache which seemed to grow worse with every jolt to his spine from the waggon's lurching.

"Why bring any plates?" he demanded curtly. "They were cracked to begin with. I told you to throw them out."

Rachael withdrew her hand from his arm. The few poor bits and pieces they possessed had served them well enough during those dismal years in Lewes and she had not had the heart to discard them.

"In any case," the new rector continued, "you will find a whole cupboard of plates at the house. Good sound stuff, hardly used. The Bishop's secretary assured me the rectory is well supplied with the usual domestic goods. It all comes to me with the living."

The waggon gave another lurch and the contents of the wicker hamper rattled uneasily together.

A further turning in the lane now appeared beyond the tunnel of trees they were passing through. Bright April sunshine threw into relief the baked mud ridges corrugating its surface. In wet weather this country byway would be a mire, churned up by the hooves and wheels passing over it. It was the same everywhere in the remoter parts of the Weald. For generations, travellers had been complaining about the state of the roads, deep sticky mud in bad weather, bone-jolting ruts in dry; but nothing was ever done about surfacing them. In fact, it was an oft-repeated joke that the reason Sussex women had such long legs was because they stretched them by having constantly to drag their feet out of the clinging wealden clay.

As the carrier's waggon swayed out from beneath the trees Esmond Bates blinked in the sudden brilliance of sunlight; and for no reason in particular there came into his mind a memory of how the sun had shafted down on to his wife's warm brown hair, the first time he had noticed her.

She had been arranging a bowl of flowers in the side chapel of All Souls, head bowed over her task, the light from the stained glass window spilling over her and turning her into such a bright and lovely vision that the fact had not occurred to him till later that her head had not been covered in church.

"Which road now, sir?"

The carrier's voice from the front of the waggon roused him from his reverie.

"I don't know the ways hereabout, so far from Lewes. I'd be obliged for your guidance."

They had halted at a crossways, one narrow road to their left, two others branching away almost ahead of them. When Esmond had ridden this way the first time, to view his new living, he had been accompanied by the agent and had taken no particular note of the route. But he recalled there had been a signpost at this junction, one arm pointing to Weatherfield, another to the neighbouring hamlet of Troy Town, a third to Shatterford, and the last indicating the direction of the town through which the waggon and its occupants had travelled from Lewes.

"There ought to be a signpost somewhere about," he called back. "Don't you see it?"

The carrier half-rose from his seat and looked around. "Reckon that be it." He indicated with his whip.

Esmond shielded his eyes against the sun's glare and stood up to follow his direction. The post had obviously been uprooted, and now lay propped at an angle against the hedge. He made a small sound of annoyance.

"That's of little use to us. Some careless farm cart, I suppose. If we take the wrong turning here it will send us right out of our way."

Just as Esmond's irritation at the absurdity of their situation began to sharpen, the carrier cocked his head to one side and said, "Now thanks be to that! Somebody's a-riding this way."

Above the chirp of hedge sparrows a rhythmical drumming became audible from the tree-shaded dip of the left-hand road, and within a few moments a horseman came into view, cantering smoothly up the slope towards the crossways.

Catching sight of the stationary waggon he reined in and approached at a gentler pace along the grassy verge until he was parallel with the passengers. The height of the bay gelding gave him an immediate advantage over them, forcing Rachael to shade her eyes to look up at him as he halted alongside. She could see little against the brightness of the sun outlining the man's figure, only that he was strongly-built and wore the clothing of a yeoman farmer.

He shifted himself in the saddle, and made a slight sketch of a bow.

"Are you in any difficulty, sir? Might I be of assistance?"

The voice was deep, and would have been cultured were it not for a slight broadening of the vowels marking him a countryman.

"I'd be obliged to you if you could set us on the way to Weatherfield," Esmond answered. "The signpost over there has been shifted. We have no way of knowing which road to take."

The rider glanced behind him, then looked back at the man in sober clerical garb.

"You're travelling to Weatherfield?"

"We are."

"I see. Well, Mr—?"

"Bates, sir."

"Well, Mr Bates, this is a poor beginning for us. A bad greeting. You'll be the new parson, I take it?"

31

"I am."

"Bashford. George Bashford." The rider raised his hat and leaned down from his horse to shake hands. "I farm over at Netherton."

Esmond introduced Rachael and Bashford repeated his bow, deeper this time. She had a better view of him now and saw that he was young, cleanly shaven, and with thick brown hair cut short above his ears. His strong features went well with his build and firm voice.

"And is Netherton near here, sir?" she asked.

"No, it's a good way beyond Weatherfield, ma'am—getting on for East Grinstead."

Bashford's eyes moved across her face, noting its fine-boned beauty, then he looked again at her husband and smiled apologetically.

"I'm sorry you've been held up like this. It's the right fork you want." He pointed out the route with his riding crop. "Perhaps I can make amends for the ill reception by going on ahead to let them know you're expected?"

"Thank you," Esmond responded. "If it is not out of your way."

"Not at all."

"Then that would be most kind of you, sir."

George Bashford smiled again, touched his hat to Rachael, and circling his horse round behind the waggon, trotted past them on the further side, calling out to the carrier to follow his direction.

Roused up by a flick of the whip, the draught horse moved ponderously after his, taking them over the crossways and into the welcome shade of a high hedge which bordered the new route for a mile or so before dwindling to give a clear view of the valley in which Weatherfield lay.

Before long Esmond Bates and his wife were able to pick out various features of their new parish and its setting: hill pastures and copses, arable land further down, scattered farm buildings; the spire of the church half-hidden amongst trees; then the first of the cottages appearing as the lane levelled out, and figures moving in the distance.

As they neared the village they overtook a small boy in a

smock slashing at nettles with a rook-scarer as he dawdled along. He stood back against the hedge as though to let the waggon go by, staring in open curiosity at the strangers; then suddenly took to his heels and dashed off along the lane, his dog leaping behind him.

Esmond's headache lifted a little. Shifting himself on his seat, he turned to look Rachael full in the eyes with an intensity that betrayed his normally well-guarded emotions.

"May I be as good a husband in this place as I hope to be a priest," he murmured.

For a long moment they looked at one another. Then she leaned forward and kissed his cheek.

"You are always a good husband to me, Esmond," she responded softly.

But her words, like her gesture, were automatic. Even as she touched him she was silently praying that the near-stranger she had lived with in Lewes might at last begin to respond towards her as she had always imagined a husband would; that the shadow on their marriage might be lifted.

By the time the carrier's waggon reached the main part of the village, the small boy and his dog had become part of a group of a dozen or so people standing at the rectory gate on the edge of the green. Of George Bashford there was no sign, but several men who had been at work in the lower fields had been hailed by him as he rode by and had come down to help with unloading the waggon.

While the job got under way, Rachael stood to one side to take in her new home.

Weatherfield was typical of many such small settlements among the woodlands of the Weald. Esmond, for whom such things were a fascination, had studied the derivation of its place-name and discovered it to be Witheranfeld; which he explained meant that their parish covered land once belonging to some Anglo-Saxon settler called Wither, or "the Ram". He would not be drawn into speculating how such a nickname might have been gained.

At some time in the past the community had shifted from

its original site, leaving the rectory and small Norman church standing in isolation on the opposite side of the green. The centre of the village was now its high street, running away downhill towards Troy Town and Shatterford and bordered by cottage rows whose gardens stretched behind to the farm lands. To one end stood the general store; at the other, the smithy overlooked a rush-fringed pond fed by a stream flowing the length of the street behind a line of railings.

The rectory itself was a handsome Georgian house whose warm brick frontage was partly obscured by climbing roses. It stood well back from the green behind a long garden, bounded on one side by the churchyard wall. Sheep were feeding among the grassy humps of graves. Rooks wheeled and cawed in neighbouring elms; and beyond the branches of an ancient yew the shingled spire of St Anne's rose into the early evening sky.

As her eyes travelled down from the spire, Rachael's attention was suddenly captured by sight of a man sitting on the churchyard wall watching the activity at the rectory. She gave a start. Surely it could not be . . . ? She stared at him, wondering whether she was possibly mistaken. Yes, of course she must be.

Then, when he jumped down and began walking towards her, she knew beyond any doubt that there was no mistake: the broad, muscular shoulders, the black curling hair, the heavy moustache. It was the same man who had been with Charlotte Smith in All Souls' graveyard that day.

Greatly agitated, she continued to stare at him; and as he came by he looked across and smiled, his teeth strong and white as she remembered them in the dark virile face. Then someone touched her arm, wanting to know whether the chairs should be put in the parlour or study, and when she looked round again the man had disappeared.

She was still standing there on the path trying to see whether he was among those at the waggon, perplexed by such an encounter, how it was possible he came to be in Weatherfield of all places, when a red-haired woman came up the garden carrying a pile of Esmond's books held together by a leather strap.

34

Immediately she saw her, Rachael abandoned her search and went over, reaching out a hand.

"Do let me take those. They're too heavy—for you. You may harm yourself."

The young woman stopped and looked over her shoulder.

"That's kind of you, ma'am, but don't worry. I shan't catch hurt. I carry a sight more'n this most days."

She shifted the books awkwardly to the other side of her swollen body.

"Even so, at least let me share the load with you."

"As you like."

Balancing the weight between them, the two made their way side by side along the brick path and in through the modestly columned porch of the house. The dark-haired man was nowhere to be seen among the group of helpers inside, either.

For the moment Rachael forced herself to put him to the back of her mind.

"Which is the study, do you know?" she asked, searching about her.

The other gestured with her head towards a right-hand door leading off the central hallway. It stood ajar, revealing the shadowy interior. Going through, she found herself in a room lighted by sash windows overlooking the garden. She lowered her burden to the floor and glanced around. Apart from bookshelves on either side the chimney breast, the place was empty. A mass of charred paper spilled from the mouth of the grate and overflowed on to the bare floor boards. On the mantelshelf above, a broken wooden calendar showing 17 January 1852 was almost three months out of date.

The red-haired woman seated herself heavily on top of the books and cast a quick look around the room.

"Old Parson Yardley died that month," she said, indicating the calendar. "Cold got on his chest. His sister come straight back here directly after the funeral and took all manner o' stuff away. Anything she reckoned to get a penny or two for, the old cat. Half of it weren't her'n to take, neither."

She glanced over to where Rachael was standing, an expression of sympathy on her young face.

"What's left's fit for naun but kindling, I'm afraid you'll find. And you wi' so little stuff of your own, an' all. Still, them shelves are built in pretty solid—she couldn't make off wi' them, leastways. Your father'll have plenty o' space for this lot."

She patted the books and got to her feet, her hands pressed against the small of her back to relieve the ache of the child within her.

"Mr Bates is not my father," Rachael said quickly. When she and Esmond were first married she had been embarrassed when strangers meeting them confused their relationship to each other. Now she had learned not to be so sensitive. "He's my husband. I'm Mrs Bates."

"Oh . . . oh, I'm sorry, ma'am! I thought—" The other looked flustered. "There, that's just like me. Always making a boffle o' things. And there's me went and told Frank . . . When I saw you outside it never crossed my mind you might be married. I hope you're not offended?"

"Of course not. May I know your name?"

"Dinah. Dinah Flynn. I live out towards Troy Town, a mile or so off. At the alehouse."

Rachael watched her as she turned away to unfasten the strap binding Esmond's books, and thought how pretty she was despite the ungainly figure. Pregnancy had lent its compensation of a healthy glow to her skin that enhanced the burnished coppery-red hair caught into a loose knot at the nape of her neck.

"Leave those," she said, as Dinah made to start putting the books on the shelves. "My husband will want to arrange them himself. You've already done more than enough."

"It's no trouble, ma'am. I like to be of help."

"Well, perhaps you'd show me the kitchen quarters? I must make a start somewhere. It might as well be there."

She followed Dinah out into the hallway and along a passage at the far end beside the stairs.

"Did Mr Yardley's sister live here at the rectory?"

36

"After she were widowed, yes. Before that, some of us in the parish took it by turns to come up and clean and do. But when Mrs Phillips come, a year back it was, she didn't want no help from anyone. Ran the place by herself till the old man died."

"And is she in the village still?"

"Lor', no! Not her. She took herself off back Chichester way." Dinah looked over her shoulder. "We were glad to be shut of her, an' all. Nobody liked her. She even tried to stop the parson baptising my little Frankie. Now then, here we are. This here's the kitchen—"

She led Rachael into a high-ceilinged room at the bottom of the passage. Like the study, it was bare of any furniture. In the middle of the floor stood the hamper from Lewes containing the plates which Esmond had sneered at for being cracked and no longer of use.

Rachael's eyes moved to the wall cupboards beside the range. They stood open and empty. Of the "usual domestic goods" her husband had promised there was nothing, not even a scrap of carpet underfoot or a piece of lace at the window.

Something of the pleasurable anticipation she had felt at moving to Weatherfield began to evaporate.

Late that night Rachael lay awake beside her sleeping husband in the wide double-bed which he had insisted they purchase new, though the meagre stipend he received as curate had been stretched very thin by such an extravagant gesture. She was over-tired and tense, and envied Esmond his ability to fall asleep so easily. It had been a long day for them both.

She turned over. As ever, her husband was sleeping with his back towards her. She laid her cheek against his shoulder and put her arm across his waist, her hand moving over the rumpled folds of the linen nightshirt. But her touch failed to rouse him.

She turned on her back again and stared up into the blackness. Perhaps it was a mercy he slept, she thought bitterly. So often she had lain beside him in the dark hours of

37

other nights, holding him and comforting him after yet another failure.

Their marriage had never been consummated. Rachael understood little of a husband's physical need for his wife, but she was beginning to recognise her own needs and suspected there should be a great deal more to married intimacy than she had ever experienced with Esmond.

He loved her deeply; she believed that. Yet at times she sensed something more in his regard, something that he seemed to be at pains to conceal from her. Even in the privacy of their bedroom he rarely used any expression of endearment, only occasionally, and diffidently, speaking of his love; seeming to reserve his passion to be poured into the frustration that came later, the muffled cries of self-reproach and anger when his kisses and caresses had ended yet again in dissatisfaction and failure.

Rachael tossed restlessly. She had made it her rule never to complain or even voice her disappointment. Only once had she dared to suggest, in as tactful words as she could find, that Esmond seek qualified advice. His reaction had been horrifying. For a moment she thought he would strike her; and then he had flown into the vilest temper, shouting accusations that she was little better than a bitch in heat, that she had never tried to understand, that she laughed at him behind his back, comparing him with other men.

Then, worse still, he had suddenly lost all control and had broken down completely, weeping like a child for forgiveness, kneeling at her feet with his face buried in her skirts, and begging her never to leave him.

Rachael had avoided any further mention of that side of their marriage, though her husband continued the unhappy circle of his attentions. Now, as she lay in Weatherfield rectory remembering the knowing smiles of the villagers as one of the women pointed out to her the long-neglected nursery, she reflected darkly that it seemed impossible she and Esmond would ever be able to fill that room with anything other than lumber.

5

For his first address in his new church Esmond had chosen to preach on a verse from the Gospel of St John: "Except a corn of wheat fall into the ground and die, it abideth alone; but if it die, it bringeth forth much fruit."

It made the basis of a good Passiontide sermon, comparing the corn of wheat to Christ and His own death; and it was an analogy which his congregation should readily grasp, he thought, being for the most part field-workers themselves.

"Nature, looked at superficially, seems to say that death is ruin . . . the ruin and end of all that is strong and beautiful in life," the rector told his listeners.

"But, my friends, Nature scanned more penetratingly, more profoundly, shows that death is but the precursor of new and vigorous life. The caterpillar forfeits its form to become the butterfly. The seed decomposes to become the plant. If the corn of wheat does not fall into the ground and die, it abides alone—intact, but dry, shrivelled, unproductive. If it dies, however, it forthwith becomes a principle of life: it bringeth forth much fruit."

He laid down his notes for a moment on the edge of the pulpit and slowly scanned the upturned faces of the congregation. All eyes were fixed upon him from the box pews crowding the nave of the small church. Despite some coughing and shuffling he was satisfied that he had their attention, and took up the notes once again to continue.

"—The power of death, the power of sin, the power of Satan . . . such powers, if we will are gone . . . if death is looked forward to, not without awe, but without apprehension, this is because Jesus Christ has died."

The isolated rustling and murmuring grew more persistent, forcing Esmond to pause again; and his listeners took this as an interlude in which to relieve their various creeping discomforts by breaking into a chorus of coughs and noisy throat-clearing which died away gradually into a single rasping sound traceable to the nearest box pew, where a stout individual was scratching vigorously at the bristles on his unshaven jaw.

Esmond drew a breath and began again more loudly.

"My friends, we each must ask ourself will the Divine Redeemer own me as one of the fruits of His death? Alas, if any one of us here present should have hereafter to reflect ... 'the shadow of sin is still so black upon my soul that His death was truly in vain.'"

At last the notes of the sermon were tapped together on the pulpit edge and laid aside.

For several moments there was complete silence.

From the back of the church someone spoke, addressing his pew neighbour in the high, tremulous tones of the very old and deaf.

"Has he done yet?"

"Aye."

"Ah." A pause. "Reckon he makes a tol'able good preacher. He doan't mumble his words, do he? Behopes he makes 'em plainer, though. They long 'uns be durned hard to follow."

The acoustics of the ancient building amplified this observation, and Esmond saw several heads nodding agreement. He cleared his throat. He would have preferred to hear something about the actual content of his sermon, and to be described as only a "tolerable good" preacher stung his pride a little, having grown used to the unstinted praise of his congregation in Lewes.

But he let it pass. They would develop a better respect for him in time.

"Let us now stand and sing together hymn number 104: 'O sinner lift the eye of faith, to true repentance turning'."

He nodded across to Joseph Green, an earnest, unsmiling individual who combined the work of sexton with that of harmonium player. Joseph was present this morning in the

40

latter capacity; though the zeal with which he now proceeded to stamp down upon the treadboards to fill the harmonium bellows with air carried precisely the same movement and force as his footwork with a spade when filling a new grave with earth.

The hymn number, as Esmond shortly observed, had been an unnecessary detail. Few of the congregation seemed to be following the words from their books; and when after verse two the voices fell away to be replaced by an almost monosyllabic drone, it occurred to him that less than half those present were actually able to follow the words at all.

The discovery vexed him. He ought to have known that he would meet with ignorance in all its forms in such a backward parish instead of blithely supposing that adult literacy at least had penetrated its rural isolation. In future, he told himself resignedly, he would have to limit the selection of hymns to those dozen or so they would be sure to know by heart.

Raising his own voice, he sang clearly and strongly, rounding out the words of the last verse to encourage those few still struggling on against the mournful out-of-tune cadences of the harmonium.

There was another disappointment. That first Sunday service had not attracted the numbers the new rector hoped to see at church. He had considered delaying the start of service; but the verger, Ezra Jolly, had assured him that all the regular villagers were present, and he had had to console himself with the thought that at least the rest had been honest enough to stay away and not turn God's worship into a spectacle for the merely curious.

His little flock of faithful parishioners was composed of no more than half a dozen or so single members and four families—Jenner, Slybody, Juglery and Stillborne—totalling some thirty in all.

He had made a remark about such outlandish names on first hearing them from the verger; but it seemed they had long been common to the district. And indeed, when he and Rachael had taken an evening stroll about the churchyard, they had noted that these were the names which figured with greatest frequency on the headstones; along with those of Hollowbone, Wildgoose and Whiskey, whose numerous descendants apparently did not see fit to be a part of the congregation.

Well, things would change now that he was in charge of the parish. He already intended to dismiss the existing churchwarden, whom he had disliked within five minutes of meeting, and appoint another jointly with a vestry overseer, to be responsible for the prevention of Sunday drinking in the alehouse and to manage the distribution of Poor Law relief where necessary.

Esmond had made time to look at the entries in the Poor Book, kept with the register in the vestry, and had been appalled by what he found there. Instead of being sent away to Heathbury workhouse, such paupers as included the elderly, children of large families unable to support them, and bastards whose fathers were unknown, had all been allowed to remain in the parish at the expense of tithe contributions which should rightly have come to the church. And this with the full knowledge and consent of his predecessor, the Reverend John Yardley.

The income of a clergyman with a living as insignificant as Weatherfield depended largely on the offerings of his congregation; and when those offerings took the form of what was known as small tithe—chickens, eggs, cheese and occasional livestock—he had little enough ready cash to spend on the upkeep of his church and graveyard. So it had angered Esmond to discover in the pages of the Poor Book such entries as:

"Elizabeth Nye, one shift . . . the late Wm Hill's children to have some shoes . . . Ann Capel to be allowed 6 shillings on condition she troubles the parish no more this summer . . . Widow Jenner a wheel for spinning . . . John Whiskey's wife to be brought back from Buckfield infirmary and be allowed 7 shillings . . . Janet Wildgoose to have 5 shillings towards support of her bastard child . . ."

Shifts, shoes and spinning wheels were the responsibility of neither the Church nor the Poor Law in his opinion; and those who needed bringing back from infirmaries should certainly have been redirected towards the inside of the workhouse.

As for the number of illegitimate children born in the district, he had held his head in his hands and groaned aloud to find again and again the same damning entry, varying only in its changes of name: "the overseer to visit Hannah Brooks and view her condition . . . that Samuel Fletcher be taken before the magistrate unless security be immediately given for a bastard child sworn on him . . ."

It filled Esmond Bates with disgust to find such gross immorality among his parishioners. He supposed it was because they were largely uneducated, insensible creatures who spent their days among brute beasts or else mired with the dirt of the fields that they must seek to satisfy their carnal lusts and appetites in such wanton fashion.

The holy estate of matrimony was ordained for a remedy against sin, to avoid fornication, that those not having the gift of continency might be married and so keep themselves undefiled members of Christ's body. Yet, to judge by the depressing numbers of bastards recorded in the Poor Book, it would seem that in Weatherfield—and doubtless not only in Weatherfield either—the act of carnal union between men and women was being habitually and flagrantly practised outside marriage.

It was a just punishment on such open and notorious livers, he had reflected, that the children they so wickedly brought into the world stayed so short a time in it; and he had derived grim satisfaction from checking the parish register against the Poor Book to verify the list of fatherless infants born dead or moribund and buried without ceremony at the foot of adult graves.

Even here, though, the lax Mr Yardley had been acting against common practice. In cases where fathers had acknowledged their base-born children and undertaken to support them, Esmond's predecessor had allowed their baptism at St Anne's. Their names included that of Frank Patrick Flynn, bastard son of Dinah Flynn and Frank Morgan.

Very well. There was nothing a new incumbent could do

to expunge the mischief permitted in the past. But no more would be permitted. "It must needs be that offences come; but woe to that man by whom the offence cometh!"

Jabez Hollowbone removed the clay pipe from between discoloured teeth and spat with great accuracy through the railings into the duck pond beside Weatherfield high street.

"I don't hold wi' furriners," he told the men standing with him. "And I won't be druv' by one, neither. Partic'ly one that won't even gi' me a civil word to my face."

"How's that, then, Jabez?" enquired a short, thickset individual whose red cheeks were lost among a profusion of mutton-chop whiskers.

The pipe-smoker sucked and spat again, then jerked his head in the direction of the rectory on the far side of the green.

"*He* catched me again this morning. Taking a short cut over his land. 'You,' he says, coming upon me very sudden from his back-door, 'you'—not even the courtesy o' plain mister, mind—'you, my man.' So I stops and waits, while he my-mans at me a while more about a-traipsing over his property—"

"Lucky he never thought fit to look in the bag you had wi' you," interjected Henry Wildgoose, of the mutton-chop whiskers. "Otherwise he might ha' found a one-or-two of his own conies to vex him harder."

"—'*And*,' he says when he were done, 'why don't I see you in church of a Sunday?' 'Why?' says I. 'Why, Mr Bates, 'tis on account o' not being a church-going habitual, if you want my reason.'"

"No more'n the rest here," put in someone else, clad like the others in the creamy-grey embroidered smock of a farm-worker. "He can't drive us nor make us, rant as he may."

"Aye, and so I tells him. 'Harvest and Christmas,' I says. 'Twice a year's enough, parson. There's no romish practice here to order a man against his will'."

Henry Wildgoose spoke up again.

"Myself, I'm done wi' him already. It'd ha' caused no

harm to let us have the marbles match in the churchyard on Good Friday, as we always have. You tell us, Wal Juglery— you tell us what he answered when you asked."

Walter Juglery, champion marble player in the village, glanced around his circle of neighbours and nodded.

"'Tis true. He forbad it. Said he'd not permit gaming in the churchyard, no, nor marbles neither."

Marble-playing was a recreation which had been enjoyed by Sussex men and boys since time out of mind. According to local legend, it was believed to date back to Calvary itself, to the Roman soldiers who cast lots with sheep's knucklebones for possession of Christ's garments; and in memory of that, Good Friday was the day on which marbles were traditionally played in the villages of Sussex.

In Weatherfield, the game was held on the greensward beside the church wall. But not this year.

"I told 'un straight," Walter continued, measuring out his words with the same care that he gave to his marble shots, "there's never a Good Friday gone past wi'out the men have a match in the churchyard."

"And how did he answer you?"

"How did he answer me? Well, he says summat about old ways bein' for the iggerant, and a few long words more, but the man talks so thin 'tis mortacious hard to follow 'un."

There was general agreement.

"Why they seen fit to send us a durned furriner for parson beats me," Jabez Hollowbone observed truculently. "Let him take hisself back off quick to distant parts, I say, and vex his own kind wi' his contrariness. He's made a bad beginning here, true enough—"

General agreement again.

"—and he's not like to change his stiffneck ways to make hisself better wanted, neither."

6

While her husband occupied himself with parish affairs, Rachael was kept busy at the rectory transmuting the disorder there as best she could into something more like a home for them both.

She had prevailed upon Esmond to employ a servant; but instead of some strong, willing person he had been constrained by his limited finances to take on fourteen-year-old Ada Slybody, who came to them very cheaply since she had a withered leg and was not much endowed with intelligence.

Not that the lack of intelligence mattered greatly: in a parish as poor and shabby as Weatherfield there was no one to come calling at the rectory to leave their cards and take tea with the new minister's wife, so that little Ada's duties were confined to the scullery and wash-house, where neither fuddled wits nor withered leg hindered her unduly.

One of the first tasks Rachael set herself was the drawing up of an inventory of the furniture and other household goods, writing each item down in her neat sloping copper plate hand, taking one room at a time. When the list was complete she found herself, as she had expected, troubled as much by its omissions as its brevity. But Esmond had to have a pony and trap to enable him to travel about the district, and since the greater part of their income was tithed, finding the money for it had meant the sacrifice of domestic comforts.

"Really, it's too much! Look at this—"

She showed the list to Dinah Flynn, who had come in one evening to help with letting down the hems of the curtains brought from Lewes.

"Only our own four chairs, and those so worn I'm ashamed

to put them anywhere but the kitchen. That wretched Mrs Phillips had no right to sell the furniture. No right at all. My husband intends making the strongest complaint about it. All she left us was an old chest of drawers riddled with the worm and one armchair with a broken leg."

Dinah looked up from the length of curtain she was unpicking. Her face was in shadow, the light from the oil lamp behind on the dresser falling over her shoulder on to her hands.

"It's not that bad, surely, Mrs Bates? Our cousin Jack'll mend the chair for you, gladly. He's a dab hand at fixing things like that."

"That makes *five* chairs, then." Rachael amended the list. "Now, what is there for the floor? If I can find the column. Oh, yes, here. One runner carpet for the hall. It's far too short, but I suppose it must do till we can afford better. The colour's still bright, at least. A square for the parlour. One for Esmond's study. A poor threadbare thing that will have to go into the front bedroom . . ."

She threw the list from her in despair.

"Oh, I can't go on. It's too depressing."

Dinah watched her turn away to take up one of the curtains from the table, setting herself resignedly to sew a new hem. She felt a liking for Mrs Bates. She was glad there was a young woman of her own age at the rectory instead of some elderly churchwife, though Mr Bates himself had obviously married in middle life. She wondered why she should have wanted to wed a man so much older than herself, especially, it seemed, one without money; what attraction she could have found in such a husband. The rector struck Dinah as a cold sort of bedfellow for someone as openly warm-natured as his young wife. He was too pale, somehow. There was something chilly about his look as well as his manner.

She hoped that Rachael Bates would favour her acquaintance. Though, of course, the fact that she had one child born out of wedlock and was about to bear another might prove an obstacle. So far, she had not admitted to being unwed, turning away any question about a husband with some offhand remark that was neither truth nor lie.

47

She rethreaded her needle and bent her head once more to the sewing. Mrs Morgan. Mrs Frank Morgan. What would she not give to have that as her rightful name. To be Frank's wedded wife seemed a state more precious than anything in the world just now. But he had taken his stallion to the hill farms further south and was not expected back in the district until after the baby was born.

She turned her mind to the farm at Netherton where she worked as a dairy maid. There was a room there full of all manner of stuff that her employer, George Bashford, had stored away a few years back. If she remembered rightly, a lot of it was just the kind of thing Mrs Bates was needing. A pity to let it lie wasted at Netherton, she thought, when it could be put to good use here at the rectory.

George Bashford called on the Bateses a few days later.

Esmond had left the house soon after breakfasting to visit one of the outlying cottages where a farm labourer's wife lay dying; and was then going on to look over a horse and trap he thought he might possibly buy.

Rachael was alone, struggling to put up a drying line between two old apple trees behind the rectory. Persuaded early into the wash-house by one of those gloriously clear dawns of late April, she had spent the entire morning with little Ada Slybody labouring over a mound of washing: a necessary task, but one she was now regretting having begun, especially as Ada was more hindrance than help, complaining about feeling unwell with what she called her 'predicament' and having to be sent home to her mother before the washing was even half done.

Esmond never assisted in any domestic capacity, spending most of his time at home in his study. Like most men of the period, he took the view that marriage provided not only a partner and companion but also an efficient housekeeper, and it was no part of a husband's duty to lend himself to those services which fell to a wife to perform. Rachael knew that it would be a waste of breath to ask if they could afford to get in someone stronger and more reliable from the village. Little Ada must do, at least for a while.

Hot and flushed from the steam of the copper, muscles aching with the effort of lifting sodden sheets and working the heavy mangle, she was stretching up in a vain effort to secure one end of the line around a tree limb when George Bashford found her. Having got no response to the bell-pull in the porch, he had taken the churchyard path round to the back of the rectory and stood watching her for several minutes, astonished to find a woman of her position at such a task.

So intent was she on her struggle that Rachael was quite unaware of his presence until he spoke.

"I think you need some help, ma'am?"

She swung round, startled.

"Oh! Oh, Mr . . ."

"Bashford."

"Yes, of course. I should have remembered."

Despite his wonder at her menial activity he found himself admiring the pink flush of her cheeks, the slight huskiness of her voice.

"Do forgive me, Mr Bashford. I'd no idea anyone was there."

"I seem to have come just in time. You'll allow me to do that for you?"

"Well, thank you, I would be grateful. It must look a trifle irregular, I know. But the girl my husband employs is unwell, so I must manage as best I can alone."

Bashford came in at the side gate and across the grass. He took the end of the line from her.

"Where shall I tie it—here?"

"That will do very well, or it will be too high for me to lift the linen."

Knotting the rope firmly about the base of the branch, he glanced over his shoulder at the double-handled wicker basket on the ground, noticing how heavily weighted it was with wet sheets.

"Is there nobody else to give you a hand with that?" he asked her. "Nobody from the village? Let me go down into the high street and send a woman over to help."

"No, please don't trouble. There are only a few things. I can see to them well enough for myself."

49

George Bashford continued to look at her, taking in her delicate build, her obvious weariness, the pallor of her complexion emphasised by dark shadows beneath the slate-blue eyes. He guessed that it was not only the laundering she saw to "well enough for herself" but much of the other domestic work. And that on top of the parish duties of a parson's wife: the care of the sick, the teaching of the catechism and collects to the village children, the distribution of alms, and all the other acts of charity she was called upon to perform.

He was frankly surprised that her husband had seen fit to employ only one servant at the rectory, when two or three would not have been excessive. Perhaps Mr Bates was waiting until later in the year when the women hired for fieldwork were paid off and an employer might have his pick of them. That is, unless what he had recently learned from one of his own workers was true, and the rector presently encumbered by a lack of funds.

"Are you sure you won't let me send someone from the village?" he asked again.

"Thank you, quite sure. It isn't necessary."

"Very well. Then I'll give you a hand myself." He removed his jacket and tossed it aside. "Come along, Mrs Bates. I can see you're thinking what good reason you can find for refusing my assistance, but it's no use. I won't stand by and watch you trying to manage alone."

Taking up one of the heavy linen sheets from the basket he heaved it deftly across the line.

Rachael opened her mouth to protest, well aware of the impropriety of his being seen helping to put out bed linen. But she was weary and a little irritable, and that brought out the wilful streak in her nature which she had tried so hard to suppress since her marriage.

It was an inherited trait. Orphaned in infancy, she had been raised by her father's sister, a woman who had epitomised everything elegant, egregious and defiantly raffish about the heyday of the Regency. In her own youth Aunt Kember had been one of the belles of the regiments stationed at out-quarters near Lewes, taking from life every free pleasure that was offered; and in·later years had kept up a disregard for the more stifling conventions, preferring as always to make her own.

Her example had not been lost on her niece.

The old lady had died, lamenting the growing rigidity of society, only a short while after Esmond Bates came to the town as curate of All Souls. Rachael had felt her loss. It was not only that she had spent almost the whole of her young life in Aunt Kember's care: there was something more, something which went far deeper. Undoubtedly one of the reasons why she felt such attraction for the new minister was her need for security, her need to be controlled by a stronger, older personality. That was the legacy of her orphaned childhood. But the root of that attraction was the desire to find someone who might be lover, father and mentor all in one.

However, she had been conscious of nothing but love when she accepted Esmond's proposal of marriage.

As she watched George Bashford effortlessly heave the sheets over the drying line she thought of her husband now, of his coldness when he disapproved of something she had done, of his unhelpfulness and captious manner.

She picked up the farmer's jacket from the fork of the apple branch where he had tossed it. It smelled of horses and saddle leather.

"I'll hang this by the door."

She moved away. From between the sheets, Bashford's eyes followed her. She was lovely beyond his experience of parsons' wives. In fact, it was some time since any woman's face had appealed to his fancy so much. He admired her slender figure, too, as she went about at the other end of the garden, spreading the smaller items of laundry over the rosemary bushes by the wall.

When the work was done, Rachael fetched him a mug of cider from the house. He drank it slowly while they stood together in the garden.

After a while he remarked, "I believe you know one of my dairy workers. Dinah Flynn."

"Dinah? Why, yes. She's been here several times. I didn't know it was you she worked for, though."

"Mm." He lifted the mug and took another mouthful of the cool cider, then drew the back of his hand across his lips. "She's been at Spring Hill for, oh, must be getting on ten years now, I reckon. She first came to us in my father's time, when she was twelve or thereabouts. She's a good worker."

"Is her husband one of your men? She never has anything to say about him."

"It's unlikely she would. Dinah hasn't got a husband, Mrs Bates."

"Oh? She's widowed?"

"No . . . no, that isn't it." He hesitated, awkwardly. "She's unwed. A spinster."

Rachael was silent for a few moments. Unmarried mothers were nothing new to her experience; but she had not thought of Dinah as one.

Slowly she said, "I see. And the child—the children?"

Bashford shrugged. "Don't judge her too harshly, ma'am. She's a decent enough girl, despite the way things have gone. She's not the first to find herself in that position, nor will she be the last."

Rachael ran a finger along the bib of the long white pinafore covering her gown. "I wanted to stand sponsor to the new baby."

Bashford watched her face as he asked, "And do you still?"

There was a pause. Rooks cawed in the elms on the far side of the churchyard. Somewhere a dog barked in response to a shrill whistle. Voices carried faintly from the direction of the village store on the street beyond the green.

"Yes. I do." She looked away. "What does the Book tell us? 'Judge not, that ye be not judged'? I hope I'm not a hypocrite, Mr Bashford."

"I didn't suppose you were."

She turned her eyes back to his face, and saw the admiration there. Something else, too—something in the way he was regarding her that made her feel strangely defensive and needing to explain herself.

"My husband . . . I'm afraid his views are very strict. He's not a tolerant man. He condemns loose behaviour of any kind, no matter what the circumstances are. If I'm to sponsor Dinah's baby it would be better if the—father were to marry her."

"But it seems he won't, ma'am. He's told me so himself."

"You know him?"

Bashford nodded. "The stallion man."

She frowned at the expression. "You make him sound a curious breed." ·

He smiled at that. "In a manner of speaking, I suppose he is. What I meant was, he's a stallion leader."

"I see," she said hastily. "I understand."

"Yes. Well, he makes a fair bit of money that way. He has a sound head on his shoulders, has Frank Morgan. Good with horses. But then, that would be the gipsy blood in him."

"And he refuses to marry Dinah? But why? She seems the kind who would make a capable wife. And the children are his?"

"The first one, yes. You've only to look at the boy to see that. As to the one she's carrying now . . . well, Dinah's not the sort to go from man to man. Frank Morgan's the one for her. I think she loves him true enough."

Rachael moved slowly away from him across the grass, pausing beside a rose bush where the first buds of late spring were starting to open. She touched one gently.

"How sad it is when love goes unappreciated," she murmured.

George Bashford was not sure he had heard her correctly. He went to speak; then thought better of it.

Instead, he said after a pause, "It wasn't Dinah and Morgan I called to see you about, ma'am. The point is, she tells me you're short of a few things here at the rectory."

A wry smile showed for a moment as she turned and looked across at him.

"Yes, there are one or two items. But they're of no importance. We can manage without for a while until my husband has settled his affairs."

"I see."

Bashford went over to the door for his jacket.

"The thing is," he continued, coming to stand closer to her, "I've quite a bit of household stuff up at my farm. It's hardly been used at all. I bought it five years back, when I married. But my wife—well, I lost my wife and the child together, you know, and after that I pushed everything away into the one room. Feminine knick-knacks . . . they're not much use to a man living by himself."

He stopped.

Rachael's eyes had filled with swift concern.

"I'm sorry, Mr Bashford. I had no idea. How tragic for you."

"Well, it happened a time back. Life has to go on. Isabelle . . . she's a memory to me now." He passed a hand through his thick hair and bent to retrieve his hat and crop from beside the basket. "But if you do need anything, Mrs Bates, you're more than welcome to come over to Spring Hill Farm and take what you want. The stuff's only gathering dust where it is. I shan't ever use it again."

"What can I possibly say?" Rachael smiled; and again he found himself admiring the beauty of her expression. "You're more than kind, sir. I'll speak to my husband directly he comes in. I hope he'll allow me to take advantage of such a generous offer."

She walked with him out through the side gate and along the path to where his horse was tethered, munching grass cropped from the roadside. Bashford pulled himself easily into the saddle, turned to give her a little bow and held up his hat to her before putting it on. He pulled the animal's head round and nudged it into a trot.

Only when he had passed out of sight down the dip of the lane did Rachael begin to worry if, after all, it had been very wise or very proper of her to have accepted his help with hanging out bed linen.

7

Esmond Bates's enthusiasm seemed no more than luke-warm when Rachael spoke to him after supper about George Bashford's visit and the nature of his offer. He had come back late to the rectory, in a sour mood, having paid out rather more than he had reckoned on for the pony and trap. And the livery rates in the village at the stables adjoining Joe Fladgate's smithy had done nothing to improve his temper.

He toyed with the idea of repairing the old outbuilding on the church-owned glebe land behind the house and keeping the horse himself. But that would mean hiring a lad, and with the cost of fodder and shoeing coming on top, his stipend would be whittled away faster than ever. At least Joe Fladgate's price included upkeep of the trap as well as the animal.

"Esmond? Esmond!"

He looked up from his calculations.

"I asked you when can we go over to Netherton, to the farm?"

"What? Oh—I don't know. I have enough as it is with my parish duties," he told her irritably, "without running about half the countryside after a few pieces of furniture."

"But Esmond—"

He put up a hand. "I understand your impatience, Rachael. But there is little to be done until the agent has investigated my complaint about our accommodation. Hopefully, some kind of payment will be forthcoming to compensate for the lack of furnishing and goods."

"But *when*? How long do we have to wait before that happens?"

Rachael came up behind Esmond's chair in the study and put her hands on his shoulders.

"I appreciate how busy you are," she went on quietly. "I do understand. But this means so much to me—to have the house made nice, to have it comfortable and right for us." A note of sadness crept into her voice. "I'm so weary of having to make do, Esmond, patching things up, everything always so shabby and threadbare. I do so want to make a good home for us here."

She leaned forward and laid her cheek against his hair. As always, her touch weakened him. He put down his pen on the table in front of him and turned his head, grasping one of her hands and pressing his lips into the soft palm.

After a moment he said, "You do not need to prove yourself a good wife, my dear. I have always been grateful for your efforts to ensure our domestic comfort. If I appear short with you, it is because I am disappointed at not being able to provide you with something better than you have had from me so far. But things will improve—" He looked up at her. "They can only improve."

"You're very considerate."

Rachael moved away from him, and the moment of intimacy was lost.

For a while she stood in silence, staring at the opposite wall. The outline of a picture which had once hung there showed up as a brown rectangle against the faded posy pattern of the paper.

"It may take many weeks before the agent investigates our complaint against Mrs Phillips," she started again. "And in all that time we must live like this . . . hardly better accommodated than our parishioners."

"Rachael—" her husband began; but she ignored him.

"At least let us borrow something to furnish the parlour, Esmond. Suppose we were to have callers? I should be ashamed to show them into the room as it is."

Esmond bowed his head.

"Very well," he said at length. "You shall have something for the parlour. George Bashford's offer was a gesture of charity, and I should not like to seem too proud to accept."

"There'll be no trouble or expense bringing the stuff from Netherton," she hastened to explain before he should change his mind. "There's a woman in the village goes out by cart each day."

"What woman is this?"

"Dinah Flynn, from the alehouse."

Barely was the name out of her mouth before her husband's manner underwent a marked change. He pushed back his chair and stood up abruptly.

"I will not have you associating in any way with Dinah Flynn," he said harshly. "She is not fit company."

"But—"

He swung round, his eyes cold with sudden anger.

"Do not argue with me! I know about that woman. And I think it best you remember your position and not encourage her with your friendship."

She faced him across the study table, amazed at his vehemence.

"My friendship? After she has done so much to help here, you ask me to deny her my friendship?"

"It is scarcely a matter of denial—"

"Look behind you, Esmond. Do you see the curtains at your window? How neatly they hang? Dinah Flynn sewed them. And the range in the kitchen, how well it draws now? Dinah cleaned the flue because Ada couldn't manage. And the scullery floor—"

"Be silent! I am ashamed at you for defending such a creature so brazenly."

Two red spots burned on Rachael's cheeks.

"Yes, I do defend her. Oh, Esmond—where is your charity? I know why you disapprove so. But is it her fault she's in such a position? Should we condemn her for that?"

"And if it is not her fault, then whose is it, pray? One illegitimate child already, and another soon to be born. Both got against her will, I suppose you would have me believe. And as for my charity,"—Esmond glared angrily at her and shuffled together the papers on his table—"my charity does not extend to condoning immorality in my parish."

Rachael averted her face from him. She closed her eyes

57

and drew in a deep breath. It would not do to cross words while he was in such a savage humour.

In a quieter tone she said, "*I* do not condone her behaviour, either. But neither will I condemn her. She has shown herself a good friend to me."

"You choose your friends unwisely—as always."

Tight-lipped, her husband turned away and looked out through the window, forcing himself to ignore the neatly-stitched hem hanging evenly below the sill which he had praised when he saw it first, taking it for her own work.

A small tick jerked at the muscle of his jaw.

His young wife's spirited defence of such a sloven as Dinah Flynn incensed him. Always she chose to favour the worst type of creature; and do it not as a duty, but in open preference to those far better deserving of her patronage.

In Lewes he had found her enthusiasm at first engaging, and the vicar had spoken in praise of her work with the less fortunate families of the parish. But then she had begun to go among the riff-raff that polluted the town's gutters—drunks and whores and their diseased kind.

It had seemed to the fastidious Esmond that Rachael sullied herself by such behaviour. What had first attracted him so much about her—purity and innocence, a flawless virtue, an almost childlike belief in the goodness of her fellow men—was in danger of becoming contaminated by too close a contact with this human refuse. Esmond himself knew only too well how easy it was for the pure of heart to be gulled into seeing only the best of these people, to believe them worthy of salvation while all the time their insidious corruption ate into the goodness like acid.

There was a period after he had left St Albans for London when he had descended into that pit himself and become the consort of creatures more wretched and depraved than it was possible to imagine. There had been no vice so loathsome that he had recoiled from practising it on one occasion or another, no debauchery too obscene that he had turned from it in revulsion.

The degradation of his life was completed on the night he had bought a child's innocent body and so tainted and despoiled that little form with his own vileness that every human instinct had cried out against such trespass.

In the bleakness of a new dawn he had looked into the still-drugged eyes of that child. And suddenly discovered himself to be poised at the very lip of Hell, staring into its foul black depths and seeing reflected there the blasphemous image of his own soul.

That dreadful moment of self-realisation had been to him a sign, a warning presenting itself as the means to his salvation. The memory of it had seldom intruded upon his conscious mind since, in expiation of his former wickedness, he had joined the Church; but there were times, times he least expected, when it suddenly all came back so vividly, so horribly, that his disgust at himself made him physically ill.

Some nights, when he lay beside Rachael in their bed, it seemed almost as though her sweet, innocent young body was subtly transformed even as he held her, and he found himself once more in the embrace of some depraved whore whose knowing fingers crawled insistently over his unclean nakedness.

At times like that he feared that he was near to madness.

He needed constantly to exercise an iron self-control to hide his fear and weakness from the world, and from himself. He had witnessed too much of the dissolute traffic between men and women, and children; had seen how purity was tarnished and besmirched by carnality. And purity, whether of soul or body, had become for Esmond Bates a thing inviolate. As a priest he had set himself a mission to proclaim the Gospel message of forgiveness, in the absolute belief that the soul's salvation lay in purity and chastity of mind and body. Man is the slave of sin, he preached. But there were too few who wanted to know.

He sighed deeply, his anger draining from him. Perhaps it had been unwise of him to bring his wife to Weatherfield so soon. She should have remained behind in Lewes, at least until everything had been properly settled here.

Turning from the window, he moved slowly back to his chair and re-seated himself.

"Rachael—" he said after a time, "Rachael, you are young

and too trusting, and people will ever take advantage of that. Be guided by me. I know the type of woman Dinah Flynn is. She will worm her way into your affection for her own corrupt ends . . . use you without your even being aware of it."

"I think not."

"Very well. But consider my position here, if you will. What kind of example do I set my parishioners if I allow my wife to become the intimate of farm drabs?"

"That is unjust, Esmond. Dinah is no farm drab."

The rector closed his eyes wearily and passed a hand across his face. He knew all too well the obstinate streak in his wife's nature, her wilfulness when thwarted of something on which her mind was set.

"The man she consorts with is a common gipsy. A horse dealer, a vagrant. I am told that his reputation with women is a byword throughout the district—"

"Then isn't Dinah more to be pitied than blamed, loving him as much as she does?"

"—and the life he leads is an insult to decency. He openly boasts of his dissolute behaviour . . . it is no secret that he maintains bastard children in other parishes than this. What creature of any honour would willingly associate herself with such a man?"

"When a woman is in love, she often shuts her eyes to imperfections."

Esmond looked up sharply at the ambiguous note in his wife's voice. He frowned, but made no reply.

"Let me say this on Dinah's behalf, since she's not here to defend herself," Rachael went on swiftly. "She remains unwed only because Morgan—this . . . stallion man—refuses to marry her. In all other things her conduct is above reproach. He acknowledges her child as his, and he pays for its support. And though their relationship may not be one that the Church recognises, the previous rector here, Mr Yardley, went so far as to bless the union by baptising the child. The entry is in the register."

"I have seen it." Esmond's frown deepened. "I am not concerned with the ill-advised actions of previous incumbents. From what I have learned of John Yardley, he set his rules by his own lax standards. The parishioners will not find me so tolerant of their loose living."

"And yet if you prove yourself too severe with them, you may lose their goodwill," she argued.

"Better to lose that, surely, than to lead them into temptation by closing my eyes to their misconduct. Do you set yourself up against me, Rachael?"

"No."

"Then do not range yourself so blithely on the side of Dinah Flynn and her like. It is not they who need your support—they can manage very well for themselves. It is *I* who need to be supported. What use is it for me to exhort my flock to conduct themselves in a righteous and God-fearing fashion if my wife aligns herself against me and is seen openly to encourage moral laxity?"

"Forgive me, Esmond, but you seem intent on turning this conversation into some kind of a judgment. When have I ever encouraged moral laxity? All I am doing is accepting the help and—yes, the friendship, of this one woman. How can that possibly be interpreted as encouraging her immorality?"

Rachael turned from her husband and moved away.

"Surely I don't need to remind you, of all people, of Our Lord's words to the woman taken in adultery."

He made no answer. Instead, as she opened the door, he said sullenly, "Where are you going?"

Without looking back she replied, "To ask in the village for directions to the alehouse."

8

It was the same Regency regiment whose members had toasted Rachael Bates's aunt in Lewes years before which was responsible for the establishment of Dinah Flynn's family in Weatherfield.

61

One of their number, buying himself out of the service, had been moved by Irish impulse to acquire the licence of the alehouse which served the neighbourhood. He lost no time in advertising the change of ownership, and the place quickly earned for itself a reputation as a "regular" for the more serious drinkers of the area.

In the early days there was frequent trouble with the local constable: it was not merely the drunken violence and illegal gaming that brought him in, but the presence of poachers and owlers and other night birds in the fume-filled anonymity of Captain Flynn's ale-room. The parish overseer was a regular visitor, too; but only on Sundays, and at some risk to his person, attempting the discharge of his duty to see that the law against Sabbath drinking was being observed on the premises.

The Captain's wife and baby daughter had followed him from Lewes camp. Three more children were to be born at the alehouse, but only one, another girl, survived infancy. When a surfeit of alcohol finally killed off Patrick Flynn, it was the elder daughter, Molly, who took over the running of the place and within a year had turned it into a well-managed and reputable establishment for the more sober and law-abiding.

She was a hard-working and disciplined young woman, careful not to encourage the familiarity of her customers. So it came as something of a surprise to the district when, in the summer of 1830, the first whispers of gossip hinted that one customer, at least, had found his way into her bed.

"What d'you think o' that Molly Flynn?" tongues had clacked in the village. "What did I tell you? Bad blood will out."

"And never a sign of her being church-cried, neither. Who was it, d'you know?"

But Molly Flynn never said.

In due time her own daughter—red-haired like the old Captain—was born at the alehouse, and named Dinah. The village gossips, sensing they had lost their quarry, abandoned the chase and set their tongues in pursuit of fresher game.

True, there had been a brief revival of old rumour when

Dinah's little Frankie was born; but this time there was no need to speculate about the father's identity when the whole of Weatherfield knew that Frank Morgan the stallion man had been lodging at the alehouse.

The setting of so much family drama stood at one side of the broad lane running from Weatherfield to Troy Town, a mile or so out from the village and separated from it by a natural boundary of fields and copses. It was an ancient building, the original shape long vanished beneath a number of rooms and winding staircases added on to it by successive generations of tenants.

The street door opened at the top of a flight of stone steps and led directly into a broad central passage. At the further end, another set of steps made a somewhat hazardous entrance down into the ale-room itself, a low-ceilinged place, one wall occupied entirely by an open hearth and flanking wooden settles. The rest of the room was furnished with stools and several circular tables, each topped with an iron rim to prevent customers carelessly elbowing their beer pots to the stone-flagged floor.

Just now, the tables were pushed back against the further wall while a middle-aged woman vigorously applied a broom to the flags.

Pausing by the hearth, she bent down.

"Get out from under there, blast you!"

At the sound of her voice, a small brown mongrel dog crawled on its belly from beneath one of the settles, showing the whites of its eyes as it looked up at her.

Molly Flynn aimed a blow at it with the broom.

"Out! Go on—clear off wi' you."

Dinah, who was wiping the table tops over with a damp rag, glanced across at the wiry, thin-faced woman.

"Let it be, Mam. It's doing no harm there. The poor thing's been out in the rain all night."

Mrs Flynn (the "Mrs" was a courtesy title only) put the broomhead beneath the cringing animal's hindquarters and gave it a sharp push in the direction of the steps. Then she turned on her daughter.

"And how am I to get this floor cleaned up wi' blessed dogs under my feet. Come on, now—look sharp wi' that you're doing, my girl. It's gone seven already. The parson's wife'll be here any minute, and you not ready for her."

Dinah squeezed out the rag into a pail.

"I've done," she said.

"Well, don't stand there. Get your pinny off and see to little Frankie afore you go. I've only got one pair of hands and you know how he needs watching wi' his milk."

Dinah lifted the pail and went slowly up the steps and along to the kitchen. The baby inside her felt heavy, a dragging weight on her body, and her legs and ankles were already starting to swell again, although it was still early in the day.

The toddler on the kitchen floor, a shock-headed, sturdy little fellow, shouted his delight as she came in and lifted his arms to her. She emptied the pail into the sluice, then bent cumbrously and hauled him up and sat with him on her knee, where he kicked and wriggled about.

"Keep still, do, Frankie!" she told him irritably. "Drink your milk up, there's a good boy."

He sucked greedily at the cup held to his mouth and a thin white trickle ran over his chin and down his plump bare chest.

"Here's that Mrs Bates come!" her mother called to her along the passage. "Stir yourself now, girl—our Jack's outside wi' her."

Dinah wiped the milky mouth clean and set the boy back down among his playthings on the floor. A dull pain curled around the small of her back. She drew a deep breath; then slowly let it out again. The pain had been nagging at her all week.

"Just coming, Mam," she called back, reaching up for her shawl on a hook behind the door. "You be good now, Frankie. Your grannam'll be along to you in a minute."

Jack Adams had halted his cart in the early morning shadow of trees opposite the alehouse steps. The son of Mrs Flynn's sister, he worked with his father, Priam Adams, as a general carter and carrier in the district; and, being still unmarried, lived with his parents in one of the larger cottages facing Weatherfield green.

Once Dinah's advancing pregnancy had made it difficult for her to walk the seven miles or so into Netherton each day, to Spring Hill Farm, her cousin had arranged his work so that he could take her there and back by cart.

Usually they were away well before six o'clock; but not today. On this particular morning he had an additional passenger to carry; Mrs Bates from the rectory.

Dinah had told him that she was going to see Mr Bashford at the farm, and instructed him to wait for her out of sight beyond the church in case the new parson should see him through the window. Jack had no idea why there should be so much bother to keep the visit a secret from the woman's own husband. But he was not one to ask questions, preferring as ever to mind his own business and let other folks mind theirs.

Now, though, sitting with Mrs Bates behind him in the cart, he was ill at ease, fidgeting with the reins and wishing they could be on their way.

Jack Adams was always nervous in the company of strangers. So many times during his young life he had been the butt of derision and cruelty because of his acute stammer that he spoke as little as possible. It was only in the company of his family and few friends that he was able to relax enough to hold an almost normal conversation.

The journey out from Weatherfield had proved uncomfortable. He appreciated that the parson's wife only meant to be friendly, asking so many questions. But he had stuttered and stumbled so much over his replies that even to his own accustomed ears he had sounded half-witted.

Jack cleared his throat unhappily and wished that Dinah would bestir herself.

"Does the place have a name, do you know?" Rachael Bates asked, breaking the lengthening silence.

He shifted himself on his seat and looked back at her. He had a delicate, almost girlish face with large eyes which usually held a wary expression and a well-shaped mouth poorly disguised by a pale, sparse moustache.

"A name?" repeated Rachael. "The alehouse, I mean. They often have a painted sign hanging up outside, but I don't see one here."

Jack flushed. He cleared his throat.

"Folks just c-call it the alehouse, m-m-ma'am. Though I believe it were once the M-m-man in the M-m-m-m-" He stuck.

"Moon?"

He nodded miserably.

"It's a fine old building."

He nodded once more; then started up in relief as Dinah appeared.

Rachael thought at once how strained she looked. During the journey to Netherton, too, she seemed subdued and quite unlike her usual self. But when asked, she only replied, "Oh, it's nothing, ma'am. I'm getting broody, I expect," and laughed a little.

However they had hardly passed the first outlying cottages and were still some distance from Spring Hill Farm, when Dinah gave a sudden gasp and clutched at Rachael's arm.

"What is it? Dinah—what's wrong?"

"I—I think the baby's coming . . . . my waters have gone."

"Your—? Are you sure?"

Dinah nodded, her face suddenly contorted with pain.

Rachael looked down at the stain spreading across the clean sacking beneath them.

"Jack—make haste! Get us to Mr Bashford's, quick as you can!"

Jack Adams was already applying his whip to the horse, forcing it into a fast trot that sent the cart lurching from side to side as it rattled through Netherton village and up the long slope of the hill beyond.

George Bashford, working with his men in the home field, saw the cloud of dust as they swerved in at the far end of his drive, and from the way Jack Adams was urging on his horse he guessed at once there was something amiss and came running down to meet them.

Barely had the cart been brought to a standstill in the yard before Rachael was on her feet, crying out to him for assistance. The quick surge of pleasure he felt at seeing her again was immediately replaced by concern when he saw how agitated she was.

Reaching the cart, he took in Dinah's situation at a glance.

"Now then, Mrs Bates, there's no cause to be so alarmed," he said calmly, helping her down. "She's not going to have the child this very minute. Here, Jack—give me a hand with her into the house."

"You'll send for a doctor?" Rachael asked anxiously, following them in.

"Doctor? There's no doctor around here, ma'am. The nearest is miles away, in East Grinstead. She'll manage well enough without, don't you worry. It isn't as though this one's her first."

Dinah was made as comfortable as possible upstairs in a starkly furnished room with whitewashed walls. Word was sent to fetch the local woman who assisted at such times, but she lay ill in bed with a flux and in need of attention herself.

"You're not to worry," George Bashford told Rachael again. "Stay here with her while I ride over to Shatterford. It's not far. I was there this week and saw someone who'll do just as well. And Jack's already started back to Weatherfield to bring Mrs Flynn."

"But . . . what if I should need help while you're gone?" she asked in a low voice, glancing towards the bed. "I've had no experience. What should I do?"

Bashford spoke to her reassuringly. "Keep calm and let nature do its work. Dinah's a strong, healthy girl. Nothing can go wrong."

But his mouth tightened as he turned away. Unspoken lay the memory of his own young wife, dying four years back in this same room giving birth to a dead child.

Isabelle's suffering had dragged on through almost three days of cruel, punishing labour. A doctor had attended her; and a midwife who constantly forced her to drink infusions of feverfew and raspberry leaf, though she vomited much of it straight back. Their ministrations had proved useless.

At the end of those long nightmare hours his son had been born, perfect. And dead. Isabelle had followed the child soon after, weakened by the exertions of her labour and the loss of blood.

Bashford looked across at Dinah, quiet on the bed. A pity she had not had the good sense to stay home at the alehouse today. Then he moved away towards the door, and as he passed Rachael he put his hand for a moment on her slender shoulder and said quietly, "I won't be long. I promise."

By midday Dinah's pains were coming harder. She bore them bravely, comforted by the other woman's presence and pathetically grateful for what little assistance she was able to give. When the contractions started, she asked for something to pull on, and Rachael went out and found a strip of towelling to tie to the brass headrail.

As the contractions strengthened Dinah had to bite her lip to keep herself from crying out; and there was nothing the other could do for her now except keep the sweat-streaked hair from her face and hold down her shoulders during the worst of the pain.

At last there was the sound of someone below, footsteps on the stairs, the door opening.

Rachael turned, relieved, and saw George Bashford there. Beside him in the doorway was another man.

Before she could stop herself, she had cried, "You—?" And then covered her mouth with her hand in embarrassment and confusion.

"This is Frank Morgan," Bashford said at once. "I expect you already know—"

"No. We've never met." She collected herself hastily.

Frank Morgan looked at her. His dark eyes moved slowly over her face and body.

He smiled, and said, "We've never met, that's true. But I remember seeing you." Then his gaze moved to the woman on the bed.

Dinah heard his voice and feebly turned her head towards him.

"Frank?"

"I'm here."

"Oh, Frank . . . I thought you—"

Then pain overwhelmed her again and she gripped the towel and hauled on it, the breath coming in sobs between her clenched teeth.

"Rest easy, now. It won't be long." He went over to the bed and kneeled down. "Breathe steady if you can, love. Let's see whether the crown shows yet."

Rachael turned away.

"Aye . . . There it is. And dry as bone." Morgan got to his feet. "Have her waters broken?"

"Yes. About—about four hours ago," Rachael replied without looking at him.

"Damn it! That means a dry birthing."

"Can you do anything for her?" asked George Bashford from the doorway.

"Oh, she'll be all right. There's enough here to see her safely through—" the stallion leader motioned with his head towards the bag he had brought into the room with him. "But I'll need hot water, a couple of jugs full. And clean cloths. And do you have any goose fat in the place?"

"I believe so," Bashford answered. "I'll let you have it directly." He touched Rachael's arm. "Come along, Mrs Bates. We won't be needed here. You can lend me a hand below if you will."

She followed him down the stairs.

"Does he really know what he's doing?" she asked. "It seems hardly—well, proper, somehow."

The young farmer made a sound of reassurance. "He's as good as a doctor any day. Better, even. I wish . . . And he does happen to be the child's father. Dinah's in good hands, don't you fret."

Rachael sincerely hoped so. And was as relieved as George Bashford himself when, a little later, Dinah was safely delivered of her baby.

It was a girl.

"Now what's up wi' him?"

"With who, mam?"

69

"That Frank Morgan, that's who. Isn't he going to stay wi' you?"

"What d'you mean?"

Dinah's face was pale with fatigue, her eyes dark-ringed as she lay in the bed, propped against a folded bolster.

Mrs Flynn stared out through the window. "He's going away down that hill as though he can't put too much distance atween himself and here."

She turned sharply to look at her daughter. "You haven't been up to any smart tricks at his expense, have you, my girl?"

"Tricks? What kind o' tricks?"

"He didn't look too pleased about that baby. Seems to me the mite would've done better wi' black hair, perhaps."

Dinah bent her head over the small form at her breast, frowning slightly at the downy auburn hair that was showing more noticeably now that the baby's skin was losing its redness. Mam was right. Frank had not seemed too happy about his new daughter.

She shivered slightly.

9

Dinah had good reason for concern. The stallion man had been dismayed at his daughter's birth.

His daughter? He wrenched fiercely at the branches in his path as he strode along. Damn it, that child was never his. Dinah had played fast and loose elsewhere. She must have done. He had never fathered a daughter in his life, not once; not ever. So blast Dinah Flynn for a faithless bitch! Easy to let some other man pleasure her while he was away, then cozen him into believing the bastard she bore was his.

When was it he had lain with her? Morgan counted back. It must have been around the end of last harvest. Yes, he had been in the district for more than a week. But he had scarcely set foot in Weatherfield—there had been a woman from one of the downland farms to occupy him.

He frowned; then suddenly swore aloud, remembering. Dinah had come looking for him one night and found him in one of the barns, the worse for drink. But damn it, drunk or sober, he had taken every precaution that no second by-blow would come of that encounter.

He turned his face to the sky and closed his eyes, his mind a turmoil. The child was full-term, he would swear, so it *must* have been conceived at that time. But a girl! It was not possible.

There was a general belief among horsemen that a mare's first stallion had so great an influence on her body that every one of the foals she subsequently dropped inherited something of him, no matter what other horse sired them. And the more a mare was covered by a particular stallion, the more completely her offspring would resemble him.

Frank Morgan applied this same belief to himself, sincerely convinced that he was so much a man, so totally masculine in mind and body and action, that he was capable only of reproducing sons, sons in his own image.

Dinah's child was a daughter, and therefore none of his. And if not his, then whose?

He stared about him for a moment, then wheeled around. She had pricked his pride, and that hurt him. Never mind that he had tired of her already—she had no right to gull him, to think him so easily deceived. One way or another, he thought grimly, she would be made to pay for this day's work.

He began retracing his steps, cutting back through a plantation of spruce and up towards Spring Hill. By a gate at the back of the farmhouse was standing a woman in white. Frank Morgan paused as he recognised her.

Mrs Bates.

He had not believed it at first when someone told him she was the wife of the new rector of Weatherfield. The moment he had set eyes on this woman, the day she came to the village, he knew instinctively that she had never lain with her

71

husband; nor any other. A man of his experience could hardly be mistaken in a thing like that.

One night, he had stood in the darkness of the rectory garden watching her brush her hair at the open window above the porch. The lamplight within the room had outlined her body through the thin material of her shift. Mr Bates had come up behind her and put his arms round her waist; but after a few moments had moved away again, and for a long time after the lamp went out his wife had stayed motionless at the window.

From the shadows below, Morgan had watched the pale reflection of her face, and the fancy had come into his mind that she was like some caged wild creature that had never known the taste of freedom.

Looking at her now, standing at the house gate above him, something quickened inside the stallion leader. He grinned suddenly. He would pay Dinah Flynn back in her own coin.

"Is she resting quiet now?"

Rachael turned her head sharply, startled by the unexpected sound of his voice. He saw her eyes widen a fraction as he came up to her. Her young face looked drawn and there were lines of weariness about her lips.

"I'm sorry—what did you say?"

"Dinah. She's resting now?"

Rachael nodded.

Morgan came in through the gate and stood beside her.

"She'll need an hour or two yet before she's fit to travel. Will you be going back to Weatherfield with her?"

"I suppose I must. I . . . I should have been back much earlier. But as things are—"

"I'll take you, if you like. I'm going that way."

Rachael raised her eyes and looked at him. This was the first time she had seen the stallion leader properly, close to. Before it had only been at a distance. The speed of his walk had made him sweat and he had pulled off his neckerchief and opened his shirt. The crisp black hair grew almost to the base of his throat.

He was not a tall man and she did not have to lift her eyes

far to meet his. Something there seemed to catch and hold her—a boldness, a sensuality that made her heart beat suddenly a little faster and sent an exciting warmth through her limbs.

She hurriedly dropped her gaze to his mouth and saw the full lips beneath the black moustache draw back in a slow smile.

"Would you like me to take you?"

His voice was very soft.

"What . . . what about Dinah?"

"Don't worry about Dinah. She'll be looked after."

Rachael drew a ragged breath. She felt utterly drained by those gruelling long hours in the bedroom. Her thoughts were in disorder, and her judgment—never her strongest point, subject as it was to sudden shifts of mood and fancy—on perilous ground. Under normal circumstances she would not for an instant have considered accepting Frank Morgan's invitation. But these were not normal circumstances; and she was a woman weakened not only by physical fatigue but by the constant mental stress of frustration and disappointment.

At this moment her natural scruples failed her. She lacked the strength to resist a man as compellingly forceful as this one.

"I'd better let them know," she said, indicating the farmhouse. "I was meant to be choosing some pieces of furniture."

"Won't it do another time?"

She nodded again.

"Right. I'll wait on for you here. Don't be long."

She went back into the house and up to the whitewashed room where Dinah lay. The girl and her mother both looked at her strangely, but made no comment when she told them Frank Morgan was conveying her back to Weatherfield.

George Bashford's reaction was more marked, and it struck her later that he had seemed unusually concerned. But then, the furniture could wait until Rachael came out to Netherton some other day, he had assured her; she was not to concern herself. It was more important that she went home to her husband before dark.

Still feeling utterly disorientated by the day's events, she went back outside to Frank Morgan and followed him down the hill path behind the house.

From the upstairs window Mrs Flynn watched them go.

When Rachael started to talk about her husband, the rector, on the walk into Netherton village, Morgan wondered for a moment whether his unerring instinct had for once misled him.

Then he had smiled to himself, shaking his head at any such self-doubt. There was a world of difference between the way an unawakened woman looked into a man's eyes and the look a bedded woman gave him. The latter was confident and knowing. The other was how Rachael Bates had looked back there at the gate. Uncertain. Innocent. Immensely attractive.

Morgan smiled again as he watched her neat figure ahead of him on the narrow lane.

By God, this was a pursuit he meant to enjoy, he promised himself. By some extraordinary luck he had stumbled upon that most irresistible of combinations, a maid who was married. And, moreover, not married to just any body, but to a minister of the Church no less. The situation had a most appealing piquancy for someone of the stallion man's appetite and humour.

He did not consider for a moment that he was committing a grave wrong to these two people. Had he stopped to think what he was doing, his amorality would have led him to argue that he was not harming their marriage in any way, but helping it rather. The Reverend Bates was obviously little use as a husband; and while two such innocents shared the same bed their union was bound to remain unconsummated.

As Frank Morgan saw it, by arousing the man's wife to the sensual sweetness of physical love and teaching her to know her own body and use it as an instrument of pleasure for her husband, he was doing both of them the greatest service.

"Have you been married long?" he enquired casually after they had walked on side by side in silence for a while.

Rachael shook her head. "Not long," she answered briefly.

"And how long is that?"

"Almost two years. It will be our second anniversary next month."

"That's nice. And are you happy with your husband?"

His question startled her. She paused. Then said quickly, "What's that to you, sir?"

Morgan shrugged. "Nothing. Look,"—he pointed ahead—"there's Padley's place through the trees."

"Padley's? Should I know it?"

"No. But I left my horse there this morning when I rode over from Shatterford with Bashford."

He turned as a thought struck him.

"You can ride, I suppose?"

"Ride?"

"Aye. No matter if you can't. I'll hold you tight."

The colour rose in Rachael's face. Her steps faltered, then stopped.

"Oh, didn't I explain?" he continued blandly. "I've no cart or carriage to convey you in. I'm sorry if you've been misled. You'll have to ride pillion with me."

"I'll—? You're not serious, surely?"

He smiled.

"Why did you not tell me this earlier?" There was a note of anger in her voice.

Turning, she began walking back in the direction of the farm.

"You wouldn't have come with me." Morgan followed.

"Of course I wouldn't! You don't really expect me to ride on the back of your saddle, do you?"

"I don't use a saddle."

She glanced back at him over her shoulder. "Lord's sake . . . what would people say?"

"Damn what they'd say."

The stallion man lengthened his stride and moved ahead, forcing her to stop. He came closer. Again Rachael was troubled by the intimacy of his gaze, the warm virile smell of his body.

75

"You want to get back to Weatherfield, don't you? How does it matter how you go—astride a horse or behind one?"

"But it does matter. You must remember who I am . . . my position . . . my husband . . ."

"How is your husband going to find out if we never tell him?"

Morgan was right beside her now, almost touching. When he spoke again, Rachael felt his breath on her cheek.

"And you'd like to come with me, wouldn't you?"

His nearness disturbed her. She closed her eyes, remembering the effect he had had on her once before, when she had watched him below her in the churchyard at Lewes. In her mind she saw him again. The image set her pulses racing.

A feeling she had never known before, or even dreamed of, seized her suddenly; and it no longer mattered in the least that this man was the father of Dinah Flynn's children, that he had kissed and caressed Charlotte Smith . . .

She felt herself succumb to an overwhelming recklessness. And when she opened her eyes to look at him once more, Frank Morgan knew beyond any doubt that she would not refuse him when the time came.

He touched her arm lightly.

"Don't worry that we'll be seen. We'll cut across the back fields. There'll be nobody about this time of evening."

Riding in his arms on the back of the great stallion proved an experience which would remain vivid in Rachael's memory for the rest of her life, despite the shadow cast over it by future events.

He held her close from behind, gripping her within his thighs, one arm strongly around her, the other brushing against her breast as he handled the reins. She had removed her chip bonnet and leaned back against him, eyes half-closed against the wind in her face.

The sun banded the western sky with colour, firing the heads of the Downs in the far distance and sinking its dying warmth into the earth of the fields. Everything around them seemed touched by a primitive magic, as though the man and

76

his stallion had taken her back through time to a pagan world.

The whole experience was so utterly unreal, so much like fantasy, that Rachael wished it might go on for ever.

But Morgan's horse, despite his massive size, covered the miles across country surprisingly quickly, and it was still not quite dusk when they reached the concealment of a copse of trees at the far end of Weatherfield churchyard.

The stallion leader slid from the Shire's back and held up his arms for her, catching her firmly around the hips. For a long moment he held her captive against him before slowly setting her to the ground. Through the branches, the roof of the rectory kitchen was just visible.

"My husband will be waiting for me," Rachael said breathlessly.

"Oh, yes . . . your husband. I'd forgotten about him."

"I must go now."

"I suppose you must."

"Thank you for bringing me back."

"It was my pleasure."

In the dimness, his teeth gleamed whitely.

"Perhaps—" she began hesitantly.

"What?"

"Oh . . . nothing."

She moved away from him into the evening shadows, straightening the crumpled gown.

Softly he said, "I'll be seeing you again—beauty!"

Esmond was not at the rectory when Rachael went into the house. A note on his study table curtly informed her that he had gone to a meeting of the churchwardens in the vestry.

She was relieved at his absence. It meant that she was able to change her clothing before he came in. And, since little Ada Slybody had already gone, there was time to be alone to collect her thoughts and compose herself. The reckless fancies which Frank Morgan had aroused in her did not belong in the sobering atmosphere of the rectory.

When her husband arrived at the house a while later,

Rachael's appearance was as neat as always, her expression as calm.

"You've been a long time, Esmond. I was expecting you home before now," she greeted him, reaching up to kiss his cheek. "What detained you?"

"I might well ask you the same thing."

He did not return her kiss, and she realised from his demeanour that something had angered him.

"I've been to Netherton, to see Mr Bashford about the furniture for the parlour," she said calmly. "You knew I was going."

He looked at her stonily.

"Dinah Flynn's baby has been born—"

"And you had to involve yourself, I suppose."

"Don't sneer, Esmond. I could hardly help but be involved. There was no one else to stay with her."

"Oh, come now. What do you take me for? No one else, indeed!"

"But it's true."

She began an explanation of the circumstances, but he cut her short.

"Enough! I have no wish to hear about it. Not another word, do you understand? Now would you go and prepare me some supper. I have an appetite."

Esmond ate his meal in silence at the kitchen table.

When he had finished he wiped his lips carefully and put the napkin down beside his plate. Rachael thought he was about to say something; but instead, he got to his feet and left the room without so much as glancing at her. In a while she heard the door to the study close behind him.

He often had these hostile moods of temper. Sometimes for days on end he would hardly speak, hardly look at her, as though he found her very presence offensive. Then, abruptly, the spell would break and he would revert again to his former self.

But each time, something in Rachael's regard for her husband curdled a little more.

She cleared the dishes from the table and took them through to the scullery to be rinsed under the pump. Through

78

the window above the brownstone sink the outline of treetops at the far end of the churchyard showed blackly against the pale night sky.

She paused at her work and stared out, remembering. Then passed the back of her wet hand across her mouth. Already the events of the afternoon were starting to seem unreal, fantastic, a dream almost. She recalled the undeniable hunger of her feelings for Frank Morgan, her incautious behaviour.

And suddenly, she was frightened.

10

"Where are you going?"

At the sound of her husband's voice Rachael paused on the stairs.

Esmond came out of the study and stood below in the rectory hallway.

"Did you not hear me? Where are you going?"

She turned and looked back at him. "I'm going to bed," she said tonelessly.

"Not yet. Come down. I wish to speak to you."

"Esmond . . . I'm tired. I've been up since before six."

His face was in shadow, the hall illuminated only by the lamplight in the room behind him, silhouetting his figure.

"I repeat, I wish to speak to you."

Rachael heard the steely expression in his voice and knew it would be unwise to resist. Blowing out her candle, she came slowly down and followed him into the study.

"Sit down, please."

He seated himself opposite behind his table and leaned forward, hands clasped in front of him, and cleared his throat.

"I have something very serious to say to you. It has come to my knowledge that you have been conducting yourself in a most reprehensible manner."

She remained silent, her eyes fixed on his face. Oh God, what if she and Frank Morgan had been seen together after all?

Esmond watched her carefully, waiting for her expression to betray her.

"Well?"

Still she said nothing.

"Come, now," he snapped, growing impatient, "surely you have something to say? You have been seen by members of the congregation indulging yourself with a man in what can only be described as improper behaviour!"

The colour rose hotly in her cheeks.

"Ah—I see by your face that you comprehend me at last."

Rachael's throat closed up in panic.

"I—I . . ."

"Yes?" he pounced.

She shook her head.

"It's not true," she managed to whisper at last.

"Not true? Not true, do you say? Woman, how dare you compound your guilt with such lies! Two witnesses saw your misconduct with this man. And you have the affrontery to say it is not true."

Rachael clenched her fists and pressed them into her lap to keep them from trembling. Her heart pounded; her stomach so tight that she felt physically ill with apprehension. What could possibly have possessed her to behave so irresponsibly with Morgan? How was she ever to explain her reasons, her feelings, to Esmond, of all men?

Desperately she said, "Who are these witnesses?"

"The wives of Joseph Fladgate and Ezra Jolly."

They must have been somewhere in the churchyard earlier.

"And . . . and what is it that I'm supposed to have done?"

"You don't know? You've forgotten, perhaps?" Esmond's sarcasm was unnecessarily heavy.

Again, she shook her head.

"Then allow me to refresh your memory, my dear. You were seen by these two respectable parishioners in broad daylight standing out in the garden here with George Bashford—"

"Mr *Bashford*?"

"—allowing him to handle the rectory laundry—"

"The laundry!"

"The laundry! Don't you realise what a compromising position that places you in? The wife of a minister of the Church, letting herself be seen by all and sundry with a man—a virtual stranger—hanging out . . . bed sheets?"

Rachael's sense of relief was so great that she almost laughed aloud. And as the nerve-wracking tension receded, she foolishly over-reacted.

"Better than being seen with him between sheets, surely? That might have given the ladies something worth complaining about."

The flippant, thoughtless remark goaded Esmond Bates into a sudden fury of temper.

"Yes, you would like that, wouldn't you!" he shouted, flinging himself out of his chair. "Someone like Bashford in your bed. That would suit you very well! Oh, you needn't look at me like that, pretending your innocence. I know you too well. Don't think I haven't seen you, Rachael, the way you looked at George Bashford—yes, him and any other man who pays you notice. And don't think, either, that you gulled me with your excuses about his furniture. Furniture! It was not furniture that took you to his house today with that wretched woman. Come, now—admit it! It was all a trick in order to deceive me."

Rachael shrank back in her chair at the savagery of her husband's tone. Roughly, he reached down and seized her by the shoulders, dragging her to her feet.

She clung to him.

"Oh God, Esmond . . . don't, please don't! I only spoke in jest. I didn't mean it. There's no truth in what you say—not a word."

He flung her away from him.

81

"You expect me to believe you? My own people come to me to complain of your infamous conduct—openly flaunting yourself before that man, encouraging him to familiarity—and you expect me to believe that you are innocent? That you had no intention of deceiving me?"

"No! No! I've never deceived you. How can you say that?"

He stared at her, pressed from him against the wall, her face pale with emotion. His insane jealousy drove him on.

"My God, Rachael. I should have left you in the stews of Lewes. A whore has better occupation there."

She flinched at that. In his vile tempers he had laid his tongue to many hurtful names, but never that before now.

"Ah—that hit its mark, did it not? You don't care to be called whore, do you, my dear."

She averted her head, feeling the tears start, reluctant to let him see how his words hurt her. In a while his vicious mood would pass, as it had done so often before, and he would become contrite, regretting his outburst, begging her forgiveness. But this time, for such a petty matter, she did not think she could grant forgiveness so easily.

She raised her face to him once more, struggling to control the trembling of her lips.

"You have no right . . . no right to speak to me in such a way," she said brokenly. "I've never once deceived you, neither in my heart nor in my actions. Your abuse is more than I can bear."

The tears spilled over, and she stumbled towards the door.

Esmond was immediately at her side. He laid a restraining hand on her arm and she could feel that he was shaking.

She snatched herself away from him.

"Don't touch me!"

"Rachael—Rachael, I'm sorry . . . so sorry. Forgive me." The pathetic pleading had begun. "Don't cry. I cannot bear to see you distressed. Forgive me. I had no right, it's true, to abuse you so shamefully."

She made no answer.

"I love you so much, my dear . . . so very much. I cannot help my jealousy. What man could, with such a wife! Of course you meant no harm. How could you possibly. You are so young, so pure in mind. Please don't turn yourself away from me like that, I beg you. Forgive me. Rachael . . . dearest . . . tell me I have your forgiveness."

He put his arms around her and pulled her, resisting, against him. She bit her lip to stop herself from screaming out at him to let her go, leave her alone, to go away—anything but what she knew he expected of her now.

Awkwardly, he lifted her stubborn chin and began kissing her, his lips and cheeks wet with his own tears.

"Let me hold you," he whispered hoarsely. "Be kind to me, Rachael."

She allowed him to lead her upstairs. The bedroom was still warm from the evening sun, and the lush scent of the climbing rose at the open window seemed to stifle the air.

Esmond began tearing at his clothes, hurling aside the clerical stock, dragging at the straps of his trousers in a fever of impatience. Rachael forced herself to feel as little as possible as she went automatically through the process of undressing. It had all happened so many times before.

Later she lay staring up at the ceiling where a moth flew drunkenly in the yellow circle of reflected lamplight. Esmond was curled up at the far side of the bed, making it shake with his sobs. Through the latticed window the evening star shone clear and bright beyond the cottage roofs, and somewhere up in the hill fields a dog fox barked.

Why did it have to be this way? Her husband's coldness, his outbursts, his contrition, his excitement; and always, his failure.

She thought of Frank Morgan and remembered the look in his dark eyes, his breath on her cheek, his body firm against hers in the copse. She remembered how his hard-muscled thighs had gripped her on the ride, how his arm had brushed against her breast. Something pleasurable began to knot in the pit of her stomach.

She rolled over and touched her husband's shoulder.

"Don't," she murmured. "Don't grieve so, Esmond. Hold me . . . please . . . put your arms round me and hold me."

He sniffed convulsively and turned to her, pulling her against him. His body trembled terribly; but gradually he grew still and after a time his breathing quietened and became regular. Rachael continued to stroke his hair, while the knot inside her pulsed a little longer, then died.

Esmond was asleep.

For a long while afterwards she lay beside him, a prey to her own misery and despair, asking herself again and again why she had ever consented to marry such a man. She had lived with him as his wife for almost two years, and still she did not know him, could not understand the reasons for his strangeness, seemed unable to penetrate into the darker side of his nature.

He was such a complex person. His swings of mood were so extreme, so erratic, that she often felt she was sharing her life with two or three totally different people. Rachael could not know—for he took great pains to conceal the fact from her—that it was his failure as a priest that oppressed Esmond most deeply during these periods of depression. The awareness of insufficiency was a constant drain on his spiritual strength, a goad with which he lacerated his conscience; and at such times he wanted only to hide himself away behind a locked door and be left alone to exorcise the demons that harried him.

These fits of bleak depression might last for days; and at the end he would re-emerge sunken-eyed and drawn in feature, surrendering himself without a murmur to Rachael's demonstrations of concern and responding with tenderness and affection, becoming once more the man to whom she had so readily given her heart those years past in Lewes.

When Rachael had first heard the new curate of All Souls preach, she had taken an immediate liking to the handsome, melancholy-looking man in the pulpit above her. When she discovered that Mr Bates was still unmarried, she imagined that the melancholy of his expression must result from the loneliness of his life, and in a short while was allowing herself

84

to admire his fair good looks, the slim upright figure so well set off by the sober cloth of his calling.

She was an imaginative young woman and one feeling followed swiftly upon the heels of another: within a month this romantic, handsome, solitary figure had aroused in her feelings of protective tenderness. Within a month more she had to confess to herself that she was a little in love with him. By the early spring of 1849 Esmond Bates was a constant fixation in her thoughts and his existence was rapidly becoming the most important thing in her young life.

Esmond noticed her. He could hardly fail to do so. She put herself so often in his way, asking his advice, offering her good services for the parish, always at hand whenever she was needed, yet never intrusive or overly familiar as some of the other young female parishioners were.

Whenever he paid her some small compliment about her work, Rachael would visibly glow with happiness and spend the rest of the day feeling that her heart was about to burst with love. If, on the other hand, he was preoccupied and neglected to speak to her, that same heart sank within her and the day was blighted with disappointment.

Her aunt was not long left in doubt about the object of her niece's affections; and she approved.

Rachael's friends were less prepared to tolerate her in this present mood. Her conversation was so interlarded with references to Mr Bates—his goodness, his charity, his scholarship, dedication and self-sacrifice, his opinions and observations—that there were several who took a perverse delight in pointing out every possible instance of his failings.

They did not long remain her friends; and their mocking criticism served only to arouse her to greater heights of loyalty and devotion.

Esmond was flattered. And also frightened. For some while now his fellow clergy had been urging him to take a wife, and he was aware that he needed to marry if he wished to be considered for promotion within the Church: a spouse was a most useful adjunct to a minister's work.

The notion of marriage had always filled him with a dread

foreboding. What might such a relationship enkindle? Might it not aggravate that side of his nature which for so long had been kept rigidly suppressed? As for any other result of such a union, certainly he did not wish for children. The thought of procreation filled him with the strongest nausea.

And yet, a wife . . . Someone to love him, to show him tenderness and consideration as a mother might, someone to care for his needs and share in his toil. If only he might have the fortune to find a woman he might trust not to betray his ideals, a woman whose purity could keep at bay that darker side of his being by encouraging his other, godly, goodly side.

Might Rachael Kember not be such a woman?

So Esmond had commenced his courtship. He took her to hear the military bands play on the castle green. He walked with her beside the Ouse. He lent her his books to read for discussion. And a little later he took tea in her aunt's parlour above the shop in Flood Street and explained that his income was very small, that he had no private means of support, that he must keep up his subscriptions to libraries and literary societies; but nonetheless with her permission he wished to be considered her niece's suitor.

The old lady made no demur.

In return, Rachael astonished him by the devotion he seemed to have aroused in such a young and beautiful creature. Something within him, something which for so many years had been repressed and denied, began to grow. As it grew, it strengthened, and in its strength became the most overpowering emotion he had ever experienced. He was in love: he loved: he was loved.

And with his love came jealousy.

At first it only manifested itself in minor ways. For instance, Rachael was not to spend so much time with her friends if it meant denying him the pleasure of her company. One by one her friendships lapsed, either through negligence on her side or pique on theirs, until there remained only one who had not dropped away—Euphemia Godman who lived two doors down in Flood Street.

Then, in November 1849, Aunt Kember died of whatever

disease had been eating into her since youth; and Esmond's proposal of marriage followed almost immediately.

As if some self-imposed restraint had been lifted by her acceptance of him, Rachael shortly became aware of a more marked change in her fiancé's attitude. Now she was forbidden to speak to men she had known ever since childhood. Now she must be less outspoken in her views since they were unseemly for a young woman of her position. Now she must behave with more modesty and circumspection and not pursue her parish work among the tenement slums of the town. Now she must practise purity of heart and mind and body at all times and not be so demonstrative of her love.

If she had misgivings, she quickly stifled them; and complied with Esmond's wishes. But when, after their wedding in the summer of 1850, and the curiously unsatisfactory few days spent at a lodging house at Brighton by way of a wedding tour, her husband's bouts of self-recrimination and depression began, those misgivings were not so easily stilled.

But Rachael had sworn before God that she would love and cherish this man until her life's end. She remembered that now as she lay awake beside his sleeping, twitching form in the bedroom of Weatherfield rectory. She could no more abandon him than she could kick away the crutch that held up a cripple.

11

Frank Morgan, too, was sleeping.

The encounter with Rachael Bates had whetted his lusty appetite and he had returned to Netherton to find some girl at Padley's farm to lie with. The girl had gone now, but the stallion man stayed on in the straw of the hay loft dreaming of a loose-breasted woman showering him with sea spray and eluding him each time he grasped for her smooth wet body.

A low whinny made him open his eyes.

In the stall below, the black Shire moved restlessly. He listened, instantly alert. A footfall sounded out in the yard and a moment later someone entered the barn and paused, holding up a lantern to illuminate the dark interior.

"Morgan?"

The stallion leader raised himself on his elbow. "Who is it wants me?"

"It's me—George Bashford. Will you come down?"

He gripped the edge of the loft trap and swung himself through, landing lightly on his feet.

"Well?"

"Dinah's still up at Spring Hill."

"So?"

"So what do you intend to do about her?"

Morgan spat on the ground. "She's no concern of mine any more."

"How do you mean?"

"I mean the brat she birthed today isn't any of mine."

Bashford stared at him in the guttering lantern light. "What are you talking about, man? You're not saying you disown the child?"

"That's about it. It's nothing to do with me."

"What makes you think that, in Heaven's name?"

Morgan looked at him. "It's a female." Then he turned away and began walking towards the barn door, brushing the straw bits from his hair and naked chest.

Over his shoulder he said, "And unless it's you that happens to be the father, I can't see that this business is any of your affair."

"Maybe it isn't." Bashford followed him out into the moonlit yard. "But it so happens that Dinah Flynn's on my farm, and I'm responsible for her. Oh, come on now, Morgan—" The farmer was taller than the stallion leader by half a head, though not so heavily muscled. He gripped the other's shoulder and shook it slightly. "She regards herself as your wife in all but name. She wouldn't be unfaithful, you know that."

"Do I?" Morgan shrugged his hand off. "Not any more, I don't."

Bashford regarded him in silence, his eyes narrowing.

After a moment he made a small sound of exasperation and said, "Well, somebody's got to take her and her mother back to Weatherfield tonight. She could stay on at Spring Hill, gladly, but she's fretting about her son and wants to get back to him."

"So what's wrong with her going the way she came?"

"Jack Adams had to leave hours ago." He paused. "Look, it's putting me out, but I suppose I could do it. If you're really so set against the girl, I mean."

"Oh, I'm set against her, all right. But I'll even the score. She'll find it doesn't pay to make a fool of me."

George Bashford could see that Morgan was spoiling for an argument. He shrugged and turned to go; but after a few steps checked himself and wheeled round.

"By the way, I should have asked—did you see Mrs Bates safely home?"

The stallion leader looked at him slyly. Then, unexpectedly, he started to laugh.

Bashford's jaw muscles tightened. "I don't see there's anything to give amusement."

"No, I don't suppose you would."

"And what's that supposed to mean?"

"Nothing. But you disappoint me, Bashford, you really do."

A hard edge came into the farmer's voice. "Do I, now."

"Yes. Don't say you haven't noticed. No? Then open your eyes, man! Mrs Bates may be married, but I'll stake my oath her husband's never laid a hand on her. Your *Mrs* Bates is still a maid."

Bashford looked at the stallion man, the blood colouring his face.

"Mind your tongue when you speak of that lady!" he snapped out.

"Oh-ho." Morgan's teeth gleamed wolfishly. "Fancy her for yourself, do you?"

"Damn you, Morgan!" The voice was steely cold, the words spaced slowly. "If I find you causing mischief in that quarter, I warn you—I'll break your gipsy neck myself."

The stallion man's fist clenched. "Are you looking for a fight with me?"

"Yes, by God I am if you start any of your tricks with Mrs Bates."

"You don't fool me, Bashford. I can see behind your game. You're only warning me off so you can have the field clear for yourself."

The other made a contemptuous gesture of dismissal and turned away.

"I'll tell you what,"—Frank Morgan called after him as he went—"you can have Dinah. As compensation."

George Bashford mounted his horse and rode back at a gallop along the darkened lanes towards Spring Hill. He was a man slow to anger, but just now his blood was up.

He had never cared much for the stallion leader, he reminded himself savagely. A handsome dog, and with morals to match. Like most half-breed dogs, he was never quite to be trusted. But he had a way about him with women and it was no idle boast that he generally got what he went after.

Bashford flicked irritably at the reins as he brooded on Morgan's insinuations about Rachael Bates. Was it possible? Might that marriage be nothing more than a shell? Damn it, he told himself angrily, it was no concern of his if it was.

Yet, he had to admit it—he had somehow sensed that the rector was a man with some secret misery, and had felt a kind of pity for him from the first. For his young wife, too. At least, he had thought it to be pity until tonight. Now he was not so sure.

He urged his horse up the final slope.

At the farmhouse a lamp burned in the upstairs room,

spilling its yellow light into the darkness. He dismounted and looked up, and the anger slowly evaporated as his mood was overtaken by one of concern. Poor Dinah . . . and what of her? She stood to lose most of all, and simply because she had borne a daughter.

Bashford did not doubt for a moment but that the child was Frank Morgan's, and he marvelled that any man could be so blindly self-deluding as to reckon himself capable of fathering only sons. Surely there was more to it than that.

He crossed from the stables into the house and went upstairs.

Dinah was resting on the edge of the bed, a shawl thrown about her shoulders. The baby lay close against her breast. As he entered the room she turned her head sharply and he saw an instant's hope fade in her eyes as she recognised him in the lamplight. At that moment he felt a great compassion surge up within him.

"Is this all you have to wrap the child in?"

He leaned over her and touched the little form gently. The texture of the swaddling material—one of his own discarded shirts—felt rough to his fingers.

The thin figure of Molly Flynn stirred in the shadows.

"It'll do till we get home. Though Lord knows, Mr Bashford, there's little better there for the poor mite."

"Hush, Mam."

Dinah glanced at her, then looked wearily away. The waxen pallor of her face was emphasised by the heavy braid of red hair falling forward over her shoulder.

"We'll manage well enough, don't you worry, sir. If I can borrow this,"—she indicated the shirt—"I'll bring it back clean when I come in to work."

"There's no hurry about work," Bashford reassured her. "Your job will be here for you when you've got back your strength."

For a moment he gazed down in silence at mother and child. Then began to say something else, but checked himself.

Finally, he cleared his throat and said awkwardly, "Look, I . . . I've a few bits of clothing you can have for the child.

They were meant for—" he made a half-gesture towards the bed. "I'll look them out for you."

Mrs Flynn waited until his footfalls had died away on the stairs.

"There, what did I tell you, our Dinah! He's going to let you have the stuff his wife got in for that baby o' theirn. There'll be some nice things there. She had taste, did Mrs Bashford."

Dinah said nothing.

Downstairs, George Bashford selected a key from the ring on his fob chain. He held it between finger and thumb and looked at it thoughtfully, then went along to the far end of the hall passage and thrust it into the lock of a closed door.

The hinges creaked back.

Inside, the small room was piled untidily with furniture and boxes, everything covered with a thin layer of grey dust, cobwebs hanging between the delicately-turned legs of up-ended chairs.

Holding his lamp high, Bashford skirted the room to the corner near the window, where a small trunk lay on a table. Beside it on the floor stood an empty wooden cradle with elaborately carved hood and panels.

The young man looked pensively from one to the other. It all seemed so long ago now, the pain, the sorrow, the emptiness. Sighing, he put the lamp down and bent to lift the cradle. Well, why not, he thought; they're only gathering memories here.

Little Frankie had never had such a thing as a cradle. Dinah had rocked him in her arms and put him to sleep in the bottom drawer of the chest in her room at the alehouse. Now, when she saw what George Bashford wished her to have for her baby daughter, the tears welled in her eyes.

"Mind, it will all need a good airing," he told Mrs Flynn. "The clothing's been in that trunk a good few years, but the room's dry enough so I shouldn't think there's anything mildewed."

Molly Flynn lifted the trunk lid and peered inside. A finely crocheted shawl lay on top of a pile of little garments, the work of the late Mrs Bashford.

"You're a good man, sir," she told him earnestly. "God bless you for your kindness."

Her sincerity, and Dinah's, touched him. A pity that Frank Morgan could not have seen fit to do as much for his child instead of running off disowning her; bragging on about other women when Dinah so obviously needed him here beside her.

What a birth day for them both.

"I've kept meaning to do something with these things for a long time. I'm glad to see them put to good use at last." Bashford glanced at Dinah's pale, drawn features. "It's getting late. Time I saw you all safely home. Are you sure you won't change your mind and stay here for the night?"

She shook her head. "Thank you, sir. But no. If I don't get back to the alehouse, our Frankie'll be screaming the place down."

George Milverton Bashford came of a line of yeoman farmers who, for generations past, had toiled to wrest their living from the stubborn clay soil of the Sussex Weald.

The family originated in the west of the country, at Dorchester; but during the troubled times of the Civil Wars the Bashford of the day, being a Parliament man, had uprooted his family and replanted it well away from the contagion of Cavaliers.

He had settled at Netherton in 1644, in a handsome timbered Wealden hall-house standing beside the road crossing Spring Hill to Shatterford. Unhappily the place was badly damaged by fire early in the eighteenth century, and was rebuilt upon the old foundations as a plain-fronted brick farmhouse after the stolid architectural fashion of the day.

Here, in 1822, another George Bashford was born to carry on the ancient line.

He grew up at a time when the country was once more in a period of transition, passing from the age of elegance into that of industry; though, even so, his childhood was barely touched by exterior change. Looking back in later years—for Bashford was a man of sentiment and such memories held especial meaning for him—that childhood seemed a time of peace and harmony, its summers never-ending days of sun in a cloudless heaven, its winters thigh-deep in snow and icicles spangling every hedgerow.

As he grew out of infancy his life, like that of any other countryman, fell naturally into the swing of the seasons and was governed by the changeless pattern of ploughing, sowing, harvesting; birthing, fattening, slaughtering.

There was little time to spare for any formal education. The dame school at Netherton taught him the collects, and his reading and numbering came from the farm office's ledgers and books of husbandry. Only once had he shown any interest in extending his learning, by purchasing a second-hand set of volumes containing the plays of Shakespeare.

His father had remonstrated at such a waste, declaring that a man's livelihood depended on the skill of his hands and the sweat of his brow, not in the stuffing of his head with useless fancies; and the books were shifted to one of the out-houses where in time their leather-bound spines grew mildewed with damp and the reddish-brown spots of foxing spoiled their unopened pages.

Despite his imperfect literary development it should not be supposed that Bashford was an uncultured man, nor in any way lacked social grace and manners. His mother had been one of the Milvertons of Arundel; and as though to make amends for marrying into an inferior class and delivering her son to the life of a yeoman and not a gentleman farmer, she had raised him to be courteous, honourable and ever well-disposed towards his fellow creatures.

He was a humane man at a time when humanity tended to be regarded as a weakness, especially when proferred to dumb beasts. Nevertheless it was an accepted fact that young Bashford would not tolerate cruelty, particularly cruelty in pursuit of amusement.

His labourers knew better than to fight their dogs in his barn, or set them to bait badgers. No hen was ever threshed to death with a flail at Shrovetide, as was the country custom. And he insisted that the snares on his land be inspected every day so that their victims would not be left too long in agony.

Some of his methods might be jeered at behind his back; but there were others which proved him a man of acumen and foresight.

It was usual for dairy farmers such as he to calve their cows in spring, keeping the animals on a meagre diet during the lean months of winter. But George Bashford held that since the business of a dairy farmer was not to keep the cows, but let the cows keep him, the foundation of his profit lay in good winter feeding, for no beast could be expected to keep its condition and produce healthy calves when its diet was little more than poor quality hay and cold water.

Weakened cows dropped weakened stock, he argued, and it was folly to increase the feed to build up condition only when calving was over and the cow had begun to give milk, for that was putting the fat upon her ribs and not into the milking pail. Therefore he allowed his beasts up to eight stone per day of the first winter green crop (kale or rape, sown after the earlier vetches), and in time the results fully justified the experiment.

More recently he had astonished his neighbours further by bringing his calving season forward. When they queried his immature judgment, he replied that it was surely more profitable to calve in winter when milk was fetching a higher price: a cow dropping her young then, and not later into spring, could be expected to yield a hundred gallons more in a year.

At the stock auctions and markets such new-fangled methods were openly scoffed at. In time, though, George Bashford's foresight paid off and the scoffers were forced to take back their words and own themselves duly impressed by the prices fetched for Spring Hill stock and the steady rise in milk output.

By 1850, when he had been master of his farm for some half-dozen or so years, he had not only paid off his late father's creditors and bought land to swell his arable acreage, but was able to invest in one of the new steam traction engines to drive a threshing machine in his stackyard.

In the management of his farm and his labour George Bashford's affairs had prospered. But it was a sadly different tale with his private life.

At the age of twenty-four he had married, and successfully. At twenty-six he was a widower. It was God's will, he supposed; but it seemed a cruelty to take both mother and child together, especially when the boy was so healthily formed and still living, so they told him, till barely an hour before being delivered.

In moments of reflection his mind often dwelt on that scene, and a sense of guilt would oppress him. How much had he himself been to blame for what happened? For he had quarrelled with Isabelle over her morbid fear and suspicion that he was being unfaithful to her while she was forced to spend her final months of pregnancy as an invalid.

On the day her labour started he had insisted on riding over to East Grinstead on business. When she called him a liar and accused him of seeing some woman there, he had finally lost his temper. A violent argument had broken out with a great deal of unkindness spoken on both sides.

In the middle of it he had flung himself out of the house without a thought for her condition and taken himself off for the day; and when he came back that night, found her already several hours into labour.

When next he was permitted to see her, she was dead, stretched so pitifully upon the blood-soaked sheets, the instruments of her ordeal discarded beside her, her sightless eyes turned towards her son. And the child, warm from his mother's body though he had been brought from her lifeless, joined to her still by the cord which had given him his brief existence.

Something had died within George Bashford himself, too; some sense of certainty, some part of his belief in the mercy of God. And he went less often to church than before, thinking it was a discourtesy to give praise and thanks with his lips when his heart still bore the bruise of his bitterness.

Since Isabelle's death he had been courted by several of his neighbours' daughters, but none that he had taken with any seriousness. He supposed that one day he would marry again and have other sons to inherit the land, living sons; but it was not a business that pressed on his attention as yet. He could afford to wait.

It was supposed by those same neighbouring farmers' daughters that Mr Bashford led a solitary sad existence with no woman's company about his house, and this imagined loneliness fuelled their romantic fancies. But the truth was quite otherwise, and would have shocked them had they known of it.

There was a woman in Tunbridge Wells—a nice woman, a young widow who took in lodgers—whom he visited from time to time for the kind of pleasure a single man may take with a good conscience if he is so disposed. He was fond of her, and she of him; but not so fond that she would grieve if he never returned to her.

And in fact he had not returned in recent weeks. He did not know why, but Tunbridge Wells had lost much of its attraction for him since Rachael Bates had come to live in Weatherfield.

12

"I always said he had a weak spot for you, that George Bashford."

Molly Flynn stood back in the bedroom of the alehouse to admire the sight of her new grandchild asleep in her cradle.

Not only had the young farmer brought them home in his trap, wrapping Dinah in one of his own best wool blankets and carrying her in his arms up the narrow stairs to her bed;

97

he had given a lift out of his way to Mary Adams who had
been at the house to keep an eye on little Frankie and serve
Mrs Flynn's customers in her absence.

"He's got a heart o' gold, he has, and lucky the girl who
wins it."

"What you going on about, Mam?"

"You and Mr Bashford, that's what I'm on about."

"Then you're wasting your breath." Dinah turned her
head wearily on the pillow. "He's not looked at a woman
since his wife died, all the country knows that."

"Time his mind was changed for him, then. You could do
well for yourself there if you played clever."

Her daughter closed her eyes.

"I've already got myself a man," she said obstinately.

"What? That Frank Morgan? Some good he's done you,
saddling you wi' children and never word of a wedding ring
out of him!"

"Oh, don't start on about that again. Not tonight. You
know how things stand between Frank and me."

Mrs Flynn gave a little tug of irritation at the counterpane.

"Frank Morgan! I rue the day he first come here. Him
and that great horse of hisn. That's all he's fit for, the
common gipsy, a-traipsing round the countryside wi' that
animal. He's no sense o' decency . . . Thinks he can please
hisself what he does, and too bad for the girl he leaves in
trouble."

"Be quiet, Mam, will you? It won't do any good to go on
about him."

"But it's true what I say, our Dinah. It's a crying shame he
won't marry you—and two such lovely babies you've borne
him, an' all. Any self-respecting kind of a man would've wed
you straight off, he would."

Dinah shifted herself on the bed and looked at her
mother.

"What about the man who fathered *me*, then? What self-
respect did he show? You've no right to speak so ill o' Frank
when that Daniel Linton used *you* no better."

Mrs Flynn bridled angrily. "Don't you Daniel Linton me,
my girl! And don't you go breathing his name beyond these

four walls, d'you hear? It's no business of any o' them up the road." She jerked her head. "You saying that—it was different wi' me. Mr Linton was a married man already. A gentleman, mind . . . he never saw me go without—"

"Neither does Frank."

"—and he'd have wed me if he was free, except he died, poor man. This Frank Morgan o' yourn, he's never had a wife at all, not one. Nor he's likely to, neither. And who can blame him when there's fools like you ready to gi' into him—"

"Mam, I'm tired. I'd like to sleep now."

"—and there's that George Bashford, such a kind man. Look what he's done for you . . . giving you so much, an' all. Now you can't tell me he'd have done a thing like that if he didn't have a care for you. A man all alone like he is needs a wife looking after him. He doesn't know what to do wi' hisself, and that's the truth. You heed my words, our Dinah. You put that Frank Morgan out o' your head and start thinking about the future. There's little Frankie to consider, and now this new 'un. Poor little mite, no father—not even a name to call her own."

Dinah turned her face to the wall.

After a time she said slowly, "I was thinking o' calling her Rachael. But I'm not so sure I like it now."

Molly Flynn trimmed the lamp until the flame was no more than a thin blue rind of light casting a faint glow in the room.

"Mr Bashford's wife was Isabelle. I've always thought that a pretty name."

Dinah made no response.

Mrs Flynn waited.

Then—"You're a cunning one, aren't you," her daughter said finally. "Never gi' a bone a rest." She turned over, and in the dim light her face wore a smile. "Isabelle. Yes, I like that. I think I'll call her Belle."

The weather changed during the night, the mild winds of May veering to the west to bring heavy rain to the district, and it was late into the following afternoon before

99

Rachael Bates was able to get out to see Dinah and the new baby.

Rather than precipitate another scene with Esmond she kept her visit secret, waiting until he had driven off in the trap on business at the other end of the parish before she could slip away along the path through the fields.

The sky was leaden with cloud, a fine drizzle gusting like smoke across the open country. By the time she reached the alehouse door her thin flat-heeled pumps were sodden and mud-caked even though she wore pattens, and her cloak wet through.

She pushed back the hood from her face and knocked louder. Somewhere a dog barked, a voice was raised. Then footsteps approached.

"Lord above! Mrs Bates!"

Molly Flynn opened the door wider.

"Come along inside out o' the wet. What a day! You'd never credit it was nearly June, would you. Here, let me have your cloak. You've come to see our Dinah, I suppose."

She led the way along to the end of the passage.

"Mr Bashford brought us back hisself from the farm," she said over her shoulder.

"That was kind of him."

"Aye, he's a real gentleman. Not like some. I'll take your things through into the kitchen. They'll be drying afore the fire while you're up wi' her. She's in the first room facing you at the head o' the stairs. I'll leave you to find your own way."

The staircase was steep and poorly lit and Rachael had to go carefully. But at the top there was a small window sunk deep into the wall to show her a door on the left.

She tapped at it.

"Dinah?"

"Who's there?"

"It's Rachael Bates."

"Oh."

There was a pause.

"Oh, come in. Mind the step behind the door."

The room was lit by a long, low window running the length

of the eaves and overlooking the wet fields behind the ale-house. A chest of drawers topped by a mirror, a button-backed chair and a large bed made up the furnishing. The floorboards were bare of any cover. It might almost have been Rachael's own bedroom at the rectory.

Dinah lay back amongst the pillows, the baby at her breast.

"I'll be done in a minute. Sit yourself down, ma'am. I'm just feeding her."

"I'm sorry . . . have I come at an awkward time?"

The young mother glanced up; then shook her head. "It was kind of you to come out on such a day."

Her voice sounded flat.

"I wanted to know how you were." Rachael picked up a shawl from the chair. "This is beautiful. Did you crochet it yourself?"

"No. Mr Bashford gi' it me yesterday. That and a few other things he'd kept by."

Rachael sat down.

After a while Dinah continued, "He lost his wife when their baby was born."

"Yes. He told me."

"She made that. The shawl. Poor lady . . . I was thinking about her only this morning, how sad it was she should spend so many hours making them things."

"Sad?"

"All a waste of her time really, when you come to consider. Now then, little 'un, let's have you up."

She held the protesting baby against her shoulder and began patting her gently.

"Would you hand me the shawl across, Mrs Bates?"

Rachael watched while the baby was wrapped.

"She's a lovely child, Dinah. Have you thought of a name for her yet?"

"I fancied calling her Isabelle. Belle, for short."

"Yes. I like that. It'll be Isabelle Rachael, I hope?"

Dinah looked at her sharply.

"I mean . . . if I'm to be a god-parent," Rachael added. "It's customary for a child to take its sponsor's name."

A closed, tight look came into the other's face. Dinah Flynn was not a jealous woman, but it had hurt her deeply that Frank should have left her yesterday, choosing instead to keep Rachael Bates company to Weatherfield. And Rachael was just as much to blame. The rector's wife should never have gone with him. It wasn't right. She should have waited for Mr Bashford with the rest of them.

Dinah had suspected for some time that she was losing Frank Morgan. Desperately not wanting to believe it, but knowing in her heart of hearts that he was growing cool towards her. For months now, she had been hoping that the new baby might bring him back.

And yesterday he had left her. Hardly spoken a word. Just gone off back to Weatherfield with Mrs Bates.

Her mother had been right. She should have given the stallion man another son.

Slowly she said, "I don't recall us saying anything about god-parents. You're mistaken surely, ma'am."

Rachael saw the expression in the grey-green eyes. It was a look of rejection. She turned away, hurt.

"Well, perhaps we can discuss it again later. When you decide about the baptism."

"When *I* decide? It's not for me to decide. The matter's settled already, I should think."

"What do you mean?"

"Your husband won't baptise this baby, Mrs Bates! You know how he feels about me. He makes no secret of it. There's nobody in the parish hasn't heard his opinion by now."

"I know. And I'm sorry—truly I am. I have tried to make him see how difficult things are for you."

Dinah shrugged her shoulders.

"It's . . . well, it's Mr Morgan my husband feels most strongly about," Rachael went on hesitantly.

"Oh?" The other looked at her. "And what about you?"

"Me?"

"Yes. How do *you* feel about Frank?"

The unmistakable hostility in her tone made Rachael feel uncomfortable.

102

"Why, I—I hardly know him. I haven't had time to form any opinion. Dinah . . . if you're upset about yesterday—"

"Upset?" She put on an expression of surprise. "Why should I be upset, for Lord's sake?"

"Because I accepted Mr Morgan's offer to bring me into the village."

"You're free to do what you like. You and him both."

"Is that why you seem to be turning against me? Because of what happened yesterday? If so—"

"I don't know what you're on about, Mrs Bates," the other interrupted shortly, not looking at her. "I was too busy yesterday having this baby to be upsetting myself about anything you and Frank might be doing together."

There was a painful silence.

Rachael got to her feet.

"I'm sorry we must fall out like this. I thought of you as my friend. I hope you are still?"

The hurt in her voice was almost an appeal.

Dinah glanced across at her. "I don't know how you can talk to me about friendship, ma'am, when your husband ill speaks me so."

"But he'll change his mind, in time. Once you're married—"

"To Frank Morgan, I suppose?"

"Yes. Of course. To Mr Morgan."

"Frank'll never marry me. Not now. He's got too many others like me around the country."

Rachael looked down at her, remembering the girl in Lewes churchyard. And herself, yesterday, succumbing to the same primitive, frightening, delicious feeling of helplessness.

"He must've tried a trick or two wi' you, as well," Dinah went on, watching her face. "Oh, you don't have to look so shocked, Mrs Bates! I know Frank too well. There's no woman safe left alone wi' him. Married or maid, he treats us all the same. Any way—" she turned away, sighing. She was starting to feel weary now and the resentment was fading—"it don't really matter any more. Yes, so he should've stayed wi' me yesterday, by rights. But that was

103

none o' your fault. It wasn't you took him away, ma'am . . . he wanted to go."

The naked look of misery on her face made Rachael immediately put her own embarrassed discomfort aside.

"But hasn't he been here to see you—or the baby?"

"No. Nor he won't. He's done wi' me."

"How can you say that? This is his child!"

Dinah held little Belle tightly against her. "Oh, he won't let that sway his mind for him. What's children, after all—"

She broke off; then, after a moment recovered herself and went on, "I always knew it'd happen one day. But he's stayed wi' me so long now . . . I just kept hoping and praying he'd come round to wedding me in the finish."

"He still might, Dinah. Don't be so desperate."

Rachael sat on the edge of the bed and clasped her hand.

"No. He's gone. Oh, he'll send me money for Frankie and Belle. But I seen it plain in his face yesterday . . . it's all over between him and me. There's nothing left."

Her mouth quivered and she averted her head, the heavy red hair falling forward across her breast.

In a choked voice she whispered, "I wish to God I knew what's to become o' me."

Almost exactly the same words were being echoed at almost the same moment by another young woman some hours' journey away. And for much the same reason.

Charlotte Smith lay across the bed in her small rented lodging in Lewes, having just vomited for the third time that day. She had been feeling queasy all the week, and yesterday had needed to be excused from giving the little ones at the school their afternoon supervision.

This morning she had been ill as soon as she awoke. The tears had run down her pale face as she stared at her reflection in the piece of mirror above the washstand in her room. There was nothing amiss with her stomach, she knew that. She was a strong healthy girl who had hardly suffered a day's illness in her life. No, the cause of her sickness lay within her belly.

She was going to have a child.

Charlotte sat on her bed and wept. When her menses had been a week late in showing, she had dosed herself with pennyroyal. When that had failed to produce anything, she had forced herself to swallow spoonfuls of thick, viscid castor oil which certainly had results, but not the one she was desperately hoping for.

Now the second month had gone by, confirming her worst fears. The morning sickness had started, just as she had seen it happen time after time with her own mother; until the thirteenth pregnancy had proved one too many for the worn-out body to carry.

Oh God, what am I going to do, she asked herself wretchedly. How could I have been such a fool as to get myself in this trouble?

She thought back to that day in March, that bright, deceptive day, and cursed herself for being so easily tempted by a handsome face and a few smooth words of flattery. How was she going to find him again to tell him? And if she did find him, would he want to know?

She had waited for him the next day, as they had planned. Then, thinking that perhaps she had mistaken the hour, went looking for him in the public houses round Lewes market. Frank, she had said. No, she didn't know his surname; he never told her.

She had given his description at half a dozen places before someone had said did she mean Frank Morgan the stallion leader? Yes, he had mentioned a horse; a stallion, something to do with his trade. In that case, she was too late, Frank Morgan had left Lewes that morning. If she went across by Buckfield, she might find him.

But where? Charlotte had asked around. And in the end, someone had mentioned a village called Weatherfield.

13

Rachael Bates fell sick with a heavy chill as a result of the soaking she got going out to the alehouse. For some days she was forced to remain indoors at the rectory, shivering and sneezing and huddled over a meagre fire, snapped at by Esmond who disliked illness, tolerating it only in those who were plainly dying, his resentment fuelled by her defiance in seeing Dinah Flynn again.

There were no visitors, apart from one: George Bashford, who called twice.

Rachael would rather not have received him, feeling as wretched as she did. But on his second visit he brought a basket of eggs and cheese and vegetables from the farm; and also a bunch of sweet-smelling pinks, which Esmond jealously threw out into the yard when he found her arranging them for the parlour.

It came as no surprise to Rachael that nobody from the village had troubled to call to ask after her. The Reverend Bates's efforts to win his parishioners' regard had so far met with scant success.

There had been several small incidents caused by his impatience with their country manners and customs which had aroused feelings of resentment on both sides: not only his banning of the Good Friday marbles match in the churchyard, and his refusal to pray over Fred Whiskey's barren sow, but his scathing attack from the pulpit following Weatherfield's May Day revels when the young women of the village had danced barefoot and white-garlanded around a stout pole on the green.

Rachael was reminded now of something Dinah had said when they were talking in the kitchen one day.

"Mr Bates don't seem to fit in here, somehow. There's folks

who doubt his heart's properly set on what he's doing. Leastways, that's what I've been hearing around the village."

Rachael had expressed her disappointment. "We thought how well people seemed to have accepted us!"

"And so they have . . . some on 'em. But it's a pity you had to move from town, if you don't mind me speaking so plain. Your husband's not a country man, ma'am. He don't understand our ways. He talks above our heads, and that's a fact. Mebbe he'd have been contenter staying amongst folks who respect his book learning more."

"But he tries so hard, Dinah. It would hurt him cruelly to think the parish was rejecting him. Poor Esmond . . . he spends almost every waking moment attending to church business, visiting, ministering, writing his sermons, letters . . . You've no idea how much he puts into his work."

Dinah had avoided looking at her, only replying, "Hard work never made a man popular if the will to like him was lacking. It seems we don't deserve your husband, Mrs Bates. He's too clever by half for us."

Rachael reported this conversation in a long letter which she wrote to Euphemia, her friend in Lewes, to help pass the solitary hours at the rectory.

She was quite frank about their situation in Weatherfield. Putting it all down on to paper, she found she was able to review her relationship with Esmond in an almost impersonal fashion: the domestic problems which had seemed to take on a bleaker aspect each time she thought them over to herself in the small hours of the morning, by being reduced to mere words, appeared to dwindle accordingly.

By the time she had completed the tenth page of her letter her optimistic nature had begun to reassert itself and she felt in better spirits than she had all week.

Going upstairs, she placed the envelope at the back of a drawer in the bedroom where her husband would not see it. Until she was able to give it to Jack Adams to deliver for her to the mails office at Buckfield, it would be prudent to keep such correspondence from Esmond's knowledge.

*   *   *

Next morning, feeling quite recovered from her chill, Rachael took George Bashford's rescued pinks and mixed them with roses from the rectory garden to take into the church for decoration.

After the bright sunshine, the old building struck almost unpleasantly cool inside; but after a while, occupying herself arranging the flowers in bowls, the sensation passed off.

St Anne's was a small church. And made to seem smaller still by the high box pews crowding either side of the central aisle. Its one notable feature was its wall frescoes, depicting saints and angels and scenes of Paradise and Hell. Unfortunately, these had been partly effaced at the time of the Civil Wars and never restored, so that the once bright colours were now faded and patched with damp and the outlines of the figures grown indistinct.

Rachael had not found the church either particularly inspiring or welcoming. It had a closed-in, fusty atmosphere, as though the place were ill-aired through lack of use; and despite all her efforts and brave displays of early summer flowers, the overall impression remained one of sombreness and melancholy. Even the light that came in through the leaded windows seemed joyless, she thought.

She had finished an arrangement of roses for the side chapel and was standing back to decide whether a few stems more were needed, when a slight sound behind her in the emptiness made her look quickly over her shoulder.

Frank Morgan was leaning against one of the box pews.

His appearance was so sudden and totally unexpected, that Rachael's heart leaped into her throat. A wave of panic seemed to engulf her and she turned swiftly, not towards the stallion leader but towards the altar, as though seeking protection from his presence. As she did so, one of the long rose stems she gripped dug its viciously curved thorns into her hand, bringing the blood welling up through deep punctures.

She gave a small cry of pain and dropped the flowers. Immediately, Morgan was at her side.

"What is it? Are you hurt?"

He took her hand and turned it over so that it lay open within his own.

"You're bleeding," he said. And bending his dark curly head, he raised her injured palm to his lips.

A shudder ran through Rachael's body as she felt his mouth against her skin, his warm tongue moving over the soft flesh. She snatched her hand away and held it clenched to her breast.

"There's no need—please, it's nothing . . . a scratch . . ."

Her blood had marked him.

He smiled at her. Then, slowly, he licked the crimson stain from his lips, never once removing his eyes from hers. There was something so primitive, so suggestive, about the action that her legs began to tremble and she swung away from him and sat down on the steps of the chancel.

He came and seated himself beside her.

"You ought to bind it up. You'll have your clothes messed. Here,"—he pulled the kerchief from his neck—"Let me do it for you."

"No! No, really. It doesn't matter."

But he took her wrist and pulled it against him, and firmly but gently bound the kerchief around her palm.

"There."

The confusion of her emotions almost choked her. She would have stood up and left at that moment, if she could. But she was helpless, unable to move, trapped by her own overwhelming physical response to the stallion man's presence.

If someone were to come into the church now, she thought desperately, and see them so close together on the chancel steps . . .

Frank Morgan looked at her. Her eyes were downcast, the lashes shadowing the flushed cheeks. She looked so vulnerable. For some reason a feeling of tenderness stole over him, and instead of taking advantage of their intimate situation to draw her to him, he got to his feet and moved away.

"I'm sorry I startled you just now," he said. "You looked such a picture, doing those flowers. I couldn't help but watch."

Rachael fought to control herself. Carefully she responded, "I didn't hear you behind me. That's why I—" Her eyes dropped to her bound hand. "I thought I was alone."

"Oh, no. I was already here when you came in."

"I didn't see you."

"You wouldn't. I was in the porch room."

Her gaze flew down the length of the aisle to a low doorway set in the thickness of the north wall. Behind it a spiral staircase led to a small room above the church porch.

"Don't you want to know what I was doing there?" Morgan went on. "No? Aren't you curious at all? Well, I'll tell you even so. I was waiting for you, Mrs Bates."

Her eyes flickered back to his face.

"Why?"

"To see you."

The feeling of panic, of shameful exhilaration, returned.

"What do you want with me?"

"Now don't get yourself worked up! I wanted to find out how you are, that's all. You've been ill, I heard."

"It was no more than a chill."

"Ah, but never underestimate a chill. It can see you off faster than many another ailment. You shouldn't have risked your health walking out in that weather to see Dinah."

She did not respond immediately. There was a long silence. Oddly, his mention of Dinah's name had aroused her to a sudden anger, and she had to make a conscious effort to compose herself.

"Why do you treat that girl so badly?" she asked guardedly after a while.

He made a small sound of amusement. "Dinah? Do I treat her badly?"

"She seems convinced you've abandoned her."

"Is that so? And what do you think?"

"I . . . I think you should marry her."

The stallion leader smiled. "You do, do you."

"Yes."

Rachael rose to her feet. Now that their conversation was on surer ground she was beginning to feel in better control of her emotions.

110

"It's the only honourable thing for you to do, surely?"

"If I were to do the honourable thing by all the women that complained about me, I'd need to become a heathen Muslim. If you catch my meaning."

She looked away from him, from the sly humour in the dark eyes.

"But I appreciate your interest," he went on. "It's kind of you to consider my welfare."

"It wasn't your welfare I was thinking of, Mr Morgan. It was Dinah's. And your children's."

"One child."

He moved across the aisle after her, following her back into the side chapel.

"The boy's mine. And don't worry, I'll see he's all right. As for the other—well, Dinah must drink as she's brewed."

"You're very arrogant, aren't you."

Rachael picked up the remaining flowers from the chair where she had left them lying and forced herself to finish her arrangement. Her hands trembled. The pulse in her neck throbbed so violently that it shook the small ear-drops she was wearing.

Before she could stop herself, she found she was saying, "I saw you once before, you know. In Lewes. In the churchyard with Charlotte Smith."

She was glad she had found the courage to tell him at last.

"Charlotte Smith?"

"Yes."

"Never heard of her."

"You didn't even ask the girl her name?"

"Now hold on a moment, Mrs Bates—"

"Lewes," she repeated, more loudly. She turned round and saw the look of blankness on his face. Somehow, it irritated her. "You were in the churchyard together."

"Oh . . . that girl." He grinned at her suddenly. "Charlotte Smith, was it? Fancy that, now. And you saw us, did you?"

The tone in his voice made Rachael lower her eyes. "Yes. It was during the service. I was in the gallery."

"And you saw us—together."

She nodded.

111

"I hope you enjoyed the show."

The blood rushed to her face. Angrily she said, "Have you no sense of shame? None at all?"

"You should talk of shame! Nobody asked you to watch."

"No. That's true. And this isn't the place to discuss so . . . so sordid a subject. Excuse me."

She pushed by him and went quickly along the aisle towards the north door. He followed; and as she reached the further end put out his hand and caught her arm from behind.

"Let go of me!"

"Not until we've finished our conversation."

Rachael struggled against the restraining grip, but he was too strong for her.

"Has anyone ever told you how beautiful you are when you're angry?" he asked. It was one of his stock expressions reserved for situations such as this.

There was no response.

He tried again. "You know, I've never met a woman quite like you before. Somehow, you're different from the others."

He felt her relax a little, and followed up his advantage.

"In fact, as soon as I saw you—you remember? I was sitting outside on the wall—I said to myself that's the loveliest creature I've set eyes on in a long while."

The triteness of his phrases, the practised ease with which he uttered them, had the effect of irritating Rachael even further. She snatched her arm away, catching him off guard.

"Thank you," she said icily. "But your opinion of me isn't of the slightest interest. You see, Mr Morgan, I am fore-warned. Dinah told me about your—your 'tricks', as she called them. I'm sure you're very successful with silly, impressionable Charlotte Smith and her kind. But I'm sorry—your false flattery has no effect on me whatever. Now, I suggest that you take yourself out of this church . . . and this with you."

She tore off the kerchief binding her hand and thrust it at him.

"You'll forgive me if I don't offer to wash it for you."

The force of her words and the manner in which she delivered them pleasantly astonished Frank Morgan. He had guessed that she would show him defiance, but never dreamed that she would react to his approaches in quite such a spirited way.

He took the stained kerchief from her, and pretended to bluster.

"Dinah said *what* about me? Tricks? What's she mean by that—tricks?"

"You know very well what she meant. You've just this minute given an example. All this insincerity . . . this pretence. It's a charade! You don't mean a word of it. It's nothing but an act you put on to trap foolish women into admiring you."

The fact that Rachael herself had been so willingly entrapped by the stallion man's virile charm on the horse ride from Netherton now piled fuel upon the fire of her vexation.

She went on. "Dinah was quite right to call such behaviour tricks. It *is* trickery. It's a low, nasty way to worm yourself into the affections of gullible creatures. Don't you ever give a thought to the heartache you cause? Doesn't it ever occur to you that your conduct is lacking in any kind of morality?" She heard herself echoing her husband's words. "The life you lead is an insult to decency!"

Morgan raised an eyebrow. "Oh, now—Mrs Bates! You're being too hard on me."

His admiration for her was increasing by the minute.

Rachael looked past his shoulder towards the altar. Then she turned away without a word more and moved to the door. As she put her hand on the massive iron ring, the stallion leader called after her, his voice echoing slightly in the stillness.

"It's very uncharitable of you to judge a man on the word of another. Won't you give me a fair trial, my beauty? You and me, now, we could be the sweetest of friends. And we will, if you'll only give me the chance to show you."

The door opened, and closed behind her.

113

Morgan grinned to himself. The chase was going to be more exciting than he could have imagined.

It was just as well that the Reverend Bates was closeted in work behind his study door when his young wife returned to the house. Had he seen her he would have demanded to know at once what had happened to put her in such a temper. And she could scarcely tell him: "Frank Morgan. He was waiting to catch me alone in the church. He imagines he can seduce me."

Far better, Rachael decided, that she say nothing, keep Esmond ignorant of the stallion man's presence in the village until someone else told him, and hope that the man himself had sense and decency enough to be circumspect about their encounter.

She did not linger in the rectory hallway but went straight along to the scullery at the back of the house to bathe her throbbing hand under the pump. Though the bleeding had stopped, the puncture marks left by the thorns were swollen and painful.

She found a piece of clean rag and tore it into a strip, binding it round her palm and tugging impatiently at the knot with her teeth. Then, lips set, she stood staring through the scullery window towards the line of trees at the end of the churchyard. Frank Morgan's behaviour had thoroughly roused her.

It was not only his presumptive manner that rankled so much. His overwhelming confidence that she could be won over by second-rate sentiments. His arrogance in daring to accost her in church, of all places, and show himself so lacking in respect for God's house. She was a married woman, her husband a member of a highly regarded profession; Morgan's superior in every way, not only class and social standing, but in background and upbringing.

How could she have allowed herself to be so attracted by such a man, she thought indignantly. How could she have let him even for a moment believe his shallow attentions meant anything to her?

She remembered the trite phrases, and her breath came

out sharply in exasperation. Who did Morgan think he was to treat her in such a familiar fashion? And worse—what sort of a woman had she shown herself to be, permitting him so freely to take advantage of her weakness?

Rachael snatched herself away from the window and went through into the kitchen. Little Ada Slybody was there, wiping a greasy face on her pinafore sleeve and complaining about the heat from the range as she prepared a midday meal; but Rachael paid the girl no attention.

Had she encouraged the stallion leader in any way, she wondered. Had he taken her acceptance of his help, her toleration of his familiarity, as an invitation? If so, what insolence! Who was he, to think that a woman of her position, with so much social duty and responsibility, could in any way be swayed or tempted by a man of such reputation!

That Frank Morgan should regard her on the same level as Dinah Flynn or Charlotte Smith, or any other woman he had gulled with his falseness and self-conceit, only added to Rachael's feeling of anger and humiliation. He had made her a fool in her own eyes. He had cheapened her. For that, she could not forgive him. Her instinctive wish was that she should never have to set eyes on him again, that he would remove himself from Weatherfield and not return. But that was wanting the impossible, and she knew it.

Pulling out a chair, she sat down, elbows on the kitchen table, staring ahead.

There was only one thing to be done, she decided at length: he must be persuaded to take a wife. That way, he would have to change himself, learn to behave in a proper, Christian manner. No more roving about the countryside. No more temptation to looseness and leading women astray. Marriage would tame his ways and teach him better conduct.

Rachael's annoyance had clouded her judgment. Had she paused to consider, she would have realised that her anger against Frank Morgan was compounded of elements of fear and frustration and powerful physical attraction. Wed to Dinah, he would no longer present a threat to her own marriage; nor to her peace of mind.

The moment for such consideration was already passing,

her vexation giving way to a crusading zeal. By the time she had finished supervising Ada's clumsy preparation of the meal, she had decided to see Charlotte Smith on her next visit to Lewes, to make some enquiry about the girl's welfare.

She had no way of learning that Charlotte was no longer to be found in Lewes. Her search for the stallion man had taken her to Buckfield; and there, as fate fell out, she had met up with a young carrier named Jack Adams.

14

Jack Adams was the youngest of what had once, years before, been a family of four sons. But disease had taken the lives of the three older ones before they were barely out of the cradle; and his childhood had been shared instead with his cousin, Dinah Flynn.

As a result, the two had grown up together virtually as brother and sister, and the bond of affection between them was very strong. The eighteen months separating them in age had meant that from infancy Dinah had always been the leader, Jack her willing follower.

When the children of the village reduced him to tears with their pitiless mockery of his stammer, Dinah had been there to slap them into silence and make them accept him in their games. During their brief years of schooling she had saved him from appearing too much an idiot. Later, when childhood had passed, she was the one with whom he shared his most secret thoughts; her faith and encouragement helped him to find his place in the community not as a poor stuttering thing to be the butt of fun, but as an ordinary, unremarkable young man.

Jack still stammered, and he was still painfully shy with

anyone outside his family group. But at nineteen he had a fair enough opinion of himself, bolstered by the knowledge that he was probably the finest woodcarver in the district. As a boy he had occupied himself making little figures—shepherds and sheepdogs, lambs, cows and dairymaids—and as he grew older this had developed into the sole occupation of his solitary hours.

He would dearly have loved to be able to earn his living in a carpenter's workshop, but the circumstances of birth had decreed that he be a general carter by trade. It was what he had been raised to. His father, Priam Adams, had been a carter all his life, as had his father before him, and it would have gone hard on the family fortunes had the only surviving son run away—as Jack sometimes dreamed of doing before he learned better sense—to apprentice himself to a master craftsman in some distant town. When Priam Adams became too old to work, Jack would be the sole provider of the family's daily bread.

For months now Jack had been working in secret to make a gift for Dinah when the new baby came. He had often made her things before, but this was to be different. It was an ambitious piece of carving, but he felt himself competent at last to attempt it and was pleased at the way it was emerging beneath his hands.

He worked late hours to complete it, finishing the delicate carving at head and foot, rubbing the piece down again and again so that the sides were as smooth as satin and the fruitwood gleamed like soft pearl in the lamplight.

A week or so after Belle's birth he wrapped the gift in a piece of sacking, hitched it awkwardly beneath one arm and let himself out through the latch gate at the end of the cottage garden.

With the intention of avoiding his aunt, Mrs Flynn, who would have found him some job to do first, he approached the alehouse through the orchard of apple trees at the back. Only the brown mongrel dog saw him arrive, sniffed at him as he passed and wagged a tail, recognising an old friend; then watched indifferently from the kennel as he slipped indoors.

There was no one on the stairs.

He set down the sack-covered shape on the floor outside Dinah's room and pushed her door noiselessly open. His cousin lay asleep on the bed, her auburn hair fanned out over the pillows.

"Dinah."

She did not stir.

"Dinah!"

His hoarse whisper roused the baby, and its muffled cry of protest drew Jack's attention to the foot of the bed, to George Bashford's cradle. His eyes widened in dismay.

The baby gave another coughing wail, louder this time.

"Wha . . . Jack?" Dinah woke with a start. "What you doing standing there?"

He looked away from the cradle and stared at her. Instead of answering, he said dully, "So you g-got one already."

"Got what? What you on about?" Her voice was still heavy with sleep.

He indicated the foot of the bed.

"Oh, that. The cradle. Mr Bashford gi' it me."

She rubbed her eyes, yawned widely, then pulled herself up in the bed.

"Well? You going to stand there all day? Aren't you going to look at her?"

"Can you g-give it back?"

"Give what back? My little Belle? Don't be daft, I only just got her!"

"The cradle, I mean." The humour in her voice was lost on him.

"Why should I? We need one, don't we?"

He nodded miserably. Dinah studied his bowed head in silence.

"You've been and made one for me yourself, haven't you?" she said at last.

He nodded again.

"Where is it, then?"

Jack fetched his work in from the landing and placed it carefully on the floor, pushing aside the sack covering.

"There," he said, moving back so that she could see it.

118

"Oh—!"

Dinah's breath came out in a gasp of delight. She eased herself from the bed, the long cotton nightgown trailing over her bare feet, and came over to kneel down beside her cousin's gift. Her hands moved over the sleek sides, traced with a finger tip the outline of the carving, pushed the cradle tentatively so that it rocked smoothly and silently from side to side.

"Thanks, Jack," she said quietly. "It's beautiful. It's the best thing you've ever made."

He said nothing, but his pleasure at her words showed in his face.

She got to her feet again and went across to the foot of the bed to lift her baby, turning the swaddling shawl back from the tiny face.

"Come and have a look at her. What d'you think? Isn't she a love?"

He moved to her side and looked critically down at the crumpled features.

"Do you want to hold her?"

"Oh—can I?"

"'Course you can. She won't break."

Jack cradled the baby against his thin chest and began rocking himself gently from one foot to another; not clumsily as so many men would have done, but with care.

Dinah sat on the edge of the bed, smiling as she watched him.

"You know, our Jack, it's high time you were wed wi' little 'uns of your own," she said after a while. "I've never known a man love children the way you do."

"I can't afford to m-marry on what I earn."

"Then ask your dad for a better wage, why don't you? Lord above, he works you hard enough."

Jack shook his head. "He don't stint me. Any way, there's no woman I want to m-marry as yet."

"Oh no? That Harriet Green from Tye Cross would wed you fast enough if you asked her."

"Then she'll die an old maid wi' waiting."

"Poor Harriet! D'you reckon she knows?"

119

"It's not that," he went on, not sharing her amusement. "It's . . ."

"What, then?"

"Oh, nothing."

He looked down at Belle and carefully put his forefinger into the little palm. The baby fingers curled around it.

"She's got your hair, all right," he said abruptly. "I can't see m-much o' Frank Morgan in her, though."

Dinah's smile faded. "No . . . more's the pity."

The sudden unhappiness in her voice made her cousin look up.

"He has seen her, hasn't he?"

"Before I did, even. It was him birthed her."

"But there's s-something wrong atween the two o' you?"

Dinah shrugged.

"There is, isn't there?" he persisted. "Has he been upsetting you again?"

"No more'n usual. He still won't marry me, if that's what you mean. Another baby don't make any difference to that, however many he might get on me."

She stood up and went to the cradle George Bashford had given her. Her cousin watched in silence as she took out the coverlet and the little moss-filled pallet and started rearranging them within the one he had made for her.

The baby hiccoughed gently in his arms.

"You d-don't regret having her, do you, Dinah?"

She turned her head and smiled at him, trying to be her old self again.

"'Course I don't. Never for a minute. I love her—don't I, my little pet?" taking the baby from him and brushing her cheek against the soft coppery-hued down on the small head before settling her into the new cradle. "There. Don't she look a treat?"

Jack nodded, pleased with the result of his work.

"The Queen herself'd envy me that. You're real clever wi' your hands, our Jack. I wonder you've never thought to sell some o' the things you make and earn yourself a bit of extra money. Why don't you?"

"There's too few folks'd buy, that's why. I'm a c-carter by

120

trade, not a wood craftsman. I can't go doing others out o' business by poaching their custom, now can I?"

"Not round here, mebbe. But further abroad, who's to know? Especially down along the coast. Now there's a notion! I'll get Frank to—"

She checked herself. Jack saw the animation drain from her face.

Reaching out to touch her arm, he asked quietly, "What is it, Dinah? Come on, tell me. What's Frank been at to upset you? I c-can see there's something up."

She shook her head, turning away from him.

Then she sighed and looked down at the baby. "Well, if you must know—he seems to think this 'un isn't his. Don't ask me why, Jack. God knows, I've never given him cause to think there's anyone else."

"He's a fine one to be talking like that! Not his, indeed—I'd like to know what b-bastards in these parts Frank Morgan *hasn't* fathered!"

"That's not true!" Dinah swung round, the blood firing her cheeks. "Well . . . some, mebbe. But none that I want to hear of!"

"It *is* true. And you needn't go putting your hands to your ears, neither. I can't understand you, our Dinah. Letting a man misuse you the way that 'un does."

"Don't you start on that tack—I have enough of it from my mother."

"Then mebbe you ought to listen to her."

"If you can't keep a civil tongue in your head, Jack Adams, you can take yourself out o' my room!" Dinah's eyes were suspiciously bright. "Whatever Frank does or doesn't do, it's no concern of anybody's but him and me."

"Him and you and a few others, I should say. You want to hear what I was told about him yesterday!"

"What? What lies are they spreading now?"

"It wasn't lies. He's got another girl into trouble, an' that's a fact."

"What you talking about? What girl?"

"A girl I m-met in Buckfield yesterday dinner time. She was at the Pelham Arms asking after your Frank."

121

"So? How d'you know it was *my* Frank? Could've been anybody. There's plenty o' Franks about."

"But only one stallion leader called Frank Morgan. It's him, all right. She described him to a spit."

Dinah bit her lip and looked away.

"Why d'you put up wi' him the way you do?" Jack went on. "He treats you worse'n dirt, he does. Here's you wi' two little 'uns by him, and there's him knocking about Lewes free as a bird, taking up wi' other women and leaving 'em in a like condition. It don't make sense to me, our Dinah. It really don't."

"What's Lewes got to do wi' it?" she asked irrelevantly.

"It's where this girl m-met Frank. Early on in March, she told me. No more'n one day, that's all it were, and she never saw hide nor hair of him again. When they found out she was having a child she lost her job. Aye, and her lodgings along wi' it."

"So now she's come looking for Frank to take the blame? Lord above, Jack, you don't half let 'em pull the wool over your eyes, don't you?"

"What's that supposed to mean?"

"Only that this poor homeless creature could've got herself in trouble by half the men in Lewes, for all you know! And she has the sauce to pick on my Frank. Well, she's made her mistake there. He's not like you, letting yourself be taken in by a pretty face and a tale o' woe." She stared at him. "I hope you didn't let on where to find him?"

Jack looked away, avoiding his cousin's eyes.

"I felt sorry for her—"

"You would!"

"—she was s-standing out in the yard, asking every man that went by. She'd been sleeping in the stables a couple o' nights . . . there were rat bites on her legs."

"Oh, she showed you her legs, did she?"

"I saw the marks when she climbed up in the cart."

"The cart? What was she doing there?"

"I give her a ride after I'd got her something to eat."

"You did what? You give her a ride? Where to?"

"To Shatterford. Well, that's where he is! Leastways, that's where he was last week."

122

"Well he ain't there now. He's gone. Lord knows where, but she won't find him in Shatterford."

"What'll become of her, then?"

"I don't know! God's sake, Jack—it's nothing to us what becomes of her! Let her find Frank if she can. Poor girl, I suppose I ought to pity her, in that condition and no home to go to. But you shouldn't have brought her round here. She'll only end up in the workhouse. What d'you have to go getting yourself mixed up in it for?"

He shook his head and looked down, his expression a mixture of uneasiness and concern.

After a moment he said awkwardly, "I'm s-sorry. Don't take on about it, Dinah. But what was I to do? I couldn't leave her there, now could I? She looked that poorly. It wasn't that I meant . . . I don't like to see a body in trouble, that's all."

Dinah made a sound of exasperation. For a time she said nothing, turning over in her mind the implications of what she had learnt. But her anger had already passed, and she did not care just now to rake over its embers.

She came over and put her hands on her cousin's thin shoulders.

"I know," she said quietly. "It's all right. I'm sorry I raised my voice to you. Let's change the subject, shall we?"

He nodded.

"What d'you think o' the baby's new name?" she went on deliberately. "Belle? It's a shortening for Isabelle. D'you like it?"

"It's as good a n-name as any, I reckon."

"Did I tell you? The parson's wife's wanting her calling Rachael, after her? She's asked to be a sponsor at the christening."

"Oh?"

"*If* she's christened." Dinah sat back on the bed and pulled the cover around her. "Mrs Bates promised she'd talk to her husband about that and the sponsoring. It still don't seem right to me, though. I mean, she don't hardly know us, does she? If you want my opinion, it's a baby of her own she needs, not a share in somebody else's. I wonder she hasn't

123

had one already—she's been married long enough." She smiled suddenly. "Perhaps it's that old man of her'n. You ought to go up to the rectory when he's not there, our Jack. Do her a good turn."

"What? Mrs Bates? Not me! There's a few wouldn't m-mind, though, from what they say. Farmer Bashford for one."

"Now what you been hearing about—"

Dinah stopped abruptly in mid-sentence, her head turned towards the opening door.

"Jack?" Molly Flynn came into the room. "What you doing up here? I never saw you come in."

"No. I used the b-back."

"Well on your way out you can use the front, and gi' me a hand shifting the barrels as you go."

"Look what he's been and made for us, Mam," her daughter interrupted, pointing. "Did you ever see anything like it? He's done hisself proud this time, ain't he?"

Mrs Flynn moved around the new cradle, examining it with a critical eye. The thin work-worn hands touched the carved hood.

"Aye. It's a nice piece o' work. You won't be needing Mr Bashford's after all, then?"

"Don't look so put out! Mr Bashford won't mind. Perhaps he'll let that Mrs Bates have it, along wi' all the other stuff he's giving her. I was just saying to our Jack, she might be needing one before long."

She looked at him slyly.

"A pity Frankie's too big for it," said her mother, anxious to hold on to the farmer's gift. "We could knock the end out, mebbe. It might fit him then."

"What, and spoil a good piece o' furniture! Mr Bashford won't thank us for that."

Molly Flynn's sharp features registered annoyance. "Well, Mrs Bates had best take it, then," she said peevishly. "An empty cradle's soon filled, and there's one there that'd be thankful of it, I don't doubt."

"You should never have brought her round here. She'll only end up in the workhouse."

Dinah's words about the girl he had tried to help preyed on Jack Adams's mind for several days afterwards.

He realised that if Charlotte (which she had said was her name) stayed on too long in Shatterford, the constable would arrest her for vagrancy, for being a charge on the parish, since she obviously had no means to support herself. If they sent her to the workhouse as a result, it would be partly his fault, he decided, because he was the one who had brought her into the district from Buckfield. And that made her almost as much his responsibility as she was Frank Morgan's.

Jack had not doubted for a moment but that Morgan was the one to blame for the girl's plight: the stallion man's reputation was too well known. But suppose she failed to find him? Or, if she did succeed in tracing him, suppose he did as Dinah said he would, and refuse to accept liability for her child? What was she to do then? There was nothing in Lewes for her to go back to; and if she applied for parish relief here, she could only stay a week at the most before the Poor Law officers sent her on to Heathbury and its dismal workhouse, to give birth to her baby and then be put out again on to the streets.

It worried Jack. He had a compassionate nature and could not bear to see a creature helpless or hurt or abandoned without doing whatever he could to alleviate its distress.

Charlotte Smith was just such a poor creature in his eyes.

His pity had been moved the moment he saw her in the yard of the Pelham Arms in Buckfield. Hungry and dirty, her hair tangled about her shoulders, calling out to any that went by in that busy place if they knew of Frank Morgan.

Most had ignored her; but there were a few who made sport of her, treating her with the coarse humour reserved for women in her wretched condition, winking at each other as they jostled her out of their way. If she had been a dog, they could not have treated her worse.

The girl had been pathetically grateful for Jack's offer of help; and for once he had been able to control his stammer in the presence of a stranger and asked her questions about herself, where she came from, how long she had been on the road. He did not need to ask why she sought Frank Morgan.

And now she was in Shatterford, and Morgan gone, moved on somewhere else with his stallion.

Well, she could not be left alone there to face the workhouse, Jack Adams decided. Not if he could help it. He would find Frank Morgan for her; or else take care of her himself.

15

A few miles from Weatherfield, at the foot of the windmill on Snow Hill, a soberly dressed figure stood looking out across the Sussex countryside. Above him the mill sweeps moved ponderously round in the blustery wind, the whole edifice creaking against the pull of the fan-tail.

The man held his high-crowned hat against his thigh and the fair hair was blown untidily forward across his forehead. Occasionally he raised a hand to shield his eyes from the stinging pieces of chaff whirled up by the gusts.

After standing there a while, he drew a deep breath, as though some decision had finally been reached, replaced his hat and was about to move off when a sudden movement on the hill path below caught his attention. He paused, watching.

Within a few moments more the movement had resolved itself into someone climbing steadily up the slope: a dark-haired, well-built man clad in the usual countryman's garb of tweed coat, neckerchief and corduroy trousers tied below the knee with twine.

Reaching the top of the slope, the man stopped to catch his breath, putting his hands on his hips and looking about him. His glance fell upon the watcher within the shadow of the mill sweep and he gave a slight start, as if surprised to find anyone there. Or perhaps surprised to see who it was.

For several moments the two men stood facing each other across the grassy space, the wind beating between them as though straining to keep them apart.

Then the newcomer was seen to smile to himself.

"Afternoon, sir," he called, walking up a short way.

"Good afternoon," the other responded.

"A rough day for the time of year."

"Yes."

"The crops'll be flattened in the fields if it keeps up like this."

"Indeed."

The newcomer drew in several more deep breaths and looked carefully at the fair-haired man, his eyes travelling over the white band, the stock and black frockcoat. He smiled again.

"Aren't you Mr Bates? The new parson at Weatherfield?"

"I am."

"We haven't met before. But I know you by name, of course."

"Then you have the advantage of me. You are not one of my parishioners, I think."

"No, I'm not. Not exactly."

"Do you live in the district?"

"On and off." The man turned and looked out over the countryside. "Fine view from up here."

"There is indeed. I'd paused to enjoy it for a while before calling on the Olivers." Esmond Bates indicated the weather-boarded cottage standing a short way beyond the mill.

"Ah. Tod Oliver hasn't been keeping too well, I hear."

"He shows improvement."

"I'm glad to learn it. I've got business with him myself."

There was a pause. Esmond stood waiting for the stranger to introduce himself.

Instead, the man startled him by saying suddenly, "It's funny we should meet like this, you and me."

"Funny?"

"Aye. That's the word."

"I don't understand . . . Why so?"

The other put his hands into his pockets, the dark eyes moving across the rector's face.

"On account of the things I've been hearing about you."

"About me? What manner of things? To my advantage, I trust?"

"Ah, that would be telling, now, wouldn't it."

Esmond frowned at the faintly sneering tone.

"I don't think I quite like your inference, sir!"

"Oh? I didn't mean to sound disrespectful. It's just my manner of speaking. You ask Mrs Bates. She'll tell you. She knows me and my little ways quite well."

The rector's senses sharpened. A feeling of hostility stole over him as he looked at the man. Was it imagination, or was there a look of insolent amusement in the expression?

"My wife knows you? Strange, I have no recollection of her mentioning you."

"Probably she forgot. You know what women are like."

"May I ask where you met her?"

"The first time? Well, according to her, it was in some churchyard in Lewes. But I wasn't conscious of the fact, as you might say, so perhaps we won't count that occasion."

"I'm sorry. I don't quite understand you. Would you make yourself plainer?"

The other shrugged. "As you wish. The first time I actually made so bold as to exchange words with your dear lady was . . . now let me think. Oh, yes—it was over at Netherton. She had the kindness to admire my stallion."

"Your . . . stallion?"

"That's right. The Brighton Regent. A beautiful beast, Mr Bates. The best stud in the southern counties. You should see him with the mares! It's a sight to stir a man's pride, it is."

Esmond Bates made a sharp, choked sound and half turned away. Then he swung back, his lips compressed, and stared into the other's face. His attitude had undergone a marked change.

Coldly he said, "Now I know you."

"You do?"

"Dinah Flynn's paramour . . . her debaucher."

"Oh, come now, sir! Those are mighty strong words for a man of your cloth to be using." There was no mistaking the mockery in the voice.

"You are Morgan. Frank Morgan."

The stallion leader removed his right hand from his pocket and held it out towards the rector.

"Frank Morgan it is."

The intended handshake was ignored. Esmond looked him up and down in disgust. All that he had learnt about this man from the reports of others had led him to regard Morgan in the very worst light, spiritual defilement personified. His moral incontinence, the open licentiousness of his occupation, his deliberate flouting of all Christian ethics, the facility with which he made use of witless females for the gratification of his lust: the indictment against him was a damning one indeed.

Esmond Bates had already pre-formed in his mind an image of the stallion man as some satyr of the pagan world, demi-beast in appearance: that image had not been too fanciful. And the knowledge that Rachael had been in contact with this creature, exposed to his corruption, filled the rector with revulsion.

He said, "What motive had you, to approach my wife at Netherton? It was while she was with your . . . woman at Bashford's farm, I suppose."

"Well, it's a free world, as they say. I meant no offence. Leastways, not the kind of offence you mean, Mr Bates. Your wife certainly took none. And before you turn any nastier with me, let me tell you something."

"Well?"

"I've broken with Dinah Flynn. It's all over between us. Finished. You'll be pleased to hear that, I'm sure. So now you can take her back into your fold and pray for her salvation as much as you want."

Esmond made no reply. His face had taken on a strange, pinched expression.

"I'll let you into a little secret," Morgan continued, grinning. "The truth is, I've found a girl I like better."

"I see."

"Much better. She's a proper little sweetheart, this one."

"And is it your intention to marry this . . . girl?"

The stallion man's laugh jarred on Esmond's nerves.

"Marry her? Would that I could, Mr Bates!" He came a few steps closer and lowered his voice. "Trouble is, she's

129

married already, you see. But they tell me her husband's a poor sort of man. If you catch my meaning."

He winked slyly.

The rector stared at him in distaste. It seemed almost as though the mockery in the veiled innuendo were being directed at him personally. The muscle in his jaw began to twitch. For a long moment he looked into the dark gipsy eyes and saw there the mirrored image of how he himself had once been, in the corruption of that other existence.

A sudden hatred seized him. An overwhelming desire to strike out and destroy.

"Have you no sense of shame? None at all?" he asked aggressively. "Do you think it right or proper to cast aside a woman—one, moreover, by whom you have had children— cast her aside to leave you free to seduce another to your wickedness? No, don't turn yourself away from me, Morgan! You shall hear me out, whether you will or not."

He reached forward, his voice rising.

"I think our meeting here today was no accident. I see God's hand in it. It was plainly intended to spare me the trouble of seeking you out. The welfare of the souls in this parish rests in my care. It is my duty to stamp out such vice and defilement as your kind introduce here. It may be I cannot force you to marry the mother of your bastards, but I *can* prevent you from carrying your mischief further. Who is this other woman you would damn with your adultery? I demand to know!"

"Do you indeed?" The sneer on Morgan's face was unmistakable. "Ask your wife. She'll tell you. You'll get nothing by preaching to me."

Abruptly he flung himself away and began walking towards the mill cottage.

Esmond Bates stared after him, his face clouded with the passion of his anger. A sudden buffet of wind caught his hat and blew it backwards to the ground; but he made no move to retrieve it. Instead, he took several half-running strides to bring himself up behind Morgan and grasped the stallion leader's arm, forcing him to turn and face him.

"You are a godless creature. Do you hear me? Godless!"

130

The wind whipped the hair into his eyes and he brushed it impatiently back with his free hand. "I forbid you ever to speak to my wife again. Ever! You are not to go near her nor have any kind of contact with her. Do you understand me? You will leave my wife alone."

Morgan pulled back from him, pushing the restraining hand aside. He looked Esmond insolently in the face, a knowing smile twisting his lips.

"Your *wife*, Mr Bates?" There was a subtle emphasis on the word.

"You will leave her alone!" the rector repeated furiously.

"Like you've left her alone?"

"What do you mean by that?"

"Oh, come. You know what I mean well enough."

"God damn you, you devil!"

"Don't you go damning me, you hypocrite! It's plain enough to any man with eyes what kind of sham your marriage is."

Esmond's face was suffused with blood. For a moment Morgan thought he was about to strike him. Then the clenched fists fell back to his sides.

In a strangled voice he said, "I don't want you near her again."

"And how d'you intend stopping me?"

"She must go away. I shall send her away." He stared fixedly at the stallion man, his eyes glittering behind the hair blown across his face. "Yes . . . that's right. That is what I shall do. Send her away from this place. It is not fit for her so long as you remain in it."

His expression altered. He turned abruptly and seemed to throw himself away from the mill's shadow as though from the shadow of evil, hastening down the slope as fast as he could towards the path.

Morgan watched him go. After a while he shrugged his shoulders and walked over to where the rector's hat lay discarded on the grass. He picked it up, brushed the specks of chaff from it and tried it on.

It was a perfect fit.

*   *   *

"Go back to Lewes?"

Rachael Bates stared in disbelief across the room at her husband. The cream and mauve columbines in her hand trembled slightly above the china vase on the parlour table.

"It would only be for a period," said Esmond. "A month or so, perhaps."

"A month or so! But . . . what about you?"

"I shall remain here, of course. I can hardly desert my duties to accompany you."

"And what of my duties? What about the confirmation class I've started? The sewing circle? And the house—who is to look after that? You know how much supervising Ada needs."

Her questions were ignored.

"Answer me, Esmond. Why should I need to leave Weatherfield? What has happened?"

Again, he avoided a reply. "Only yesterday at breakfast you were talking of returning to Lewes," he said instead.

"But not now—not yet! I meant some time in the future, for a short visit only. Not a month or so. What will they think in the parish if I disappear for such a length of time? They'll surely wonder—"

"Let them wonder! Your absence is no concern of theirs."

Rachael continued to stare at him. Some days ago Esmond had come home in a vicious ill humour which he would not explain; and that night had cried out repeatedly in his sleep. Much of it had been an unintelligible ramble. Except for the word "Morgan", spat out several times with great vehemence.

Now she had a dreadful suspicion that her husband's sudden desire to get her away from the district had something to do with the stallion leader. Had they met? Had Esmond learned the nature of their encounter at Netherton, what had happened between them in the church?

She said carefully, "Nevertheless, it will seem to our parishioners that you are sending me away."

"I am not *sending* you away. Do not try to twist my decision into a cause for argument, Rachael. If you wish for a reason, you shall have it. You have been looking somewhat strained these past weeks . . . the change, the burden of responsibility. Obviously you have overtaxed your strength." This was the pretext Esmond Bates had hit upon once the heat of his rage against Morgan had cooled to the more rational level of cold hatred. "Arthur and Emily have already indicated their willingness to have you stay with them for a while."

"Arthur and Emily Collins?" Rachael's voice expressed her swift dismay. "Oh, not the Collinses! Please, Esmond . . . you know I've never been at ease in their company."

"Nonsense. I can think of no one better to look after you."

His wife threw down the spray of columbines.

"Why should anyone need to look after me? I don't understand. I feel perfectly well, yet you wish me to be treated like an invalid. Tell me the truth. I think you should. What has happened? Why do I have to go to Lewes in such an unseemly hurry?"

Esmond reacted with a sudden show of temper.

"Because *I* wish it! And if you were any sort of dutiful wife you would accept my wishes as reason enough and not seek to argue with me. I expect your obedience, Rachael. And I will have it. The matter is settled. Arthur Collins expects you in Southgate Street on Friday."

Rachael bit her lip in vexation. Head averted, she said sullenly, "If I must go—since you are so very insistent— does it have to be to the Collinses? Effie and Ralph would be more than—"

Her words were cut short by his interruption. "Such an arrangement is out of the question. I do not approve of the Underwoods. You know that. They are a poor influence."

"And *I* do not approve of the Collinses! They are"—she sought for the term she wanted—"stuffy. Yes, that's it. Stuffy! Stuffy and dull."

"That is enough, Rachael. Remember they are my friends."

"And Effie is *my* friend. The only one you ever let me keep. And even then, your dislike spoiled everything. Why, I hardly dare even write to her."

Esmond made a gesture of irritation and turned away towards the empty fireplace, frowning.

It was true, of course. He had resented anyone who claimed a share in his new wife's affections. Euphemia—Effie—Godman in particular, since she was closest. She and Rachael had been inseparable since childhood. She had been the bride's maid at their wedding (Arthur Collins was the groom's man); and a short while later Rachael was maid of honour when Effie wed Ralph Underwood, son of Underwood the draper in Lewes high street.

Esmond had soon put an end to any idea of his young wife's that they and the Underwoods make up a social quartet. He had disliked Effie's husband from the moment they met, sensing in him exactly the kind of corrupting influence he feared would taint Rachael's innocent purity.

This was a man who clearly preferred to spend his Sundays gambling at illegal cockfights or bare-knuckle matches; and when he did attend church the smell of liquor on his breath was always noticeably stronger by the end of the service than it had been at the start.

Esmond was politely regretful, but he could no more accept Rachael's friends than she seemed willing to accept his. In particular Arthur Collins, of Holy Trinity in Southgate Street, who had known him since he first took Orders, and had been instrumental in his obtaining his curacy in Lewes.

Arthur had married the elder daughter of Holy Trinity's vicar, and had stayed on as perpetual curate in the confident expectation of inheriting his father-in-law's living when the old man died. He and Emily both shared Esmond's high Christian ideals and bookish tastes; and it had wounded her husband deeply when Rachael made it plain that she did not enjoy their company.

"A pair of dusty old blackbeetles," she had once scornfully described them; and Esmond had never forgotten that.

He turned back towards her now, watching in silence her tight-faced expression as she finished her arrangement of the columbine sprays. The downward turn of her lips warned him that she was resentful of being sent away.

But she had to go. Better that she be kept safely in Lewes under the protection of Arthur than remain here to be lusted after by lewd and conscienceless creatures like Frank Morgan.

134

"Friday, then," he said finally. "I will drive you myself in the trap as far as Buckfield and arrange for you to be taken on from there."

16

That night Rachael slept particularly badly.

Tossing and turning from one side to another, she managed to doze only fitfully, waking each time the dull chimes of the church clock disturbed the stillness. The dragging hours seemed endless. And the darkness served only to exaggerate her worry and fear so that she could not tell which was worse: to lie awake thinking, or drift into brief dreams which turned rapidly to nightmare.

She longed to be able to still her mind, shut off its clamouring; but it was too insistent.

At one point her restlessness woke Esmond. He took her in his arms and murmured a few incoherent words, but was soon asleep again, his mouth slack against her cheek.

His unconscious touch only increased the feelings of tension. She began to think about the way this marriage had cheated her, deprived her of the satisfaction of a woman's fulfilment, and found herself wondering what it must be like to be loved by a man . . . a man like Frank Morgan.

The thought of the stallion leader roused her.

It mattered not at all that she disliked him, feared him even, had planned to reform him by marriage to Dinah Flynn. Physical passion had little to do with affection or respect. Just now the image embraced in her mind was of the power of a hard muscular body, strong arms, black hair damp with sweat, lips pressed insistently against hers.

She gave a soft cry and turned over, hugging herself to her sleeping husband. The only response was a grunt.

For a while she tried to imagine that this was Frank

Morgan beside her, that any moment he would move and touch her in the darkness, his rough hands moving over her naked flesh. The fantasy sent a tingle of unfamiliar pleasure coursing through her.

Then Esmond grunted again and rolled on to his back and began to snore.

Frustration made Rachael desperate. Her body ached for the caress of a man and it was torment for her to lie here beside a husband who had so little physical use for her. She pitied him his inability to consummate their union; but pity could not deaden her need for the satisfaction he denied her.

Beyond the shuttered window the midsummer dawn was just beginning to break. A solitary bird had started its hesitant song among the boughs of one of the apple trees in the garden below. Unable any longer to bear the tension, she got up from bed and pushed open the shutter. Everything outside was shrouded in a pale mist.

Suddenly she felt a compulsive need to get away from this room, from this house, out into the cleansing air. Slipping off her nightgown she looked at herself for a long moment in the mirror beside the window; then turned away and began to dress quickly and silently, not bothering with restrictive undergarments or whalebone-stiffened petticoats.

The village lay still and ghostly beyond the green.

Rachael paused at the rectory gate but there was no one else about at this early hour, and she started to walk along the lane towards the farm lands. In the eastern sky a pallid sun hung half over the horizon, its bloodless light shining thinly through the persisting layers of ground mist, and the air was filled with dawn song from invisible birds all about her in the trees and hedgerows.

How long she walked she had no idea. By half past five the sun was fully risen above the tree tops, but veiled still, casting a diffused glow across the countryside.

She started to descend from the hill pastures, fearing to stay any longer in case Esmond should wake and miss her. But in the mist she lost her way. The hedge she thought would lead her back towards the village took her instead to a high bank, topped by wooden palings, and as she stood there hesitating she heard the unmistakable sound of horses whinnying in the field beyond.

Walking on beside the bank she came to a five-bar gate. The mist was starting to lift a little now, sucked up by the growing warmth of the sun, and looking out across the field she saw there were half a dozen mares running free with a stallion, their coats wet with night dew, eyes glistening as their dark shapes loomed towards her.

A sudden strange fancy seized Rachael as she watched them. She had the sensation that she was the only human being alive in this fresh new day, quite alone in a world of mist and sun, bird song and galloping horses. Slowly the tensions of the past hours dropped away and she drew in deep lungfuls of air, marvelling at this heady feeling of freedom.

The black stallion threw up his head and neighed harshly; then nuzzled one of the mares, nudging her neck and rubbing his gleaming flanks against her. They moved together side by side across the field and in a while he reared up against the skyline and began to mate with her.

Rachael had never seen this act between horses before. Dogs, yes. But dogs were ridiculous, uncouth creatures, embarrassingly vulgar in their street antics, whereas this display between mare and stallion had a most powerful beauty about it.

She watched them, bewitched.

And in turn was watched herself.

Frank Morgan had risen early to make a check on his horse. Walking up in the lee of the bank he had seen a figure standing at the gate of the horse pasture, and paused. Then, recognising the woman, had experienced a sharp, swift excitement that made him catch his breath.

He did not stop to wonder what she was doing here at such an hour. It was enough that she *was* here. He had looked around to make sure that she was alone, and keeping out of sight, moved up the slope of the bank and crept along by the palings until he had a clear view of her face.

Her eyes were fixed upon the Brighton Regent, her lips parted a little, her arms crossed over her breast, the brown hair falling loosely about her shoulders. She was not wearing

137

any petticoat and the sunlight outlined her long legs through the thin material of her skirts.

When the horses moved apart she gave a soft sigh and leaned forward against the gate as though what she had just witnessed had taken all the strength from her limbs.

Morgan felt the surge of desire quicken within him, his throat going dry. This was the moment he had waited for, the moment he had longed to come. There would never be another so suited to his purpose.

He stood up.

Rachael heard the sound and looked quickly over her shoulder. Above her on the bank a man was staring down at her. She knew at once who it was, but she felt no disquiet. The spell of the horses was still too strongly upon her. She looked back at him calmly, waiting; and he slithered down the bank and came over to where she stood.

Neither spoke.

The expression in his dark eyes was of hungry excitement, the look a greedy child wears when it has a whole cake but cannot decide where to take the first bite. His gaze moved over her face, her shoulders, the soft swell of her breast, and the urgency mounted within him until he could no longer contain it.

Slowly he reached towards her.

Rachael stepped back, but the high wooden gate trapped her. There was no escape.

Frank Morgan followed, moving so close that their bodies almost touched; his hands on either side of her gripping the bar. Still, neither of them said a word. He pressed himself against her, feeling her body yield as his mouth brushed her cheek. Her breath smelled sweet and there was a faint scent of violets on her skin. She turned her head away but he persisted, and when at last he found her lips she gave a low moan and clung to him, her mouth quivering against his.

His arms tightened around her and she strained herself to him, returning his kisses with a passion that made his senses swim. He had never known a woman so desperate. After a while she leaned back, breathless, and he took her

138

face between his hands, his eyes moving over her features as though she were the most precious creature on God's earth.

His voice broke the spell.

"Come on, we'll go into the barn. It'll be more private." He kissed her again, and laughed. "You won't regret it, I promise."

Rachael pulled away.

"I . . ."

"What's the matter? Are you frightened? You needn't be. I know it's your first time. I'll be gentle, I swear I will. I won't hurt you."

"No . . ." She struggled to free herself.

Morgan gripped her tightly by the arms. Her face had lost the look of abandon that had first aroused him so much, and now she seemed like any other young female nervous about surrendering herself to a man.

He began to coax.

"Don't be coy. You don't have to be modest with me. You were made to be loved, d'you know that? You're as hot for it as I am. I know. I felt it when you kissed me. You're like a ripe fruit just waiting to be plucked from the tree."

He pulled her to him again and pressed his mouth hard on hers. But this time her lips would not open for him and her body stiffened in his embrace.

His desire for her was so achingly strong that this show of resistance angered him. He had never forced a woman in his life—never had cause to—but just now he felt that if she would not yield to him willingly he would be driven to take her against her will. Nothing else mattered but the urgency of his need to gratify himself, to complete the satisfaction she had promised him until a few moments ago.

"What's wrong with you?" he repeated hoarsely. "Is it your husband? Are you bothered he'll find out? Is that it?"

Rachael shook her head. "Let me go. Please let me go. I'm sorry. I shouldn't have . . . behaved as I did."

"It's too late to be saying sorry now, my beauty."

He pressed his lips roughly to her mouth, her face, her neck, and she felt his hands move down to her hips and grip her hard against his body. It frightened her and she struck out at him, realising too late what an uncontrollable state she had roused him to by her foolish, wanton conduct.

A sudden noise startled them both. It was a high-pitched giggle.

Morgan cursed under his breath and looked about, trying to find its source; and Rachael seized her chance to free herself from his grasp. Before the stallion man had time to react, the giggling broke out again, nearer.

Along the side of the bank came a young couple, children almost, their arms entwined around each other's waist. Every few steps they paused to exchange kisses, immature caresses that were barely more than a touching of lips to lips. Then their faces drew apart and the girl would give another little laugh and lower her eyes, her cheeks flushed with pleasure, while the boy cast sidelong bashful glances at her.

Neither appeared to have noticed the man and woman by the gate.

Their innocence, in comparison with the embraces she had exchanged with Frank Morgan, made Rachael feel sick with shame. Her craving for a man's touch, her feverish imaginings, the frustration that had driven her from her husband's bed into the arms of the stallion leader, had been nothing more than lust; and she was no better than one of those loose women she had so often pitied, mauling at their drink-roused partners in alleys and public-house passages.

Averting her head she moved away from the gate; and then suddenly took to her heels and ran as fast as she could down the hill and across the cart track into the opposite pasture.

There she paused briefly to get her bearings, and glanced back. Morgan had not moved. The boy and his girl were still totally absorbed in each other as they passed in front of him, hiding him from her sight.

She turned and went on. Never again, she promised herself in an anguish of self-reproach, never again would she so jeopardise the decency of her life by allowing herself to succumb to such base temptation. Thank God she was leaving

140

Weatherfield. In Lewes at least she would be beyond the stallion man's reach and the memory of this morning could be wiped from her mind.

<h1 style="text-align:center">17</h1>

"And is dear Esmond well?" Emily Collins enquired. "We were so concerned, Arthur and I, when he had to go into the country. Such a change after his years of devoted work in urban parishes."

Rachael sat stiffly upright on a straight-backed chair in the Collinses' cheerless parlour in Southgate Street. The seat had split at the edge and the horsehair padding pricked the backs of her legs through the thin material of her skirts.

"Thank you, he's settled very happily," she said politely. "His health is much improved by the move. The air in the country is so good for him." She put down her cup. "He's beginning to lose that awful town pallor at last."

"Pallor?" queried Arthur Collins, whose own sallow complexion betrayed too many hours closeted indoors.

His wife, a tall bony woman in black, pursed her lips and looked critically at Rachael.

"Another cup of tea?"

"No, thank you."

"Esmond's letter told us you've been over-tiring yourself. She does look a trifle peaky, doesn't she, Arthur? We must ensure that you have complete rest whilst you're with us. No excitement, Esmond said."

"Oh?"

"We think therefore, Arthur and I, that you should limit your social entertaining. In fact, it might be best if you do no entertaining at all."

"But I *am* allowed out?"

Mr Collins, a middle-aged, balding man with steel-rimmed

spectacles clamped on a long, thin nose, leaned forward and patted her hand.

"I see no reason why not, my dear. A short stroll after dinner to take the air, perhaps. I shall be glad to accompany you for the exercise myself."

Rachael stared at him, dismayed.

"But . . . may I not go visiting? I've not seen my friends here in Lewes for some time." She had already drawn up plans to call on Charlotte Smith, as well as the Underwoods and a few others.

"Remember what your husband has advised." Mrs Collins smiled thinly. "No excitement. I feel sure that your—friends will understand that you must have rest. Visiting may be a little unwise in the present circumstances."

Rachael's eyes darkened. So that was the arrangement. To keep her closed up in this gloomy house with the Collinses as her guardians. It was as she suspected, she thought guiltily. Somehow Esmond had learned about the stallion leader.

It was inevitable, she supposed. Gossip and speculation flourished like contagion in such a small community as Weatherfield, and her encounter with Morgan at the church could hardly have gone entirely unobserved: someone surely had seen him follow her out. It needed only one casual remark, one passing reference, for Esmond's jealous nature to interpret the incident in the very worst light.

How typically in character that he should retaliate not by confronting her directly, but by turning her over to his precious friends for a period of 'corrective instruction'—one of his favoured expressions.

Well, it would not do to cross them too soon. Her time here would be difficult enough as it was.

She stood up. "With your permission, I'd like to be shown to my room now. The travelling has tired me."

"Of course." Emily Collins pulled on the bell-rope. "We have given you a room at the rear of the house, overlooking the grass. Such a restful view, I always think."

The view was, as she said, most restful: rows of lichen-stained gravestones creeping unevenly from below the window towards the flint-knapped walls of Holy Trinity

Church, and the sweeping branches of a clump of evergreens spreading a dense shadow across the grass. The only cheering sight, to Rachael's eyes, was a glimpse of Lewes marketplace between the roofs beyond the churchyard wall.

She drew her shawl around her chilled shoulders and turned away from the window to examine the room.

It was functionally furnished with an iron bedstead and a set of deal drawers, and a rag rug to cover the floorboards. There was no mirror, she noticed. The only decoration was a large framed motto in woolwork hanging above the bed. "The Fear of the Lord is the Instruction of Wisdom," it read.

Downstairs in the front parlour Emily Collins sighed regretfully and looked at her husband.

"I'm afraid she is going to prove stubborn, Arthur. Her expression when I said she might not visit!"

"I have every confidence that you will be able to discipline her, my dear."

A flicker of distaste passed across Mrs Collins's strong features.

"Such a silly, wilful creature. What on earth possessed Esmond to marry her? Helen would have suited him so much better."

"Undoubtedly. As I've often said, nothing would have pleased me more than that he should marry your sister. But"—Arthur Collins shook his head sadly—"it was not to be. He took it into him to make that young person his wife, and no argument of mine could dissuade him."

"Such a waste." His wife rose from her chair and stood for a moment looking out through the lace-netted window at the horse traffic passing along Southgate Street. "Even for Esmond's sake, I would not have welcomed her into the house had Father not taken to his bed again. She can make herself useful looking after him. Reading to him, perhaps. She has a pleasant enough voice, I'll say that for her. A little throaty for my taste, but quite clear."

"An excellent arrangement, my dear. He seems less restless when there is someone to sit with him. Perhaps the young person will be good enough to attend to his other requirements, do you think?"

143

Mrs Collins moved away from the window.

"I rather had that in mind when we answered Esmond's letter."

The Reverend Frederick Kingsley, vicar of Holy Trinity, in the fortieth year of his incumbency and the seventy-fifth of his life, pulled fretfully at the covers on his bed.

What was Emily about to keep him waiting so long for his breakfast? Had she no control over those idle girls they kept as maids? And where was Helen—why was she not here to assist Emily, like a dutiful daughter, instead of taking herself off to London after that ridiculous little curate from St Michael's?

He struggled for a while to ease his dropsical body against the mound of pillows surrounding it, but the effort proved too great and he lay back, panting slightly. Devil take the lot of them!

There was a knock at the door.

When it did not open immediately, he called out testily, "Come in, come in!" The voice was hoarse and thick, a poor echo of what it had been in former days when his pulpit oratory had swayed congregations.

An unfamiliar young woman entered the room. Mr Kingsley inspected her. A little brown-haired thing in one of those Scotch checks the Queen was making so popular. Nasty material in his opinion.

"Well?"

"Your breakfast, sir—"

"About time!"

It was hot in the room and the odour of the sick body was strong.

She put the laden tray down on the side table, intending to draw it closer to the bedside.

"Don't fuss over me, woman. I can see after myself."

Irascibly, the old man reached out for plate and fork. Rachael passed them to him and he immediately began stabbing at the thick pieces of meat. After several greedy mouthfuls he looked up at her.

"Well? And who are you?"

"Rachael Bates. Mrs Bates, that is."

"Bates? Bates?"

"My husband is the Reverend Esmond Bates. He was formerly curate of All Souls."

Mr Kingsley digested this information with another slice of gammon. A thread of grease ran down one side of his chin. She held out the napkin to him, but it was ignored.

"I remember him. One of Arthur's cronies. Heard he'd left the town."

"Yes, several months ago. He has the living of Weatherfield now. It's a country parish beyond Buckfield."

Mr Kingsley chewed on, washing the meat down with gulps of porter. Rachael stood uncertainly beside the bed, wondering whether she should go or stay.

Finally he spoke again.

"And what were you before you married, Mrs Bates?"

"What . . . was I, sir?"

"You heard me correctly. Your speech has the local accent, which leads me to conclude that you are from the area."

"Oh, indeed, yes. I lived here in Lewes with my aunt, sir. Miss Kember. She kept a shop in Flood Street."

"Kember, d'you say? Kember? Not Fanny Kember?"

"Why—yes. Yes, that was her name."

"Fanny Kember!"

A tremor ran through the bedclothes and the old man's body was shaken by a series of low choking coughs. He seemed to be laughing.

Rachael stared at him.

Then a sudden sound from the doorway made her turn sharply, in time to see Emily Collins come into the room.

Glancing across at the bed, the older woman tutted with impatience.

"Come along, Father! Are you not finished yet? Arthur will be up directly to prepare you for Dr Carroll."

Mr Kingsley struggled among his pillows.

"Carroll and his damned leeches . . . he'll have every last drop of blood from me before he's done. Here—take these things." His curious reaction to the name of Fanny Kember appeared to be forgotten.

145

Rachael removed the plate and beer-pot and placed them on the tray to take them down to the kitchen.

"I'll see to that," Mrs Collins said sharply. "My husband will require you to assist him here."

"Here? But . . . I'm no sick-room nurse!"

"Nevertheless, you will please stay and help Mr Collins."

"To do what?"

"Mr Kingsley needs to be washed and his bedding changed."

Rachael made no attempt to disguise her astonishment.

"I am expected to do that?"

"I see no reason why you should refuse. You've surely done as much for the sick among your husband's parishioners?"

"For the womenfolk, yes. When it was necessary. But you will forgive me, Mrs Collins. I've no experience of carrying out such intimate tasks for . . . for men."

Two high spots of colour appeared on Rachael's cheeks.

"What's this, what's this?" Mr Kingsley called out peevishly. "What're you saying to upset the girl, Emily?"

Mrs Collins ignored him.

"Indeed, I consider it a most unusual request," Rachael continued. "Naturally, I have no objection to helping with Mr Kingsley's meals. But you surely cannot expect me to undress and wash him?"

"I would not have thought you so fastidious," Mrs Collins replied acidly.

The other's eyes widened. With some difficulty she suppressed the bitter response that comment provoked.

Instead she said, "You will excuse me?"

"Where are you going?"

"Have I a choice? I believe Mr Collins has set me some reading to do in my room."

That, it appeared, was how she was intended to pass her days here: shared out between Bible study, Mr Kingsley, and the pious instruction of such works as Francis Newman's *History of the Hebrew Monarchy* and *Phases of Faith*.

Mrs Collins's lips tightened.

"Very well. You may go for the moment. But I assure you,

this unhelpful attitude will not make your stay with us any the pleasanter."

Rachael picked up the tray a second time. On her way to the door she said quietly, "I never imagined, ma'am, that it was intended to be pleasant."

"Is that him?"

"Yes. That's the man."

Jack Adams drew his companion gently back behind the stable wall.

"You're sure?"

"It's him, all right." Charlotte Smith's young face was flushed. "I'd have known him anywhere."

She shifted herself so that she could see once more into the yard, where Frank Morgan was supervising the mating of his stallion to a chestnut mare. The horses hid his view of the stable block where she stood, and she watched him unobserved. He was just as she remembered him from that day in Lewes: handsome, self-assured, easy-going, laughing as he called out something to one of the men with him.

She felt suddenly dizzy and put a hand against the wall to steady herself.

"Here, hold up, now—" Jack took her arm. "You're n-not going to faint on us, are you?"

She smiled weakly, shaking her head; and he smiled back at her.

She had so much to thank Jack Adams for, she told herself. She had been truly destitute, reduced to living off whatever she could beg or steal when he had come back to Shatterford in search of her a few days ago. He had taken her to a place called Spring Hill Farm. He knew the owner, a Mr Bashford, and had arranged with him for her to stay in an empty cottage there.

"We'll wait till they've taken the horses out," Jack said. "They'll be done in a m-minute."

Charlotte looked down at the slim, strong hand grasping her arm. Then her eyes moved slowly upwards and their glances met, and held.

"You're very kind to me, Jack. I don't know why you bother."

"I like you," he told her frankly, astonishing himself.

"I like you as well."

They continued to gaze at one another; and the smiles slowly faded. It was as though they had never seen each other properly before this moment.

"I don't know what makes you care for me . . . not in the state I'm in."

"I don't m-mind that. It wasn't any fault o' yourn."

"No. You're right." Charlotte looked away. "I'm glad you told me about him. I think I knew from the start I was wasting my time, looking for him. But I thought—well, I suppose I thought there was a chance he'd be different. What a laugh, eh? Your cousin Dinah and all them others . . . I chose myself a right 'un to be took in by."

Jack gave her a little shake.

"I told you n-not to worry, didn't I? Come on. We'll miss him altogether if we don't look sharp."

Still holding her arm, he walked with her from the shadow of the stable wall out into the open yard.

Frank Morgan turned towards them, wiping the sweat from his face with his neckerchief. Seeing only Jack Adams and a young woman, he nodded a casual greeting and started re-tying the cloth. Then paused, and looked again. There was something vaguely familiar about the girl.

"Hello, Frank. Remember me?" she said.

The dark eyes travelled quickly over her face, noting its paleness, the shadows under the eyes, the hollowed cheeks emphasised by dull hair scraped back into a knot.

"I don't think so," he said warily. "Any reason why I should?"

Charlotte placed her hands across her belly. "Here's your reason."

The stallion man's glance dropped.

"She's w-with child," Jack put in, unnecessarily.

"*Our* child, Frank. Yourn and mine. Started in Lewes." She gazed at him fixedly. "You remember me now?"

148

Yes, he remembered her now. Charlotte something-or-other. The one the parson's wife had seen him with.

"You expect me to believe that's my doing?"

"What d'you mean?"

"Oh, come on! You know what I mean all right."

Her face grew paler still, and more strained.

"I wasn't the first man you've been with," he went on. "You were no maid when I took you, so why come picking on me?"

"Because this is your baby I'm carrying."

"Oh, don't give me that. What kind of a blasted fool d'you take me for?"

"But it *is*," she insisted. "Don't you think I know who fathered it?"

"Prove it."

"How c-can she?" Jack interrupted again.

Morgan turned on him. "You keep out of it! What did you have to bring her here for anyway?"

"She's g-g-got every r-r-right to b-b-be here."

"Oh, shut up, you stammering half-wit! If you can't make yourself plain, keep yourself quiet. Any other man and I'd think the pair of you had got together on a purpose to snare me. But seeing it's only daft Jack Adams,"—Morgan looked him up and down—"who can't even talk straight, let alone—"

"You leave him be!" Charlotte broke in. "He's worth six o' you any day."

The stallion leader threw back his head and gave a mirthless laugh.

"What—him? He's as brainless as he's beardless. Still in short breeches, living at home with his mam. Just goes to show how your taste runs, my wench, fancying the likes of him."

Jack Adams caught at his arm. "D-d-don't you d-d-d-"

But the words of anger refused to come clearly and he flung himself away, cursing his useless tongue.

Morgan grinned.

The mockery of his expression twisted something within Charlotte Smith as she reminded herself how falsely this man had played her. Savagely she turned on him.

"Yes, that's right—smile! You've got plenty to smile about, haven't you, Frank Morgan? It isn't you that's lost your job and your lodgings, is it? It isn't you that's carrying a bastard and has to hear its father deny it's his! It isn't you that's got to give it birth and hope it dies before it draws its first breath!"

She stared at the stallion man and hit herself hard on the body.

"This is yourn. Nobody else's. It was you got it on me. And if I wasn't a maid when you took me that day, it's only because there's other men like you knocking about, ready to promise a girl the world if she'll part her legs for 'em!"

The amusement died from Morgan's face.

"And I still say it wasn't me that got you in trouble. I'll own I used you badly, though. I shouldn't have left without saying goodbye." He paused. "What will you do? Have you thought?"

"You won't marry me?"

"No."

She looked down, shaking her head wearily. "Then I don't know what I shall do. At least gi' me some money, for God's sake."

"No!" Jack pulled her round to face him. "Don't you b-beg from him."

Contemptuously Morgan said, "You keep quiet. Don't be a greater fool than you are already. I reckon I owe her a bit for the pleasure she gave me. Here,"—he reached into his pocket and pulled out a handful of coins—"here's something to be going on with."

"She don't need your m-money." Jack struck out at him, knocking the coins to the ground. "I'll be the one to look after her if you won't."

"Don't, Jack," Charlotte said. She bent down and began picking up the scattered pieces of silver.

Morgan watched her. Then his glance moved back to the younger man's face.

"What d'you mean—you'll look after her?"

"I mean I'll m-marry her. If she'll have me."

Charlotte looked up at him, startled.

"And as for the baby," he continued doggedly, "I'll be a b-better father to it than you could ever be, Frank Morgan. So you can clear off, d'you hear? You're nothing to us any more."

18

The stable interior struck cool after the heat of the yard, the light subdued where it came in through grimed panes of glass set in the slope of the roof. Swags of dusty cobwebs festooning the rafters overhead undulated slowly backwards and forwards in the through draught from the open door.

"Have you rubbed him well?"

Frank Morgan glanced at the farmhand holding his stallion's halter rope, and received a nod of affirmation. He passed a hand down the gleaming black flank.

"Good. Fetch us over a flat iron from the house, will you? I'll give him a drench while we're waiting for Bucknell's mare."

When the man had gone Morgan carried his bag to a work-bench against the stable wall and took from it a folded sheet of thick brown paper and two smallish blocks, each done up in clean rag. Opening out the paper he measured a piece off with his eye, turned it down and sharpened the crease with his thumbnail before tearing it neatly.

The larger piece was pushed aside out of the way; the other was folded carefully in half and left on the bench in front of him.

Untying the rags, he used his pocket knife to cut a lump the size of a walnut from the block of resin and another from the block of soda, sandwiching both between the two halves of paper and pressing them down well with the heel of his hand.

While he waited for the flat iron he tidied away what he no longer needed and checked the stable for something to stand on to do the drenching. A portable mounting block beside the door appeared to meet his requirement.

The farmhand returned. "Will this 'un do, Mr Morgan?"

The stallion leader hefted the flat iron in his hand.

"Aye. That's heavy enough. Now catch hold of the horse again while I pound this lot, in case the racket startles him. I don't want him getting agitated."

Raising the iron, he brought its face down hard upon the paper square, crushing the lumps of resin and soda until they were reduced to fine granules. The paper was rolled up into a tube. Then, indicating to his assistant to lead the horse out of the stall, he dragged the mounting block into the middle of the straw-covered floor.

"Right—bring him up and hold him steady there. Back a bit . . . a bit more. That's it," climbing up. "Now slacken your rope off as I take his nose."

In his right hand Morgan grasped a small, thick piece of wood, drilled at one end to take a loop of cord. Passing the loop over the soft part of his horse's nose, he gave it a sudden sharp upward and backward twist, forcing the Brighton Regent to open his mouth and so enable him to pour the crushed contents of the tube smartly to the back of the throat.

"Hold him!"

He released the loop and slapped his hand against the muscular neck before jumping down from the block.

"There. That's soon done. I'll take him now."

Leading the horse out to the trough in the yard, he stood by to let him take sufficient water to wash down the drench— a conditioner which he regularly used to ensure the animal's strength and potency. With two more mares still to be served that afternoon, the Brighton Regent would need it.

If required, the stud could cover up to a dozen mares in a day; but Morgan seldom allowed so many, preferring to keep his Shire fresh and in peak condition for as long as he could. He had known of too many stallions worn out by over-mating in what should have been their prime; and that on top of a circuit of sometimes up to sixty miles in a week.

A stallion leader would generally set out from his base on a Monday and walk an advertised route, spending each night at a different town or village. His stops—usually a farm, a smithy, or, preferably, a public-house yard—would be known in advance to draught-horse owners on the circuit and they would arrange to bring their in-season mares to be covered. Occasionally a club might hire the stallion to stand for several days at one yard; but generally a leader could expect to have completed his round by Saturday and be back again at his base.

Frank Morgan's work took him mainly into the north-eastern Weald and Kent, since the majority of Sussex farmers still preferred to follow the centuries-old practice of using oxen as draught animals. In recent years he had also started to build up business in areas to the west of the Ashdown Forest as progressive agricultural methods there favoured the faster manoeuvrability of the horse. Though he had heard it predicted that the coming of steam power to the land would mean the end of draught animals altogether, he doubted that it would ever prove a serious rival to the muscle power of a team of Shires.

His stallion, the Brighton Regent, was much in demand by farmers wanting strong young animals for gelding or later breeding. The horse was from the stock of the almost legendary Fen Blacks, a ponderous breed of enormous weight and size developed out of the old Great Horse which had carried men into battle since the time of the Norman Conquest. It was in direct lineage to the most famous Black of all, Wiseman's Honest Tom, foaled in 1800, and had inherited its grandsire's massive build, sooty colour and flowing mane and tail with a profusion of long, coarse hair on the cannons, fetlocks and coronets.

Morgan had purchased the Brighton Regent from an East Midlands breeder five years previously, when the stallion was a yearling. It was his second horse: the first, a three-quarter bred Suffolk, had had his back broken during a mis-mating when the mare had kicked out and sent him rearing over off-balance.

The stallion season generally got under way in March and

Morgan travelled round all the mares on his circuit every three weeks to try them. Those ready to be covered would be served on the first visit; the others were brought back to be tried subsequently.

The method of trying, to find whether the mare would accept the stallion, varied little from one place to another. A strong barrier of some kind—known as the trying, or teasing, bar—would be set up securely in the yard and the mare brought in from the field. The stallion was led up to the other side of the bar to get her scent, and allowed to tease her by rubbing his head against hers or biting her playfully on the neck.

If the mare were properly in season ("in song", as the horsemen called it) she would submit to the teasing and could safely be brought out from behind the bar to be covered.

But if she were not ready the men holding her often had to look lively to escape being kicked; and only an inexperienced or careless leader would try to put his stallion to a mare likely to use her shod hooves on such a vulnerable target. The injuries could well be severe enough to spoil a stud animal for good.

Morgan had held himself bitterly to blame for the death of that first horse. It was the kind of accident a stallion man dreaded; and it had been caused by his own laxity, by paying too much attention to a woman watching him work and not enough to what was happening at the trying bar. "Business first, pleasure after" henceforth became his unwritten motto. He loved the Brighton Regent too much to risk a repetition of that earlier tragedy merely for the sake of a woman's inviting glance and moist red lips.

"Up. Up, boy. That's enough. You've taken all you're getting."

He shortened the Shire's halter rope and pulled his head away from the water trough, brushing at the flies clustered around the eyes. The wet fleshy mouth nuzzled his shoulder, leaving thick threads of saliva on the mat blackness of his moleskin waistcoat.

"They two're still about here, Missus says," the farmhand

informed him conversationally when he led the horse back into the stable.

"What two?"

"They two as come in the yard to speak wi' you just now awhile. Missus seen 'em go round the back o' the barn together."

"Well, they won't be up to any harm, tell her. Belikes they're only after a bit of privacy."

He returned the other's broad grin with a shrug of indifference. If Jack Adams wanted to go burdening himself with the responsibility of a pregnant female, that was his affair. Morgan had paid his own due to her, and as far as he was concerned the business was at an end. Let them marry, and good luck to them, he thought. Give them a year and Jack would be wishing he'd not been so hasty to rush into wedlock with a woman who had little choice but to take the first man who offered himself.

How much simpler life would be if men and women behaved as horses did. Coming into season, meeting and mating, then going their separate ways. With horses there was none of this nonsense about trapping a man into marriage; no second thoughts, pleas, recriminations, tears and demands. When they were not being accommodating in bed, women were an infernal nuisance.

Morgan picked up the curry comb and began grooming the Brighton Regent's jetty coat. His thoughts shifted to Rachael Bates.

Since that encounter with her up at the horse pasture the rector's wife had rarely been out of his mind. He had not attempted to follow her when she ran from him: it would have been a mistake. Had he caught up with her he would have taken her by force there in the grass of the fields, and it would have been a brief, rough business giving pleasure to neither.

She would come to him again in time, one way or another. The heat of her passion had been so strong that she would not be able to hold out against him when next he got her alone. If he could take a room somewhere. Not too close to Weatherfield or she would fear her husband's discovery; but then, again, not so far distant that her absence would be remarked on.

Yes, a room for the night was all they would need, somewhere safe and private. Once they were together he would rekindle her wild passion to such a pitch that its intensity would burn them both through to the very marrow of their bones.

Frank Morgan hugged the image to himself as he worked. He had never met a woman who affected him so much. What did it matter that she was married to a churchman? What were churchmen after all but caretakers, money-grubbers, full of pious cant on Sundays and pompous wind the rest of the week? They served God, maybe; but he had known too many who served Mammon first to have much respect for the sanctity of the Church. Esmond Bates was no better than the rest: a mealy-mouthed cleric who was quick to condemn in others those natural activities which he himself so unnaturally failed to appreciate with his own wife.

Did the man love her? Morgan wondered. He had never had much patience with love himself: it was a cloying emotion that women seemed to catch like a sickness after spending a night in a man's arms. But somehow, the notion of love and Rachael Bates did not arouse his usual cynicism. If the inclination took him, it might be quite easy to harbour something other than honest lust for a woman like her. She had virtue as well as beauty; and a passionate nature that any man would welcome the mastery of in his marriage bed.

He cursed under his breath and threw the curry comb aside. Was ever a man so bedevilled by his own nature? He wanted that woman; but not casually, to be tumbled in some corner like a common doxy and forgotten the moment she left his arms. He wanted to spend time with her, look at her, talk to her . . .

Someone outside shouted his name, and the vision fled.

Frank Morgan thrust his hands through his hair. Blasted mooncalf, he told himself savagely. You're getting soft, man. She's only a female like all the rest, waiting to twist you the moment you show any weakness. Save your finer feelings for

156

your horse, like you've always done—and be damned to Rachael Bates.

"What he needs is a good smearing o' raddle, that 'un."

Henry Wildgoose cut himself a thick wedge of cheese and bit into it. His dog, sitting some yards away, shifted its gaze for a moment from the flock of sheep feeding halfway down the field.

"You reckon?"

Henry's fellow shepherd, the marble-playing Walter Juglery, took the cheese from him and reduced it by a further wedge. The dog's gaze flickered again.

"Aye. 'Tis the only way, surely. Else how's this new parson to uncover the truth o' the matter?"

Walter grinned.

"See now," Henry went on, winking broadly. "You have a field o' twenty–thirty ewes and you put the ram in among 'em. You need to keep a count which it be that old ram's a-served. So what means d'you use? You give 'un a good smear o' red raddle all along his chest and belly afore you free him. Am I right? Come morning you take yourself around the flock. And there they be. Every sheep that old ram's a-covered, he's marked her back wi' raddle, clear as day."

Walter lifted the stone bottle of cider from between three large flints keeping it upright in the shade of the hawthorn hedge behind. He drank in silence and handed the bottle over to Henry.

"So, 'tis like I say—" Henry drank in turn. "Parson Bates needs taking a raddle brush to that Frank Morgan." He wiped his whiskers with the back of his hand and winked again. "He'd mighty soon know where his missus's been!"

"But you doan't know for certain sure it were Mrs Bates you seen up at the horse pasture. You were a good step on from her."

"So I were."

"And she were backturned when you seen her. It might a'been any other."

"So it might."

"An' she were running, an' all."

157

"Aye, so she were. But backturned or no, Wal, running or standing, I'd take my oath that woman were Mrs Bates. And Frank Morgan up by the gate a-looking after her."

Walter shook his head.

"And Mary Stillborne seen her an' all, doan't you forget," Henry sliced the heel from the long loaf lying between them in the grass and pushed it into his mouth. After several hard chews he went on indistinctly, "a-going in at the rect'ry gate the very same hour . . . fair flogged wi' running."

"Mebbe. But that's not to say she were up to anything wi' Frank Morgan. Belikes they met by chance."

"Belikes they did."

There was a silence.

Then Walter's mouth twitched itself once more into a grin. "It ain't right. Not the parson's young missus. Somebody should be a-telling him."

"Who, then? Not me! I'm no nabble-trap to go running wi' tales to Mr Bates. It's neither fat nor wool to me what she does wi' herself whilst he's abed. If there's aught atween Morgan an' her, it's none o' my affair."

"Aye, well. I'd not bring her to harm, neither. She's always treated me an' mine fair an' civil, dear soul."

"Then we'll let it lie," said Henry.

He divided the remaining wedge of cheese and carefully pared off the thick rind and tossed it away. The waiting sheepdog caught it in mid-air with a snap of its jaws.

"The Devil's storing up enough trouble in that quarter," he added sagely, "wi'out needing us to gi' him a hand."

19

For a third time the Reverend Esmond Bates read through Arthur Collins's letter from Lewes.

". . . Your wife has been with us eight days, and I believe is more easily settled now. No doubt she felt somewhat strange at first to be in our house; though we are, of course, no strangers to her. But the intimacy which we share with you, dear friend, is, alas, lacking in her regard towards us. Emily and I hope, however, that she will be more ready to give of her friendship when she has been with us a while longer.

"She speaks most touchingly of your place there at Weatherfield, and is quite naturally anxious to return once her health permits, fearing that you may not pay due heed to your own care whilst she is absent. I know that she frets against the stringency of our management, but Emily and I dutifully bear in mind your wish that she remain beyond the influences of those of her former acquaintances who might encourage her restiveness . . ."

Esmond laid the letter aside on his desk and passed a hand over his eyes. Rachael . . . Lord God, how he missed her. The house seemed so bleak without her presence, especially on such a day as this when leaden clouds and a thin, miserable drizzle darkened the windows and made the rooms depressingly gloomy.

He looked around him. The study was a muddle: papers scattered across the desk and floor, books left lying to gather dust in corners, a plate of half-eaten food still on the chair where he had left it yesterday; or it might have been the day before.

The place was beginning to look like his bachelor lodgings in the years before his dear young wife had come to lighten the darkness of his unhappy life. Without Rachael's supervision, little Ada Slybody was proving herself more of a sloven with each passing day. She would have to be dismissed. If he cancelled his subscriptions to the various institutes and literary societies of which he was a member, the money thus saved could be used instead to employ someone more reliable.

Esmond went out of the study into the rectory hallway, and a growing sense of disgust possessed him as he wandered about the house. He had promised that it should be kept clean—and look at it. The columbine sprays Rachael had arranged in the parlour were dead, their withered petals scattered on the dusty table surface. He had not been inside that room since she left. The scullery was a mess of dirty crockery and stale food. And upstairs, the bedroom disgusted him with its scattered articles of clothing and thick, frowsty air.

Was this how he fulfilled his promise?

He sat down at the foot of the unmade bed and leaned his arms on the brass end-rail, staring out through the window across the deserted, rain-sodden green. Poor Rachael, he thought bitterly. Poor girl. What had she ever had from him that was not mean or shoddy or cast aside by others? The only new things he could recall buying for her were a wedding ring and this bed. And what happiness had either brought her? Surely she deserved better from him.

He had often behaved badly towards her. Badly and selfishly. There was a devil in him still that provoked him to abuse her innocent, artless affections and reward her patience with the incivility of his moods. Why had he sent her away to Lewes when she had no desire to go? Had she really been at risk by remaining here? Or had he allowed his loathing of such men as Frank Morgan to blind him to the reality of her situation? Surely Rachael was too good, too pure in spirit ever to let a creature like that gain any influence over her.

His own fears, his anger against Morgan that day on Snow Hill, had confused and disturbed him so at the time he could scarcely recall now what he had said or done. He only knew that Rachael must be protected. Except for Jerusha, his mother, she was the only woman who had ever given him real affection, and to lose her through persuasion or temptation to any other man would well nigh drive him out of his mind.

Esmond got up and went below again to the study. He picked up the dirty plate from the chair and took it along the passage to the scullery. No need for Rachael to remain any longer in Lewes, he decided. She should come back here, where she belonged, at her husband's side.

But not just yet, perhaps. Not while the place looked so neglected.

Going into the parlour, he opened the window and threw the dead flowers into the garden. He had never given her much material happiness, but it was not too late. He would go over to Netherton himself and see George Bashford about that furniture. And find someone more suitable than little lame Ada to come in and clean and tidy up the place, ready for Rachael to come home. Home to him.

Esmond Bates smiled, his attack of conscience working its own redemption.

Leaving the rectory he walked through the drizzle across the green to Weatherfield high street. A call at Isaac Taylor's general store sent him further on along the road, past the dame school to a cottage isolated by a prim little garden at the far end.

Half an hour later he was back at the rectory, his spirit lighter than it had been for some time.

The two sisters who lived at the end cottage, Comfort and Charity Poole, had been awaiting such a visit for months. Pride in the beginning had held them back from going in person to offer their service at the rectory; followed shortly by pique when the new rector's lady failed to approach them herself for the same purpose. Why should she pass them over when there wasn't a body in Weatherfield didn't know how diligent and thorough they both were?

There were many behind their backs to call the Pooles over-diligent and over-thorough, with their meddlesome nosing into everything that was not their concern.

Not that the pair gossiped. On the contrary: the titbits of information they gleaned from their prying and poking were probably safer with them than with most other females in that small community. Ferreting out the secrets of others (and the more secret the better) may have been the sole occupation of the two sisters, but at least they brought the skeletons rattling out of family cupboards purely for their own private enjoyment.

Now, standing side by side in the hall of the rectory, the two stout, middle-aged women smiled contentedly at one another.

"You see," Esmond Bates was telling them, "this is a large house. Maintaining it is not an easy task."

Comfort and Charity nodded understandingly. They

seemed to exude an air of motherly kindness with their soft voices and pleasant country faces.

"You understand, I hope, that I am not able to offer much," continued the rector. "As you will find, we live very frugally here. But my wife will be most grateful to you for any lightening of her burden."

"Poor young lady," Comfort said. "And her so delicate, too. Never mind, things'll be easier now you've got us in to help."

"That's right, sir," added Charity. "Don't you fret yourself. Mrs Bates won't hardly know the place when she comes back from—from—" She paused. "There now, I've forgotten where it was she went off to."

"Lewes," said Esmond.

"Ah." Charity looked knowingly at her sister. "Lewes. Didn't I hear she had a brother living there?"

Comfort frowned. "Was it her brother? I thought it were a cousin."

"An aunt, actually," Esmond said again. "Though the lady has been dead for some years."

"Oh? Then Mrs Bates'll be staying wi' friends of the family?"

"Yes. Well—that is to say, friends of my own."

The rector hesitated, and the sisters looked at him expectantly, waiting. He cleared his throat.

"The Reverend Collins and his wife. In Southgate Street. I've known them both for many years."

Comfort and Charity smiled and nodded, satisfied.

"If you will excuse me now, I will leave you to get on. You know your way around the house, I believe you said?"

"That's right, sir. We used often to help the old parson out afore Mrs Phillips come."

They worked throughout that afternoon and began again early next morning, their soft voices sounding in the empty rooms as they moved from one floor to another, uncovering the history of the Bates's brief marriage along with the dust and cobwebs.

By Wednesday evening the rectory had yielded up all its secrets to them, discovered in the pages of Esmond's diary in

162

the study desk, a book of poetry with verses heavily under-
scored, a sketchbook, letters from Rachael to Effie
Underwood pushed away out of sight at the back of a bedroom
drawer. Little things, innocent in themselves, but together all
telling the same sad tale.

"She's not happy wi' him," murmured Comfort.

"No wonder, such a harsh, jealous man he must be,"
whispered Charity. "Looks like Frank were right all
along."

And they glanced slyly at each other and hid their smiles
behind their hands.

It was the middle of the following week before Esmond Bates
could find time from his parish work to make the journey to
Netherton. July was drawing to an end and the crops stood
heavy-headed in the fields awaiting the start of the harvest
season. No need to send advance word of his calling: George
Bashford would not be far from the farm at this time of the
year.

It was a warm drive out. With no breath of wind to stir it,
the air seemed trapped within the narrow lanes. On either
side among the banks of gorse, the dried seedpods burst in
the heat with little sharp cracks of sound, like miniature
musket volleys.

The rector's black frockcoat soon became uncomfortable
and after a time he halted the trap to remove it. Threads of
sweat ran down his temples, darkening the fair hair, and he
raised his hat (his best—the everyday one was annoyingly
mislaid and he could not think where) to dab at them with
the cuff of his shirtsleeve, briefly envying the field workers
around him the broad cabbage leaves they wore to protect
the backs of their necks from the sun.

By the time he had driven through Netherton village and
reached Spring Hill Farm, he was thoroughly over-heated
and very thirsty, and was relieved to find Bashford at the
house.

"First things first, Mr Bates," the young farmer declared
when the rector had explained the purpose of his visit. "The
furniture can wait a while longer. Come inside and take

163

something to refresh you. You look parched after that journey."

He caught up his coat and followed Bashford through into the coolness of the farm's living quarters, and was directed to a well-cushioned chair in the kitchen.

"Here, sit yourself down, sir. This heat is enough to turn a man's legs into jelly."

Esmond put his hat to one side and wiped away the dampness left by the rim.

"His brain, too. But you should have a good harvest this year. The church can look forward to a bountiful offering at its Thanksgiving."

"'Tis to be hoped so. Unless we get a thundery August. Now, what can I offer you? I've some excellent ale if you'd care for a pot."

"Thank you. I can think of nothing more welcome just now."

Bashford went out, returning in a short time with two brimming tankards, one of which he passed carefully across to the rector.

"Your good health, Mr Bates."

The ale was a strong, dark brew and refreshingly cool to Esmond's dry throat. Within a few moments he had drained more than half of it, and paused to catch his breath, drawing it in appreciatively between his teeth.

"It has been some while since I last tasted beer as good as this. I am not a drinking man as a rule, but—"

A violent hiccough caught him unawares in mid-speech, the fumes stinging the back of his nose and making his eyes water.

Bashford smiled. "Yes, it's a good drop. Drink up, sir, and join me in another."

Esmond blinked away the tears. "Just another half-pot, I think. And then I must look over this furniture of yours."

Since Rachael Bates's visit to Spring Hill in May, Bashford had made time to clear out the store room and put to one side the things he thought might be of some use to her at the rectory. It had been a task long put off, but one which proved not as painful as he had feared: the stuff seemed to have lost

164

its old associations at last and become so much unwanted lumber taking up useful space.

"You're welcome to any of this," he told Esmond when the second ale was finished and they had gone along to the store room. "The pieces I thought Mrs Bates might fancy are over here by the window."

In the half-light, the furniture looked fragile and outdated: a small couch with slender curving legs and arms, and a pair of matching chairs, all upholstered in pale green stripes; a Chinese lacquer cabinet; a day-bed patterned with garlands of faded roses; two little side-tables; a delicately carved rosewood mirror; even a toilet set with ivory handles and silver tops, now blackened for want of cleaning.

"You needn't have that, if you don't wish," Bashford said, indicating this last item. "It was never used, though. I dare say once the silver's had a cloth to it, it'll come up very nicely."

Esmond nodded, a little bemused by the scene. The effects of the strong ale were beginning to reach his head, making him feel suddenly curiously elated.

"Well? What do you think, sir? D'you reckon Mrs Bates would care for any of the stuff?"

"My dear Bashford, she will be delighted! She has a woman's taste for just this kind of thing." The rector gestured around the room. "Graceful. Flowery. Yes, I think she will be most pleased."

He moved forward.

"Mind your foot on that roll of carpet," Bashford warned.

He stepped over it, with the sensation that a jump might have sent him floating several inches above the floor.

"Is the carpet part of the rectory consignment also?" he asked humorously.

"If you'd like it. There's another square to go with it— over there against the wall. I've had them both out to air. You won't object if I don't open them up again in here?"

"Not at all."

There was a pause. The farmer looked expectantly at his guest.

165

"You'll take the lot, then? I can arrange for Jack Adams to deliver it, if you wish."

"My dear fellow, you're uncommonly obliging." Esmond experienced an unfamiliar surge of emotion. Why were not some of his parishioners as honestly straightforward and good-natured as this young man? "But before we go any further, there is surely a small matter of payment to settle?"

"If you're about to offer me money, I'd rather you didn't," Bashford said bluntly.

"No, no. I insist! Look, I have it ready by me—" He pulled his purse from his pocket.

"Put your money away. I don't want it," the other repeated firmly.

"Then I am afraid, sir, that I cannot accept your offer of this furniture."

"Oh, come now, Mr Bates. I don't want the stuff. It's no use to me, standing here. What d'you expect me to do with it if you won't take it? It's too flimsy to be of use to anyone round here, and it'd be a shame to break it up."

Esmond looked uncertainly at the Chinese lacquer cabinet. Rachael had once seen one exactly like it in Lewes, and the look of yearning on her face came vividly to his mind.

"I'll tell you what," Bashford went on. "Let's have another pot together and see if we can't reach some agreement about this. What do you say? I've something of an idea that won't cost you anything, but would satisfy me greatly."

The rector's third tankard was taken quite slowly, so he thought; but it still seemed to empty itself surprisingly fast. He leaned back among the cushions of his chair in the farmer's kitchen and felt himself more at ease with the world than he could remember.

Casually he said, "Now, sir. Let us have this suggestion of yours."

"It's soon said. I'd be obliged if you'd baptise Dinah Flynn's child."

He sat up again quickly, frowning. After several moments' cautious reflection he said carefully, "Baptise the Flynn child? That . . . in exchange for your furniture?"

The other nodded.

166

"This is an extraordinary bargain you hope to drive with me, Bashford!"

"It's no bargain, sir. A request, that's all."

"And if I refuse?"

Bashford shrugged.

"You don't think I have the right to refuse?" Esmond pressed him.

"I see no reason why you should. The girl's done no harm."

The euphoria evaporated a little.

"In the eyes of the Church she has committed great harm. She and that—that stallion man of hers."

Bashford regarded him patiently. "I'm sure he'll wed her before long. You wouldn't raise any objection to marrying them, I suppose?"

Esmond raised his tankard to his lips. It was empty. He looked across at the farmer and for a moment had slight difficulty in focusing on his face.

"Why should I object to marrying them? It would regularise the union. The quicker it's done, the better, in my opinion. And no doubt the parish council would agree."

"Then why refuse to baptise their child?"

The rector wavered. "It was born out of wedlock . . . a bastard . . . the fruit of their fornication."

"So was the other one, young Frankie. Yet you'll find his name in the register."

Esmond grunted and sat in silence for a while. His head wobbled slightly. It struck him that he was starting to feel pleasantly detached about the whole business.

"You know, sir," Bashford continued, "that thing about the sins of the fathers. It's a harsh judgment, I've always thought."

There was no response.

"Well, look at it this way. You'd be doing me a personal favour if you'd agree to the baptism."

The rector grinned at him suddenly. "Then I'll do it just to favour you, my dear fellow."

He banged the tankard on the arm of his chair.

"There! It's a bargain between us. Your fine furniture to please my wife. Dinah's brat Christianised to please you."

Bashford leaned forward and held out his hand, meaning to shake on the agreement. But the other misinterpreted the gesture and thrust forward instead his empty tankard.

"A toast, Mr Bashford!" he said, a shade too loudly. "Let us drink a toast to our bargain."

"Mrs Bates'll be chiding me for sending you home half-foxed, sir."

"Foxed? Nonsense!" Esmond reached out and caught his host's hand, pressing the tankard into it and closing his fingers around it. "Fill her up, there's a good fellow, eh? There's nobody at home to see whether I'm foxed or not—so be damned to it."

Half an hour later the two men sat regarding each other in a somewhat hazy fashion, though George Bashford, who had a harder head for strong ale than the normally abstemious clergyman, was far the more sober of the pair.

"So Mrs Bates isn't back yet from Lewes?" he asked when another round was underway.

"Not yet. Won't be long, though."

"I should think you miss her."

"Yes."

There was silence.

"I know I missed my wife after she'd gone," Bashford continued. "Missed her sorely for a while. But there. You get used to being alone. A man can't grieve for ever."

Esmond frowned, trying to focus clearly; but his eyes insisted on slipping sideways. He closed them.

"I don't mind being alone," he announced in a slurred voice. "'fact I'm happiest alone. But must look after Rachael. Rachael, that's my wife, y'know. She doesn't like being alone."

"No. I don't suppose she does. Women don't as a rule."

"I worry about her all the time, y'know. She's hardly more'n a child . . . yes. I mean . . ." He hiccoughed loudly. "I'm forty-one. Twice her age. Y'know that? Shouldn't have married her. That's the truth, m'friend. Should never have married her. All a mistake."

168

"Now, Mr Bates! There's many a man of your years married a young wife and lived content enough."

They discussed this for a time.

Then the rector leaned forward and waved his hand vaguely. "Tell you something. Never told anyone before."

He looked with some difficulty at Bashford and laid his finger against his lips.

"Private, mind . . . a personal matter, y'understand. Just between you an' me."

The other watched him carefully, wondering that a man could be so drunk on five pints of ale.

Esmond lowered his voice to a hoarse whisper. "I don't much care to be married. There. That's the truth. Shameful thing for a man of my standing, eh? But y'see, marriage . . . marriage's an institution needs working at. Husband an' wife, y'know, working together. That's my trouble. Can't work at it. No good as a husband."

He raised his tankard to his mouth and drank noisily, spilling ale down his chin on to the black stock.

Bashford looked at him in silence.

"When I was a young man, m'friend . . . young man . . . I was not as you see me now. I led a wicked an' sinful life. London. Evil place, London. You ever been there?"

"No. Never. But now Lewes has the railway—"

Esmond paid him no heed. "Cursed place. Every vice imagin'ble. But I paid for my tansgess,"—he paused, correcting himself carefully—"transgressions. That's the word. Transgressions. Y'know, it was God in his inf'nite wisdom punished me. Yes. Cleansed me . . . made me see the error of my ways."

Tears gathered in his eyes.

"Y'know what I did? You want to know? I swore to m'self . . . swore to turn away from wickedness. Christ's blood in the firmament, y'know . . ."

He gulped down several more mouthfuls of ale but appeared unable to recover himself sufficiently to continue.

"Here," said Bashford, concerned. "Don't take on so, sir. Have another pot to cheer you."

Esmond was too maudlin drunk to refuse.

For a while afterwards he talked in a wild, incoherent fashion which was hardly intelligible of the guilt he carried within him, his nightmares about the physical intimacy of marriage, his inability to perform the proper duty of a husband. The other let him ramble on, feeling a great pity and compassion possess him not merely for this unhappy, self-tortured man, but for the vulnerable young girl he had married.

Finally the rector's speech became totally disjointed and ceased altogether.

Bashford looked down at him slumped in the chair, his head fallen sideways on to his shoulder, the tankard lying on the floor where it had rolled from his inert hand.

Not ungently he said, "Reckon it's just as well your poor wife's away, Mr Bates. I never saw a man more mazed in my life. Behopes you'll have forgotten this conversation when you come round."

Retrieving the fallen tankard, he closed the kitchen door behind him and went out into the yard to give his head a thorough dousing under the pump before overseeing the evening's milking.

Twilight had given way to the warm darkness of the summer night. Weatherfield high street was deserted. At its far end, where it narrowed into a country lane, a figure detached itself from the shadows of a cottage garden and moved quickly off, away from the village.

While Esmond Bates lay stupefied with drink at the farm at Netherton, Frank Morgan had been visiting Comfort and Charity Poole. And now he was on his way to Lewes.

170

20

Rachael Bates closed the book, marking the page, and laid it quietly aside.

The Reverend Kingsley was asleep, his head fallen forward on to his chest and his breath coming in little bubbling snores. She eased the pillows at his back, then moved away towards the tall windows and stood for a time gazing listlessly down into Southgate Street and wishing it were possible to open one of them to let out the stale heavy air and the odours of ill-health.

Reading to the old man was the highlight of her dreary day. He had, she discovered, a surprisingly romantic taste in authors, favouring Jane Austen and the poetry of Keats. But his greatest pleasure was just now to be had from Thackeray's new novel, *Henry Esmond*, parts of which she was reading aloud between three and five o'clock each afternoon.

Rachael's growing affection for Mr Kingsley, and his for her, had come about through her late aunt, whose name had earlier provoked in him such curious merriment.

It transpired that he had known her well many years before, when Fanny Kember was a leading beauty in Regency Lewes and the Reverend Frederick Kingsley one of her many admirers.

"Of course, this was long before your time, m'dear. She was living in a house on School Hill in those days," he had told Rachael one afternoon when a slight headache kept her from reading. "Her people were in business there, were they not?"

Rachael's grandfather Kember had been a seed merchant, trading through the port of Newhaven a few miles down river from Lewes, with a warehouse beside the wharf at the foot of School Hill. His only son, Richard, had worked for him as a shipping clerk; but on his marriage in 1829 Richard had removed to his wife's home town, Lowestoft, and taken a position there with a firm of cigar importers.

Rachael was born in 1831.

One public holiday, when she was not quite eighteen months old, her parents arranged to spend a pleasant afternoon boating on The Broads. The child would have gone with them, but she was fretful with some trifling ailment and so was left in the care of a neighbour.

Richard and Sarah Kember never returned. Their bodies were discovered some days later by a thatcher, tangled together in the rushes. A short way downstream was their upturned boat. Verdicts of death by drowning were returned at the inquests; but the circumstances of the tragedy were never uncovered.

Fanny Kember had travelled up to Lowestoft as soon as the news reached her in Lewes. She had never been very close to her dead brother—a gap of seventeen years separated them in age, for Richard was the last-born and only survivor of numerous children born after Fanny—but she was ready to fulfil her Christian duty to her orphaned niece.

She herself had not married. She was of the kind, she once told Rachael, who loves only once in their life: like paper hearts, they blaze fiercely, yet briefly; and what remains is a scattering of dead ashes.

She had not allowed her private disappointment to turn to rancour, and her niece's upbringing brought joy as well as purpose into her life. Nor was she lonely at her linen shop in Flood Street. She retained admirers still from her distant youth, though as the years went by they were an ever-dwindling number and she grieved for each as age and its attendant infirmities removed them from her life.

The Reverend Mr Kingsley had not been of that circle. His intimacy with Fanny had lasted only during that brilliant burst of hedonism known as the Regency.

"I was already married, more's the pity," he had confided to Rachael that afternoon. "A family man. A churchman. But by God, ma'am, in those days we men of the Church had blood in our veins, not colourless pap like the young milksops

172

who pass themselves off as ministers today! I tell you, there was a time or two when I was damn' near tempted to give it all up for her. Told her so, too. Wife, profession—the lot. But Fanny wouldn't hear of it. Not a word. She was a good creature."

He looked sadly down.

"She did care for me in her fashion, you know. But after a period, once she'd made it plain her regard for me was cooling, I believed she might have married. I must confess I missed her." He paused, sighing. "I didn't know about her . . . illness."

"I knew little about it myself, sir. She seldom mentioned it."

"Even so, it seems strange she never took a husband, a woman like that. D'you think it might after all have been for love of me, eh?"

Rachael humoured him. "I'm sure it must have been."

He patted her hand affectionately. "No, no. Take no heed, my dear. An old man's fancy. But what a waste! Half the men of the town—half the regiment—all ready to die for her. Or nearly so. She could have taken her pick of any of 'em. And now what's this you tell me? Poor Fanny ending her days in a little shop in Flood Street?"

"I like to think she was content, though. She had her memories."

"True, true. As have we all when we grow old. And she had you to care for her, Mrs Bates. A great comfort, I'm sure. A breath of her own youth to remind her."

"I don't think she wished to relive anything through me. She kept me very sheltered."

"But you had admirers, suitors? Devil take it, my dear, there's enough of Fanny Kember about you to bring 'em on!"

Rachael had shaken her head. "My aunt discouraged callers. I don't know why. I sometimes wonder whether it mightn't have been better if she'd allowed me a little more social freedom. But there, no matter. I became Mr Bates's wife."

She recalled that conversation now as she turned away from the windows.

Yes, the wife of Esmond Bates. Yesterday he had written to Arthur Collins requesting that she be sent back to him within the week, as perfunctorily as he had despatched her. What weathercock notion had moved him this time, she wondered bitterly. Was he truly as heart-sick without her as his letter implied? Or was this some strange new urging of his unfathomable mind?

Quietly, so as not to disturb the sleeping invalid, Rachael let herself out of the room. The passage was refreshingly cool and scented with the perfume of jasmine from the bush outside the stairwell window.

She lingered there, reluctant to go up to the loneliness of her bedroom. Everything was quiet. The maids employed in the house were somewhere below in the basement area. The Collinses were both out. Since receiving Esmond's letter they appeared to have lost interest in her and relaxed their supervision, and this afternoon had gone visiting in Southover.

With Mr Kingsley asleep so much earlier than usual, there was nothing to occupy her until their return. It seemed as good a time as any to slip out to see Effie Underwood.

Well, and why not, Rachael asked herself? There was no one to stop her. It would not take long, an hour or so at the most. She could be back at the house before evening, and if Emily Collins made a fuss, it hardly mattered. Now that Esmond had summoned her home to Weatherfield she regarded herself as being quite free of any obligation to stay confined here.

Her generous mouth compressed itself into a line of determination as another notion occurred to her. Why should she not pack her box of belongings and leave the house today? Go to Effie and Ralph for a while? A note could be left with one of the maids. Esmond would be furious; but she could deal with that when she saw him.

She turned the idea over in her mind. Then rejected it. It would be unkind to leave Mr Kingsley with no word of farewell. And Arthur and Emily Collins were her hosts, however poorly they had treated her. No, she would have to return. Effie would understand.

She freshened herself in her room and threw a shawl

174

around her shoulders, then put on her bonnet and slipped out by the front door into the tree-shadowed street. Turning left she began to walk rapidly in the direction of Pelbrook Place.

"Ma'am! Ma'am!"

Effie Underwood straightened herself up from the flower bed and looked irritably towards the figure of her maid, waving to her from the rear of the house.

She raised her own voice. "Must you shout so, Mary Anne?"

The little maid continued to wave and call, but Effie resolutely turned her back on her and applied herself once more to the weeds.

Silly, noisy girl. How many times had she been told to behave in a quiet and orderly manner, as befitted Mr Underwood's household, instead of crying out their business so that half the neighbourhood heard it?

The house door closed and footsteps approached across the gravelled path.

Effie gave a sigh of relief. Mary Anne had remembered her training, for a change. There was hope for her yet.

"That's much better," she said, without looking round. "Now—what is it?"

"It's me," someone said. Certainly not Mary Anne.

Effie Underwood twisted her head sharply; then leaped to her feet with a cry of pleasure.

"Rachael!"

The two young women fell into one another's arms.

"Dear Lord!" she said at last, pushing Rachael away and holding her there at arm's length. "I can't believe it. Don't tell me The Husband has finally condescended to allow you near us at last?"

"He doesn't know I'm here. He's still at Weatherfield."

Effie screamed in mock horror. "You've left him? You've run away."

Rachael tried to keep her face serious. "No. And don't look so disappointed! I've been staying with the Collinses in Southgate Street—"

"But you loathe the Collinses."

"Esmond insisted I go. Don't ask me why. One of his sudden brainstorms. It's been awful. They haven't let me out of their sight for a moment. I couldn't even get a message out to let you know I was there."

"And how long *have* you been there?"

"Over a fortnight."

"Oh, you poor darling. A fortnight with Arthur and Emily! Ugh—it's too horrible to contemplate." Her expressive face contorted itself into a grimace of pure horror.

Rachael regarded her friend affectionately. Effie had not changed in all the years she had known her. Slim, small and dark in appearance, she exuded good humour and vitality in everything she did.

Effie seized her hand. "Come, do let's sit down."

She seated herself beside Rachael on the pretty little cast-iron garden seat. Hardly pausing to draw breath she went blithely on, "And how is dear Esmond? Your letters have been very discreet about him. Hardly a hint of a black mood or tantrum. Lord, do you know, he sounded quite the re-formed character from your last letter. Yet now what's this I hear? He's banished you to the Collinses!"

Rachael said nothing.

The other shook her head impatiently. "You should have married some sweet-natured person your own age, not tied yourself for life to that ill-tempered, jealous old—"

"Don't. Please, don't."

The little cry of hurt silenced Effie.

"Oh, it's true. I'm less than happy with Esmond. You know that. There's no point in pretending otherwise no matter how much I might try to delude myself. You were right to warn me. And I wish I'd listened, instead of closing my ears to you. But it's too late . . . He's my husband now, and nothing is ever going to change that."

Her hand was squeezed sympathetically.

"My poor darling. I know. But oh, how I wish—" Effie looked down, sighing loudly. "Still, there we are. We make our beds to lie on them."

It was a conversation the two young women had had

176

together more than once before, and always with the same outcome. There was nothing left to be said.

They fell silent, each a prey to her own thoughts. Until the sudden sound of a man's voice raised in laughter brought Effie Underwood to her feet.

"There's Ralph! Oh, what luck. I wasn't expecting him to be home for another hour at least. Come along. He'll be so pleased to find you here."

There were some things about her friend's husband which, from the start, had made Rachael uneasy in his company. He was a large, jovial man who laughed a good deal; but she had noticed that his eyes seldom reflected his amusement. They remained watchful. And whenever he touched her to greet her, as now, his hands seemed to linger a trifle too long about her waist, and his lips were a fraction too close to her own for propriety.

Yet Effie clearly adored him, and for that reason if no other she was prepared to suppress her uneasiness. Especially when he was in such apparent good spirits, having spent most of the day at the races recouping his losses of the previous week.

"But Ralph, the shop!" Effie protested.

"Be damned to the shop. What does Father pay his people for? They're quite capable of running the place without me. Who in his senses wants to be in a drapery shop on such a glorious day? Racing's the thing! Besides, Robert Radley had just come in from drinking with one of the trainers, so we knew our money was assured."

"I hope it wasn't the shop's money—"

"God damn it, my dear, d'you have to start that again? Rachael's here. We haven't seen her in months. She doesn't want to listen to us falling out over a guinea or two."

His eyes were cold despite the affable tone. He seated himself beside their visitor, putting his arm casually across the back of the seat just so that his hand brushed her shoulder, and went on, "So let us hear how Rachael's going along, shall we? Let's have the news of dear Esmond. I can't tell you how sorely we've missed him in his absence."

Forcing herself to ignore the veiled sarcasm, she proceeded

177

to give an account of her husband's new parish, enlarging on the details described in her unavoidably infrequent letters. Had Ralph not been there she would have liked to talk to Effie about Frank Morgan, and Dinah, and her concern for Charlotte Smith. But his insistent presence limited her conversation, and she could do little more than mention Charlotte in passing, asking Effie to go on her behalf to the schoolhouse in Frog Lane and enquire about the girl.

"Of course I'll go for you," the other said at once. "What was her name, did you say?"

"Charlotte Smith."

She felt Ralph Underwood shift uneasily beside her.

"Charlotte Smith," repeated his wife. "I'll remember."

Ralph cleared his throat and moved his hand away from Rachael's shoulder.

"Do you know the girl?" she asked him.

He appeared surprised at the question. "Know her? No. No, why should I? Never heard the name in my life before. Why d'you ask?"

"No reason. It was only that—"

"I've had the most taking idea!" Effie interrupted brightly. "Of course—we can use the carriage! Father won't object if you have one day away from the shop, will he, Ralph? We'll convey Rachael to Weatherfield ourselves. It won't take more than a day and a half, surely? And we can stay overnight."

"Where, overnight?" her husband asked carefully.

"Where? Why, at the house. At Rachael's rectory."

"Oh, no. No." He shook his head. "I mean no offence to you, Rachael my dear, but I cannot for a moment imagine Esmond Bates making Euphemia and me welcome in any house of his."

Rachael looked down at her clasped hands, and her silence was an eloquent enough answer to his criticism.

"Don't worry, though," he continued. "I'd give him the same treatment myself. My feelings and that gentleman's are entirely mutual. I wouldn't accept his hospitality though he offered to throw in the Bishop's wife as bedweight."

Effie screamed with laughter.

The hilarity sounded so artificial to Rachael's ears that she glanced sharply up at her friend and said, "It isn't amusing. It's true. Esmond would be the very last to give you a welcome if you returned me to Weatherfield. In fact, he's more likely to place me permanently under lock and key for daring to invite you."

Effie's expression turned to a grimace. "Lord, what an ogre. He allows you no freedom at all. But at least spend a night with us here? I'll send Mary Anne to cry it across the neighbourhood to the Collinses."

Rachael smiled faintly; but shook her head. "I dare not. I'd like to so much, you know that. But really, I mustn't."

"Really, I mustn't," Ralph Underwood mimicked her. "Well, you shall have my opinion, Rachael. Esmond Bates is spoiling you. And I don't mean spoiling you with kindness. He'll be the ruination of your sweet nature before he's done. What's wrong with you staying here for one night? Aren't we good enough family for him? My God, I remember Master Bates snivelling around my father because he couldn't even afford to pay off his debts for second-hand shirts at one time! And now he's grown so high and mighty he looks down his long nose at us because we're Trade. Who the deuce does he think he is? Just some threadbare tub-thumping hypocrite—"

"Ralph, be quiet!" Effie said sharply. "That's enough."

His eyes narrowed.

Then the flash of anger was gone and he threw back his head in laughter. Seizing his wife around the waist he joked, "Tell you what, my lovelies—we'll have an exchange. Effie can take herself off to wherever it is, to the baleful Bates. And you, Rachael my darling, can stay here with me in her place, eh?"

Effie cried out in mock affrontery and pummelled his broad chest with her fists.

"You brute, Ralph Underwood! You horrible brute to condemn me to such a fate. Cooped up miles from civilisation all alone with Esmond Bates? Lord, I couldn't bear it. I'd have to run away and follow the gipsies."

Rachael made no attempt to join in their laughter. She sat

quietly, wishing desperately they would stop treating her husband with such open contempt. It did not help her. It only served to make her realise more than ever how shallow her marriage was, how stark the future facing her with him.

Effie touched her hand.

"Don't look so down. We didn't mean any of it. It's only our fun."

"I know." She forced a smile. "I was thinking . . ."

"What?"

"Oh, that it was time I returned to Southgate Street. The Collinses may have returned themselves."

Ralph made a sound of derision. "Be damned to the Collinses."

"But they'll be expecting me. They may even have made some arrangement for me to leave Lewes." She got to her feet, trying to make light of the situation. "Who knows, there's possibly someone waiting to collect me at the house this very moment."

There was.

At least, as Emily Collins lost no time in pointing out, there had been. And if Rachael had behaved with any responsibility and remained in her room, she could have been packed and gone by now. As it was, the man could hardly leave his vehicle in the street to create an obstruction. He had driven it round to the market square and left a message that he would be waiting outside the Crown and Anchor.

"But how shall I know him?" Rachael asked anxiously.

"There should be no difficulty. He's from Weatherfield. He told Arthur so."

"What's that, my dear?" Arthur Collins looked up from his correspondence.

"The carrier Esmond sent this afternoon. Mrs Bates is concerned she may not recognise him."

"Did he give a name?" Rachael wanted to know.

The clergyman removed his spectacles and frowned. "Dear me, no. Not that I recall. How very remiss of me not to ask. But you will know him, surely? One of your husband's parishioners?"

It must be Jack Adams.

"Whoever he is, the man's already been kept waiting quite long enough." Emily Collins's tone was curt. "I suggest that you put your things together and make yourself ready without further delay. You'll hardly wish to be travelling after dark."

"May I have a few moments to bid farewell to Mr Kingsley?"

"That will not be necessary."

"Very well. Mr Collins, perhaps you'd be kind enough to convey my good wishes to your father-in-law? Tell him . . . tell him I think it unlikely we shall meet again."

21

It was five o'clock. The day's trading was coming to an end and the market crowd thinning.

Around the stalls hung a distinct aroma, a mingling of odours from raw meat, wood smoke, horses, and vegetable waste pulped underfoot on the cobbles.

Dealers were starting to dismantle their displays and roll up canvas canopies, while those with perishable goods were still crying out the lowest prices they could sell at with any profit. The ones with more durable stock—the old clothes men, the timber merchants, the traders in hardware and haberdashery—were leaving their families to load up the handcarts whilst they took themselves off to the public houses facing on to the square.

Frank Morgan wiped the froth from his moustache with the back of a hand and stood watching the activity from inside the open door of the Crown and Anchor. He had positioned himself so that he had a clear view of the corner of the churchyard wall where the lane from Southgate Street ran into the square. He had been watching that corner for well over an hour, and was starting to wonder whether his plan had misfired.

He shifted himself uneasily, leaning back with his elbows on the mahogany bar-top behind him.

Perhaps Mrs Bates intended to spend the whole evening with her friends. Damn it, he should have asked their address from the parson she was staying with. Not that he would know it, dithering old fool, but his wife looked a sharp one. She could have told him. Almost fell over herself to get shot of the girl.

The stallion leader drained the last of his ale. If Mrs Bates did not show up soon he would have to return to the house to enquire. The couple had swallowed his story easily enough. No odd looks. No questions asked. He had been worried that the Reverend Bates might already have fixed something to get his wife back to Weatherfield; but the risk was worth the gamble. And it had paid off.

Morgan smiled to himself. There was an inn just this side of Buckfield. A room for the night and all the privacy you wanted so long as you showed the colour of your money first. It would do very nicely.

Rachael Bates paused as she came out of Church Twitten into the square, shifting the weight of her small box of belongings so that it rested more comfortably on her hip. A covered waggon blocked her view of the Crown and Anchor and she waited impatiently for it to move on before she could look for any sign of Jack Adams. It had to be Jack, of course. Or possibly his father. There were no other carters in Weatherfield parish.

The waggon passed and Morgan saw her standing there, shielding her face against the dust from the wheels. He recognised the straw bonnet with its brave display of scarlet poppies as the one she had worn the day he rode with her from Netherton. He waited, never taking his eyes from her as she came on uncertainly towards the coaching inn, looking this way and that and frowning slightly.

His lips twitched.

Rachael hesitated as she neared the Crown and Anchor. There was nothing to be seen of Jack Adams. Probably he was inside, drinking with the other men at the public bar; but if so, she could hardly go looking for him, not alone.

She tapped her foot, a little movement of vexation, and glanced around. Then wondered whether she might have mis-heard the name of the inn, whether she should return to Southgate Street to make sure. The thought of having to stomach more of Emily Collins's superior airs kept her standing where she was. She could always go back to Effie and Ralph.

Two of the market traders walked past, eyeing her with interest. After a while they came by again, this time lingering deliberately in front of her. One of the pair, a foxy-faced little man, cleared his throat and spat copiously into the gutter. Rachael looked the other way, hoping they would move on if she ignored them.

"What d'you reckon?" the little man asked his companion, a younger and slightly taller edition of himself.

From within the Crown and Anchor Frank Morgan watched them closely, guessing their intention and wondering how it might be turned to his own advantage.

The younger man shrugged and looked Rachael up and down in a lazy, insolent fashion.

"A bit green. Don't look too expensive, though."

"Go on, then. Might be worth a try."

"You reckon so?"

"Go on. Ask her." The little man nudged the other forward.

"I dunno. She ain't a regular."

Rachael experienced a growing sense of alarm as the pair continued to stare at her. She picked up her box and moved a little way off, promising herself that she would wait for another few minutes, then start walking towards Pelbrook Place.

A hand touched her arm and she swung round.

"You hanging about here for anybody in particular?" It was the younger of the two.

She looked at him coldly. "I'm waiting to be met."

The man's pale eyes were fixed on the bodice of her gown, visible under the loosely-tied cloak.

"So what's he offering you?"

"I beg your pardon?"

"Oh, come on. You know the score."

She stared back at him, uncomprehending, and he made a sound of impatience and looked away for a moment.

"God blimey, you *are* green. You're walking Dolly's patch, ain't you? You one of her new girls?"

The colour flooded into Rachael's cheeks. "Please . . . please leave me alone." She was beginning to feel frightened, threatened by the man's over-familiar attitude.

"Let it be, Eddie. Like you said, she ain't a regular." The older one moved between them. "Come on, I'll buy you a drink in the Bear."

"No. I like her. She's playing hard to get, that's all. Ain't you, darling?"

Rachael started to panic and turned hurriedly away, but the man caught her round the waist, restraining her. Her box fell to the ground, spilling its contents over the dirty cobbles, and he stumbled over it pulling her roughly against him to keep himself from falling. She gave a thin scream and beat at his shoulder with her fists.

"That's right, darling—hit me! I like a bit o' temper."

The next moment someone was shouting something at her side and her molester was wrenched away and sent reeling backwards into one of the empty stalls, blood spurting from a split lip.

Rachael stared about in confusion, unable to take in what was happening. Then she was pushed violently from behind and almost fell. A well-built man with black hair staggered past, the foxy-faced little trader clinging to his back with one arm hooked around the muscular neck in a throttling grip.

The whole market square seemed suddenly to erupt in a babble of noise as people came streaming out of the public houses to watch the fight.

She screamed again, an hysterical note in the sound, and looked on in horror as the fellow on the cobbles got unsteadily to his feet, spitting blood and broken teeth, and lunged out at her rescuer with a heavy piece of board. The dark-haired man, still wrestling to prevent himself being choked from behind, swung round at the last moment and his assailant's

184

blow landed painfully in the ribs of the little trader clinging to his back, making him swear obscenely and loosen his grip.

A second later he had been shaken off like a rat and knocked against the wall, arms flailing wildly as he tried unsuccessfully to keep his balance. His partner swung a second blow, but this time missed completely and in return got a cracking punch to the chin which sent him down on his back yet again. He rolled to his side and stayed there, moaning.

There was a ragged outburst of cheering from the crowd of onlookers and Frank Morgan grinned at them, rubbing his bruised knuckles. Then he turned and went over to where Rachael Bates was standing amongst her scattered belongings, her face buried in her hands.

"I'm sorry you had that bother," he said. "I don't think that pair'll be troubling you again, though."

At the sound of his voice she gave a visible start and looked up quickly, but her eyes were blurred with tears and for a moment she could not see his face properly.

Then she recognised him. The blood drained from her cheeks, leaving them deathly pale.

The stallion leader bent down to gather together her things and put them back in the box.

"I blame myself," he went on smoothly, looking up at her. "I should've waited where I said. I hope you'll forgive me. I only went round the back to check on the horse. I wasn't gone above five minutes."

He secured the lid and stood up.

Speechless, Rachael continued to stare at him through her tears.

"Here—" he pulled a large handkerchief from his coat pocket and held it out. "You've had a nasty shock, Mrs Bates."

When she made no move to take the handkerchief from him, he reached towards her and very gently began to wipe the tears from her face as though she were a distressed child.

"You need a drop of something to calm you. No, don't pull

185

your head away like that. I'm not going to hurt you. There. That's better. Now come on, give me your arm. We'll go across to old Alice and get her to make you a soother."

It was then that Rachael found her voice.

"Where's Jack?" she whispered.

"Jack?"

"Jack Adams. Where is he? I—I must find him."

"Now, don't go exciting yourself again." Morgan spoke calmly. "Suppose you tell me why you're so anxious about Jack Adams?"

She looked about her in desperation. "Have you seen him? He should be here to meet me . . . to go back to Weatherfield."

"No, ma'am. No. It's me that's doing that. Didn't you take in what I said just now?"

Her eyes moved over his face, widening. "You—?"

"Aye. It's me that's been sent to bring you home."

"But I don't understand. I thought . . . oh, I don't understand! Everything is so confusing."

Helplessly, she began to weep again and Morgan put a comforting arm about her shoulder.

"Come on. Alice'll give you something to calm your nerves."

"But, Jack—?"

"Jack isn't here. All right? It's me that's looking after you. Now give me your arm and we'll just take a step across the square."

Obediently she allowed him to lead her over to one of the small shops neighbouring the churchyard where, above a low doorway, a hanging sign read "Druggist".

The room inside was divided by a long counter and on shelves behind it the contents of heavy glass bottles glowed in the gaslight like the colours of jewels.

Frank Morgan helped Rachael to a chair beside the door and placed her box on the floor beside her. In response to his call, a stooped old woman appeared from behind a wall-hanging at the rear of the shop. Morgan leaned across the counter towards her and there followed a murmured conversation between the pair, too low for Rachael to overhear even had she cared to listen. He gestured in her direction several times and the old woman's eyes examined her knowingly; but she felt too shaken, too wretchedly confused to respond. She hoped desperately that once they were finished here Frank Morgan would take her straight to Effie's house.

The old woman retreated once more behind the wall-hanging, and Morgan turned back to Rachael.

"There you are, Mrs Bates. She says she knows just the thing to buck you up. You'll be feeling as right as a trivet in a minute."

A sudden wave of vertigo attacked her. She put both hands up to her pounding temples and closed her eyes, saying with some difficulty, "Please—please take me to Mr Underwood's house in Pelbrook Place. It isn't far ..."

The stallion man looked at her sharply. We'll have none of that kind of talk, my beauty, he thought.

"Now then—let's wait to see how you are when Alice's soother has done its work, eh? Have patience, she won't be long with it."

The herb-wife made up the draught with care, choosing those ingredients which her sisters had used for centuries to bring a deep and healing sleep to a distressed system. Badly shocked by the sudden death of a much loved child, the customer said the young lady was. Hysterical with grief. Couldn't rest. In danger of causing injury to herself.

Old Alice nodded thoughtfully and reached down a stone jar containing a powerful nervine. That should do it. The poor little dear would sleep for hours.

There was a tooth-edging bitterness to the draught beneath the sweetness of the honey, but Rachael drank it down quickly, intent only on escaping from Morgan to the haven of Pelbrook Place. She could not believe that Esmond would have sent the stallion leader, of all people, to fetch her. But there seemed no other immediate explanation for the fact that he knew where to find her in Lewes, knew that she was leaving at precisely this time.

He paid for the draught and solicitously helped her up from the chair. For a moment the vertigo returned and she had to support herself against him in the doorway, holding tightly to his arm until the dizziness passed.

187

"D'you think you can manage the other side of the square?" he asked, thinking that old Alice's brew worked extraordinarily fast.

Rachael drew in several deep breaths in an effort to clear her head.

"I—I think so."

Still clinging to his arm, she walked slowly beside him through the now-deserted market stalls to the stableyard entrance at the rear of the Crown and Anchor. A short way in, standing against the wall, was a covered van with empty shafts. He led her across to it and helped her to climb up inside, where a wide seat took up the space at the back of the vehicle.

"You'll take me to Mr Underwood's now?" she begged, her eyes fixed in appeal on his face.

Morgan pulled down the flaps of the canvas hood and began lacing up the opening.

"You just rest easy now, Mrs Bates. It'll not take me a minute to put the horse in the shafts." He regarded her carefully through the remaining gap in the canvas and added, "I'd lie back on the seat for a bit if I was you. You're losing your colour again."

Rachael watched the laces weave in and out through the eyelets at the top of the opening, enclosing her within the dark interior of the van. Her sight suddenly began to blur. Outside, Frank Morgan walked away up the yard, whistling carelessly, and as if from far off she heard someone calling out to him.

She shook her head, trying to clear the dizziness. A low buzzing had started up in her ears and she seemed to be growing strangely weightless; while at the same time her eyelids felt as though they were hung with lead.

Gasping, she concentrated on staying upright on the seat; but the whole van was slipping sideways now, and ahead, beyond the empty shafts, the rows of bricks in the end wall had started to move in slow, undulating waves.

A single tear ran down Rachael's cheek. And that was the last thing she was conscious of before the spiralling blackness sucked her into its depths. She did not hear Morgan return with the hired horse, nor was she aware that he had secured it in the traces.

After a while he lifted the flap and looked inside at her. She lay slumped on the seat, quite motionless except for the rapid rise and fall of her breast. Ducking his head against the canvas roof he stepped over the driving seat and very gently shook her shoulder.

"Mrs Bates?"

There was not the slightest response.

The stallion leader smiled. Good. So far, things had worked out better than he could possibly have hoped. He lifted Rachael's feet on to the seat and smoothed down her skirts, his hands moving lightly over her long legs. The muscles in his jaw tightened suddenly as desire for her gripped him; but he restrained the urge to touch her again. Wait till Buckfield, he told himself. It would be worth it. There was little pleasure to be had from taking a woman unconscious in a drugged sleep.

He got down from the van and backed the horse out into the market square. Regaining his seat he gave the reins a sharp flick and the animal moved obediently forward.

At much the same hour, the Reverend Esmond Bates was sitting slumped forward in an upright chair in the parlour of Weatherfield rectory. Since waking late this morning in his own bed (they had brought him into the village late last night flat on his back in Jack Adams's cart, along with the new furniture) he had had the most sickening headache, far worse than anything he normally suffered. This was no result of strain or tiredness. No, this was more like a severe megrim. And worse, his eyes pained him and so did his stomach, and he had the most insatiable thirst. He wondered miserably if George Bashford's wretched ale had not poisoned his system.

Esmond could recall his visit to Bashford's farm the day before quite clearly. That is, he recalled it clearly up to a certain point, where they had reached some agreement about the Flynn child—a bizarre exchange involving its baptism for the farmer's furniture. From there his memory tended to play tricks upon him.

189

Dimly he seemed to hear echoes of himself talking. Talking at great length about his wife. About his marriage. About his past. If he had indeed spoken of such deeply personal things, what in God's name had possessed him?

Feverishly he ran his fingers through his hair. What exactly had he said? If only he could remember! What was Bashford about to make him deliberately so drunk that he had babbled on like an idiot of matters which for long years he had scarcely even allowed himself to think of, let alone speak aloud?

Yet now to let his tongue become so loose with liquor that everything had come spilling out, all those dreadful, wretched, shameful things. To a man he hardly knew, a country farmer who might at this very moment be entertaining half the district with his drunken disclosures . . . everyone laughing at them, sniggering at his impotence, lewdly defiling his wife with their filthy tongues.

Dear God in Heaven, forbid that it was true!

A chill sweat stood out on Esmond's forehead and he groaned aloud. How he had failed himself. Almost he could welcome the throbbing headache, the sickness and the trembling limbs as a just punishment for such self-betrayal. How easily he had allowed himself to slip into temptation after so many long years of rigid discipline. At least, thank heavens, Rachael was not here to witness this disgusting exhibition of shame. By tomorrow evening, when she was expected back from Lewes, his physical malaise would have passed. He trusted in prayer and God's mercy to ease his spiritual anguish.

22

The Devil's own luck must have been with Frank Morgan that day.

He had had precious little time to plan his seduction of the rector's wife, and he was aware that he ran the risk of a genuine carrier already being engaged who would turn up to ruin his game. So, obedient to the promptings of his native cunning, he had played safe and made enquiries at all the coaching offices and livery stables around Lewes.

He had drawn a satisfying blank. No one, it seemed, had been hired to convey a young woman from Southgate Street to Weatherfield.

In fact, Esmond Bates had requested George Bashford to engage a man; and Bashford, having business in Tunbridge Wells (though not at the house on Mount Ephraim) made the hiring from there. His man would have been in Southgate Street shortly after noon but for the mischance of being run into a ditch just outside Lewes by a loaded brewery dray.

So it was that while the genuine article stood at one side of the road supervising the repair of a wheel broken in the upset, Frank Morgan and his unconscious passenger passed him by on the other, going in the opposite direction.

The carrier's eventual arrival in Southgate Street ruffled Emily Collins; but, as she told her husband, the matter was surely more of an inconvenience than any cause for concern. Their maid, Mary Reed, had already reported to her mistress that she had seen Mrs Bates crossing the market square "very loving-like" on the arm of the man who had called at the house earlier. Mrs Collins, ever ready to think the worst of Rachael, had put two and two together and pursed her thin lips in righteous disapproval.

And that would have been an end of the whole business, had not the Reverend Frederick Kingsley chanced to learn of it when Mary Reed brought him up his early evening physic.

"Yes, sir. Ever so loving-like they was, sir," the girl informed the old man earnestly. "I thought p'raps he were Mrs Bates's husband, the way she were a-clinging to him, but then you don't hear o' clergy gentlemen wearing fancy checked trousers and sprigged weskits, do you now, sir? And any way, I told meself, unless I'm much mistook this here's the very same man what called at the house early on and said as how he'd come to collect Mrs Bates to take her off home. I

mean, that didn't sound like no husband, did it, sir, or he'd
ha' been invited in to take tea wi' Mrs Collins, seeing as how
she's known to be so fond o' Mr Bates an' all."

Mr Kingsley frowned and shifted uneasily in his bed.

"Checked trousers, d'you say? Sprigged waistcoat?"

"Oh, yes, sir. Real handsome he were."

"And Mrs Bates was holding his arm, is that correct?"

"Holding on to him and laying her head on his shoulder,
sir. S'elp me, that's the truth."

The old man tapped a rapid tattoo on the glass containing
his physic and looked the maid up and down in silence.

Then he shook his head. "No," he said. "No. I don't like
it."

"But—sir!" Mary Reed's voice rose in alarm. "Mrs Collins
says you're to drink it all, every last drop, or she'll be on to me
for not making you."

Mr Kingsley made a sharp sound of impatience.
"Confound you, girl, what're you babbling about now?
Here,"—he swallowed the physic in a single gulp, grimacing
at the sour taste—"now tell me, how did Mrs Bates appear?
Was she smiling at this man? Think carefully now."

Mary Reed shrugged her narrow shoulders and looked
around the room.

"She weren't smiling exactly, sir."

"Well? Was she crying, did you notice?"

"Oh no, sir, she weren't a-crying. Though now I come to
think on it—"

"Yes?"

"She did look a might bleary."

Mr Kingsley sat a little further up in his bed and fixed his
gaze intently on the girl.

"Bleary, d'you say?"

"Yes, sir. Like she'd ha' been crying, but now were just
plain miserable wi' herself." Mary Reed lowered her voice.
"To speak honest, sir, she'd likely had a drop or two and been
took bad. The drink can do that to a female, y'know, 'specially
the gin. Why, my old granny used to weep like a babby when
she'd seen off a bottle o' Daffy's Elixir."

Mr Kingsley shook his head.

"No," he said emphatically. "Not Daffy's. Not Mrs Bates. Never takes spirits—told me so herself. Like her aunt for that, you know."

The maid gave another little shrug. "Well, it's how she looked to me, sir. Real bleary-like."

The old man sighed heavily and plucked at his lower lip.

"Something is wrong. I know it. I can feel it in my bones. Something somewhere is wrong. That dear child is in need of assistance."

He fell silent for a few moments. Then suddenly—"Mary Reed, fetch Mr Collins here directly. Directly, I say!"

Arthur Collins was not overly impressed by the force of his father-in-law's conviction that Mrs Bates was in danger. Yet neither did he feel inclined to accede to his wife's view that the girl had planned some shameful liaison with the swarthy fellow who had come asking for her. Why had she been holding his arm? A sprained ankle, he suggested; a fit of dizziness, perhaps; or some other natural disorder to which the weaker sex were prone.

Mrs Collins was not convinced.

While she, downstairs, pooh-poohed the whole affair and pursed her lips even tighter, her father, upstairs, struggled to heave his dropsical body out of its feather-bed wrapping, insisting most furiously that unless his son-in-law took some action to have Mrs Bates traced, he would go out himself in search of her, and damned to the consequences. He owed it to Fanny, he kept on insisting. It would be failing dear Fanny if something were not done immediately to find the girl.

Alarmed by the rapidly purpling hue of the old man's complexion and his panting exertions to raise himself, Arthur Collins agreed that enquiries of some kind should be made about the town.

"At once, if you please!" Mr Kingsley's voice was raised loudly in his concern. "And her friends—yes, yes, you must seek out her friends. What were they called now?" He beat his fists against the bedclothes in his frustration. "You *must* know them, Arthur. In the high street. Drapers, didn't she tell me? Oh, what the deuce was their name . . . Underwood? Yes, that's it. Underwood! Quickly now, my boy, there's not a moment to be lost. You yourself must go down to the shop."

Mr Collins began voicing his protest, but was waved into silence.

"Yes. That's the thing. You must go at once. It's not yet struck seven, there'll be someone there to give directions to the house. Pray God they may know something of the poor child's whereabouts!"

In the end, to quieten the old man as much as his own uneasy conscience, Arthur Collins went down to the high street—letting himself out through the side door to avoid the delay of explaining himself to his wife. Something in his father-in-law's fevered concern had sufficiently discomforted him to be prepared, if necessary, to go in person to Pelbrook Place in the hope that Rachael Bates's friends might be able to shed some light on this curious business.

"Ma'am! Ma'am!"

Effie Underwood threw aside her needlework sampler and gave a loud sigh. Mary Anne was letting them down yet again, shouting out from the front hall in that coarse manner.

She looked appealingly at Ralph, but he remained resolutely bent over the accounts ledger at his desk in the window embrasure.

"Very well," she said, addressing herself to the bowed head. "I see I must go myself."

"Ma'am!" came Mary Anne again.

At that moment the door of the drawing room burst open to reveal her clutching a black stove-pipe hat to her chest. Behind her in the middle of the hall stood the tall, spare figure of the Reverend Arthur Collins.

"Beg pardon, but there's this 'ere gentleman come a-calling to see the master."

Effie rose at once to her feet. "Thank you, Mary Anne. Please show the visitor in."

She glanced over her shoulder at her husband, who returned the look, one eyebrow raised in question, before moving out from behind his desk.

"My dear sir!" He extended a hand towards their visitor.

"Why, how very kind of you to call on us. Do be seated, won't you? Mary Anne, put the gentleman's hat on the hall table. And close the drawing-room door. Quietly."

"What an agreeable surprise, Mr Collins," Effie said brightly, showing him to a chair. "We so seldom have the pleasure of a visit from you."

He cleared his throat nervously.

"No, indeed, ma'am. I believe this is actually the first occasion. That is, the first occasion I have had the pleasure myself."

"A glass of brandy, sir?" Ralph suggested.

"Thank you, but no. I was about to add that it is a pity my visit must be so brief. The fact is, Mr Underwood, I believe a lady of your wife's acquaintance may be in some—er, difficulty."

There was a moment's silence.

"Someone we know?"

"Mrs Bates."

"What? Rachael?"

Arthur Collins nodded, and immediately proceeded on an outline of the afternoon's events, giving them details of his maid's report of seeing Rachael and the stranger together and his father-in-law's distressed reaction upon the arrival of the second carrier.

"And this man—the one who came later—knew nothing of the first?" Effie asked, concerned, when he had finished.

"Apparently not."

"But it *is* possible a genuine mistake could have been made," Ralph Underwood suggested, "the two men each being hired at different times. Perhaps the explanation is that Mr Bates neglected to cancel the first hiring after making the second?"

"Even so," Effie interrupted, "that still does not explain what Rachael was doing to be seen arm-in-arm in the square."

Arthur Collins cleared his throat again.

"My wife is of the opinion that Mrs Bates had schemed to—well, to practise a deception of some kind. That is not my own view, of course," he added hastily.

"Deception? What kind of deception?"

"Ah . . . well . . ."

"You mean she may have gone off with this fellow with the intention of deceiving her husband?" Ralph asked bluntly.

"Quite so."

"Heavens above!" Effie stared at the clergyman; then gave a little laugh of embarrassment. "If Rachael had been planning any such thing, she would have said so, Mr Collins. There are no secrets between the two of us. None at all. I swear that when she left this house this afternoon her only thought was to return to Southgate Street to avoid giving concern by her absence."

"I am inclined to believe that, ma'am. Which makes this entire business so—er, so very alarming."

"You say this man told you he was one of Mr Bates's parishioners?" said Ralph.

"Not exactly, no. Let me see now, what were his words? Hmm—ah, yes. I believe he said, 'She will know me. I'm from Weatherfield.' "

"That seems clear enough!"

"But what did he look like, Mr Collins?" Effie's tone reflected her growing anxiety. "Had you seen him before?"

"No, not to my knowledge. May I remind you, ma'am, Mr Bates has not long had this living, and I've yet to visit him there. It is highly unlikely that I would know any of his new parishioners. As to the fellow's appearance—well now, let me think. Middling stature. Strong build. About your own age, Mr Underwood. Swarthy features, with heavy black moustaches. Gipsy blood, perhaps. Yes—yes, definitely some gipsy about him."

Ralph shrugged and looked at Effie.

"Fair enough. Two of our own carriers are gipsies. They're a common breed among horsemen."

She returned the look with a little shake of the head. "But to be seen on his arm—?"

"The man was no stranger, Mrs Underwood. He was already acquainted with Mrs Bates," Arthur Collins reminded her.

"Yes, but that's not the point. To be seen on another's arm in public when one is a married woman . . ."

196

Ralph stood up.

"There's probably a perfectly simple reason for this behaviour in the square, just as there's an explanation for the confusion over the hiring. But I think that for the sake of our own peace of mind we must try to find Rachael—"

"I agree absolutely," put in Mr Collins.

"—and I propose to make a start by riding out to the turnpike on the Buckfield road. They've surely left Lewes by this time, and it's that road they would take for Weatherfield. Someone may recall them passing through. I'd be obliged for a description of the vehicle this fellow is driving, Mr Collins. And his horse, too, if you know its colour. Once we are sure which road to look on, I'll get up a party of my friends and we'll ride after them. They can't have gone far."

Ralph Underwood was not acting entirely out of concern for his wife's dearest friend.

He was a young man who relished the unexpected, and the idea of escaping from the tedium of the accounts ledger to a gallop by night with his cronies along the turnpike road appealed to him enormously.

So, on learning from the tollgate keeper that a covered van driven by a man fitting the description he gave had indeed passed through earlier, his sense of civic duty was heightened by enthusiastic pleasure for the pursuit that was now on.

It did not take long to collect four of his boon companions and over a glass or two of brandy embroider the details. Infected by his mood, they were soon roused up themselves to a pitch of indignation; and within a short time were into their saddles and away at a canter down the steep cobbled hill out of Lewes, their handsome young faces cruelly eager and their spirit veering dangerously towards recklessness.

Hunting down a gipsy made fine sport.

It was a warm, clear evening.

Once the sun had set, Frank Morgan halted briefly to see to the candles in the lamps at the front of the van; and as they went along the lights flickered unsteadily, casting the horse's shadow in sudden jumps across the road and attracting clouds of insects into the beams.

Every once in a while the stallion man looked over his shoulder to check his passenger, but Rachael was still in a deep sleep. He nodded and grinned to himself, pleased with their progress. At this rate they would be at Buckfield within the half-hour.

23

"Aye. I've a quiet enough room." The fat woman looked at the stallion leader carefully. "How long d'you want it?"

"Just the one night."

She nodded, her plump dirty fingers rolling together the coins he had given her.

"Just the one night, then."

Behind her, the rumble of voices from the open door of the taproom rose to a sudden hubbub of argument.

"It *is* a quiet room?" Frank Morgan had to raise his own voice against the din. "Only the lady's not too well. The noise might disturb her."

The fat woman thrust out a moist lower lip and shrugged.

"It's as quiet a room as any you'll get in this place."

There was the sound of glass breaking. As swiftly as it had started the uproar behind her ceased, stilled by a single deafening bellow. The owner of the Fordhouse at Buckfield was more respected for the power of his lungs than that even of his fist—and he was a man who had once gone twenty-eight rounds in a bareknuckle fight with the legendary champion, Jem Ward.

Morgan jingled the remaining coins in his pocket and looked carelessly about him while the woman turned away to unhook a key from a board on the passage wall.

He put out a hand to take it; but she held it tantalisingly back.

"You've been here a few times before this, I think." Her black eyes, sharply bright in the lardy face, held a knowing look as they took his measure. "Aye. I have it. I remember you now. Last time you come here you had Farmer Copper's wife, from out Barkham way. You left without paying for the sheet you tore."

The stallion man returned her look boldly. "That's right. Farmer Copper's wife it was. I'm sorry about your sheet."

She nodded. "See you pay for it in the morning, then."

"I'll do that." He smiled slyly. "And for the one I mean to tear tonight."

The bright eyes watched him unwinking. "I hear tell you've given her a fine daughter."

"What? What's that you say?"

"Old Copper's wife. Had a daughter Easter-time."

Morgan forced a laugh and shook his head emphatically. "Then it was none o' my getting. Leastways, not if it was a girl."

"Oh?" Amusement showed in the eyes now. "Then I wonder who it was give it her? Not her husband. Not that poor sandy-coloured dribble of a man. The child don't resemble him in the least, they say."

"It must favour its mother, then."

"Nor her neither. Betty Copper was never black-haired in her life."

Morgan frowned. And remained silent.

"Aye. Well. Here's your key. The room's away at the back, over the store." She clinked the coins together in her hand. "Perhaps you'd best pay me in advance for that sheet."

The stallion leader looked at her for a moment, then shrugged.

"If you throw in the price of a bottle for me and the lady?"

"I dare say I could do that. For a consideration, mind."

He handed her most of his remaining cash. "Make it a bottle o' the best, eh? This one's no farmer's wife. She's worth a damned sight more than that."

"What's it to be tonight, then? A bit o' quality?"

199

He glanced quickly up and down the passage, then leaned forward and lowered his voice.

"She's a piece o' church property. But keep that information under your skirt."

The fat woman gave a sharp snort of cynical humour. "You whoring dog! Church property, is it now?"

"Aye. Married to the vicar of All Fools." Frank Morgan laughed and kissed the key he was holding. "But tonight it's me that will be with her in Paradise."

At first, Rachael Bates thought there must be a swarm of insects inside the van. Then, as she became more conscious, the buzzing quietened to a low-pitched hum inside her own head.

Slowly, she sat up in the darkness. Beyond the hum was the sound of many voices, shouting, laughing. And water. Was that running water she could hear somewhere nearby?

Her throat was parched and it was a painful effort to swallow. What had happened to her? Where was she? The thirst became suddenly intolerable. For the moment nothing else mattered but that she reach the water outside.

Unsteadily, she moved across to the driving seat, her senses reeling and the voices reaching her in waves of sound. She clung there for a moment, shaking her head in an effort to clear it, then tried to find the step to climb down.

The impact of the fall knocked the breath from her body and left her stretched on the ground below the shafts, half-stunned and gasping in pain. She must have lost consciousness once more, because the next thing she was aware of was a light shining into her face and hands pulling at her body.

"Mrs Bates! Mrs Bates!"

She made an effort to open her eyes.

"Oh, God—what have you done to yourself, woman?"

"I'm . . . very thirsty," she managed to whisper.

"What's that?"

"I'm thirsty. Please . . . water."

Frank Morgan stood up, cursing under his breath. He looked back towards the lighted doorway of the Fordhouse across the stable yard. The fat woman was standing there, watching him still.

He ran over to her, the lantern swinging wildly to and fro in his hand.

"She's hurt herself! Can someone give me a hand to get her inside?"

The woman regarded him, mirthful slyness dimpling her features.

"Damaged Church property is it, now? So much for your chances of Paradise."

His expression betrayed his swift anger, and she instinctively made the age-old sign of protection, clenching her fist and extending the fore and final finger towards him.

"Don't you go putting the Eye on me, gipsy! Get back to your woman. I'll fetch a couple o' the lads."

Rachael was trying to crawl towards the stream at the far end of the yard when Morgan found her again. The blood from the graze on her cheek had mingled with her tears and streaked her face.

"God almighty!" he exclaimed, looking down at her in the lantern beam. There was little desirable about her just now.

Moved by the pity that he had for all hurt creatures—an emotion seldom wasted on his fellow men—he kneeled down and took her into his arms, carefully and tenderly, and cradled her head against his chest.

"For Christ's sake, hurry up there!" he called out. "And bring us a jug of water while you're at it."

When it came, he held it to her lips just as he would were she a mare lying injured in the road, measuring the amount so that she could swallow enough to satisfy her thirst without choking herself. When her need for water was eased somewhat, he supervised her removal to the room above the store and made her comfortable on the bed before getting rid of his helpers.

Seeing Rachael lying there, her hair loose over her shoulders and her clothing in disarray, one of the men tried to joke with the stallion leader about what he'd like to do with his woman were he given his luck. But the dark anger in the other's eyes silenced him and he went away down the stairs smirking at the others, leaving Frank Morgan and Rachael alone together in the dimly-lit, dusty-smelling room.

For a time Morgan sat silently on the edge of the narrow bed, his arms stretched out on either side of her body, staring in front of him at the carved board that made up the bed-head.

He remembered it from the last time he was in this room. Adam· and Eve separated by the Tree, with the Serpent winding its way down the trunk, its sinuous curves following the grain of the wood. There was even a date. 1737.

Morgan gazed at it moodily. Betty Cooper had made some joke about the leaf-skirted figures, so inappropriately modest for a bed. Damned if he could recall what it was now, though.

Betty. He had had word from her that she was pregnant. It was late to be having a first child. Her husband had never given her one in all the years of their marriage. He remembered now that she had joked about that, too, drawing his attention to the date on the head-board. Thirty-seven. Her own age.

"D'you reckon it might be lucky for me, Frank?" she had asked. And now she had a black-haired daughter.

Morgan shook his head. That was the second one they had tried to foist on him. First Dinah, now Copper's wife. Two women he could have sworn he might depend on, in one way or another. Perhaps he ought to call in and see Dinah at the alehouse next time he passed through Weatherfield; just to satisfy his curiosity.

There was that other one, too. Charlotte Smith. It would be interesting to know what her child turned out to be— another little Morgan or some other's nameless bastard. Though either way, she was Jack Adams's problem now.

Between his arms Rachael moved slightly and half-opened her eyes. He looked down at her. There was a faint flush on her cheeks and her lips were parted moistly, almost volup-tuously.

The stallion leader drew a ragged breath. God damn it, had he spent so much trouble and time over this girl only to sit gazing at her all night like some nervous bridegroom? The sudden anger made him bunch up the sheet in his clenched fist. He stared at the face beneath him, his eyes moving slowly to the slim, bare throat and down further to the white skin left exposed where he had unbuttoned the high neck of her gown.

He had imagined her like this so many times in the past weeks. The memory of their meeting at the horse pasture had been deliberately fed in his imagination by the emotions she had aroused. No woman could respond as she had to his kisses unless she was ripe for seduction.

The knock at the door made him jump sharply.

"Yes?"

"Your refreshment—sir." Not even the thickness of the wood could disguise the mockery in the voice.

Morgan got to his feet and went over to unlock the door. The fat woman was standing outside, a tin tray with a bottle of spirits balanced carelessly on one hip.

"Thank you."

He stared coldly into the lardy face as he took it from her.

"It's the best we have, mind."

"Yes."

"Looks like you'll be needing it, as well." She glanced past him into the room. As he began to close the door on her she added cynically, "I'll wish you both a very good night."

He shut the face out, cursing at her to himself, and carried the tray over to the bed and put it on the bare boards by his feet. Rachael stirred again; but this time he took no notice, concentrating on pouring himself a generous measure of the spirit.

The colourless liquid seared his throat and made him cough. He had tasted better gin than this in the worst knocking-house in Brighton.

"Esmond?"

The voice held a note of confusion.

He drained the glass and looked down at the woman on the bed beside him.

"He's not here."

Her slate-blue eyes moved slowly up to his face, and for a moment they held an expression of fear.

"Esmond?"

"I told you. He's not here."

"Not . . . not here?"

"No!"

Morgan poured himself a second glass and tipped it sharply back, clenching his teeth against the bite. Then he shook his head, and when he spoke again his tone was softer.

"Hush, now. Don't fret yourself. You're all right."

Rachael moved her head from side to side on the hard pillow. "Where am I?"

The stallion man put out a hand and carefully brushed back the hair from her face.

"You're in a safe place. Nothing's going to happen to you now."

She frowned slightly. "Will Esmond be here soon?"

"In a bit. He's asked me to look after you."

"Oh . . ."

She lay back motionless for a while; then made an attempt to raise herself on her elbows.

"Aren't you comfortable?"

"Help me, please. I . . . I feel so weak."

Morgan put down his glass and reached to grasp her on either side of the waist. He had meant to help her to sit up, but the feel of her body beneath the thin material of the gown made him hesitate; and his hands moved up to rest beneath her breasts. He clasped her there and with his thumbs began stroking slowly backwards and forwards across the swell of her bodice.

Rachael's lips parted.

"Mr Morgan . . ."

"Frank."

She gazed up into his darkening eyes and a sudden leap of desire pulsed inside him.

"Frank," he repeated hoarsely. "Say my name. Frank. Say it for me."

She murmured something.

Without hurrying, he began unfastening the rest of the buttons at the opening of her gown, and when they were undone pushed his hand inside and cupped it over her breast, feeling the nipple firm against his palm. Rachael made a small, soft sound, somewhere between a sigh and a moan, but he silenced it immediately, bending over her and touching her lips gently with his own.

Then the gentleness gave way to a more urgent emotion and he pressed his mouth down hard upon hers, forcing her head backwards into the pillow. There was a movement of instinctive response and she gripped his shoulders, pressing herself against him.

Somewhere below voices were raised, but Frank Morgan paid them no heed. With a deftness born of long practice he drew Rachael's bodice down over her breasts, exposing them to him, tantalisingly soft and white in the dim light of the oil lamp. Beneath the left nipple were two small birthmarks.

As he bent his head to kiss them, footsteps pounded up the stairs outside and the stallion leader turned, cursing aloud, to see the door burst back on its hinges and a crowd of men come at him through the opening, bringing with them a smell of night air and horses.

"—And Ralph took one look at you and positively flung himself on the brute—"

Effie Underwood's face wore an expression of dramatic horror.

"—and that wretched gipsy hit George Protheroe so hard on the side of the head he swears he'll never be right again—and dear brave Fred was just about to take a hold on him from behind when the most enormous man like something from a travelling fair came bursting into the room—it transpired he was the owner of that dreadful place—and began bellowing at the top of his lungs and laying about him in all directions. And Ralph says there was some awful woman standing out on the stairs to watch—and laughing! Though I can hardly believe such a thing. And you, my poor darling, right in the thick of it all, too ill and confused to know what was happening."

Effie touched Rachael's hand reassuringly, trying her best to smile.

The other lay quite still in the canopied bed, dressed in one of Effie's elaborately embroidered nightgowns and propped against a deep pile of lace-edged pillows. The casement window was opened wide to let in the sound of birdsong from the garden below, and the warm air was scented with the perfume of rose bowls on polished surfaces. The contrast between this pleasant room and that of the previous night could not have been more extreme.

Effie's eyes moved over Rachael's pale, expressionless features. When they had brought her on horseback to Pelbrook Place in the early hours of the morning she had seemed almost in a trance, allowing herself to be undressed and bathed like a child. Afterwards she had fallen immediately into a deep sleep; and for the next twelve hours Effie and the maid, Mary Anne, had taken it in turns to look in on her and if she seemed troubled, stay for a while, watching the traces of fear come and go in her restless dreams as she whimpered and moaned and tossed herself ceaselessly from side to side.

Effie Underwood gave a sudden shiver, and began again.

"Ralph told me that the man was standing over you with a broken bottle in his hand, swearing to kill anyone who so much as laid a finger on you. But Fred threw a tray—of all things—and caught him on the brow. And Robert Radley—you remember Robert Radley, don't you? From Cliffe?—well, he hit the wretched brute a terrible blow and knocked him to the ground. And do you know what Ralph said? That the woman on the stairs laughed louder than ever. All that blood, and she stood there laughing. It's unbelievable!"

Rachael moved her head sharply.

"Oh, now don't let the thought upset you, my darling. There wasn't so much blood, I'm sure. Why, when they carried him outside he was able enough to hit Robert Radley in return."

Then Radley and the others had dragged the stallion leader across the darkened yard and down the slope to the stream, where they repeatedly held his head beneath the water until he lost consciousness. It had been fine sport. A broken rib or two besides would help the fellow to remember his place in future.

But of this final assault as Morgan lay helpless on the ground at the mercy of their boots, Ralph Underwood had told his wife nothing. Nor of the intimate scene they had interrupted in that room.

"Effie . . ." Rachael's voice was barely more than a whisper. "Effie . . . I'm so frightened."

"Oh, my poor dear, of course you're frightened! It was a dreadful experience. But there's no need to worry any more. You're with us. You're quite safe now."

"I feel as though I'll never be safe again. Anywhere."

"It's natural. You've had such a terrible experience. But you'll feel better in a while, you'll see."

Rachael slowly shook her head; and there was a look of such utter misery on her face that the other felt tears of sympathy prick her eyes.

"Hush, now. There. You mustn't dwell on it."

"Oh, Effie . . . you don't understand. How can you?" She gripped her friend's hand and clung to it despairingly. "It's not so much what happened to me yesterday. I know this will shock you to hear it, but I must say it. I—I would gladly have stayed with him in that place."

"Lord above—Rachael!"

"But it's true. He made me feel . . . oh, I don't know what it was. Something I've never experienced before, not in all the time I've been married to Esmond. Can you understand that? Does it make sense? He made me feel that nothing else mattered in the world but being there with him. No—don't look at me so, Effie. No wrong was committed. I almost wish to God there had been. Perhaps I'd be able to face Esmond with more courage. You see, it's him . . ." She closed her eyes and turned her head away. After a moment she went on in a low voice, "it's not the stallion man . . . it's my husband I'm so afraid of."

Effie stared at her. The shock of the abduction must have had a more serious effect than they had thought. To wish that that brute of a gipsy had had his way with her! There would be every reason to fear Esmond's violent jealousy if that had happened and somehow were to reach his ears.

She said briskly, "Now don't start worrying about Esmond. Ralph has already sent word that you're indisposed and staying here with us for a while."

"Yes, with you. Not the Collinses. He's bound to think that strange. And my box, my belongings . . . left behind last night. How am I to explain that to him? Oh God, Effie, I feel so wretched. If he learns about the Fordhouse—"

"*If* he learns. Who is going to tell him? The Collinses? They know nothing. Ralph has already been to see Mr Collins and said only that you've been found and are safely with us. In any case, how could Esmond possibly hold you to blame? None of this was your doing. If blame must be laid anywhere, let it be on that wretch who tricked you."

"You don't know Esmond. He's not a reasonable man." Rachael covered her face with her hands. "Were he ever to find out about last night, I truly believe something terrible would befall us all."

24

Rachael need not have been so apprehensive.

At least, not at that particular time. Later she would have good reason to fear her husband; but for the moment, she was safe. The Reverend Bates was himself suffering, from a lacerated conscience, and the news from Lewes served only to plunge him deeper into self-reproach and morbidity.

Perhaps it had not been wise of him, he reflected, to force the poor girl to go to the Collinses. They were an excellent couple in many ways, but impatient of her youth and possibly too careful about observing his stricture to keep her from company in the town. It would not have harmed her so very much to go out a little, and Euphemia Underwood for all her giddiness and regrettable choice of husband was nice enough company.

It was a depression of spirits caused by his own selfish behaviour which had brought on his wife's indisposition, Esmond told himself harshly; and it was only right that he should make amends by allowing her to stay with her own friends until she was recovered sufficiently to come back to Weatherfield.

But when Rachael received her husband's letter she had no way of knowing his reformed state of mind. The episode at the Fordhouse had left its mark deeper than they knew, and the constant tension began to tell on her already strained nerves. She grew noticeably edgy, unable to sit for long in one place without being driven to get up and walk aimlessly from room to room. Her appetite suffered, too; and though she slept well enough she frequently awoke tired, the rumpled bedclothes strewn about in disorder.

Effie, concerned by her increasing restiveness, urged her to consult a doctor.

Rachael was unusually short with her. "A doctor? Nonsense. I'm not ill."

"You think not? Then look at yourself!" Effie seized her arm and swung her round to face the long cheval glass in the bedroom. "Just look. You eat hardly anything. And it shows."

Rachael stared at the reflection. It was true, she did seem to have grown thinner. In her face especially, where the dark hollows beneath her cheekbones emphasised her paleness.

"And your poor wrists—" The other pushed back the cuff of the borrowed gown. "You're turning yourself into a starveling in front of our eyes. And yet you declare you're not ill. What's the matter with you, Rachael? You won't eat, you snap at me and Ralph whenever we speak to you, you wander about the house like a ghost, you refuse every invitation to visit . . . My dear, it simply isn't like you to behave in this fashion."

Rachael turned her back on the glass and stared morosely out through the window.

"You know what is the matter. This wretched business. The waiting. Not knowing whether Esmond has learnt anything. Wondering if he will. When he will. What he will do to me."

She did not mention Frank Morgan, though the stallion man was seldom out of her mind. Asleep or awake, her thoughts were fixed upon him in a kind of dreadful fascination, one half of her drawn irresistibly towards him, the other half repelled by the very notion of seeing him again.

"Esmond!" Effie threw up her hands. "Always Esmond. In Heaven's name, why are you so frightened of him? Why don't you simply tell him the truth, and have done with it?"

"I dare not!"

"But you've nothing to hide, nothing to be ashamed of. Oh Rachael, what has changed you? You were always such a happy, confident creature before you married that man."

Her hands began to tremble and she gripped them tightly together. "I dare not tell him," she repeated in a low voice. "Effie—you have no idea how he would treat me. His jealousy makes him so cruel."

"Then why not leave him? Oh, don't look so pained. Surely you must have considered it yourself before now? Leave him! Stay here with us in Lewes instead of going back to him."

"I can't do that." Rachael turned from the window, her eyes full of despair. "He needs me, despite everything. I could never desert him. I haven't the—"

She stopped abruptly as Ralph Underwood entered the room.

He looked at her; and slowly shook his head. "I'm sorry," he said. "It's gone. The whole lot. They've got rid of everything, even your aunt's Bible."

Rachael sat down on the bed, her last hope gone.

Ralph had ridden out that morning to Buckfield to retrieve her box from the Fordhouse. But, as he told her now, the owner had claimed the contents as compensation for the damage caused to his property. And it was already too late to offer him money instead: the stuff had been sold. Rachael's two gowns and her best shawl had gone to a group of hop-pickers passing through on their way to the Kentish fields; her nightgown had been taken by a woman from Hailsham way; and the remainder of her bits and pieces were dispersed among the motley crowd who patronised the Fordhouse.

She left Lewes for Weatherfield the next morning.

Effie's cousin, "dear brave Fred", was returning home to Tenterden after an extended stay in the town and agreed to take her as far as Heathbury in his trap. From there she would be able to go on by carrier. Ralph Underwood had offered to convey her himself, but she firmly refused him. She had already caused more than enough inconvenience, she insisted.

The true reason for her refusal was more personal: she had felt uncomfortable in Ralph's presence ever since that night at Buckfield. Several times she had found him staring at her, in a way which caused her embarrassment. Moreover, Esmond would not be best pleased to find him with her, and she wished to keep her peace with her husband more than anything just now.

In the soft, clear light of an August dawn, she stood beside Effie at the foot of the porch steps. Neither spoke until Cousin Fred, a slim, mousy-haired young man with glossy whiskers framing a long face, called impatiently from the trap that he wanted to be away in good time and was Mrs Bates ready to leave?

At that, she roused herself.

"Write as soon as you reach home. Promise me," Effie whispered against her cheek. "And don't forget, there's a place for you here if ever you need somewhere."

Rachael pressed her hand one last time and turned away. How could she ever tell her that Ralph Underwood's house had ceased to be a refuge?

She went quickly across to the trap and got in, and the vehicle started away down the drive. She did not look back, and in a few moments was gone from sight, hidden by the laurel bushes on the bend.

Cousin Fred spoke little on the journey to Heathbury.

211

Rachael sensed that he had accepted her company reluctantly, and so was inclined to share his relief when by noon they had reached her destination.

"I'll set you down near the Cross-in-Hand," he told her, negotiating a side lane to take them into the main street of the busy market town.

"Thank you."

He flicked the reins unnecessarily.

Then, in a sudden burst of words—as though the long silence had been a mask and only at this final moment had he found courage to remove it—he said rapidly, "It was none of my fault, you know. Tell your man I did my best to stop them. Do you understand? I did my best, but they wouldn't listen to me. I had no part in it, I swear I didn't. You will tell him that from me, won't you?"

Rachael stared at him, uncomprehending.

The young man glanced nervously sideways. "Well— damn it, I'm no kind of hero, but I do draw the line at kicking a chap once he's down. Especially when the odds are so against him. Hardly fair play. Five on to one was too much, and I did tell them. But you know how it is in a mellay like that. Look,"—he pointed ahead with the whip—"I'll set you down at this corner. It's handy enough. Ask at the store about a carrier. They'll put you right."

Reining in the pony, he brought the trap to a halt outside a double-fronted general store and jumped smartly down to assist Rachael to the ground. Then turned to remount; but she restrained him, keeping her grip on his arm and asking in a bewildered way, "Why do you call him *my* man?"

Cousin Fred looked startled. He had not wanted to involve himself in any of this business in the first place, but Ralph and the rest had egged him on to join them. And he had certainly not wanted to entangle himself with the gipsy's woman afterwards. This conveying of her to Heathbury had been Effie's idea: she had been so insistent that he could find no way of avoiding it.

How did one explain to a female relative that her closest friend was not quite the virtuous party she believed her to be?

212

No woman of any virtue would be lying half-naked with a man in the upstairs room of such a disreputable place as the Fordhouse.

He gave an embarrassed laugh.

"Oh . . . just a manner of speaking, you know. No offence meant. But you won't forget to tell him, will you? There's a good girl?"

Rachael continued to grip his arm and Cousin Fred glanced awkwardly around. Damn it, what was wrong with the woman? He hated public scenes and passers-by were beginning to stare.

A man, a country farmer in corduroy breeches and waistcoat, came out of the store and looked across at them. He went to move away; then paused, shading his eyes against the sun to make a better scrutiny; and finally came purposefully on down the steps on to the foot-path and walked over.

"Mrs Bates?"

There was a note of doubt in the deep voice, as though he were not quite sure he had the right person.

Rachael released Cousin Fred's arm and swung round, startled. Then she cried out in relief.

She was in such a low, nervy state, so miserably unhappy, so much in need of kindness and reassurance, that had anyone asked her a moment before who, in all the world, she most wished to have by her, she would have answered without hesitation—George Bashford.

And here he was.

"Mr Bashford!" She made no attempt to disguise her swift joy. "Oh . . . thank God!"

Bashford's smile faded. He looked over at the young man backing towards the trap.

"Is anything wrong here?"

Cousin Fred shook his head emphatically and proceeded to offer a hasty explanation.

"I see." The farmer consulted his pocket watch. "Well now, I've only one more transaction to put in hand before I'm done here myself. No need to find a carrier. Mrs Bates can travel back with me."

Thankful to be rid so easily of the responsibility, Cousin

Fred wished them both a quick good day, and was whipping his pony into a fast trot down the street before he had barely seated himself in the trap.

Rachael did not look after him but kept her eyes fixed upon George Bashford's face.

"If I may?"

He took her gently by the arm and walked with her a little way into the shade of the trees, concerned that she might be uncomfortable standing here in the full sun. He noticed that the chip bonnet and shawl she wore looked almost new (they were, in fact, both borrowed from Effie Underwood) but her other clothing was darned and shabby. Also, it seemed odd that she should have nothing more than a reticule with her. But he made no comment.

"Well, ma'am. This is a nice coincidence," he said pleasantly. "Though on second thoughts, perhaps coincidence is the wrong word. I'm so seldom here in Heathbury that it seems more like—well, Fate, you might say, us meeting like this."

"Yes. Yes . . . Fate indeed."

He would surely think her too forward were she to put into words her deeply felt gratitude for his arrival.

"I generally do business with a firm of corn chandlers at East Grinstead, but I heard of a dealer giving a better price at Heathbury 'change. The harvest should be a good one this year, so I'm looking to do a profitable trade with him."

"Oh. I see."

Bashford paused and glanced down at her, concerned. "You're trembling, Mrs Bates. Are you not well?"

"No. It's nothing."

She certainly looked unwell, he thought. He had not seen her for a couple of months and the change in her appearance had struck him immediately: she seemed so much slighter, and thinner, as though a few good meals would not go amiss. Though he was not a man given over to fancies, he thought he detected something melancholy—haunted, almost—in her expression.

He took her hand and placed it within the crook of his elbow.

214

"We'll go on, then. If you're sure there's nothing wrong."

"Quite sure."

"Good. I've only this business at the 'change. If you'd care to rest, there's a place for the ladies inside. Perhaps you'll take something to refresh you at the same time?"

Rachael managed a faint smile.

Holding his arm, she walked beside him along the hot, dusty streets whose surfaces were patterned with the dark trails of water carts, on towards the crossroads at the centre of the town. She looked at the faces of people passing—women with their children, tradesfolk, labourers, couples arm-in-arm beneath the trees—and envied them their peace of mind. To them, no doubt, she and George Bashford must appear no different; just one more couple like the many others about them.

The notion brought an unexpected pleasure.

Then she was reminded of the last occasion when she had walked in public on a man's arm, when Frank Morgan had escorted her to the herb-wife in Lewes market. The recollection of that, and what had followed, was almost intolerable. She started to tremble again and had to clench her fist on Bashford's arm in an effort to control herself.

He glanced down and smiled, reassuringly. But the smile hid a growing unease. Something was wrong here: Mrs Bates was ill, whatever she said. Or if not ill, then greatly agitated.

He wondered what might be the cause. There had been, he knew, some idle speculation in the district when she went off so suddenly to Lewes all those weeks back. Then there was that perplexing business with her husband at the farm, drinking rather more than he could govern and talking so wildly afterwards.

George Bashford had thought often about the Reverend Bates's curious confession; and had tended charitably to dismiss it as a lot of self-pitying nonsense. But what if it wasn't nonsense, after all? Drink frequently brought out the true state of a man's mind.

He looked at the small fist bunched on his arm, recalling some of the things this young woman's husband had said, telling himself that it was none of his business. But still thinking what a sad thing it was if those drunken disclosures should prove to be no more than the truth.

A short while later, well pleased with the way his business at the Corn Exchange had gone, he drove with her in his trap away from the town.

She was looking less strained now, he thought; and in his good humour was inclined to laugh at his earlier concern and tell himself that he had exaggerated her plight. She was a little tired perhaps, nothing more.

It was true, Rachael did seem better. Refreshed by the rest and a light meal, she made an effort to share her companion's pleasant mood, encouraging him to talk of his plans for extending the farm at Netherton and buying a second team of oxen to work the top ridge where the old copse had been grubbed up last winter.

But after a while her conversation flagged and as the miles to Weatherfield decreased she fell silent, a prey once more to her own private anguish.

Their way took them along the valley of the Rother, whose wooded slopes rose gently on either side of the broad, shallow stream keeping company with the road, an ancient route now falling into disuse since the opening of the new highroad further west. The morning had been clear and hot; but August weather is treacherous and as the afternoon wore on the clouds thickened and darkened and large, isolated drops of rain began to fall.

Bashford cast an anxious look at the sky.

"Seems like we're in for a bit of a storm. We'd best pull off the road till it's passed over."

A short distance away, the road curved through a green tunnel formed by the long leafy boughs of an arch of trees. They had barely reached this natural shelter when the dark clouds overtook them and the valley landscape was blotted out by a heavy downpour.

Bashford guided the horse through the gloom towards a high bank just off the road where the smooth grey trunks of beech trees rose to form part of the tunnel wall.

"We ought to be dry enough here for a bit."

216

Rachael removed her damp bonnet and glanced up at the massive arch above her.

"Yes."

"It's a mercy we weren't caught out in the open."

"Yes, it is."

"We seem to have had luck in several respects today, don't we?"

He leaned back on the seat, letting the reins lie slackly in his hands, listening to the steady drip of the rain falling through the leaves.

"We'll soon be on our way again. These summer storms don't last long."

She merely nodded.

Bashford started to say something else; then thought better of it. A silence fell between them. Beyond the tunnel the rain swelled the stream to a noisy torrent and the air was filled with the sound of falling water.

Try as he might to concentrate his mind on the business of his farm, he found his thoughts wandering constantly back to one theme, and after a time he shifted in his seat to look at the woman beside him.

There was an expression of such sadness on her young face that his concern for her instantly welled up again and he asked, gently, "Won't you tell me what is the matter?"

Rachael gave a start; but continued to stare ahead, making no reply.

Bashford waited a few moments, then went on, "Forgive me for prying. But I can't keep silent when I see you upset like this. Would it help if you told me what has happened?"

She lowered her head and said something, but the words were lost in the sound of the rain.

"Is there anything I can do for you?" he persisted.

A tremor seemed to run through her body. He saw at once that he had trespassed too far on her emotions and put out a hand, discomforted by her evident distress. She ignored the gesture, averting her face from him. The lump in her throat almost choked her. If he said one more kind word, she knew she would lose all control and break down into tears.

217

He frowned and looked away. It was none of his affair. Best keep out of it.

The restless horse moved forward a step and he checked it, then sat back despondently, feeling his humour evaporate in the gloomy atmosphere.

Then told himself sharply that, damn it all, the girl *was* unhappy and would get scant sympathy from her husband, if half the things the man had ranted on about came anywhere near the truth.

He tried again.

"Mrs Bates . . . I've always thought of us as friends, you know. And it grieves me hard to see you so troubled. Please, won't you let me help you?"

The force his words unleashed—the suddenness, the utter nakedness of her despair—shook him. Before he had stopped to think what he was doing, he had put his arm round her and pulled her to him, stifling her sobs against his chest, protecting her, comforting her in such terrible distress.

They stayed together like that for many minutes.

Gradually her shudders lessened and eventually she began to speak, her face still hidden from him, the sentences torn from her in deep involuntary gasps. She left nothing out; not even her willingness to give Frank Morgan whatever it was he had wanted of her.

George Bashford listened without interruption. Her story stirred him to such a deep, immediate anger that he could not trust himself to speak, Inwardly he raged at the stallion leader for being the man he was—seducer, profligate, deceiver—cursing him for his thoughtless, selfish greed in using this innocent creature so ill.

And in the midst of the anger came revelation.

It was then that Bashford discovered the truth of his feelings for Rachael Bates, realised that what he had for so long taken to be pity and impersonal concern was something far, far greater; something he had no right to harbour for this woman. It disturbed him more than anything he had ever known.

When at last she finished speaking, he continued to hold her. Beyond the arch of trees the rain had almost ceased and the sun, bursting through the edge of the storm clouds, filled the tunnel with subdued green light.

"There. There, now. It's told," he said quietly at length. "Don't fret yourself any more, my dear. It's over now. It'll not happen again. I promise you. I'll see you're kept safe from now on."

Rachael lifted her head from his shoulder and looked up into his face. He smiled: a slow, gentle smile that seemed to envelop her in its warmth and heal the hurt in her mind.

For the first time in many long days she felt at peace with herself again.

25

"Hello, my beauty."

The unexpectedness of the familiar voice startled Dinah Flynn from her reverie. She drew a sharp breath and looked quickly over her shoulder, checking for a moment the pull of her hands above the milking pail.

On the other side of the wooden partition separating the cow stalls, Frank Morgan stood among the shadows watching her.

"Oh. It's you, is it." It required some effort, but she made the response as casual as she could. "We thought you'd cleared off for good this time."

He leaned forward, resting his elbows on the ledge. "You've missed me then, have you?"

"I can't say we have." She turned her back to him again, resting her forehead against the cow's warm flank. "Not seeing as who we've got marrying into the family."

"Somebody's getting married?"

"Aye. And you needn't pretend ignorance. Jack said he'd told you weeks back."

"So he's going ahead with it, then?"

Dinah got up with the milking stool and pail and moved out into the next stall, not looking at him.

He followed, and waited till the milk was flowing well before asking again, "So it's going ahead?"

"Soon as ever they've called the banns."

"He's wasting no time, your Jack."

She threw him a dark look. "There's not much time to waste, seeing the condition you left her in."

"Me? She's been giving out that tale again? A few hours, that's all I spent with her—"

"A few hours are more'n enough. You've caused our family some trouble, Frank Morgan. Behopes this'll be the last. Our Jack's real taken wi' that girl. And I'll say this, she's a nice enough creature now we've had a chance to know her. But when he first come home to say as how he'd set his mind on marrying her—a foreigner he hadn't known above a week and carrying another man's bastard . . ." She shook her head. "It's good of him to pick up your leavings, that's all I can say about it."

Morgan shrugged.

A silence fell between them.

After a while he said casually, "What's become of the other dairy workers?"

"They're out helping wi' the harvest."

"So you're all by yourself here?"

"Not now you've shown your face I'm not."

The stallion man smiled and glanced around the shed. Then he shifted himself a little closer.

"How's our Frankie keeping? And the new one—what did you name her in the end?"

"What's it to you what she's named? You haven't shown yourself in much of a hurry to find out before this."

"Now—Dinah!" A note of hurt crept into his voice. "What a thing to go accusing a father of."

She hesitated, taken off guard. Then, thinking he was being flippant with her, flung back over her shoulder—"Call yourself a father, Frank Morgan? You've not been near us for nigh on three months, not since Belle's birth day. No money from you, no news. Nothing. You might've been dead for

220

all we knew. And now to come here acting as calm as you please—!"

In her vexation she jerked at the cow's udder. The sharp movement made the animal stamp its rear hoof against the stall floor, catching the rim of the pail and slopping milk over the straw.

"Oh, now look what you've made me do!"

Angrily, Dinah dragged the pail back into place; then forced herself to speak quietly to the cow, soothing it until the swish of the tail ceased and she could carry on with the milking.

"So it's Belle, is it?"

"Yes."

"A pretty name. But then, she'll be a pretty little thing altogether."

"How would you know? You've not set eyes on her since the day you birthed her."

Morgan smiled. "If she's anything like her mother in looks, she'll be a regular beauty."

"Words cost you nothing, Frank."

"But it's true. She's got your face, hasn't she?"

"And your manners!"

Dinah gave him a quick look and saw that he was still smiling. She went to add something else; then stopped, her heart beginning to race.

"Do you . . . do you want to come back home wi' me to see her?"

"Why else d'you suppose I'm here?"

"Well,"—she finished the milking and stood up, moving the pail out to the side of the stall—"there's always a chance you might've wanted to see me."

Morgan came round the partition into the light and stood in front of her in the doorway. In a soft voice he said, "I always want to see you, my love."

"Seems like it, don't it?" She looked at him defiantly. Then caught her breath. "Lord almighty, Frank! What you been doing to yourself? However did you get your face so marked?" She grabbed at his arm. "Let's have you out in the yard and get a proper look at you."

He allowed himself to be pulled into the sunlight, standing patiently, humouring her, while she turned his dark head this way and that between her hands, examining the injuries sustained at the Fordhouse, the yellowing bruise on his cheekbone and the ugly swelling that still surrounded the long cut above his left eye—the legacy of Cousin Fred's attack with the tin tray.

"Oh, Frank, how in the world did you manage to get yourself into such a state?" Her hands moved down over his body. "And your poor ribs strapped up as well! What in God's name have you been doing?"

He shrugged, and made a grimace. "A fight. It was nothing."

"Nothing!"

"Well . . . I'll live, don't fret yourself. They didn't damage me that much."

"*They?* Lord, Frank, how many of them was there?"

"Half a dozen, give or take." He smiled wryly. "I didn't stand around long enough to count."

Dinah stared at him in disbelief. "And you all by yourself? Oh, Frank, you ought to have more sense."

He reached out and drew her into his arms, holding her carefully against him, and kissed her lightly. "I'd almost forgotten what a charmer you are when you're riled."

"We'll have none o' that!" Dinah put up a token resistance, twisting her head from side to side to escape his kisses. "There's still that girl o' Jack's—"

"Be damned to her," he whispered against her lips. "I owe her nothing." He kissed her again; then again, harder and longer, feeling her body begin to respond to him. "Anyone likely to be around here for a while?"

"No." She looked up into the dark eyes. "Why?"

"Guess."

"You don't waste time, do you? What about your ribs?"

"It's not my ribs I'm concerned with." On the far side of the dairy yard the door to the storehouse stood invitingly ajar. "D'you reckon George Bashford would mind if we sat talking in his loft for a bit?"

She smiled, brushing the auburn hair back from her forehead. "Depends what you want to talk about, don't it? Any road, he ain't around to mind. He's gone off to Heathbury for the day. And Jackson's got everyone working the top field."

"Good." Morgan pressed his face into the thick hair, smelling the warm milky aroma of the dairy mingled with the scent of her skin. "Let's not waste any more time, then. We've got a lot of making up to do for these past few months."

"Oh . . . now then, don't cry, Frankie! Here's your dad come to see you. Look. See? He's brought you a florin for your very own."

The child lifted a tousled head from his grandmother's shoulder and turned his tearful face towards the dark stranger standing beside his mother in the kitchen of the Flynns' alehouse.

"You remember your dad, don't you, Frankie?" Dinah coaxed him. "Be a good boy now and gi' him a nice smile. He's come all the way here just to see you."

The child wavered; and greed won. The desire to have the silver coin held out to him proved stronger than his distrust of the man who offered it. He slid down from his grandmother's lap. One hand still clutching her skirts, he reached cautiously towards the bright piece.

Frank Morgan laughed and got down on his haunches in front of his son.

"Here you are, then. There. Got it tight? Good lad. Now don't I get a kiss for that?"

The child hesitated.

"Go on, Frankie," Dinah urged. "Gi' your dad a nice kiss."

The dark eyes stared unwinking into the identical ones of his father. The small chin tightened and the bottom lip began to tremble again.

"Well, if you won't give me a kiss you must give me back my florin," the stallion man told him. "Fair's fair, now."

The notion of giving up his new possession was unthinkable. Little Frankie had inherited his father's mettle. Leaning forward, he pressed his mouth quickly to the stranger's cheek, feeling the rough moustaches tickle his chin, then pulled away to hide his face against his grandmother's knee.

Mrs Flynn stroked his hair, and looked across at Frank Morgan. The thin lips made a bitter line. Trust him to turn up again like a bad penny. Just when they thought they'd seen the back of him and Dinah was getting her sense at last. And now here he was, thinking he could get his boots back under their table without so much as a by your leave, and expecting them all to behave as though he'd never been gone.

And the sight of him! No wonder the child was frightened, seeing that face so knocked about. A pity he'd had to show up to bother them again. Aye—her mouth twisted vindictively—a pity whoever marked him hadn't finished the job properly.

"Now then,"—Frank Morgan stood up and gave Mrs Flynn his most winning smile—"let's have a look at this new daughter of mine."

He was all too well aware that Dinah's mother hated him like poison. But the old woman would not be around for much longer. And he had been turning over in his mind this last week or so the idea of taking on the running of her house himself.

Well, why not? In a few years he would be forty years old. The alehouse was exactly the kind of work he could settle happily to once his champion Shire, the Brighton Regent, grew too old for the mares and the days on the stud circuit were finished.

Other stallion men sometimes started afresh with a young horse. But it was arduous work, and not for Morgan now. He already had plans in mind for expanding the alehouse, livening the place up, introducing some gambling perhaps, attracting a bigger custom. The fact that he would have to marry Dinah to inherit her mother's property was something he reckoned he could come to terms with.

*   *   *

The setting sun shone directly in through the bedroom window and lit the room with a warm glow, picking out the gleam of woodwork in one corner.

"That's a handsome cradle you've got her," Frank Morgan said approvingly.

Dinah sat on the edge of her bed, watching his face as he bent to look at the sleeping baby.

"Yes. Our Jack made it."

"Did he, now." He ran a hand over the smooth-grained wood. "He'll be starting a regular cottage industry soon, won't he? Charlotte'll be needing one herself come December."

"December, is it? You're very sure of your dates for a man who claims it's naun to do wi' him. And what's all this about Charlotte? How d'you know her name's not Rose or Mary or Polly?"

"She told me her name. That's how."

"That day, I suppose?"

Morgan looked across the room at her. "Are you by chance jealous of that girl?"

Dinah answered him frankly. "Yes."

"You needn't be, you know. I'll be honest with you. I went with her the once, no more. I was lonely and I felt like a bit of company."

"And that's all there was to it?"

"That's all. I'm sorry the girl's in trouble, but she's only herself to blame. She could have said no. But she didn't. That was the sort she was." He paused. "There's nothing more to say about her, Dinah. All right?"

She stared at him for a while longer; then lowered her head. She had been prepared to hate Charlotte Smith, but when Jack brought her to his parents' cottage on Weatherfield green and she had gone there to meet her and heard her story, she no longer had the heart to feel resentment.

The girl was no more than seventeen years old, and already had been worse used by life than most. Her mother dead, her father a drunkard, her surviving brothers and sisters scattered. Little wonder she was so grateful to the Adamses for taking her into their home as wife to their son.

225

"I don't know what I've done to deserve so much kind-ness," she had kept on saying. "Everybody's been that good to me. You can't think how it feels to have someone offer you a chance of real happiness . . . to give you a roof above your head and tell you this is your home for as long as you want."

"Our Jack's always been one to do a good turn where he can," Dinah had acknowledged.

"Oh, it weren't Jack as said that."

"No?"

"No, it were his dad. Mr Adams. There'd been a vestry meeting to see about getting me shifted out of the parish back to Lewes. On account of me not being able to support myself, I suppose. The overseer come round here to see Mr Adams, and Mr Adams straight up and gi' him his warranty he was willing to have me in his house and make me family."

"Then it's settled, isn't it."

Dinah's glance transferred itself to Lottie's thickening waistline. After a pause she asked carefully, "Our Jack's dad knows, does he, who it is that's responsible for getting you in trouble?"

"No. No, he don't. Jack said as not to tell."

"Ah. Then you'd best do as Jack says and not let on, my girl. Not if you want to stay under this roof. There's precious little love lost atween this family and Frank Morgan. If they knew it was him, likely you'd find yourself back in Lewes after all."

"Jack'd never let that happen! Would he?"

Dinah shrugged.

"Oh . . . then *you* won't tell, will you?" the other had pleaded, seizing her hand. "Perhaps I shouldn't be asking, seeing as how it was you he was cheating when Frank went wi' me that day. But you won't pay me out for it, will you? He never told me he was all but wed and had children already—"

"No. He never does," Dinah said bitterly. "He has a quick way of forgetting our existence when he's out of our sight."

"I'd never have gone wi' him if I'd known, I swear I wouldn't. You won't let on to Jack's folk it was him that

226

wronged me, will you? Not if it means they'll put me back out on the street."

"I won't . . . on a condition."

"What condition?"

"That you tell me the truth."

"What truth's that?"

Dinah had looked Lottie steadily in the eyes. "Is this coming baby truly Frank Morgan's? You can tell me. I want to know. If you own up to it being another's, well, that's your business. But if it's Frank's—"

"It is . . . it is! There was nobody else. Not then. Oh, he weren't the first I'd been with. How could he be? My own father abused me often enough that way when he'd drunk too much to care what he was doing. You'd think I'd be put off men for good, having him at me. But I wasn't. There were two or three I fancied—one especially. His people had a shop in Lewes high street, so he'd always got money to spend. And then when I went to work at the school, the woman who run it, well, her brother used to come up to my room—"

Dinah broke in sharply, "So this baby could just as well be his'n?"

"No, it couldn't. He were a poor creature of a man, he were. He used to gi' me half a sovereign to beat him with one o' the canes from the schoolroom. Can you imagine? I made him stuff his mouth wi' his handkerchief in case his sister heard the noise." She grimaced. "And what help did he gi' me in return when I needed it? None at all. Couldn't wait to have me out o' the place he couldn't when he found I was carrying. No references. Nothing. Just pushed me out on the street in the clothes I stood up in, and told me to choose between workhouse or whorehouse—it was all the same to him."

Dinah remained silent.

"But there, that's all behind me now," Lottie had gone on after a while. "I don't want to remember it no more, not now I've got Jack. He's all I care about . . . just him. Nobody else. He's done me such a kindness, looking after me like he has and making me respectable. Never mind what's gone, Lottie,

227

he says. What's to come's all that matters now. So I'm going to put that Frank Morgan and the rest of 'em clear out o' my mind, like I've promised."

"There's no mistaking whose daughter she is."

Frank Morgan's words startled Dinah out of her reverie.

"What? What you say?"

He indicated the baby. "The look of her. So like you. What's the matter? Aren't you pleased I've come to see her?"

"'Course I am, Frank! It's just . . . well, I didn't think you wanted her, the way you went off when she was born."

The stallion man bent over the cradle and slipped one hand under the baby's head, the other beneath her tiny body, raising her in the bend of his arm to lie against his chest. The little eyelids fluttered open and then closed again. He examined the sleeping profile, admiring the pearly skin framed by auburn hair already beginning to thicken into her mother's curls.

"Beautiful Belle," he said softly, almost to himself. "My beautiful girl."

Dinah's eyes betrayed her relief, filling with tears; and in her heart she thanked God that she seemed to have won her man back, when she thought he had gone from her for ever.

She drew a deep, unsteady breath.

"Parson Bates has agreed to baptise her, Frank. That's good news, ain't it? I think his wife must've talked him round to it. He were so set against me at first, I thought we'd never get it done. Mrs Bates has been real generous. You've no idea." In her sudden happiness she was ready to forget the jealousy she had felt towards Rachael Bates after the baby's birth. "She even wants to be our Belle's sponsor."

"Oh? When did she tell you that?" Frank Morgan turned away so that his face was hidden. Carefully he laid the baby back within the cradle.

"When? Oh, before Belle was born. But you'd . . . you left the village so sudden-like, it give me no chance to let you know."

228

Harshly he said, "She's probably changed her mind by now. What with one thing and another—" He swung back to face the woman on the bed. "Has she been here lately?"

"No. We ain't seen her for weeks now. She went away to Lewes. Didn't you hear?"

The stallion leader shook his head.

"What's the matter, Frank? You look so queer all of a sudden."

"I'm all right!"

"Would you rather she weren't sponsor, then? Is that it? I can tell by your tone o' voice you ain't that struck wi' the notion."

He shrugged. "It makes no difference to me."

Without looking at her he walked past the bed to the long, low window and leaned forward, hands pressed down on the ledge, staring out over the fields towards the distant village. Outwardly his manner was calm; but the mention of Rachael Bates's name had caught him defenceless, and he needed a moment or two to collect himself and master his emotions.

Try as he might, he was still unable to rid himself of her presence within him. Ever since that humiliating night at the Fordhouse he had been nagged by the ache of desire for her: the taste of her still in his mouth, the touch of her on his fingers, the memory of her lying there waiting for him, wanting him to take her.

He clenched his trembling fist against the ledge.

To have come so close, so close, only to have her snatched from him at the very last moment—God! He had not trusted himself to think about it, even. He had burnt the murder from his anger by imagining his vengeance on the men who had so misused him, who had tracked him down like a pack of dogs and lay in wait outside the door of that room, picking their moment to take him.

Morgan rested his burning forehead against the window-pane. Thanks to those whoreson bastards he had had to forfeit the woman he desired. But he was not finished with her yet. The harder the chase, the sweeter the quarry.

He turned from the window.

"Perhaps it's not such a bad idea, after all. A parson's wife for sponsor."

26

The Reverend Esmond Bates removed his hat and ducked his head beneath the low, dirt-encrusted beams of the cottage ceiling. The door stood ajar, opening directly on to the rough track outside, and daylight crept in to fall across the open coffin supported on two chairs in the middle of the room.

He went over to it and paused, looking down at the gaunt figure of the old shepherd lying stiffly within. The hands were crossed decently, as convention demanded, one lying rigidly open against the shrouded breast, the other clenched on a hank of sheep's wool.

The rector frowned and turned to the man who had followed him into the cottage and whose features were a reflection of how the deceased must have appeared in life.

"What is this?"

"What may that be, sir?"

"This,"—he gestured towards the coffin—"in your father's hand."

The other came across and glanced down.

"Sheep wool, sir."

Esmond's response was unnecessarily sharp. "That I can see for myself, Jenner. But what is it doing in the coffin? It seems to have been placed there deliberately."

"So it has, sir. 'Tis to be buried wi' him."

"Indeed?"

"'Tis the custom hereabouts, sir. A shepherd's always buried wi' a hank o' wool in his hand."

"Indeed." The tone hardened.

230

"We've always done it. You wouldn't know, p'raps, coming from the town, but 'tis tradition. Else how's the good Lord to know this be a shepherd he be a-gathering into Heaven? A man must show his calling, sir. And the cause for his absence from church."

"What superstitious nonsense!" The rector made no attempt to disguise his irritation. "Surely you cannot believe that? To think that the Almighty is incapable of recognising and receiving each of his creatures without there is this— this—"

He gestured contemptuously.

A frown appeared between Jenner's eyes. "'Tis the custom, as I say. Each man in our family, going back I doan't know amany years, each one's gone into the ground wi' his bit o' wool. Aye, and all other shepherds in these parts."

Esmond shook his head dismissively and turned away.

Then, after a long silence, he said shortly, "Well, I suppose I must allow it."

"Indeed, and I hope you will, sir. It does no harm, surely."

"It's the principle that may do the harm, Jenner. But then, I don't expect you to understand that."

He moved away towards the door and was in the act of replacing his hat when his movement was checked by a sudden outburst of barking from outside and a high-pitched voice shouting to the unseen dog to hold its noise.

A moment later a young boy appeared at the doorway, panting with the exertion of his race across the fields.

"Dad?" He pushed back the door and peered into the cottage gloom.

"Aye?" Jenner turned from the coffin. "That you, lad? What you a-doing here this time o' day?"

The boy held a hand against his labouring chest and took several deep gulps of air.

"Farmer Bashford. Looking for Parson Bates. They told 'un at the rect'ry. Likely here wi' grand-dad."

Esmond started forward. "Bashford, you say?"

"Aye. You're here, sir?"

The question was ignored. "Is there a message?"

The boy gulped again. "I've to let you know Mrs Bates is come home, sir."

The rector's manner betrayed nothing of the sudden leap of agitation within him.

"I see. Thank you." A pause. "Well, I must be on my way, it seems. Half past ten o'clock, did we say, Jenner, for the burial service?"

"Aye. Half past ten Sat'day morning."

"Yes. Well, I'll wish a good day to you."

The boy stood aside to let him pass, looking expectantly for some reward for his errand.

He looked in vain. Esmond's mind was already totally preoccupied with his wife's arrival. He was grievously disappointed that he had not been there to greet her. The scene he had rehearsed so many times in his imagination—welcoming her at the rectory door, leading her inside, showing her how everything had been made ready for her homecoming—all this had been denied him now. The fact that Bashford seemed to have appropriated his rôle and played the part for him galled him.

Charity Poole nudged her sister's arm and inclined her head in the direction of the rectory parlour, from which she had just emerged from serving a tray to Mrs Bates and Mr Bashford.

"There's something going on there," she murmured.

Comfort's eyes widened with interest. "You reckon so?"

Charity nodded.

The footfalls of the pair made scarcely a sound as they crossed the hall and went down the side passage to the kitchen. Charity closed the door behind her and looked at her sister. The plump, rosy-cheeked faces wore an unpleasantly eager expression.

"I could feel it atween 'em soon as ever they come in the house. You mark my words, Comfort. She's out to pay Mr Bates back for his neglect."

"Did she let fall anything about herself?"

"Not she!" Charity bit her lip, her eyes wrinkling in sly amusement. "But what a way to arrive. That raggedy old gown. Did you ever see the like? All she's got left to stand up in, seemingly. Give her such a start, it did, finding us here. Didn't know where to put herself for a minute. And that George Bashford right behind her—"

"—hoping they'd find the place empty, I dare say—"

"—silly pair. They didn't fool me. I could read their faces like an open book."

Comfort nodded. "And what's become of her box, I'd like to know. And all the things she took away wi' her?"

A sudden shiver of pleasure caused Charity to hug her clasped hands to her apron-covered bosom.

Softly she cried, "Ooh . . . there's something going on, for sure. And here at the rectory, an' all! A fine thing. What will the parson say when he hears?"

"*If* he hears."

"Her coming home so unexpected. Wi' Farmer Bashford. No box and looking a sight. Bursts into tears soon as ever she sets eyes on those bits o' furniture. *His* furniture, mind. And clinging to his arm for all to see."

"Shameless, I call it."

Charity drew a deep breath and smiled knowingly at her sister.

"You recall that night Frank Morgan come to visit?"

"That night he come to the cottage? Aye. What you getting at now?"

"Nothing. Only wondering. Maybe putting two and two together." She paused. "That poor Parson Bates. And him such a jealous man as he is."

Hands went up to mouths, and the knowing smiles turned to stifled chuckles of mirth.

In the parlour at the front of the rectory Rachael and George Bashford sat side by side in silence on the green-striped couch which had come, with the two matching chairs flanking it, from the farm at Netherton. Bashford was gazing thoughtfully at the floor; Rachael staring ahead at the red lacquer Chinese cabinet against the wall near the doorway. The cup rattled nervously in the saucer in her hand and she put it down on the small table in front of her.

233

Bashford cleared his throat.

He knew that he ought to leave before her husband arrived. But he had no wish to go. He wanted only to stay here beside her, not talking, not looking at her, even. Merely being with her. It was a bad sign, he knew. Somehow, he did not care.

He cleared his throat again.

"How long have the Pooles been helping in the house?"

She raised her eyes and looked quickly into his face. Then frowned.

"I'm sorry. What did you say?"

"The Pooles. They're lending a hand around the place?"

"I don't know. I suppose they must be."

"Perhaps Mr Bates engaged them during your absence?"

"Yes. Yes, that must be it. Of course. He dismissed the girl we had. He mentioned it in one of his letters."

There was another period of silence.

"Are you feeling a little better in yourself now?" he enquired gently.

Rachael nodded. Her face was still very pale and her eyes heavy, bruised beneath by dark shadows.

"I feel . . . quite well. Thank you."

But it was not the truth. Her emotional outburst during the rainstorm had completely drained her, emptied her of all feeling except a sensation of being at a great distance from everything. Her mind seemed to have closed itself so tightly that nothing mattered any more: not Frank Morgan, not the Fordhouse; not Esmond, even.

The only flicker of warmth in her numbness came from the man beside her now. George Bashford.

She clenched her hands in her lap.

"The cabinet . . . It's very fine. There was one exactly like it in Lewes some time ago. In the high street, in a shop near the top of the hill. Perhaps you know it? A cabinet maker's, next to the pawnbroker's?"

"Oh, yes, I know the place you mean."

"I used to go each day to admire it. We couldn't possibly afford to buy it, of course. But I did so enjoy looking at it through the window."

"Perhaps this may be the very same."

234

"Oh—?" She glanced at him uncertainly.

"I got it in Lewes."

In fact, the red lacquer cabinet had belonged to his wife's mother, who had presented the Bashfords with the piece at the time of their marriage. But he was happily prepared to lie, if it would give a little pleasure to Rachael.

"And there can't be many Chinese cabinets around this part of the world."

"No. Not many."

She got up and went over to stand in front of the piece, trying to concentrate her mind on something, if only some small detail which might match this to that other. It was no use. She found she could not even recall which side of the cabinet maker's window it had stood—only, for some reason, that the pawnbroker had given her much less for her aunt's rings than she had hoped for, and that Esmond had never gone back to redeem them.

That had been the cause of their first serious disagreement. One ring in particular, a thin gold band set with a little heart of pearls, she had cherished greatly. But, as Esmond coldly reminded her, all her property and possessions had become his the moment they were pronounced man and wife; and therefore he was at liberty to do what he liked with anything that had been hers before their marriage. In any case, he did not like jewellery on a woman. A wedding ring was ornament enough. The money was far better spent on the renewal of his many subscriptions to societies and Christian institutions.

Rachael turned slowly to look at George Bashford.

"You're very kind to me. All this . . . so much. You know, when I went away to the Collinses, this place was a house. A shell. Four walls, a roof, rooms. Nothing more. But because of you, your goodness and generosity, it's suddenly become a home." There was a catch in her voice. "I feel . . . I have so much to thank you for."

He was on his feet in a moment.

"Oh, now, Mrs Bates—my dear! You've already thanked me more than enough. Please do believe me when I say that your pleasure in these few things is more than I—"

Abruptly he broke off.

"What is it? What's wrong?"

"Listen . . . isn't that your husband now?"

Beyond the closed door she heard her name being called. She started visibly, the colour going from her lips. For a long moment she stood beside the cabinet as though transfixed, though under what emotion Bashford could not guess. He hoped that it was not pleasurable; then immediately chided himself for such an unworthy sentiment.

At the sound of Esmond's voice, a stab of terror had pierced Rachael's heart. She had to make a physical effort and force herself to put a hand to the doorknob and turn it, force her trembling legs to carry her through the doorway out into the hall.

Bashford turned away. But not before he had witnessed the dishevelled figure of the Reverend Mr Bates seize his young wife in his arms and crush her to him, the eyes closed and the face bearing an expression that was little short of naked anguish.

"Rachael. Rachael . . ."

Esmond kissed her feverishly.

She pulled away from him. "Mr Bashford is here still."

He released her at once, his mouth tightening as he glanced quickly towards the open parlour door. He took a step away; and then stopped, his eyes moving over his wife's pale features.

"Dear Lord—!"

"Don't be dismayed, Esmond," she said, as calmly as she could. "I've . . . I've not been well. But it will pass."

He nodded, almost embarrassed by the alteration in her appearance. The indisposition he believed she had suffered in Lewes had left its mark upon her more savagely than he could have imagined.

He drew a deep breath; and the familiar sense of guilt—and something more—dragged heavily on his spirits as he went ahead of her into the parlour.

"Mr Bashford?" He extended a hand, avoiding looking the other directly in the face. "Please—please be seated, won't you. I apologise, I had no idea my wife was not alone. I thought you had already gone."

"I'll not intrude further on your hospitality, sir. Mrs Bates'll be glad of a rest now, I'm sure, after that journey."

"Ah. Yes. The journey." He paused, glancing back at Rachael. "Forgive me, I don't quite understand. It was you, sir, who conveyed her from Lewes?"

"No, not Lewes. From Heathbury."

"Heathbury? But that's entirely in the wrong direction. I think I had better be informed of the details, if you please. How exactly did my wife come to meet with you?"

Rachael was the first to reply. "It was purely good fortune, Esmond—"

"My question was directed at Mr Bashford."

"Even so,"—she moved away from the open doorway into the room—"the story is mine, so I should be the one to answer. A relation of Effie's was travelling to Tenterden and offered to take me from Lewes as far as Heathbury."

"Which is on the way, of course," Bashford put in.

Esmond frowned. "But hardly in *this* direction."

"From there I had intended travelling by carrier," Rachael went on quickly. "It was quite by chance that Mr Bashford had business in the town and . . . and we met."

"I was coming out of Turner's. The general dealer near the Cross-in-Hand. D'you know the place? No? Ah. Well, I'd just come out from there when my eye fell directly on Mrs Bates standing beside a trap at the roadside."

"And you brought her on from there."

"Yes. That's right, sir." No mention of the storm and their halt to take shelter. "We arrived back in Weatherfield about an hour ago. Oh—" He put up a hand as though suddenly recalling something important. "Perhaps I'd best explain about Mrs Bates's box."

"Her box?"

For the first time in their conversation, Esmond looked directly at the young farmer.

Rachael, too, was staring at him. On her face was an expression of open dismay.

"Yes, her box. I'm afraid it's gone missing. It's still in the trap. The one your wife travelled in this morning."

237

He looked back at her as he spoke, and was relieved to see the sudden comprehension in her eyes.

Esmond Bates intercepted the look. And feared the worst. It was the kind of glance people gave each other when they shared a secret. He knew what that secret must be. Ever since discovering that Rachael had been in Bashford's company he nursed the fear that she'd been fully informed about that shameful afternoon at the Netherton farm. Obviously that was why she appeared so ill at ease, so reluctant to look him straight in the face, so forced in her behaviour.

He felt a surge of animosity towards George Bashford. It had been fine entertainment, no doubt, to ply a man with drink until he was incapable of using any judgment; and then sit back and encourage him to make a foolish laughing-stock of himself.

"Mr Bates—?"

Esmond blinked and stared across at his betrayer.

"I was saying, sir, about Mrs Bates's box. It was sheer carelessness, I'm afraid. You see, I neglected to remove it from the trap before the driver went on his way to Tenterden."

Rachael, watching her husband's expression closely, observed the tight, angry look. He hated waste of any kind, she knew; and replacing her clothing would cost money he could ill afford to spend.

"I am sorry, Esmond," she said quietly. Then—"I can't have you taking the blame, Mr Bashford. It was hardly your fault." She smiled at him gratefully. She had been sick with worry about that wretched box, wondering how on earth she was to explain its loss to her husband. And now, so simply, so smoothly, the burden had been lifted from her. "It was my property, after all. I should have had more care of it."

Bashford returned her smile. "We'll have to look out for it. There's no knowing when it might turn up again."

Esmond cleared his throat. "This fellow—this relative of Mrs Underwood's. I presume he will return the box when he discovers it to be still in his trap."

"No doubt. In the meantime, sir, perhaps I can make some amend for my neglect of your wife's belongings by

238

inviting her to make use of whatever she fancies from my own Isabelle's wardrobe?"

The other's nostrils took on a pinched look. "Isabelle's . . . wardrobe?"

"My late wife, Mr Bates. I still have at Spring Hill a number of her finer gowns. Silks and satins—you know the thing. Mrs Bates is very welcome to have them for her own wear if she wishes. That is, until her own are returned."

A little colour crept into Rachael's cheeks. "Mr Bashford . . . I couldn't possibly!"

He looked across at her. Perhaps he had been too forward. But his offer was genuine. It pained him to see such a lovely woman so shabbily clothed when it was within his power to dress her in something better.

He said quietly, "I've offended you, ma'am?"

"No. No, not at all. But you've already given so much. This furniture—"

Her husband interrupted her sharply. Bashford's spirit of generosity was beginning to irritate him.

"We thank you for your offer, sir. But really, we cannot be further beholden to you. My wife and I are too much in your debt as it is."

"Not at all, Mr Bates." The other followed him towards the door. "I like to be of help where I can." He glanced once more at Rachael. "Well, I'll wish you both a good day. Joe Fladgate'll have my horse ready. Thank you for the tea, ma'am. I'm glad I was able to be of service to you."

Beyond the open parlour door Charity Poole stood in the hallway, as she had been for some while, holding his hat and stick.

George Bashford closed the rectory gate firmly behind him and set off along the path across the village green, making towards the street of cottages on the further side.

A grey dusk had overtaken the day. Mothers were calling their children in from play to their supper, and the first farmworkers—those from Godsell's, the nearest farm—could be seen making their way down the lane from the hill fields.

239

The young man walked slowly, disregarding this homely scene.

He had always been more than ready to feel sympathy for Esmond Bates, he told himself; but not any more. The man was a fool. Worse, he was eaten up with self-pity. It was impossible to feel sorry for someone like that. There was something almost unhealthy about him. He loved his wife, yes. But it was not what one could call an honest love. There was some strange obsession there. And his behaviour at the rectory just now had been markedly odd.

Just as well that nothing had been said about that ugly business at the Fordhouse.

George Bashford himself was no stranger to jealousy. His late wife Isabelle had been four years his senior and had allowed this difference in their ages to dwell too much upon her mind.

She had been an attractive, lively woman and he had loved her sincerely. But she was also vain and quick-tempered, inclined to fly into sudden rages over trifling incidents. Bashford had been as faithful and as attentive a husband as most, yet Isabelle frequently accused him of admiring other women more, of staring too long at one or talking too much to another at the various assemblies they went to while staying with her family in Lewes.

Sometimes her accusations were not entirely without ground, for he was a man who enjoyed a pretty face and the stimulation of attractive company.

Her pregnancy had quietened her a little. But towards the end, when the coming child distorted her figure and bloated her features, the old jealousies returned, now directed at the women working about the farm since Bashford seldom went far from the house.

He never understood what it was she needed. If he said he loved her, she would either cling to him, or start to cry, swearing he didn't mean it. If he said she was beautiful, she would rush to a mirror and weep over the puffed reflection, calling him liar. If he praised her fine needlework, even that was not enough.

It was insecurity, he supposed. Though why she should be

240

insecure with a good home and no financial worries baffled him.

There was something about Isabelle that he sensed now in Esmond Bates, something indefinable. A tone of voice, a look, a facial expression, a gesture. He could not place it quite, and it disconcerted him.

He came off the green and began walking along the cobbled footway edging the street. Greetings were called out from several of the open cottage doorways, but he answered distractedly, his thoughts still with those at the rectory.

No, he would waste no more of his time in sympathy with the Reverend Mr Bates, he decided. His feelings lay entirely with the dear, defenceless creature who bore his name, and little else. Certainly not the happiness of being his wife.

Had it been anyone but her, Bashford would have said that Frank Morgan was welcome to cuckold the man. But as it was, Morgan needed checking sharply. There must be no risk of the affair at Buckfield becoming public knowledge.

And what was even more important, there must be no danger of the stallion leader trying his game on Rachael Bates a second time.

27

Not all farmworkers were making their way directly homewards. There were some whose route led them not down, but across the top of the hill pastures and beyond the boundary of Weatherfield to where a gnarled hawthorn marked the start of a winding track, now worn to a hollow way, descending between furze-dotted banks to a gap in the hedge bordering the lane.

Across the way, the door to the alehouse stood ajar, spilling yellow lamplight out into the dusk and drawing the thirsty workers moth-like through the gap and over the lane to its haven.

By eight o'clock, when George Bashford drove up in his trap, the ale-room already contained most of its regulars. A haze of fresh pipe tobacco hung on the air of the flagged passage and the rumble of country voices came from the further end.

The voices were silenced for a moment as he opened the ale-room door, and several of the customers made haste to touch their hat brims.

"Evenin', Mr Bashford. Evenin', sir."

He responded, greeting many by name as he came down the steps into the room and made his way over to the counter. Conversation broke out anew in his wake. A labourer leaning an elbow against the counter straightened up and nodded deferentially to him, then rapped on the wooden surface with his beer-pot.

"Mrs Flynn! Are you there? You're keepin' a customer a-waitin'."

A voice from somewhere beyond shouted an indistinct reply.

"She won't keep you more'n a minute, sir. Just fetchin' us in a barrel."

A faint vibration started up in the passage outside and grew to a reverberating clatter as Jack Adams pushed in through the side door, rolling the new cask in front of him. With a dextrous heave he set it up on end, then moved aside to make room for his aunt, following in behind, to set about tapping it.

George Bashford watched, thinking to wait until she was done before getting her attention; but Jack noticed him there and stammered out a greeting, and Molly Flynn glanced up sharply over her shoulder.

The surprise in her face changed swiftly to a smile of welcome.

"Mr Bashford! Well, and how are you, sir?"

She completed her task and got up to face him across the counter.

"I'm well, thank you, Mrs Flynn. And yourself?"

"Fair. What can I get you, sir?"

"A pint of your cider will do me nicely."

He spread out some coins.

She nodded to Jack to attend to a customer waving an empty beer-pot for service at the other side of the room, and served the farmer herself. The cider was cold and sharp and he drank it with evident enjoyment while she watched, her shrewd gaze never leaving his face.

He set the half-drained pot down at last and wiped the back of a hand across his mouth.

"I'm looking for Frank Morgan—"

"That devil!"

"—is there anyone here can tell me where to find him, d'you know? I want to see him tonight if I can."

"I'll ask for you." She raised her voice above the hubbub of conversation. "Harry! Harry Davies!"

"Harry Davies!" several voices echoed. "Mrs Flynn's wantin' you."

A short rotund figure in leather gaiters detached itself from a group occupying the settles around the open hearth and made its way over.

"Farmer Bashford's asking after the stallion leader," said Mrs Flynn. "You were drinking wi' him Tuesday last, didn't I hear?"

"Aye." The horse dealer nodded. "Likely he'll still be up at Padley's place. His stallion's been kept here these past weeks."

"He's not at Padley's now," said Bashford. "I've enquired already."

"Then I can't be of help to you, sir. He said nothing to me where he might be moving on to." The little man glanced mischievously across the counter and winked. "Mebbe you should be asking Dinah."

Mrs Flynn bridled up at once. "You leave our Dinah out of it, Harry Davies! She's not kept informed about him any more'n the rest of us."

"No. Wait." Bashford put out a restraining hand. "Is Dinah here?"

Her mother jerked her head. "Aye. She's in the back."

"D'you think I might have a word with her?"

"Of course you can, sir. Surely. Take your drink through wi' you. She'll be pleased to see you, she will. Jack! Leave that for a minute. Show Mr Bashford along to the kitchen."

Nodding his thanks to Harry Davies, the farmer ducked under the counter and followed Jack Adams through the side door.

The alehouse kitchen was a spacious room, furnished with a scrubbed-top table and several old but comfortable chairs. A large oak cupboard stood against one wall, a long-case clock against the other, and the hearth and baking oven took up the remaining wall space. The stone-flagged floor was covered with rag rugs and there were pots of geraniums set out along the window sill at the far end by the outer door.

Dinah was sitting in a low chair, her back to the lamplight, her baby at her breast.

When Bashford came into the room she covered herself with a corner of her shawl, but otherwise made no attempt to conceal herself from either her visitor or cousin. There was nothing immodest or improper about a young child feeding in company.

Even so, he said at once, "I've come upon you at an awkward time. Shall I—?"

"No, no, Mr Bashford. Please stay. She'll be finished in a minute. Sit yourself down, why don't you, and finish your drink."

The baby made little wet smacking noises and gave a sleepy cry of protest as her mother lifted her from the breast.

"There, little 'un, that's enough. You're growing as fat as a tunky pig, you greedy madam." Dinah looked up at Jack. "Take her from me, will you, love? Walk her round a bit till she's got her wind up. And don't you look at Mr Bashford like that, neither! You'll need to be used to doing it once Lottie's baby's come."

Jack took little Belle gently in his arms and set her against his shoulder.

244

"You know he's marrying, don't you, sir?" she added, pulling up the neck of her blouse beneath the shawl.

"I had heard something about it."

Bashford nodded at Jack before draining the last of the cider. The other grinned back, sheepishly.

"It was good of you to let her stay on at the farm cottage those weeks."

"The place was standing empty. Look"—he put the empty beer-pot on the table—"I won't stay long, Dinah. I merely came in to ask if you know where I can find Frank Morgan."

"Frank?"

"Aye. It's—er, a private matter."

Dinah finished fastening the long row of buttons.

"He's moved out the other side o' Weatherfield."

"Where, d'you know?"

"Stillborne's."

Bashford was surprised. "Stillborne doesn't breed. He buys his horses in. Why should Morgan go there?"

She looked down at her hands and after a moment answered quietly, "He's been hurt. Got in a fight a while back. He needs to rest up a bit afore he starts the autumn fairs. I'd have had him here to look after, Mr Bashford, but my mother's so set against him."

"I know."

"Mr Stillborne's gi' him a place for a week or so. Just till his ribs mend."

"Well, thank you for the information." Bashford moved towards the door. "I'll ride over and see him first thing tomorrow."

"Will you . . . that is, would you be kind enough to gi' him a message from me? It's about our Belle's christening."

He hesitated. What he had to thrash out with the stallion leader was hardly a piece with family messages.

However—"Of course. What is it you want to tell him?"

"It's the time o' the service. We've settled it now. Straight after evening prayer on the fifth o' September. He said not to expect him to show up . . . but I'd like him to know when it's to be, even so."

"Then I won't forget. Evening prayer. September the fifth."

"We're having a bit of a celebration here after. You'd be—"She hesitated; then went on quickly, "You'd be very welcome to join us, sir, if you'd care to."

"Thank you." He smiled at her. Then remembered something. "Mrs Bates is to be sponsor at the christening, isn't she?"

"Yes, that's right."

"Is she the only one?"

"Oh, no. There's Jack's Lottie."

He looked thoughtful. "Didn't you tell me you were calling your little girl Isabelle?"

"Belle. That's right, sir. You said at the time you'd not mind her being named after Mrs Bashford."

"I remember."

He fell silent for a moment or two; then smiled again. "What would you say to me being a third sponsor? It's usual, I believe, for a girl child's god-parents to include one to be god-father." It would be nice to share in this young life with Rachael Bates. "It seems only reasonable. I mean, if the child's to take the name of my late wife."

Dinah stared at him. "Oh . . ." Her eyes shone. "Jack! D'you hear that? Mr Bashford's asking to be sponsor wi' Mrs Bates and Lottie!"

"That's very k-kind of him. Very kind indeed."

"What's more, she was born in my house, so it's fitting I should have some responsibility for her. Good. We'll call that settled, then. I'll inform the rector of the new arrangement."

"And you'll be coming along after to wet Belle's head wi' a drop o' mam's best?"

"Gladly."

He nodded to her, pleased; then, turning, walked over to the passage door.

"Oh—don't go through the back!" Dinah called out. "Jack—here, gi' me the baby. Show Mr Bashford out the front way, will you?"

A little while after he had gone, Molly Flynn came in from the ale-room.

"Where's Mr Bashford?" She looked around the kitchen, frowning. "I was wanting a word wi' him. Never mind, it'll have to do another time."

She sat down on a chair and pressed her hand against the small of her back, grimacing a little at the dull ache. "He come asking after that blasted Frank Morgan."

"I know," Dinah said patiently. "Private business, he told me. Oh, Mam . . . you'll never guess what he's said. He wants to be Belle's sponsor, along wi' Mrs Bates!"

"Lord above!" Mrs Flynn's sharp features took on a look of astonishment. "Why ever should he do a thing like that?"

"It's on account of us calling her Belle. Like his poor dead wife. And being born at the farm, an' all."

"Well!" Her mother began to smile. "You were clever there, our Dinah, and no mistake. What did I tell you? You play your cards right and who knows but there won't be another Belle Bashford up at Spring Hill."

The other looked up quickly from the baby asleep in her arms.

"What you going on about, Mam?"

"Getting yourself in wi' Farmer Bashford. That's what I'm on about, my girl."

"Oh, don't start on that again. He's not interested in me. Not that way. Don't you think I'd know it if he was?"

"Now look, our Dinah. Use your head. Think. He didn't come here tonight just on account o' that dratted Frank Morgan. And you can't tell me he started on about being this little 'un's sponsor just on a whim o' the moment. Not a man like that. Can't you see it yet?"

"See what?"

"He's trying to get hisself closer in wi' you, that's what."

Dinah let out a peal of laughter. "Oh, Mam! You an' your notions. It's that Mrs Bates the man's struck with, not me."

"Mrs Bates? The parson's wife? But she's a married woman."

"I didn't mean it that way. Lord, how your mind does jump. I only meant he has a fancy for her, that's all."

247

"Now don't you start on that tack again, Dinah. It won't wash wi' me. It's *your* chance, not her'n at the rectory. And you take it whilst it's offered, my girl. Show the man you're willing."

Dinah made a sound of impatience and turned her head away. When she spoke again, her voice had grown suddenly weary.

"Let it drop now, Mam. Will you? It's no use you going on so. If you want the truth, I'll tell you. I'm to be married already. Frank's finally asked me."

Mrs Flynn sprang up from her chair.

"What! I won't believe it!"

"It's true. He asked me when he was here last."

"And you said naun of it to me—your own mother?"

"I was going to tell you. Oh, sit down and stop working yourself into such a pet! I did mean to tell you. I didn't suppose you'd be too pleased to hear about it, that's all."

Molly Flynn re-seated herself angrily and stared at her daughter in silence.

After a while she said in a bitter voice, "What's he up to now, eh? What's he planning on? He hasn't made you wait all this time only to ask you so sudden-like, not wi'out there's some reason behind it."

"He loves me, Mam!" Dinah cried out in protest. "He loves little Frankie and Belle. He wants us all to be together, a proper family. He told me so."

"That's his story, is it? The black devil!" Her mother glared at her. "Well, I'll soon change his tune for him. You see if I won't."

When George Bashford went after the stallion man the following morning, Morgan was out in the pasture behind the Stillborne farm buildings exercising his Shire.

Catching sight of him from the lane, Bashford walked his own animal as far as the gate before dismounting, and waited until the black stallion had turned at the head of the field before waving to get the rider's attention.

The great horse was brought at a canter towards him, clods of earth flung up behind the powerful hooves. His

248

leader rode bareback, gripping him behind the shoulders with his knees, his hands buried in the flowing jet mane.

Skilfully he guided the horse to a side-stepping halt beside the gate.

"Mr Bashford?"

The other touched his crop to his hat. "I'd like a word with you, Morgan, if you have the time."

"A word about what?"

"It would be easier to talk if you dismounted."

"Very well." The stallion leader swung himself down and faced him across the gate. "Now then, what's it you want with me?"

"I see broken ribs don't keep you from riding."

"My ribs—? They're mending well enough."

Bashford nodded. "A fight, I believe."

"A fight it was."

"I heard about it."

"Did you, now?"

"Buckfield, wasn't it? The Fordhouse?"

Frank Morgan stared into the other's face, the dark eyes narrowing.

"Where did you learn that?"

"From the woman you tried to debauch."

"What? Oh, now, Mr Bashford . . ." Morgan made a poor attempt at a laugh. "What story's this you're trying to sell me?"

"It's no story. That poor creature is near out of her mind with the shock of it. Aye, and the shame, too. You couldn't leave her alone, could you? There's a devil in you, Morgan, that drives you on to satisfy your lust when and where you will—and be damned to the damage you do!"

An angry flush coloured the stallion man's face.

"You've no right to talk to me that way, Bashford. What bloody business is it of yours, what I do with my women?"

"Rachael Bates is not one of your women." The other clenched his fist on top of the gatepost. "Never mind that she lives a respectable life, married to a clergyman. In her own right, she's a sweet, innocent young creature and what you tried to do to her that night was nothing short of rape."

"Oh, so it's rape, is it? You weren't there, so why get so excited about it? How d'you know she didn't *want* me to have her? I don't know what tale it is she's been telling you, but she'd hardly admit to wanting it as much as me, would she, now? I mean, it wouldn't sound right, coming from such a 'sweet, innocent creature'."

"Damn you, Morgan," Bashford said hotly. "By God, I wish I'd been there myself to smash your ribs. You wouldn't have got away so lightly, I can tell you!"

"You may threaten me as much as you want if it helps to salve your injured pride." Frank Morgan hitched the leather belt at his waist. "Don't think I don't know which way the wind blows with you, Bashford. You want her for yourself and you're put out that some other man's beaten you to it."

For a long moment the two glared tensely at each other across the barrier of the gate; and it was the stallion leader who dropped his gaze first.

"She's taken it badly, has she?"

"Bad enough."

"Nothing happened, you know."

"Not physically, may be."

"Well . . . what's a few kisses?" Morgan looked out over the pasture. "You mustn't hold me too much to blame. She's a very desirable woman."

The other said nothing.

"That husband of hers can't be much of a man. I might've done him a good turn there."

"Leave it!" Bashford said harshly.

The stallion man pushed aside a clod of turf with the toe of his boot. "You didn't mention any of this business to Dinah, I hope."

"No."

"Thanks. I'm grateful."

"I don't want your gratitude. Dinah's a fine girl and I don't like to see her hurt."

"Did you know I've asked her to wed me?"

"About time."

There was another silence.

A blackbird alighted on the hedge beside the gate and began a trial run of notes. Then thought better of it and flew away.

"You'll keep it to yourself, Morgan, won't you? This affair?"

"Yes. It wouldn't do for Dinah to find out. Not now."

"Not just Dinah. The whole village."

Morgan nodded.

"And that's an end of it? You won't go trying any more of your tricks?"

"No," the stallion man lied, smiling. "The field's all yours, Mr Bashford."

The other frowned and started to speak, but thought better of it.

After a pause he said as casually as he could, "I called to see Dinah at the alehouse last night."

"I was wondering how you knew where to find me."

"I've a message from her. About the little girl's baptism. The service is to be held after evening prayer on September the fifth. She'd like you to be there."

"Then I'll have to disappoint her."

Bashford's horse shook its head irritably to clear the flies from its eyes, jerking the reins. He checked it, and looked back.

"*I* shall be there. I suppose you ought to know, since you're the child's father. I'm to be sponsor, with Mrs Bates."

A cunning expression came into the other's eyes. "Is that a fact, now? Sponsor with Mrs Bates?"

"Yes."

"I see. You're interested in my daughter's religious welfare, are you, sir?"

"I shall make it my interest, yes."

"That's uncommonly generous of you." The irony in Morgan's voice was not lost. "You and Mrs Bates as god-parents! I hope she realises how fortunate she is."

28

"Dost thou, in the name of this child, renounce the Devil and all his works, the vain pomp and glory of this world, with all covetous desires of the same, and the carnal desires of the flesh, so that thou wilt not follow nor be led by them?"

Esmond Bates lowered his book of Offices and looked at his wife, standing before him with Dinah Flynn's baby daughter in her arms.

"I renounce them all," she responded in a clear voice.

He turned to Charlotte Smith beside her, repeating the question of renunciation; and then to George Bashford. Bashford cleared his throat noisily before making his response, but his eyes never wavered from the minister's.

"I renounce them all."

The service of baptism continued, with further prayers and exhortations to those present to be God-fearing and vigilant, that the child might be brought up to lead a godly and Christian life.

Then, at a nod from her husband, Rachael stepped forward to the carved stone font and carefully laid the baby in his arms.

"Name this child."

"Isabelle Rachael."

It had been sorely against Esmond's wishes that she should be given his own wife's name, and he had argued at some length with her to change her mind and call her by some other. Rachael had been obdurate; and it was with something of a bad grace that he now removed the shawl and lowered the plump infant into the font.

At the touch of cold water on her naked flesh, Belle let out a scream of indignation and continued to bawl lustily throughout the act of baptism.

Molly Flynn, among the witnesses, said with some satisfaction, "That's the Devil out of her," and was promptly hushed by the verger, Ezra Jolly.

Holding her in a practised grip by the ankles and the nape of the neck, the rector lifted the dripping, screaming infant into the shawl held ready, and then took the towel Jolly handed him to mop at the soaked cuffs of his white linen surplice.

The remainder of the service was now concluded and the baby removed to one of the box pews to be dried and dressed. The woollen shawl, damp with holy water, was carefully rolled up and put safely by. It would later be placed at the foot of Belle's cradle to protect the sleeping infant from the forces of evil.

The act of immersion appeared to have filled the small congregation not so much with spiritual thanksgiving as with a united thirst for the free ale now awaiting their consumption. And it was with some rancour that Esmond observed how they could scarcely bring themselves to wait for his final amen before surging out of the church porch.

What had this service been to them, after all, but an act of superstitious observance? They were happy now, he supposed, that the seal of respectability had been set upon another of their village bastards; just as they were happy that he was calling the banns of the marriage between Jack Adams and a woman already heavily pregnant with the fruit of her unchastity.

He made a sound of distaste, and turned away.

It had already been arranged that Rachael was to share Jack's waggon with the Flynns. They were the first vehicle to start away from the church; followed by George Bashford in his trap and behind him, strung out along the narrow lane to Troy Town, carts and vans conveying what seemed to be half the population of the district.

Esmond Bates, not unnaturally, had been unwilling to accept any invitation to attend the alehouse celebrations.

"Is this not carrying your obligation too far?" he had earlier admonished Rachael. "I have exercised the utmost patience over this business—though the Lord knows, it is irregular enough for the wife of a minister to sponsor a bastard at baptism."

"A bastard is still a soul to be saved," she had answered coolly. "Or does the state of holy matrimony in some way advance the unchristened soul further along the path to salvation?"

Her argument had only served to increase his annoyance.

"Notwithstanding, you are sponsoring the wretched infant and it will bear your name for the rest of its life. Surely that is honouring the Flynns sufficiently without needing to be present at this . . . this junketing?"

"I wish to go, Esmond. For pleasure. For amusement. Do I have to give a reason? And since it might seem odd if I went alone, I venture to suggest that you accompany me. Most of the parish will be there to celebrate. Don't you think it would be a nice gesture for you to be seen enjoying yourself amongst them for a change?"

He had reminded himself that she was still not recovered from the indisposition suffered in Lewes; and, against his better judgment, had at length given in to her request.

His critical attitude remained unaltered, however. And on the day itself he believed he had the perfect excuse for being absent from the gathering: the sudden onset of a severe chill combined with one of his headaches. After the service he had intended to find Rachael to explain how feverish he felt, and suggest they return instead to the rectory. She could prepare a hot posset for him and read aloud while he rested in the darkened study.

But the tiny pearl buttons fastening the surplice cuffs stuck in the sodden material of the loops and the verger's thick rough fingers made a slow job of getting them all undone. By the time Esmond had finished changing in the vestry and put on frock-coat and hat, Rachael had already left with the rest, and he stood alone at the lychgate staring angrily along the deserted lane, his head throbbing and a nervous tick jerking the muscle of his jaw.

A short while later Ezra Jolly drove him out to the alehouse in pursuit of his wife: an act of Christian charity, because it was far out of the verger's way and the old man held neither with drink nor with the Flynns nor with the baptising of their bastards.

As the cart neared the house, the ale distributed by Molly Flynn could already be making itself heard in snatches of song and cheerful shouts of laughter; and no sooner had Esmond alighted than Jolly drove away, whipping his horse into a shambling trot as though the Tempter himself might suddenly appear at the open door and beckon him inside.

The clergyman stood for a time in the gathering dusk of the lane, then crossed slowly to the alehouse steps. Inside the doorway a couple broke apart, startled by his silent appearance, and seeing who it was, let him go past before returning to each other's embrace.

He continued along the passage, faster now, intent only on finding his wife and taking her back at once to the rectory. He had never set foot inside the alehouse before and had no idea where he should begin his search.

So it was that he found himself standing at the top of the steps leading into the crowded ale-room.

"Why, 'tis Parson Bates! Look 'ee, the parson's here!"

Through the haze of drifting pipe smoke he could make out little but a bank of faces turned towards him.

"Come on away in, sir. Have a drink wi' us!"

"That's right, Mr Bates. You come an' sit yourself in here for a bit. Joe! Fetch the man a drink. And look sharp, now. There'll soon be none left at the rate it's going."

"No—no, I won't stay . . . most kind, but I'm looking for my wife."

Esmond made his apologies firmly, but none of the men seemed to hear him. Hands reached out and took him by the arm and he was drawn down the steps and into the crowd.

Someone pushed a stool into the back of his legs and he sat down on it awkwardly.

"There y'are, sir. Get that into you."

Someone else closed his fingers around the handle of a beer-pot, the ale slopping over the rim and on to his frock-coat.

255

"Good health to you!"

He looked around. Heads were turned expectantly, waiting, beer-pots upraised. The heat from the packed bodies and the rank smell of sweat mingling with lamp oil, tobacco and ale fumes were beginning to make him feel nauseous.

"My wife—"

Those nearest thought he was proposing a toast and there immediately went up a cry of "The parson's wife, God bless her!" echoed in various forms by those around and drowning the rest of his words.

"Drink up now, Mr Bates. Let's see the bottom o' that mug!"

Esmond took a deep breath. If he drank, perhaps they would let him go. He raised the pot to his lips, drawing a cheer from his audience. He drank again, taking long gulps of the ale until his head was tilted back and the beer-pot upside down to show that it was empty.

"That's the way, man! Enjoy yourself. Go on. Have another. It's all free tonight."

"No. Thank you. That was enough. I have to be on my way now."

But again, no one heard him and when he attempted to stand up the crush of bodies forced him down again on to the stool. His head ached intolerably.

"Please! I really must insist," he said loudly.

"But you've only jus' this minute come in." A red-faced man, grinning slackly, thrust another pot into his hands. "Why d'you wan' a go leavin' us so soon, eh? C'mon now, I'll gi' you 'nother toast."

He raised his voice to a drunken bellow.

"The Queen, lads! The Queen!"

The rest responded with enthusiasm. But then, seeing that the rector did not drink, they gradually fell silent. He looked about him. And shamed by his own apparent disloyalty, forced himself to gulp down a little of the tepid ale.

There were murmurs, but the renewed swell of voices covered them and the red-faced toper behind patted him familiarly on the shoulder.

A dull rage began to build up within Esmond Bates. He did not want to be here. He did not want to be in this crowded, stinking place, surrounded by drunken peasants, being forced to share their coarse enjoyment and their company. From the bottom of his heart he despised them all, the lot of them, with their stupid slow speech, their superstitions and their uncouth country manners.

"Wha—!"

The man at his shoulder reeled backwards, ale slopping down his clothes as the clergyman suddenly sprang up, knocking the stool sideways. Gaping, he reached out to steady himself, but Esmond thrust him roughly away and began pulling at the men in front, struggling to get through to the steps.

They moved aside. And though there was some good-hearted banter, the less good-hearted comments were louder.

"Oh, let him go if he chooses," someone shouted. "He's never liked our company, that 'un."

"Aye, let him go, damn him—"

"All the way back to wherever he come from."

"But he can leave his little wife. We don't mind her!"

The last sally provoked much laughter, and Esmond paused at the top of the steps and looked sharply round to try to identify the speaker. They fell silent under the chilling anger in his face and there were some heads turned away and throats noisily cleared.

Icily he said, "You would be well advised to curb your ignorant tongues. My wife's good name is to be respected here."

The taunt had heaped further fuel on his anger and he did not trust himself to say anything more, but swung on his heels and went out into the passage, walking blindly until he reached the open kitchen door.

Dusk had drawn in and the oil lamps lit, illuminating the group of women inside the room with a soft radiance.

In the shadow beneath the scrubbed-top table, little Frankie, dressed in long white petticoats, played with his new toy, a little wooden horse on wheels which Jack Adams had made to keep him quiet during the church service.

257

As Esmond Bates came in through the door, Frankie pushed the toy along the floor towards him. In his haste and his distraction the rector failed to see it in time and kicked against it with his foot, sending it crashing into the table leg.

Frankie let out a wail of anguish and stared up at the strange man, tears filling his dark eyes. With an unsteady finger he pointed at his broken horse, then looked back again; but the man ignored him.

"I am searching for my wife," Esmond said before anyone had time to react; and his sharp tone brought wondering glances from the women. "Where is she?"

Dinah Flynn was the first to speak. Taken aback by the curtness of his manner and his tense expression, she said, concerned, "Why . . . last time I saw Mrs Bates she were out in the garden. Is anything the matter, sir?"

He ignored her question. "The garden. How do I get to the garden?"

"Just go back through the passage the way you come, sir. There's a wicket gate at the side o' the house and a path beyond." She stared at him, and asked again, "Is anything wrong?"

"No, no. That is . . . I feel unwell. We must leave at once."

The acrid taste of the ale fouled the back of his throat and he grimaced.

"Oh, dear. I'm sorry about that." Dinah hushed her tearful son, holding his face against her skirts. "Just when everybody were enjoying themselves, an' all."

"Perhaps you ought to sit yourself down for a bit, sir?" suggested one of the other women, and he saw that it was Charity Poole. "You do seem flushed."

"No. Thank you, no. I must find my wife."

He turned away from them and hurried out again through the door, leaving the group to glance at each other in silence, eyebrows raised; and then, once his footsteps had died, break into speculative gossip.

The alehouse garden and the orchard beyond had been especially prepared for the christening celebrations. Tables and benches were set out on the grass and the apple trees

258

hung with lanterns whose glass had been masked with coloured paper. Now that evening had fallen these were lit, and the whole area prettily transformed into a miniature pleasure ground.

The lantern light lent a theatrical glow to the rowdy scene taking place. Groups of children whooped and screamed in play, running in and out among the trees; their parents sat at the tables, engaged in the more serious activity of drinking and becoming increasingly more affectionate, or morose, or argumentative, as their individual natures moved them; while Molly Flynn and her helpers passed to and fro with half-gallon jugs of ale to refill the fast-emptying pots.

Not only local families were there. A large group of hop-pickers, travelling back into Sussex from the fields of west Kent, had stopped earlier in the day at the alehouse to break their journey and had lingered on.

The screams and shouts, the outbursts of laughter and singing, led Esmond Bates directly to the scene and he stood on the brick path, frowning, looking quickly from table to table and from one knot of figures to another.

Suddenly he checked and raised himself on his toes, craning his neck to see better over the heads of those standing. Then began weaving his way hastily towards a small group standing in the glow of an uncovered lamp which lit the steps to the house cellar.

Its light fell directly upon a young woman whose back was turned to him, but he would have recognised anywhere the India shawl she was wearing. It was one he had bought for his wife as a betrothal gift, and to get it had meant the sacrifice of some of his most prized books and his silver inkstand, presented to him on his ordination. The shawl was of cashmere, woven in an unusual pattern and fringed with silk, and Rachael always wore it—as now—over the same gown, a dove-grey wool which matched its soft colours.

Relieved to have found her so soon, Esmond came up behind and touched her shoulder.

"Rachael—"

The young woman turned, startled. It was not his wife.

Finding a complete stranger in these familiar clothes threw

him into momentary confusion and he stood stock still, staring as though he were seeing a ghost.

"Yes?" The woman looked him up and down in a drunken, unsteady manner. "What d'you want?"

He somehow found his voice. "I . . . I apologise. I thought for a moment you were my wife."

"Your wife? God help us!" She started laughing and turned away to the others saying, "D'you hear that? A parson's wife? I ask you—do I look that respectable?"

She was dark-eyed like a gipsy, and though she was the same height and build as Rachael, Esmond Bates could see now that she was some years older. Belatedly he recalled that his wife had attended the church wearing a gown of violet silk which had come from the late Isabelle Bashford's wardrobe.

He bent forward and examined the India shawl closely under the light. No, he had not been mistaken: this *was* Rachael's.

Angrily he said, "Where did you get this?" and reached out as though to snatch it from the woman's shoulders.

Immediately, one of the men in the group, a short thick-set fellow, pushed forward.

"What's it to you where she got it?"

"The shawl is my wife's! Yes—and the gown is hers also. I demand to know what this woman is doing wearing them!"

She tossed her head and glanced at him warily out of the corners of her eyes.

"They're mine. I bought 'em."

"Where did you buy them?" The notion flashed through his mind that Effie Underwood's relative, after bringing Rachael into Heathbury, must have disposed of her box of belongings when he found it still in the trap. "I repeat, these clothes belong to my wife and you have no right to them."

"An' I'm tellin' you, they're mine. I bought 'em."

"In Heathbury?"

"Heathbury?" She nudged her companion. "Who said anythin' 'bout Heathbury?"

"Where, then?" Esmond persisted angrily.

"Buckfield".

"Are you certain?"

The thick-set man spoke again. "She's certain. An' I was there to see it. Fair an' proper, it was. Nothin' shady. Cost her a week's wages, didn't it, girl?"

She nodded, watching the rector's face. "If these 'ere clothes belong to your missus," she said slyly, "then it must've been her what was up at the Fordhouse that night."

"Which night? What do you mean? I don't understand. What is this—this place?"

"The Fordhouse? It's an inn, o' sorts. We put up there on our way to the hop-fields, start o' last month."

"I still fail to understand what this has to do with my wife."

The woman gave him a loose-lipped grin. "It's like I said. If these 'ere clothes were hers, then she must've been the one caused all the trouble that night."

"Trouble . . .?"

She nodded again. "Though it's hardly likely, is it, now? A parson's lady in a place like that."

A red mist seemed to pass before Esmond's eyes. He felt suddenly light-headed and groped behind for some support. His hand met the cold metal of the rail surrounding the cellar steps, and he gripped it tightly.

"What kind of . . . trouble was it?"

"Oh, you don't want to hear 'bout that! A gent like yourself! It ain't the sort o' thing to go talkin' of in a public place."

The woman winked at the other hop-pickers with her, and they each looked at the rector with a cruel humour in their dark eyes.

"Anyway, it was nothin'. All over an' done with in half-an-hour."

"What was the trouble?" he repeated hoarsely.

"Well, all right. If you must know—" She brought her face closer. "Mind you, I weren't there meself at the time. I only heard 'bout it the next day. Some man had got a woman up at

261

the Fordhouse an' a crowd of her pals turns up fom Lewes an' takes her off him. That was the long an' short of it. Weren't it, Charlie?"

The thick-set man nodded; and she added, "Seems there was a bit o' damage done in the fightin', so the fellow what runs the place, he kept her box o' things and sold 'em off to pay for it all."

"Her . . . box of things?" Esmond echoed woodenly.

"That's right. She left a box. Her clothes, y'know, that sort o' thing. I paid him for this 'ere gown an' the shawl an' a few other bits o' stuff. What become o' the rest, I can't say, I'm sure. But it couldn't have been your wife, now, could it? I mean, not a gent like yourself! It's like I said, you've made a mistake, dearie. One piece o' clothing looks much the same as another, 'specially in the dark."

She pulled the India shawl closer about her shoulders as though defying any further attempt by this stranger to take it from her. He looked capable of anything. There was a sharp, cold glitter in his eyes and his lips were drawn back from his teeth.

Despite herself, the woman shivered suddenly, wondering what she might have stirred up and wishing now that the drink had not made her talk so freely.

For some moments Esmond Bates remained completely motionless, his eyes staring, his whole body rigid like something about to strike out at its prey. But it was not the creature in front of him, decked in his wife's clothing, that he saw. It was Rachael herself, betraying him, gulling him with one wicked lie after another to cover her sinful guilt.

Harshly he said, "Who was the man?"

"The man?"

"The man with her in that place."

The woman shrugged nervously and looked at her companions. They shook their heads.

"We don't know. We weren't there."

"And the others? Her friends from Lewes?"

"That's all I heard!" she protested. "I wasn't there. God's truth. None of us was. We didn't get to hear 'bout it till it was all over!"

The man called Charlie pulled her by the arm. "Come on," he said. "Time we was gettin' back on the road."

He looked curiously at Esmond, but the rector was staring past him; and even when the others picked up their various bundles and moved off across the grass, he remained where he was, his hand still gripping the cellar rail and his eyes gazing sightlessly ahead.

29

So much had happened during the past weeks to distract and unsettle Rachael Bates that her concern about Charlotte Smith had been pushed away to the back of her mind; and if she gave the girl any thought at all, it was no more than a vague remembrance that Effie Underwood had promised to enquire about her at the school in Frog Lane.

She had no possible way of knowing when she first returned to Weatherfield that the young woman referred to, affectionately, as Lottie whom Jack Adams was to marry, was one and the same person as Charlotte Smith. Even when she learned the truth, it seemed such an incredible coincidence that for a time she readily believed this must be some other girl of the same name.

But once Rachael had been told something of the circumstances, and the reason why Charlotte had come to the district, everything became suddenly, distressingly clear.

Dinah Flynn had been her informant. She had been quite open about Frank Morgan's rôle in the business; and if she wondered at all why the rector's wife should look so uneasy at the mention of his name, or why she was so certain that the stallion man must be the father of Lottie's baby, she said nothing. Now that she and Morgan were to be married themselves Dinah wanted only to wipe clean the slate of his past, efface from her mind even the fact that the coming child might be half-brother or sister to her own.

Rachael's first meeting with Charlotte Smith came after the baptism service, when they shared Jack Adams's waggon to the alehouse. She had not seen her since that fateful day in All Souls churchyard, and it discomforted her to have to sit so close to the girl, unable to avoid swaying against the pregnant body and being forced to remember that she had witnessed the actual moment of this child's conception.

She had made an effort at conversation, expressing her regret at the ill fortune Lottie had suffered. But like Dinah Flynn, the girl wanted only to forget the past in her new-found happiness as Jack's betrothed; and Rachael's discomfort had been eased a little by a sense of relief that everything seemed to be turning out so well.

Now, sitting at a table in the lantern-lit garden, she was beginning to take some small pleasure in her own life once more.

The day had been fraught with apprehension for her. Throughout the service she had been dreading the moment when she must turn around and see Frank Morgan standing with the others. But he had not been in the church. When she first arrived at the alehouse she had been tensely expecting at any second to find him beside her. So far, again, there was no sign of him.

Her fear of the stallion man had driven Rachael to seek the protection of George Bashford's company and she welcomed his invitation to sit with him out in the garden. He had been most attentive during the past half hour; and the cider she had drunk was having a pleasantly relaxing effect.

What had become of her husband she could not think. She presumed that he was somewhere in the crowd, and hoped that he would not wish to return to the rectory just yet.

"It's a good thing we chose this particular table," Bashford remarked suddenly, smiling at her over the rim of his beer-pot.

"It is?"

He nodded, gesturing with his head towards a group of merrymakers sitting nearby.

"If we'd sat across there we'd have had the light from that blue lantern in our faces. And you must agree, it scarcely does much for the complexion."

Rachael studied them, and had to admit that he was right.

"As for the red lamp this way,"—he gestured in the other direction—"I could be charitable and say it makes old Juglery look flushed with health. But since I know full well from watching him that it's ale he's aflush with, I must give the old fellow his due for having picked on a light that best disguises his bloom."

Rachael leaned forward and cupped her chin in her hands, her bonnet tilted a little back on her head, her eyes on her companion's strong, regular features.

"And what of our own choice?"

The young man peered up at the lantern suspended from an apple bough above his head. Then his glance returned to hers and he gave a wink.

"I was cunning. I marked this table out especially on account. You see, I reasoned it this way: if you saw me in the wrong light, it could easily miscolour your memories of me. But pink—that's a flatterer."

She smiled. "And how will you remember me?" she asked innocently.

Bashford's expression grew serious. He looked directly into her eyes.

For a moment he did not reply; then he said softly, "I'll always picture you as you are now. A rose. A pink rose. The sweetest blossom I ever saw."

The blood rushed into her cheeks and she lowered her gaze.

"It's true," he persisted gently. "I shouldn't say it, I know. But I can't help myself, so you must forgive me. No—don't turn your head away. I haven't offended you, have I?"

"No," she replied in a low voice. "I'm not offended. But you oughtn't to say any more."

265

"Very well, I won't. I'd do anything rather than displease you. You know that, don't you?"

She looked at him again. "Yes. I do." Then, to cover her embarrassment—"Did . . . did I thank you, by the way? For the gown? It's a beautiful fit. And it goes so well with the shawl I borrowed from Effie. Don't you think?"

His gaze never left her face. "To be honest, I hadn't noticed the shawl. Only the gown itself and how well it becomes you." He reached out a hand tentatively across the table. "Rachael, won't you accept it as a gift from me? Please? I want you to have—"

He broke off, staring past her shoulder. His expression fell.

"What is it?"

"Your husband. I think he's searching for you. Shall I— do you want me to go over and fetch him?" It was hard to keep the reluctance from his voice.

Rachael turned to look behind and saw Esmond a little way off, standing alone.

"Yes . . . Perhaps you'd better. If you wouldn't mind."

The young man got up, ducking his head to avoid their lantern.

"You won't forget what I said just now, will you?" he said earnestly. Before she could reply he was walking quickly away towards her husband.

In the shadows at the far end of the garden, beyond the glow of the coloured lights, hidden from the revellers' eyes by the angle of a stone wall, Frank Morgan stood watching the noisy scene.

He had not meant to be anywhere near the alehouse this evening, not after an argument yesterday with Dinah when she told him hotly that if he could not stir himself to be at the church for the service, she did not expect him to come showing his face for the beer afterwards.

He had spent the afternoon in his temporary billet at Stillborne's farm, lying in the straw of the hay loft and getting thoroughly drunk on a bottle of spirits.

Damn Dinah, he had told himself. Damn her scold's

temper. There was a lot he meant to change once they were married. Besides, what made her think he preferred old mother Flynn's watered ale when he had a bottle of strong liquor all to himself? Much better to lie happily here with his horse for company than have to suffer a rowdy, drink-fuddled crowd at the alehouse.

He could talk to that stallion, say out loud things which he would never in the world have told another living soul: his fear of growing old, of losing his man's strength and virility; his need to be loved, coupled with the opposing force that drove him to treat that love with such callous indifference; his feelings of rootlessness, of not belonging, which had haunted him ever since childhood.

This afternoon his thoughts had been drifting in haphazard fashion between Rachael Bates and George Bashford (whose attachment to Mrs Bates he was beginning to resent), and his baby daughter, born at Bashford's farm; and thence to another girl-child, born at another farm.

The attack at the Fordhouse had taken him completely off his guard. When his assailants had ridden away, he had been carried half-conscious into the taproom and at length attended to, thoroughly if ungently, by the gorbellied ex-prize fighter who ran the place.

Reviewing his situation in the early hours of the morning, he had decided that he needed somewhere not too far off where he could rest up while the worst of his injuries mended. There was only one such haven he could think of. At dawn, helped into the covered van in which he had arrived so blithely the previous evening, he had turned the horse's head in the direction of the village of Barkham, and Copper's farm.

His luck, it seemed, was starting to come back to him. Old Copper was lying abed with a fractured thigh where a bullock had caught him during a bungled slaughtering, enabling his wife—the companion of that earlier, happier night at the Fordhouse—to keep Frank Morgan's presence on the farm from him.

He had spent much of the following week holed up in the barn loft while flaxen-haired Betty Copper divided the long, uneasy days between her invalid husband, her former lover, the farm work, and her baby daughter.

On the third evening she had brought the young child to the loft for him to see, a black-haired, dark-eyed sturdy infant, the very image of the stallion man's gipsy mother.

His already injured pride had taken a sore blow, but he acknowledged the child as his. As he cradled her in the straw of her proxy father's loft, he had ruefully consoled himself with the thought that even his Shire—the finest stud horse in the southern counties—had occasionally been known to lapse and likewise sire a filly foal.

Now, lying in this other loft at Weatherfield, his thoughts returned once more to Rachael Bates; and the temptation of seeing her again had finally proved too strong to be resisted.

Cursing himself for his weakness, he had thrown the bottle aside and gone out into the failing light and over the fields by the hill track. For the past half-hour he had stood silent and unseen, a melancholy mood depressing his spirits as he watched the dumb show being enacted in the alehouse garden between Rachael and George Bashford.

So absorbed was he by the obvious fancy that had grown between the pair that he did not notice the arrival on the scene of the Reverend Mr Bates, not until Bashford got up to go over to him.

He saw at once that the clergyman was greatly agitated about something, and appeared even more so on finding his wife alone in the farmer's company. Pulling his arm sharply away from Bashford's hand and wheeling about, he strode across to the table where his wife was sitting, and as the light caught his face, Morgan beheld its expression quite clearly.

He moved forward a short way out of the shadows, disquieted by the naked anger he saw there.

Esmond Bates's voice was raised, but the stallion leader could not make out the words. Bashford seemed to be remonstrating with him. He was pushed to one side as the older man reached out and seized his wife by the arm, jerking her so roughly to her feet that her chair fell over backwards and she almost lost her balance. The shawl slipped from her shoulders and Bashford reached down to retrieve it. But before the woman had a chance to take it from him, her husband thrust her away, causing her to stumble again and this time fall clumsily to the ground.

Morgan cursed under his breath and ran across the grass to the darkness of an unlit tree, perplexed as much as disturbed by this extraordinary scene.

He heard George Bashford cry out something and saw him kneel to help the fallen woman to her feet. Then the young man turned on the rector and appeared to be arguing furiously with him. Their raised voices had already attracted the attention of people at the nearby tables, and others were starting to gather round to see what was going on, enabling the stallion leader to come up behind them unobserved.

By now, Rachael was in tears and Bashford, still holding her shawl, had moved in front to shield her from her husband. Savagely, Esmond Bates snatched the wrap from his hands and thrust it towards his face.

"This—this is what I am talking about!" he shouted, loud enough for Morgan to hear him clearly. "You lied to me, Bashford. You and she both. There was no box left in that trap at Heathbury!"

Bashford replied in a quieter voice, but his answer only served to inflame the rector further.

"I can show you where her clothing is. On some other woman's back! There—over there!" He jabbed a finger towards the house.

There were murmurs from the onlookers, and some ribald comments that roused laughter. Ingoring them, Bashford tried to reason; but the other would not listen.

"Move out of my way. This is not your business. Move away from my wife."

"I'll move when you tell me what you mean to do with her. I warn you, sir, if you intend her any harm because of this—"

With a cry of fury the rector lunged out at him, catching him in the chest and sending him staggering backwards into a table. There were shouts of encouragment from those nearest, sensing a fight might be starting, and at the back of the crowd two drunken men began their own noisy argument.

Esmond turned on Rachael and threw her shawl to the ground in a gesture of disgust. Grasping her by the arms, he pushed her in front of him and forced her to start walking, jostling her roughly through the onlookers. Despite her tears she tried to go bravely, but the pain of his fingers digging into the soft flesh grew so unbearable that she cried out.

It was this that finally broke Frank Morgan's control. Shoving aside those in his path, he ran after the couple. But hardly had he gone halfway towards them when someone caught him by the wrist and dragged him aside.

"No! For God's sake, keep out of it!"

"Leave go of me, damn you—" Morgan struggled to loosen George Bashford's grip on him. Over his shoulder he caught a glimpse of Rachael's stricken face turned for a moment towards him at the edge of the crowd.

"Come back!" he shouted.

His cry was either ignored or never heard. Still propelling his wife forcibly in front of him, Esmond Bates disappeared into the darkness at the side of the alehouse.

He renewed his efforts to free himself.

"In Christ's name, man—let me go after them or I'll kill you!"

But Bashford held firmly on to him. "Keep out of it," he repeated between his teeth. "If Bates ever learns your part in the Fordhouse business, God knows, it may well be you that's killed."

Cursing, Morgan swung round and before the other could stall him, struck him a winding blow to the midriff, doubling him up with pain. The onlookers raised a cheer and shouted out to the farmer to get off his knees and fight back.

He staggered up, gasping. As Morgan started to run across the grass, Bashford hurled himself forward and caught him round the legs, bringing him crashing headlong to the ground. The stallion man twisted under the hold and tried to kick his assailant off, but the farmer had him pinned down in a moment and Morgan cried out in agony as the other's knee jarred sickeningly against his injured ribs.

"What's this? What's going on out here?"

Above the hubbub of voices and the screams of children,

270

Molly Flynn could be heard calling sharply from the house steps. The crowd fell back as she pushed through from behind and stopped short, hands on hips, surveying the scene.

"Drunken fighting! I thought so. Come on, break it up. I'll have no drunks fighting on my property!"

Seizing a pint-pot from the nearest table she marched across to the two men still struggling together on the ground and emptied the contents over their heads.

"Jack! Billy!" she shouted over her shoulder. "Move yourselves, wherever you are, and get over here. See this pair off. And I don't want 'em getting back in again, neither."

Frank Morgan held his ribs and groaned.

"Oh, so it's you, is it?" Mrs Flynn glared down at him in the lurid glow of the lantern light. "I might've guessed you'd be mixed up in it." She turned as Jack Adams ran up. "Get him off my property. Damn troublemaker! And his friend as well."

"I can get myself up, thank you."

George Bashford shook off Jack's hand and got to his feet, brushing grass and dirt from his jacket. He glanced at the irate woman in front of him. Recognising now who it was, her expression altered in an instant and she snatched a hand to her mouth.

"Lord above, Mr Bashford! Oh dear, sir, I am sorry. I never realised it were you, or I wouldn't have acted so hasty. Here, let me—"

"I can manage, Mrs Flynn," he answered shortly, wiping the beer from his face and neck with a handkerchief. "There was no need to waste good ale."

Then, turning to the stallion leader still nursing his ribs on the ground—"D'you need a hand, Morgan?"

"Aye, blast you. I think you've cracked me up again."

Bashford bent and helped him to his feet. "I'll see you back to Stillborne's place."

"I can make my own way."

"As you will. I'm sorry if I caused you any hurt."

"Don't you be sorry about hurting that 'un!" interrupted Mrs Flynn at once, glaring at the stallion leader. "He's

271

nothing but trouble. I wish to God he'd clear off for good and never show his blasted face here again."

"You keep out of it, old woman," Morgan said savagely. "The quarrel's between me and George Bashford."

"That's as may be, my lad. But it's my property you've picked to quarrel on—and that makes it my business as much as any. And what's more, I'll not have you brawling wi' the likes of this gentleman when he's an honoured guest here. I'll have the constable on you, see if I don't!"

"No need for the constable," the farmer reassured her hastily. "It's a private matter. I'm sorry we chose such a public place to have it out."

Molly Flynn's face took on a look of suspicion as she glanced from him to Morgan and back again.

"It's not over our Dinah, is it?"

"It's nothing to do with Dinah," said the stallion man curtly.

"You hold your tongue and keep out of it! You're in enough bad water wi' me already. Mr Bashford's done us the kindness to sponsor that baby o' yourn—yet here you are fighting wi' him. And you tell me it's naun to do wi' our Dinah! If it's not over her, why else should you pick a quarrel?"

"Now, Mrs Flynn. Don't go working yourself up into a state about it. As I said before, this is a private matter between Morgan and me, and Dinah doesn't come into it." Bashford gave her a look of reassurance; then called out to the young man standing awkwardly to one side—"Jack! Bring my trap round to the front of the house, will you?"

"Well, go on—do as he asks you! And you lot,"—Mrs Flynn raised her voice to those still looking on—"the fighting's finished, so there's no point in wearing out the grass wi' boot leather. I'm serving no more ale till you're all seated decent at them tables, you hear?"

They responded good-humouredly and she turned again to George Bashford, shaking her head.

"It's best if I don't go in to say goodbye to your daughter," he said. "Not in the state I'm in. Tell her from me that I was sorry to leave without seeing her, will you?"

"I'll do that, sir. And we'll keep the nabble-traps shut on this little business."

He nodded his thanks, and went over to Frank Morgan.

"Come on. Let's get you back. Oh, come on, man—don't push me off like that! You can't walk all the way to Stillborne's as you are."

"I'll manage," the stallion leader said sullenly. "Sore ribs never stopped me yet, so don't go concerning yourself. A brush like that is nothing to me."

He walked away a few steps, then wheeled around.

"But mark what I say. This affair over Mrs Bates isn't finished yet. You look out for me, George Bashford, because by God, I shall be looking out for you!"

30

"Esmond—please . . . You're hurting me!"

Rachael tried to pull free of her husband's grasp, but her plea was ignored.

"Esmond . . ."

She could barely make out his face in the darkness of the lane; but as he turned his head towards her there was sufficient moonlight between the high clouds for her to see the cold glitter in his eyes. Something there froze her. She stood perfectly still, and the fear that had sprung so swiftly upon her in the garden tightened its grip.

This is a nightmare, she told herself frantically. In a moment it will end and I'll wake and find everything quite normal. This is not really happening. I'm only dreaming. I'll open my eyes and see the daylight at the window and Esmond asleep beside me.

The night breeze rustled amongst the trees bordering the lane and she shivered a little as it touched her uncovered shoulders. From the back of the alehouse a short distance away the sounds of celebration carried clearly; and nearer, tethered to cart and van in the next field, the revellers' horses shifted restlessly.

Esmond Bates felt his wife tremble, but her discomfort had no effect on him.

In the dim light he observed coldly that tears streaked her cheeks. Normally it would be more than he could bear to see her in such distress, but now he remained quite unmoved. She would never again have the power to arouse him to feelings of tenderness. She had been so infinitely precious to him, her innocence so dear. A child, almost, to be protected and cherished. His love for her had been the greatest thing in his life.

And now . . .

He swallowed suddenly; and without realising what he was saying, spoke aloud.

"She is as rottenness in his bones."

Rachael started. "Esmond?"

Disregarding her, he spoke again, his voice little more than a whisper.

"A virtuous woman is a crown to her husband. But she that maketh ashamed is as rottenness in his bones."

She bit her lip. She had never known him to be like this before, not even in the worst of his moods. What had happened? Who had he been talking with back there at the alehouse? Was it Frank Morgan? What had they said? How much had he learned?

The questions hammered at her mind. Everything had started so quickly, had changed so fast: one moment she had been happy, at ease, she and George Bashford together enjoying the infectious gaiety of those around them.

And suddenly . . . Esmond. Pulling at her. Shouting. Shaking her. "I have found you out—whore!"

She shivered again.

"Can't we go home now? Please, Esmond? Anything that needs to be said will be better discussed there. We can't stay out all night. Do let's go home."

"Oh . . . yes . . ." The glittering eyes came closer and she smelled the sourness of ale on his breath. "There is much that needs to be said, is there not, my dear? A story? About a lost box? That's it. You shall tell me a story."

Someone came out through the wicket gate at the side of the alehouse and crossed the lane to the field entrance. They heard him whistling in the darkness, the small circle of lamplight swinging this way and that, and then the sound of a horse and trap being led out. It was halted before the house and soon afterwards another figure emerged from the gate and climbed up.

There was the slap of leather.

"Hoa! Get up there!"

The voice was unmistakably that of George Bashford.

As the trap approached, Esmond pulled his wife back into the deeper shadows of the hedge and she had to fight with herself to suppress the cry that rose in her throat, telling Bashford that she was there. He would have helped. He had promised as much, and she believed him. But instinct warned her that to alert him now would only make her situation the more serious; to involve him any deeper in her troubles might well turn Esmond's insane fury upon him, too.

The spark of rebellion died. In silence she shrank back against her husband and the trap went past them into the night.

Esmond Bates remained motionless until the last faint sounds of its progress had ceased. Then he stepped out into the middle of the lane, dragging Rachael with him, and raised his fist.

"You, too!" he called hoarsely. "Yes, you, too, must answer for so much treachery. For it is said, 'Cursed is he that smiteth his neighbour secretly. Cursed is he that lieth with his neighbour's wife'!"

He is mad, she thought frantically. His mind is unhinged. Whatever I say to him now he will not believe. God help me, what am I to do?

Hesitantly she laid a hand on her husband's arm, and in the light of the moon saw his teeth show palely in a death's-head smile as he turned to look at her.

Softly she pleaded, "Esmond . . . it would be best if we went home now. I fear you are not well."

The smile lengthened and became a snarl.

"Not well? Not well, do you say? And who has made me unwell? Answer me. Who is it that has brought me to this condition?" Seizing her by the shoulders he began to shake her. "Whose falseness and deceit have robbed me of my peace of mind—answer me that! I will tell you. My wife. My own wife. That wife whom I trusted to love and obey me always!"

He released her, thrusting her roughly away from him, and they stood facing each other in the lane, silent but for the sound of their rapid breathing, Esmond's face a mask, Rachael's whiter even than the moonlight could bleach it.

After several long moments he started to speak again, his tone now altered and become sinisterly conversational.

"You are right, of course. We cannot spend the night out here, like gipsies. Or hop-pickers. My head burns. I have a chill, you know. I looked for you after the service but you had already left without me. Left without me . . . left me. If only you had stayed behind for just a little while. I am not well. It is your duty to care for me. And yet you gave me no thought. Why did you not wait?"

Rachael cringed back from him. "I thought you would follow."

"And so I did. And I found you. Yes, I found you. And more—"

He broke off. Then, suddenly, swung round and began walking rapidly away along the lane.

She hesitated, looking back towards the alehouse; then slowly turned and followed after her husband.

For fifteen minutes or so they walked on in this fashion, Esmond striding blindly forward, his wife stumbling behind over the dried cart ruts, trying to keep up but falling further and further from him in the darkness. Occasionally she called out to him to wait, but her cries went unheeded.

The night seemed to close in. At first all she could hear was her own sobbing breath and the distant sound of her husband's footfalls. Soon she grew aware that there were unseen things in the high hedges on either side. Sudden rustles and thuds; pattering and scratching; small sly sounds that ceased as soon as she stood still and started up again when she moved on. At one point a sudden loud cough from close by made her cry out in terror.

It was only a cow; and the thought of this warm, harmless creature standing so near had a calming effect on her raw nerves. For a while longer she stumbled forward, still frightened, but less afraid now of the darkness and night noises than she was of the threat which lurked ahead on the lane.

She paused again and turned, listening, alerted by a new sound. A vehicle was approaching from behind.

Relieved, Rachael called out to her husband, ran back a little until she could make out the oncoming cart and stood back against the hedge, waving to attract the driver's attention without startling their horse.

"Who's there?" It was a woman's voice. "Come forward a bit so's we can see you better."

Rachael came on until she was level with the candle-lamps. "Are you by chance going into Weatherfield?"

"We might be, depending on who it is wants to know." The voice was full of suspicion.

"Mrs Bates. Mrs Bates, the rector's wife."

There were two figures in the cart. She peered at them.

"Lord above, Mrs Bates!" cried the nearest. "Whatever be you doing along here at this hour o' the night? 'Tis us—the Pooles."

She grasped the side of the cart in her relief. "Oh, Miss Poole! Thank heavens it's you."

"Just as well it is," said the other, Charity. "You never can tell who might be on the roads after dark. Nobody's safe these days. Come you along, Mrs Bates—" She climbed down and assisted Rachael into the cart. "Wherever is your husband? Don't he know you're out here by yourself?"

"Oh . . . he's gone ahead a little way. He's . . . he's feeling unwell. He wanted to go back to the village as quickly as possible."

"And leave you behind to follow?" Comfort Poole chucked the reins and the pony started forward. "That weren't very sensible of him, if you don't mind me saying."

"Here, now——" Her sister produced a cover from beneath the plank seat and wrapped it around Rachael's shoulders. "You must be perished, walking about wi' no shawl nor nothing on you."

"Yes—oh, yes, my shawl!" She tried to make light of it. "I must have left it behind at the alehouse. Esmond was in such haste to be gone."

"We saw you there," Comfort said, "earlier on."

"Oh?"

"Aye, before you went out to sit in the garden wi' Mr Bashford."

"I didn't notice you."

"No, likely you wouldn't. Mr Bates come into the kitchen after you."

"It isn't my place to say, I'm sure," Charity broke in. "But it's not like your husband to be so careless o' your safety, ma'am. He must know the risk, surely, leaving you alone here?"

Rachael remained silent, and Charity glanced at her sister and went on, "Why, my blood runs cold to think what might've become of you if Comfort an' me hadn't happened along. Suppose now instead of us there'd have been two or three men——"

"Yes. I'm thankful indeed it was you."

"A good thing we made up our minds to come away before trouble started. That Molly Flynn ought to have more sense than go making so free wi' her ale. Not even watered it wasn't, neither. Stands to reason there'd be some as couldn't take it. Soon as ever we heard there was fighting out in the garden, that was it. Away we come."

"Look—there!" Comfort, at the reins, pointed. "Isn't that Mr Bates up ahead?"

They peered forward and in the dim moonlight saw a dark shape moving beneath the overhanging trees.

Rachael called out to him.

The figure paused, allowing the cart to come up alongside and slow to a halt.

"Esmond? Is that you?" She tried to make out his face in the shadows. "The Miss Pooles overtook me on the lane."

"That was convenient." The expression in his voice sounded perfectly normal.

"I'm afraid we can't offer to take you on board as well, sir," said Comfort. "There's not room enough for four. But we'll be glad to see Mrs Bates safe home for you."

"Yes. Please do that. I shall be along directly."

The cart moved on, leaving him standing alone by the side of the lane. He waited until it was some distance off, then began to walk after it, taking care to keep well behind.

Somewhere in the woods to his left a vixen screamed suddenly, piercing the still air with her mating cry; and Esmond Bates smiled joylessly.

"Now—we shall have the truth!"

It was more than an hour later, and Rachael had had time to undress and brush out her hair before she heard her husband's step in the porch below. The house door was slammed behind him and he came straight upstairs to the bedroom and halted in the doorway, facing her, the oil lamp beside the mirror casting his shadow in sharp relief against the open door.

"The truth, mind. Nothing less will content me."

She put down her hairbrush.

"Can't we discuss this in the morning, Esmond?" she begged. "You say you are ill . . . and Lord knows, I'm weary enough myself. A night's rest will benefit us both."

He came further into the room and his eyes moved from her face to their bed, its counterpane neatly folded back and his nightshirt laid out on top.

"So. You expect me to swallow my righteous anger and lie meekly beside you. Is that it?"

She lowered her head.

"Yes, you do well to look ashamed! There will be no sleep for either of us tonight until we have had this matter out."

"What matter? My box, do you mean?"

"Your box, just so. Left so very carelessly in Heathbury. That was what you told me, was it not?"

Rachael swallowed and gave a little nod.

"Answer me! Did you not tell me that your box of

belongings was left by accident in the trap which conveyed you from Lewes? Left, moreover, on the very day you arrived back here with our over-generous friend Bashford?"

"Yes."

"Speak up! I want to hear your lies clearly."

She raised her head and looked directly at him. "Yes, that was what I told you."

"It was a lie."

"Yes, Esmond. It was a lie."

"What then, in fact, had become of this box?"

"I—I—"

"Well?"

Rachael bunched the neck of her white linen nightgown in her hand.

"I . . . mislaid it."

"I already know that you mislaid it," her husband said menacingly. "*Where*, precisely, is the question I wish you to answer."

"And if I do not answer?"

He came swiftly towards her across the threadbare carpet and struck her savagely across one cheek with his open hand. The force of the blow jerked her head backwards.

"I think you *will* answer, Rachael," he told her coldly. "Now, I ask you again. Where did you mislay your belongings?"

Tears of pain, and of fear, ran down her face and soaked into the smocked bodice covering her breast. She nursed her numbed cheek in her palm and fought down the choking sobs to answer before he should strike her again.

"At . . . at Buckfield."

"Ah, now we are getting a little closer to the truth! Come—control yourself. I cannot hear what you say when you cry so noisily. When were you at Buckfield?"

"I . . . I don't recall."

He gripped her by the hair and forced her head over to one side, making her cry out.

"I repeat, when were you in Buckfield?"

"It—it was the day I left the Collinses."

"So." He released his grip and stepped back from her.

"You absconded from the place where I had sent you—sent you, moreover, for your own good. Turned your back on my friends, in whose safekeeping you were—"

"I did not turn my back on them! It was they who . . . who . . ."

"Be silent, I have not finished! How dare you spurn their kindness and charity and desert their house in such a fashion!"

"Esmond—"

"Who was waiting for you at Buckfield?"

"No one!"

He slapped her across the face a second time, knocking her sideways. In an effort to save herself from falling, Rachael grabbed at the chest of drawers behind her; but her hand only caught the lid of the toilet set George Bashford had sent and it fell with a crash from the chest top, scattering its contents over the floor.

She crouched down, her face buried in her arms, but her husband's insane jealousy and anger had driven him beyond all compassion. Reaching down, he hauled her roughly to her feet and pushed her against the side of the bed.

Hoarsely he repeated, "Who was waiting for you at Buckfield?"

Rachael clung to the brass rail at the bed-foot, her body shuddering with uncontrollable sobs. She lifted her face to him, bruises already beginning to swell her cheekbone.

"In God's name, Esmond . . ." The words came in jerks.

"Was it Bashford?"

"No!"

"Who, then? I know there was a man there. I even know the place of your assignation—the Fordhouse." He stared down at her, his fists bunched convulsively. "Answer me. Who was the man?"

"It . . . it wasn't the way you think. No—please, Esmond, don't hit me again." She raised an arm to protect herself. "For God's sake, believe me! It was a trick!"

He stared at her.

"It's true . . . please, please, you must believe me. Arthur Collins himself told me a man had called to fetch me home."

For a while she was overcome by sobs and unable to continue. Then——"I had to go to the marketplace. There—there was a fight. It upset me and—and he gave me something to drink . . . a drug."

Esmond pounced. "*Who* gave you something to drink?"

Rachael shook her head.

"*Who?* Answer me! By Christ, if I have to kill for it, I shall have this man's name."

"It . . . it was . . . Frank Morgan."

The sound he made was the snarl of an animal.

"Morgan. Now we have it!"

"Yes. He—"

"How did he know where to find you?"

"I don't know. Oh, please, believe me . . ."

Esmond Bates walked slowly to the door; turned there, paused, and came back again. His forehead and upper lip were beaded with sweat and the muscle in his eyelid started to twitch.

When he spoke again, his voice trembled with an uncontrollable anger.

"You sent him a message. That—that woman, that Underwood creature, she assisted you, I suppose. Oh, don't try to deny it! It would be like her. She has always hated me."

"No! Effie had nothing to do with it. I swear she didn't."

"And it was her husband—yes, of course. I see it all now. It was her husband and his crowd of wastrels who caused the trouble at Buckfield that night."

Rachael bowed her head.

"They . . . they saved me," she whispered.

"What was that? What did you say?"

"They saved me," she repeated in a stronger voice. "I had been drugged. I told you, Esmond. Why won't you believe me? Morgan had drugged me and . . . and taken me to that place. Arthur Collins—"

"Oh, yes, blame Arthur! It was he engineered the whole sordid business, I suppose?" Esmond sneered.

"He went to Effie's house—"

"That is hardly likely."

"He went to Effie's house. And . . . and then Ralph Underwood came after me."

"Arthur knew, of course, where you had been taken?"

"No. Oh, I don't know. I can hardly remember what happened after Lewes. I—I was in a room with Frank Morgan . . ."

She paused.

Her husband's face tightened. "Yes? Go on."

"He didn't touch me! Nothing happened between us. Oh, Esmond, I swear to God nothing happened . . ."

Sobs overwhelmed her once more and she clung to the bed rail, shaking her head mutely, the long hair sticking in rat's tails across her wet cheeks.

"I don't believe you," she heard him whisper hoarsely. "You were alone with him. Tell me. Were you alone together?"

She nodded.

"And this room. There was a bed? A couch?"

"Nothing happened between us. Nothing . . . nothing . . ."

"He made you his whore."

"No, no! Nothing happened!"

All self-control gone now, Esmond pulled her by the arm towards him and ripped open the bodice of her nightgown, exposing her shoulder and breast. Rachael tried to stop him. He hit her viciously on the side of the head and she fell backwards across the bed. In a frenzy of madness, he began tearing at his own clothing.

"We shall see whether you are a whore or not," he rasped.

"Esmond! Esmond—no!"

He flung the frock-coat from him into a corner of the room and tore the black clerical stock away from its collar-band.

"In all the time of our marriage I have never violated your purity. You were innocent. Untouched. I respected your body . . ."

His trousers were thrown aside and he wound the end of the broad belt round his hand.

". . . this filthy, tainted body!"

Rachael screamed in agony as the leather lashed across the soft flesh of her thigh.

"I will teach you to let other men near you!"

He struck at her again, and again.

"Taking what your husband has always denied himself—"

The belt fell to the floor and he flung himself on top of the weeping, sobbing girl and began ripping with savage force at her nightgown.

Her screams were muffled and she struggled violently under him; but the force of his body held her down. Her shoulders were pressed backwards and his mouth was against her throat. The pain of what he was doing to her was worse than anything she had ever known. For a moment she lost consciousness and then, in the next instant, heard him cry out as though he himself were in agony.

Suddenly his wild movements were stilled and he lay gasping, supine on top of her.

Rachael stared up over his shoulder. The shadow of the lamp flame flickered to and fro across the ceiling. Tears trickled slowly down her throbbing temples into her hair. Her body ached in every joint. Her flesh burned.

After a time her husband shifted himself and she stiffened immediately, fearing he was about to start some fresh assault upon her. But instead, he slumped to one side and began very quietly to weep.

31

The eyes watched him from the shadows. Eyes staring out of the darkness; faces thrusting blindly towards him. The light from the candle in his hand touched them as he passed, throwing grotesque shadows sideways along the wall so that mouths gaped and leered and chins wagged up and down in soundless laughter.

Another man alone in the silent, unlit church at this late hour might have been filled with a superstitious dread at the eerie movement of these nocturnal shades; but Esmond Bates ignored them. And as though his neglect deprived them of their substance, the animation from beyond the grave faded: once he had moved on, the memorials to the dead became shrouded again, their profiles serene, their sightless eyes turning once more upon eternity.

He continued until he reached the end of the south aisle, and stood there for a time, motionless. Then he went a few paces further and the narrow door to a box pew creaked faintly as he swung it open and went inside.

Raising the candle, he found the brass candle-holder on the wall beside the seat, and sat down. The flame flickered uncertainly, steadied, grew higher; and Esmond's eyes became reflected pinpoints of light as he stared unblinkingly ahead into the blackness.

Fingers tightly interlaced between his knees, he hunched himself forward. The frock-coat was unbuttoned, revealing his bare neck, and without the dignity of clerical band and stock he looked shabby, his hair unbrushed and falling forward across his forehead. The candlelight glistened on his skin, showing up deep shadows beneath the eyes, the downward turn of the mouth, the stubble on the cheeks.

Anyone seeing him there might have been forgiven for mistaking him for a much older man, tired and careworn, defeat showing plainly in the slump of his shoulders.

Were Esmond Bates capable of any rational feeling just now, doubtless he would have agreed. But his feelings were not rational and had nothing to do with normal emotions. Once the initial numbness of the attack on his wife had passed, he had been overwhelmed by a terrible sense of loss, as though something fundamental to his self-pride had been forced from him and was gone for ever; followed by a desperate need to find solace, spiritual sustenance, something he might cling to until this fearful madness had lifted from his mind.

Throwing on his clothes, not caring how he dressed, he had left the rectory and stumbled across to the church. Rachael had neither looked at him nor spoken to him; and he had made no attempt to touch her again. He needed to be away from her, away from that room, from the sound of her weeping.

Lifting his eyes, he gazed steadily ahead past the candle flame to the communion rail and the altar beyond. There was nothing there for him but darkness and silence. He inhaled deeply, and smelled the decay in the old fabric of the building, the closeness of the air, a musty staleness as though the breath of countless congregations had been trapped within this little space.

His thoughts fluttered, refusing to settle on anything but one single image: Rachael and Frank Morgan together.

Esmond lowered his head into his hands. He made an effort to clear his mind, to pray. His lips moved, whispering, "Vengeance is mine, I will repay, saith the Lord"; repeating the words over and over again until they became meaningless. Try as he might to concentrate, to reach out beyond himself, that haunting image intruded constantly, shifting and expanding until it filled his whole sight with the vision of his wife lying in the arms of the stallion man.

In the candlelight her naked flesh seemed to gleam like pearl against the swarthiness of Morgan's body, her hair falling loosely over his chest, her hands moving in slow sinuous caresses that made Esmond groan aloud in torment.

What should he believe? Where was the truth in it all?

He did not know. Some corner of his mind, where sanity still held, clung to the thought that Rachael was innocent, the hapless victim of savage circumstance, that her protestations had been genuine, that her only guilt had been to keep him so long in ignorance.

But then again came the sly, insidious whispering to mock him: no, she lied, she tricked and deceived you, laughed behind your back, dishonoured you, lay with that man, gave him her body. Whore, whore . . .

At the back of the church the door opened.

And yet, urged the voice of sanity, that had not been the body of a whore tonight. All those years ago, in London, these evil times, so long ago now, those women . . . Tears began to trickle, unheeded, from his eyes. Oh God, that had been no whore's body tonight.

286

The light of an oil lamp drew nearer, swinging from side to side along the aisle.

Esmond shook his head, trying to still the whispering, to separate fact from his mind's fancy. He had to be sure. Had to find out—

Someone spoke.

"Who's there? Who is it?"

The suddenness of the voice so close to him jerked him upright. He looked frantically around, and lamplight fell across the box pew where he sat.

"Come on—come out of it!" the voice called angrily. "I can see you, so don't try hiding yourself in there."

"Wha . . . what's happening?" As the light caught his face, Esmond put an arm across his eyes.

"Come on, I said. Out of there, whoever you are."

He recognised the owner of the voice now. It was Robert Hogben, one of the churchwardens. He got to his feet, supporting himself with a hand on the edge of the pew.

Hogben made a sound of surprise. "Mr Bates? Is it you, sir?" He seemed unsure, holding the lamp higher to be certain that this haggard-faced, ill-dressed individual was, indeed, the rector of St Anne's. "I—I'm sorry I've disturbed you, sir. I saw a light from the cottage and thought I'd best take a look." He paused, but there was no response. "It *is* gone midnight, sir."

Without moving his head, Esmond looked towards the stout, grey-bearded warden.

"Too late," he said softly.

"Well, yes it is."

"Too late. No going back now."

"What? What's that you say, sir?"

Esmond leaned forward and blew out the candle on the pew wall. A thread of smoke curled up from the blackened wick and he followed it with his eyes until it had faded on the air.

Hogben studied him, frowning, disquietened by the minister's curious behaviour.

"Mr Bates,"—he ventured after a moment or two—"might you be leaving shortly?" The sooner the church was re-locked and the man in his bed, the better.

287

Esmond pondered the question. "Leaving? Oh, yes . . . I dare say I shall be leaving. There is little enough to keep me here now."

He opened the pew door and stepped out into the pool of lamplight, seemingly unaware of Hogben's critical examination.

"Yes, I must leave, I suppose. Where do you suggest I might go?"

"Go, sir? Well—well, back to your home, of course."

The other's expression altered in an instant. Like an animal laying back its ears, his whole face tightened.

"No! Never! That is one thing I cannot do."

Hogben stepped hurriedly back a pace, alarmed by this sudden change in manner. His lamp swung in a wild arc, sending shadows chasing across the width of the nave.

"I will tell you where I mean to go," Esmond went on, ignoring the movement. "I have to find . . . a man."

"A man? At this hour o' night?"

"The hour does not matter. You see, I have no idea where he may be lodged. If I begin the search now, it is possible I shall have him by morning."

The warden scratched his head with his free hand. "What man is this, then, sir?"

Esmond looked at him slyly. "*You* know him."

"Me? Well, I dare say as I do. But wi'out a name it's hard to figure which particular man you have in mind."

"I mean . . . Morgan."

"Ah."

"Frank Morgan."

"Aye, I'm wi' you now, sir. The stallion leader. And it's him you're wanting to find?"

"You have it exactly, Mr Hogben."

"I can't help you much there, I'm afraid. He comes and goes the whole o' the time, that 'un." The churchwarden paused; then—"The only folk I can think of who'd mebbe know are the Pooles."

Esmond gave a start, and stared at him in silence; and Hogben hurried on, "I—I mention them because they're

288

related. Only distantly, you understand, sir. But Morgan's round at their place from time to time. There's not much goes on in these parts that they don't know about."

The rector's eyes closed. His whole body became rigid. Slowly he raised his head until his face was in shadow and from his throat there came a long, low groan of anguish.

Hogben gaped at him, then started forward in concern.

"Mr Bates? Is anything wrong? Are you ill, sir?"

The other fell silent; and but for a visible tremor in his limbs, remained quite motionless for a time.

Then he drew an unsteady breath, lowered his head once more and said in a voice which seemed to be breaking with emotion, "So that was it. That was how he knew where to find my wife. Those two women. Those Judases! And they learned it from me. Oh God . . . is there no one I can trust?"

Hogben looked away, embarrassed by the naked suffering revealed in his face.

"Why don't you go on home to the rectory, sir? I can see you're in a bad taking about something."

Esmond shook his head. "You do not know, Mr Hogben . . . can have no idea what that man has done to me."

The warden's bushy eyebrows rose a fraction. From what he had just heard, he could guess all too well what Frank Morgan had been up to. But Mrs Bates—? The stallion man had poached too far this time.

"Look, sir. I tell you what I'll do. You go on back to your wife, now,"—he saw the other turn away, but persevered— "and in the morning I'll ask in the village and find out for you where Morgan is. That way's the best, don't you agree, now?"

There was a period of silence.

Then Esmond said carefully, "Thank you, Mr Hogben. But I have a better plan. I shall wait for you here whilst you enquire at the Pooles on my behalf."

"But you can't stay in the church all night, sir!"

"I do not intend to."

The warden started to speak again; then paused, frowning. "You mean . . . you mean I'm to go *now*?"

Esmond nodded.

"But, Mr Bates—it's almost one in the morning. They'll be sound asleep in their beds."

"No matter. The wicked are soon woken."

He looked at Hogben intently, and the lamp sputtered and flared up, exposing the grief in his eyes.

"Do this for me. I beg you. Do it for me. I would go myself this very moment, but I would not be answerable for my conduct towards those women. Not after such treachery. It was they, Mr Hogben—it *must* have been they—who told Morgan where my wife was staying when she was in Lewes this summer. And he went after her. He went after her and . . ." His voice broke and he covered his face with his hands. "Oh God, I am a man in despair. Which way am I to turn? That devil has robbed me of the one thing I prized most, and I am left in Hell."

Hogben felt a welling of pity for this miserable, humiliated man. There had been a time, years ago now, when his own wife had admitted to being unfaithful, and he recalled vividly the pain it had caused him. He had beaten her soundly so that she lost the child she was carrying, and that had been an end of the matter. He had not considered such treatment to be harsh or cruel: it was, after all, a man's right to administer what punishment he saw fit, since God had created woman to be the inferior, weaker vessel.

"Wait in the porch for me, then," he told Esmond. "I'll not be long." At that he took the rector almost gently by the arm and led him back through the body of the church towards the door.

Once again the carved faces of Weatherfield's dead flickered in momentary amusement.

Robert Hogben was wrong.

Charity and Comfort Poole were in their beds, true; but far from being sound asleep. The events of the evening, the service of baptism, the entertainment at the alehouse, and especially their meeting with Rachael Bates on the lane, had given them material for several hours of animated conversation, during which "Who would've thought . . ." and

290

"I wonder why . . ." and "D'you suppose . . ." were repeated often.

Even after they had shooed out their several cats, placed the chair against the door and carried their candlesticks up the steep and narrow staircase to their bedroom, the speculation continued at odd intervals, so that neither allowed the other to doze off for more than a few minutes at a time.

So it was that both heard the lifting of the latch on the garden gate and footsteps approaching the door.

"Now who d'you suppose that can be at this hour?" Charity wanted to know as the sharp rap of knuckles on wood sounded downstairs.

"Might it be Frank?" suggested Comfort, re-lighting the candle beside the bed. "Open the window and call down."

Her sister did so; and a moment later turned back into the room.

"It's Robert Hogben."

"Hogben? What's he want? Is his wife took bad again?"

Charity's cap-covered head went out and in at the window a second time.

"There's a message from Mr Bates!"

"Oh? Well, now, that's different." Charity threw back the bed cover and pulled her wrap around her shoulders. "We'd best let him in. We might be needed at the rectory."

Her disappointment on learning downstairs that they were not was, however, short-lived, lasting only until Hogben spoke the name of the stallion leader.

"But can't it wait till morning?" Charity demanded, puzzled. "Why does Mr Bates need to know this very minute where Frank's lodged?"

The burly churchwarden stood just within the door, shaking his head, wishing only to get this foolishness over and done with and himself home to his bed.

"He's fixed on knowing it tonight. I tried to head him off but he won't be shifted."

The Pooles pulled their wraps tighter about their matronly figures and exchanged glances.

"What's afoot, then?" Charity wanted to know. "Is there trouble, Mr Hogben?"

He shrugged. "There might be for ought I know. The rector's wandering in his wits, if you want my opinion."

"Why? What's happened?"

Briefly he told them how he had seen a light from the church while checking his poultry against foxes, and had gone in to find Mr Bates slumped inside one of the box pews.

"Only half-dressed, he was. Mumbling on about something being too late. I couldn't get a word o' sense out of him for a bit."

"And what of Mrs Bates?" Charity asked.

"He won't go home to her, seemingly. Turned quite nasty-like when I mentioned it."

The eyes of the sisters opened a fraction wider.

"I knew there was something queer," Comfort declared. "Soon as ever I seen that poor creature out there tonight, I knew in my bones there was something going on."

"We ought to go up to her, don't you think?" suggested her sister. "She might be in need of help."

"That's true. She might. Especially the way her husband's disbehaving. I'll go and—"

Hogben interrupted her impatiently. "It's Mr Bates that needs the helping, not his wife. D'you know where Frank Morgan's to be found, or don't you?"

"Wait on. Gi' us a minute to get properly dressed and we'll come across the green wi' you. I'd like to hear from Mr Bates hisself why he's so desperate to get at Frank."

The churchwarden reacted sharply. "Oh, I shouldn't be doing that if I was you, Miss Poole! He's in a rare taking against you pair. Told me he couldn't be answerable for his behaviour if he come near you."

"He said that?"

"He did. Something about you letting on to that Morgan where he might find Mrs Bates in Lewes."

The two women looked at one another again. For a long moment there was silence.

Then—"But we're not to blame for what Frank gets up to!" protested Comfort.

"No, indeed," echoed Charity. "Behopes Mr Bates don't hold *us* responsible for whatever he's gone and done. I mean, it isn't as though we're that close connected. Frank's father was no more'n our cousin, after all."

"Well, whichever way, he does hold you to blame, seemingly," Hogben told them bluntly. "And what's more, he called you a couple o' Judases for talking so. Treachery—that's what he said it was."

Hands were raised to mouths in dismay.

"Indeed, Mr Hogben," said Comfort, recovering, "you're right. Mr Bates *is* wandering in his wits!"

"So where is Morgan? D'you know?"

"He's lodged over at Stillborne's farm," Charity said decisively. "And you can tell the rector from me that I'm glad to be able to help him. If Frank's caused trouble and put him into such a state that he goes turning on us, who've done so much for him these past weeks, then all I can say is, I hope he gives Frank what he deserves."

"*And*, if you please, tell Mr Bates we meant no mischief by passing on his wife's address," put in Comfort. "If it were such a great secret, why tell us hisself in the first place?"

Why, indeed, thought Hogben. "Stillborne's, you say? Right, I'll be away back to let him know. He's waiting for me at the church."

"And we'll go on up to the rectory," said Charity, seeing him out through the door. "This is a queer business, and no mistake."

But you pair'll get to the bottom of it, I've no doubt, the churchwarden added to himself.

Slowly, clumsily, like an old woman crippled with pain, Rachael Bates moved away across the room from the bed and bent down to the bottom drawer of the chest to drag out her one remaining nightgown. The other, torn and soiled, lay where she had let it fall on the floor.

Unsteadily, not trusting her trembling legs to support her, she hauled herself over to the washstand in the corner and grasped its edge with one hand while she poured the contents of the ewer into the basin.

The water seemed like ice against her burning skin, turning to fire where it touched the scratches on her shoulder and breast and the long weals on her thigh.

Carefully she eased on the clean nightgown and then sought around on the floor for her hairbrush. It lay against the wall among fragments of glass from the silver-topped toilet bottles. The girl suppressed the sobs that threatened to rack her again, and forced herself across the room to pick it up, crawling on hands and knees, scarcely aware of the splintered glass like needles in her flesh, raising beads of blood.

Holding on to the brass rail at the foot of the bed, she dragged herself to her feet again. Then before the mirror on the dressing table by the window she began mechanically to brush at her tangled hair, her eyes fixed on the image that stared back at her.

From below voices were lifted, calling; but she made no response.

In a while they moved nearer, on the stairs and then approaching the closed door of the bedroom.

At the sound of the knock the brush strokes faltered and Rachael's eyes moved to the reflection of the door behind her, watching dully as someone outside slowly turned its handle and eased it open.

"Dear Lord above!" Comfort Poole stepped back to take in the scene that confronted her within the room. She turned to call out—"Charity! Come at once!"—then looked again.

In the drab lamplight the room seemed a shambles, bed-clothes pulled from the mattress, clothing strewn across the floor, shattered ornaments underfoot. And in the midst of it all—

Comfort drew in her breath sharply as Rachael turned from the mirror towards her.

"Oh, Mrs Bates . . . Mrs Bates! Oh, you poor dear. Whatever has he done to you?"

She came over and took her by the arm, looking in un-feigned concern at the swollen, bruised and tear-stained features.

Rachael opened her mouth, but could only make a choking sound.

"It's all right, my dear. You take your time, now."

The woman glanced over her shoulder as her sister entered the room and said, angrily, "Did you ever see anything like it! It's a wonder he didn't kill her."

Charity surveyed the scene, shaking her head and tutting loudly at Rachael's appearance.

"We ought to fetch the constable, by rights."

"No . . . no, please . . ." The girl found her voice at last. "There's no need."

"But after what Mr Bates has done to you—"

"We . . . we had an upset . . . a disagreement." She was close to tears again. "It was nothing more."

"Nothing, Mrs Bates? Nothing?" cried Charity. "When your poor face has been knocked black and blue and your house turned upside down and your husband skulking out there in the dark?"

Rachael turned her head away. Dully she said, "These things sometimes happen between . . . between husband and wife."

"Well,"—Charity looked at her sister—"we'll say nothing more, if that's the way it was."

"He'll leave you be now, that's for sure," Comfort added. "You've seen the back of him for the night, so there's no need to worry yourself further, my dear. Why don't you come and lie down for a bit while Charity and me clear up some o' this mess?"

She turned Rachael gently towards the bed, but the girl pulled sharply away.

"No! No, I . . . I'd rather not."

Comfort's eyes moved down from the rumpled bed to the ripped and bloodstained nightgown on the floor beside it.

"Well, just as you wish. Shall we find your wrap and Charity'll take you downstairs and sit wi' you in the kitchen?"

"Yes. Thank you. I'd prefer that."

"And then we must think what to do wi' you. You won't want to stay here for the rest o' the night, I don't suppose."

"No."

Rachael took the wrap and eased it about her shoulders. She moved awkwardly to the door with Charity close behind her; then paused in the open doorway and after a moment asked hesitantly, "Do you know where my . . . where Mr Bates has gone?"

"No, we don't," Charity said at once, forestalling her sister. "It were Robert Hogben who told us we were needed here. He's found Mr Bates in the church, and that's all we know o' the matter."

Rachael nodded. She appeared to consider something further. Then, finally—"I must go back to the alehouse. Would you take me?"

"The alehouse?"

"Yes. Please, it is important. I have to speak to Dinah."

She had no need to mention the name of the stallion man.

32

Frank Morgan opened his eyes, and groaned.

On the bale at his head a hen busily pecked amongst the hay. He rolled over on to his back, and the sudden movement caused the bird to take fright and fly squawking to the floor of the loft. In its wake a cloud of fine dust hung in the shafts of early morning sunlight streaming in through gaps where roof tiles had slipped.

Morgan groaned again.

Had he not felt so wretchedly ill he might have been glad to wake to such a fine morning. But the sunlight, the birdsong and the distant sounds of the farm grated on nerves that were raw from too much alcohol followed by not enough sleep.

To one side of his makeshift bed the hen began a throaty cluck. Groping blindly about, he found the empty spirit bottle and threw it clumsily towards the bird, causing it to se up another squawk and make off to join its companion scratching about on the floor of the barn below.

The stallion leader's head fell back against the rolled-up sacking which served as pillow. He passed his tongue over his dry lips and grimaced at the sour aftertaste left by last night's drink. Beneath his bare shoulders pieces of straw had worked their way through the blanket and pricked uncomfortably, drawing his attention to the ache in his muscles; which in turn reminded him of the tussle with George Bashford and the reason why his head now throbbed so intolerably with the lingering effects of the liquor he had drunk.

Passing a hand through his rumpled hair, he leaned up on one elbow. He remembered staying on at the alehouse after Bashford had left, keeping well out of Molly Flynn's sight and helping himself (more from spite than from pleasure) to her ale. But how in God's name had he got back here to Stillborne's?

He frowned, trying to piece together the blurred events of the night. Then it came to him: Jack Adams. Of course. Jack waiting for him in the lane, arguing with him, hoisting him into the back of a cart to lie noisily unhappy, watching the stars spin in circles above him all the way back through the deserted village.

No, not quite deserted. He recalled now Jack saying there was a light burning in the church, and someone still about at the rectory. Morgan had wondered, bemusedly, whether Rachael Bates needed his help still, had tried to make Jack stop the cart; and when he refused, made a grab at the reins. But the drink had robbed all the strength from his legs and he had fallen down again, cursing uselessly, to be driven on to Stillborne's and half-carried, half-dragged up the ladder to his bed in the loft.

Morgan grunted. He was a good type, Jack Adams, for all that he'd stopped him from paying Mrs Bates a visit. Just as well. He'd been in no fit state to do anything, and she was probably the sort of woman who hated to see a man in drink.

'Drink. Yes, that was it. He'd been a fool to insist on downing the rest of that bottle of spirits; especially after so much ale. Vaguely he remembered Jack in the barn below making sure that the Brighton Regent was racked up and tethered for the night.

What was it they'd talked about? Something important.

Morgan frowned again. Then nodded to himself. Belle. That was it. Little Belle. Good to know Jack would be keeping an eye on things whilst he was away doing the rounds of the Michaelmas hiring fairs to advertise his stallion ready for the start of the next stud season.

And that girl. Charlotte. Lottie. Yes, they'd talked of her, too. Well, and why not—they would all be related one way or another after the wedding. Jack Adams was first cousin to Dinah, which made him Frankie and Belle's . . . second cousin? And if Charlotte's baby turned out to be any of Morgan's own, then Jack would be fostering the children's half-sibling.

The stallion leader shook his head, unable to concentrate on such a ravelment, and winced as a stab of pain arrowed through the top of his skull. He felt in a poor way, what with the old ache back in his ribs again, and now this infernal pounding inside his head, a taste like sand in his throat and his eyes giving the impression they'd been rolled in grit.

Grunting with the effort, he pulled himself to his feet and fumbled with the buckle of the thick leather belt holding up his trousers. Lurching across to the ladder, he let himself gingerly down through the open trapdoor, cursing aloud as his foot slipped on a rung. The barn door stood ajar, letting in enough daylight for him to avoid the bales and rick ladders into which he had staggered last night, and the chickens scratching about in the straw flew clucking from under his feet as he made his way outside.

He had only the briefest glance to spare for his horse, tethered at the further end of the barn, and therefore failed to see the figure standing in the shadows beyond the stacked bales, watching him as he stumbled out into the yard to sluice his head and shoulders at the pump.

The cold, clear water revived him.

When he had finished he stood for a time in the early sunlight, his eyes half-closed, enjoying the warmth on his wet skin and thinking about riding his horse on the hill pasture before breaking his fast in Stillborne's kitchen.

It was only as he turned back to the barn door that he realised he was not alone, that someone was there just inside.

"Hallo?" he called uncertainly. "Is that you, Mr Stillborne?"

Without stopping for any reply he came back into the barn. The other's face was obscured by shadow, and after the brightness of the sun Morgan's drink-bleary eyes could make out little except that he was untidily clothed and bore no resemblance at all to the neatly-groomed farmer. His impression was that this must be some vagrant who had made a bed for the night among the bales.

"What's your business here, friend?" he asked.

The man remained silent.

Morgan had the instinctive feeling that there was something familiar about the shadowed features.

"Do I know you? You've been around here before, surely?"

Again, there was no response; and after a moment's hesitation the stallion leader walked down the barn towards his horse, using a sack from one of the bales to wipe the pump water from his hair and face.

The other followed behind a short way, but paused when he reached the foot of the loft ladder.

Keeping his back to him, Morgan made a show of checking his animal's legs. Some sixth sense had begun to sound a small bell of warning in his mind, cautioning him to be on the alert. As though sensing his unease, the powerful black Shire backed suddenly, jerking the rope tethering him to a ring post in the wall.

"Easy, boy—easy there!"

He spoke quietly under his breath, stroking the horse's neck to calm him. Then, without looking round, raised his voice a little and said, "Was it at one of the horse fairs we met, maybe? My memory's not my own this morning, so you must forgive me if I seem offhand." He paused, listening, then continued, "We celebrated my daughter's baptism last night and the drink's still making merry with my wits."

299

Mechanically, he carried on moving his hand over the horse's gleaming coat and waited for the stranger to respond.

But again, there was nothing.

Morgan began to lose patience. Over his shoulder he said, "Well, come on, man! Let's hear your voice. Is it Farmer Stillborne you're wanting, may be?"

"No. It is you I came to speak with." The words fell tonelessly.

He swung round. "Speak, then. Who are you? I haven't the time to waste just now guessing at names and business."

The man came on towards him and paused once more, this time beside a pile of heavy plough chains thrown down by the wall. Even from this distance and in such poor light, Morgan was aware that he was being stared at in a most extraordinary way and wondered uneasily whether one of Stillborne's workers might be within hailing shot in case there was trouble.

"You know my name. It is Esmond Bates."

Morgan gave a start. For a second he stood dumbfounded, mouth open, not knowing what to say; embarrassed, almost. Then—"Of course! I should've known. I recognise you now. But—"

"And my business with you here concerns my wife."

"Your wife?"

"I will be brief. I have good reason to suppose she is your creature."

"My . . . creature?" Morgan eyed him warily, attempting a laugh. "Now what kind of word is that?"

"It is as fitting as any other. Or do you prefer whore?"

"I prefer neither, Mr Bates! In God's name, is this any way to talk of your own wife?"

"I speak no more than the truth." The rector smiled suddenly, an unnerving thing to do in such circumstances. "Come, let us not play games with one another. I know about the night you spent with her at Buckfield, you see."

The stallion man's head went up sharply. His pride was touched there.

Defensively he said, "Then you know everything there is to know."

"Yet I would prefer to have an account from your own lips."

He shook his head and turned away, realising suddenly that he was caught in a trap; and not sure how he could get out of it. Damnation, he thought resentfully. Why do I have to be fuddled with drink at this, of all times? Suspicious husbands had had him cornered before now, but factors had always worked to his advantage, enabling him to gain the benefit of the doubt.

But this time . . . this time he sensed it would not go so easily for him.

In an effort to divert the conversation, he forced himself to say lightly, "You look all in, man. How long is it since you last slept?"

Esmond Bates would not be drawn.

"Spare me the hypocrisy of your concern, Morgan. Because of you, I have been out walking the country since before daylight."

"Because of me?"

"I needed time—and space—to think. I had to be sure."

"Be sure of what, now?"

"Of the exact nature of the wrong you have done me."

"Ah. I see." Morgan tried to clear his thoughts, hampered by the dull pounding ache in his head. "This wrong . . . it's to do with your wife, of course?"

The other looked at him in silence.

For a while they remained thus, without speaking, the quiet inside the barn broken only by the clucking of hens scratching in the patches of sunlight by the door and the chirp and flutter of sparrows in the rafters overhead.

Then Morgan took an unsteady breath. Perhaps, after all, honesty would be his best approach.

"Well, Mr Bates. I'll admit you've put me in something of a quandary. If I tell you the truth of the matter, you may not believe me. And if I lie to you, your wife must suffer for it."

Again, there was that cold, unnerving smile. "My wife has already suffered for it. Now it is your turn to pay. I have come here to see that you make proper reparation for the harm you have done me."

The stallion leader moved back a step, a little unmanned by the threat underlying those words. He was no coward, but the confrontation was rapidly turning ugly.

He began to bluster. "Now look here! I don't know just what it is you've been hearing about me and Mrs Bates. But it strikes me you've got hold of the wrong story. I don't deny we were together at Buckfield. But is it such a crime as you make out for a man to lend assistance where it's needed? She had to get back to Weatherfield, didn't she? And I happened to be in the right place to oblige."

"Don't compound your guilt with further lies, Morgan. You followed her to Lewes. You deliberately put yourself in her way."

"Who's been telling you so?"

"The very ones who gave you the information where to seek her. Yes, the Pooles! I see that makes you pause. God knows what was in your diseased mind when you planned to go after her."

"No—no, you're mistaken. I made no such plan. I had to be in Lewes myself, d'you see. It was chance, no more, that your wife and me were in the town at the same time."

"Do you take me for such a fool? The only thing I am prepared to believe is that my wife was not at first aware of your dishonourable intentions. That when she left this village there was no previous arrangement between the pair of you to meet at Southgate Street."

"Of course there was no previous arrangement!"

"Not then, perhaps."

"There was never any. In Heaven's name, Mr Bates, why insist I'm lying? I'd only met the lady once before, and that on the day my daughter was born. Hardly the circumstance for the kind of intrigue you're suggesting! No, believe me. It all fell out exactly as I've told you."

Esmond stared at him, and the stallion leader swallowed nervously.

After a long pause, the clergyman said in a more conversational tone, "Do you find my wife an attractive woman?"

"Attractive? Well . . . well, yes. I suppose she is. I mean she has a pleasant face. I've not give it much thought."

"And do men find her desirable, would you say? Do you find her so?"

"Damn it, man. What kind of questions are these? How would I know whether others find her desirable or not—" In the middle of his bluster Morgan saw a chance to turn the conversation from his own involvement, and seized upon it. "You should be asking George Bashford that, not me."

Esmond reacted sharply. "Bashford? What has he to do with it?"

"Oh, now, Mr Bates! I'm not one to go blabbing tales out of turn. You'd best go and ask him that yourself."

"The Devil I will!"

A spasm of naked fury passed across the other's face. Clenching his fists, he moved closer. Morgan's horse sensed his rage and began to show the whites of his eyes, frightened by the growing tension in the air. The iron-shod hooves struck loudly against the straw-covered brick underfoot as he jerked a second time at the tethering rope, dislodging one of the nails holding the ring to the post.

"Careful, man!" warned the leader sharply. "Keep away. You're unsettling him."

"Then control the brute. Or perhaps you cannot? After all, you have little enough control over yourself."

"Oh, I can manage him well enough. Within reason, that is. But he doesn't like strangers at the best of times. And he hates sudden noise or movement even more. Makes him nervous. Panicky. You'd be well advised not to come too close."

The rector examined the restless Shire suspiciously before he spoke again.

"I repeat my question. What has Bashford to do with my wife?"

"As far as I know, nothing."

"Then why mention his name just now?"

"When I say nothing, what I mean is, there's no actual relationship between them . . . as far as I know."

"No?"

"Not yet."

303

"Oh? You think there may be something between them in the future, is that it? You are a seer, too, amongst your other attributes?"

"Well, Mr Bates. Let's put it this way—" Morgan was beginning to feel more confident. "You've just proposed that other men may find your wife desirable."

"Yes?"

"Last night, as it chances, I happened to be watching her and Farmer Bashford sitting out alone together in the ale-house garden. This was before you arrived to interrupt the pretty scene, of course. Now, I've lived long enough to know when a man fancies a woman. The way he looks at her, the way he touches her hand—"

Esmond's eyes narrowed.

"—and if you want my advice, you'd be wiser paying attention to what may be going on there than come wasting time and breath on me."

"Perhaps so." The answer came sharply. "But then, it was not George Bashford who spent the night with my wife at the Fordhouse at Buckfield. Ah, yes. I see that takes the smile from your face! That he lusts after her in *fancy* is indeed a grievous sin before God. And I grant, you are right to surmise that his attentions are over-warm. But there is no dishonour in *fact* until physical concourse has occurred between them." Again, that sudden unnerving smile. "I think Mr Bashford is most unlikely to be encouraged so far. We may discount him."

"Why so?" Morgan asked warily.

"I have taken . . . certain steps, shall we say."

"What steps?"

"Whatever has happened privately between my wife and me need not concern you, sir."

"Why? You've done something to her? No. Oh, no. Don't tell me you've finally become man enough—"

The stallion leader gave a shout of laughter.

"Christ above, is that what you meant by her suffering already? Poor woman, you've kept her long enough waiting for it!"

Esmond Bates tensed himself. All the loathing he

harboured towards this man was beginning to well up inside him to such an extent that he felt he must choke on it.

Thickly he said, "I know her—now."

Something flashed within Frank Morgan: a frustration, a disappointment, a grief, almost, born of despair that the prize he had so lusted after was now lost for ever. Flinging himself forward, he seized the rector by the shoulder and thrust him backwards against the wall.

"You poor fool! You think bedding her will stop other men wanting her? Don't you realise what it is you've done? You don't know women, that's obvious!"

Esmond pulled away from the restraining hand. For a brief moment the memory of Rachael, weeping, crying out, struggling beneath him, seared his mind.

Then he came back, snarling—"I did no more than was my duty."

"Your duty? God in Heaven, man. That's a *woman* you're wed to! A healthy, normal, natural, warm-blooded female. What's the matter with you? Any other man would've bedded her with pleasure on the marriage night—aye, earlier if he'd had the chance. And she'd have given pleasure back, because that's the woman she is. She has the mark of Venus on her—here, on the left breast—" Frank Morgan struck himself with his fist. "Or maybe you've never noticed? Never even looked at her to see? And what of the children you've denied her? Had you been even half a man she'd have delivered you a son by now—and taken pride in the begetting of him, too!"

The stallion leader paused. An expression of uncertainty, of disbelief, passed across his face.

"Is that what you'd demean by calling mere duty? What kind of creature are you? What do you want in your bed? A boy?"

The final link with sanity snapped within Esmond Bates.

Out of the corner of his eye he saw the plough chain lying against the wall. His passion lent him a strength far beyond that of the normal. In one swift movement he bent, snatched a length of the chain, straightened up to his full height and holding the metal like an axe between his hands, lashed out at the stallion leader's head.

The heavy iron rings caught Morgan across the temple and he fell, unbalanced, stunned by the savage force of the blow.

As he lay half-conscious on the barn floor the rector struck at him again; and he continued to strike, dragging the chain back and up and down like a flail until the man beneath him lay without movement.

The violence of the blows, the hatred that delivered them, the raw smell of blood in that confined space, sent Morgan's horse into a panic. Kicking and plunging, he dragged the remaining nails from the ring post and freed himself.

Esmond appeared unaware of what was going on. He stood over the body of Frank Morgan, the bloodied chain gripped tightly in his fists, waiting for a leg to move, an arm, as though this were some insect he was crushing the life from.

The Brighton Regent reared up above him and brought his massive forehooves down on to his left shoulder.

The clergyman staggered sideways under the force of the blow.

The horse reared again, striking him this time on the back, causing him to fall forward on hands and knees, the breath knocked from his body. He attempted to move, to crawl, but his shoulder was smashed and he screamed out in agony as the splintered bones gave way.

The pain cleared his mind. A sudden, terrible, paralysing fear gripped him. He realised, too late, what was happening, the jeopardy he was in; and he screamed again, a thin, tearing sound, and tried to drag himself from under those murderous, iron-shod hooves.

The maddened horse rose up once more on his hind legs pawing at the air. For long moments he seemed to hang there: a giant black shape suspended above the crouching man.

Then the full force of his weight came down upon Esmond Bates's head, dashing in the back of his skull against the blood-spattered straw.

33

Rachael Bates was at the alehouse when news came of the double tragedy at Stillborne's farm.

"They say it looks like Frank's horse went m-mad and trampled 'em both," Jack Adams told them in the kitchen. 'It took the men nigh on half-an-hour to get him from the b-barn so they could see to the bodies. Proper smashed, they were. Parson Bates . . . he were d-dead already."

"And Frank?" Dinah cried.

"He still had some life in him—"

"Did he speak? Did he say what happened?"

Jack shook his head. "He didn't last more'n a few minutes. He went just after they g-got to him."

Molly Flynn, sitting by the kitchen range with little Frankie on her knee, tightened her lips and pressed the child's head against her shoulder.

"But why? Why?" Dinah cried out again. "Why should the horse turn on him? Frank treated that beast like his own flesh an' blood—"

"Better, some would say," her mother broke in bitterly.

"Always so kind and gentle wi' him, he were. He thought the world of him. Never raised his hand, never mishandled him . . . What could've happened, Jack? In God's name, tell me."

"Nobody seems to know. Farmer Stillborne's pigman were crossing the yard, heard all the commotion in the b-barn, and he went in to take a look. Couldn't see much, he said, except the horse playing up there. Called Frank. No reply. So he made off to tell 'em at the farmhouse."

He paused, and glanced over at Rachael Bates.

She sat apart from the others in a chair by the window and had barely spoken a word since the news came; only stayed as she was now, her head bowed, her arms clutched tightly across her breast.

"They c-couldn't find Frank anywhere. So old Stillborne, he went in hisself with a couple o' men . . . and it was then they found . . ."

"Oh, if only that Mr Bates had kept away!" Dinah wailed. "If he hadn't have gone after Frank this'd never have happened."

Her mother reacted sharply. "There you go again, shifting the blame. If anyone's the cause o' this, it's Frank Morgan hisself."

"No! That's not true. Don't say such a thing, Mam."

"It's true enough, my girl, and well you know it. He brought it on his own head, carrying on the way he did. You see what Mrs Bates has had to suffer because of him. He was a bad lot, that 'un."

Dinah wiped the tears from her face with the back of a hand and looked resentfully at Rachael.

All this had started with her. Arriving at the crack of dawn in the Pooles's cart, running about the place and going on something about Frank and the trouble he was in. And the Pooles saying as how the rector had knocked her about on account of it all. Thank the Lord her mother had kept them out of the way down here in the kitchen. The pair of them were itching to find out what Frank had got to do with it. One way or another she'd seen them off before Mrs Bates started letting on all that had happened.

Not that she'd made much sense at the time. Something about her husband being in a terrible taking against Frank and making off in the middle of the night to find him.

Dinah thought it was unfair of her to come here, dragging her misery with her as though it was anyone's fault but her own what her husband did.

But Rachael Bates had not unburdened herself of the full story. Even in such a deeply distraught state as she was, she had had the presence of mind to gloss over the episode of the Fordhouse. All that she had disclosed, and later repeated more coherently to Mrs Flynn, was that Esmond suspected Frank Morgan of pestering her with his attentions, that h had flown into an ungovernable rage after last night's scene here in the garden, and had gone to Stillborne's to have it out with him.

To Molly Flynn, it appeared that Rachael's concern was solely for her husband's safety. And who could wonder. Morgan was by far the stronger of the two. If it came to an argument between them, blows would surely follow and the rector, not being a man used to violence, would come out of it the worst.

At the time, Mrs Flynn had privately thought this would be no bad thing to happen. They would be bound to bring a charge against the stallion leader as a result, and with any luck he might see the inside of Lewes Gaol for a term.

Even now that she knew he was dead, her attitude had not softened. She had always disliked Morgan. But for him, Dinah might well have been wed and settled long before.

"Ah, well . . . One shouldn't think ill o' the dead," she said grudgingly, aloud.

Dinah sniffed back her tears. "He's beyond your malice now, wherever he is."

There was a slight sound from the window as Rachael Bates stirred at last. Her hands fell to her lap and she clasped them there. The Poole sisters had helped her to dress and tidy back her hair, and the neatness of her appearance served to emphasise the bruises marking her pale face.

"What . . . what have they done with the . . . bodies?"

"The b-bodies, ma'am?" Jack Adams's eyes flickered towards her, then away. "Oh, they were carried to the house, I believe. Harry Ovenden were there, and he told me. It was him as fetched the sheep hurdles to lay 'em on."

"Did he say anything else?"

"Only that Farmer Stillborne sent to tell the authorities what'd happened, and the doctor's being g-got from East Grinstead."

"A bit late for any doctor," interjected Mrs Flynn.

Rachael said faintly, "He will still be needed. They must find the cause of death."

"The cause o' death—oh! Oh, Frank!" Dinah burst into noisy sobs. "That blasted horse . . . I never did trust it . . . oh,

Frank! . . . I was thinking o' making him gi' up the round once we was m-married."

Grief overcame her and she began to rock herself backwards and forwards in her chair.

Little Frankie, frightened by his mother's tears, set up his own plaintive wail and in turn awakened the baby in her cradle by the wall.

Jack picked her up and began nursing her. "They'll have to shoot the horse, I dare say. Nobody'll buy him once word g-gets round what he did. A pity, really. You might've proved a claim on him, our Dinah. You'd have been able to sell him for a tidy bit."

"They won't shoot the creature out of hand," said Mrs Flynn impatiently. "Not till there's been some kind o' enquiry."

"Maybe not. But I can't see a d-dealer wanting to pay good money for a stallion that's trampled its own leader."

Rachael Bates spoke again, her voice low but controlled.

"Regent would never have turned on them deliberately. Something must have frightened him. Mr . . . Mr Morgan did tell me that he hated loud noises near him." She hesitated. "If they were arguing . . . in the barn . . . something happened to make the horse panic."

The others looked at her in silence.

"It wouldn't be fair to shoot him. The horse wasn't to blame."

"Wasn't to blame, indeed!" Dinah shouted, her voice distorted by sobs. "If I had a gun I'd go right this minute an' shoot him meself!"

Reaching up, she snatched little Belle from Jack's arms and pulled the baby to her breast, rocking and weeping over her while Belle raised her own thin sound of protest.

"It's all your husband's fault."

The tear-smeared face was turned back to Rachael.

"It were him did for Frank . . . going there, all on accoun' o' something he'd worked hisself up over. Why couldn't you keep him away? Why didn't you stop him?"

"That'll do, my girl!" her mother said sharply. "Mrs Bates has to bear a heavier grief than you, remember. She's los everything. Home as well as husband. You never had any-thing to lose but your good name. And that went the day Frank Morgan walked into this house."

"He *would've* married me," Dinah sobbed.

"Aye. If he'd wanted. He *could've* married you afore Frankie was born, but he didn't. No, you count yourself lucky you're spared any more of his faithless words and empty promises."

"Oh, how can you be so heartless? What about my babies? It's their own father has died . . ."

Her mother shot her a look of contempt. She passed a hand over little Frankie's swarthy curls.

"They'll be a better sight off wi'out him. Especially this 'un. And pray the Lord *he* don't turn out another blasted Morgan."

The blood rushed to Dinah's face. "And I'll hope and pray that he will, despite you! Every time I look at our Frankie from now on, I'll be watching for his father—"

She stopped.

George Bashford stood in the kitchen doorway.

As soon as he had heard the news in Weatherfield, Bashford had gone directly to the rectory; only to find the place empty and no sign of Rachael Bates anywhere about the village.

His second thought was to ride out to the alehouse to learn whether the Flynns knew of the tragedy.

He was vastly relieved to find Rachael there with them. Though his condolences at the double loss and his expressions of shock at the manner of its happening lost much of their warmth when he saw the marks on her pale, bruised face.

"I'm afraid you'll be required to make a positive identifi-cation," he explained to her later. "It won't be pleasant for you, but you must be brave. It won't take more than a minute."

"And what about me?" Dinah Flynn sniffed back her tears.

"You don't have to be there. Someone else can identify Frank. Jack will do it for you, perhaps."

"No. I'll do it meself. It's my right to see him. Nobody was closer to him than me."

Jack Adams looked at Bashford. "What's to be done about the b-burials, d'you know, sir?"

"Well, if the authorities decide to hold an enquiry into the deaths, the coroner will need to view the bodies. I believe that's the usual procedure. No doubt they'll be taken to the mortuary at East Grinstead. You recall when the Margery boy was found drowned a year or so back? There was an inquest to uncover the circumstances, and the body kept at the mortuary in the meanwhile. So I'm afraid there's no knowing how long it'll be before something can be done about funerals."

"Nor who's to conduct them, neither," Molly Flynn observed. "We'll need to send out for somebody since we've no parson of our own any more."

Bashford's face tightened. He could understand the old woman's lack of distress over the stallion leader, but at least she might show more sensitivity about the harrowing circumstances of Rachael Bates's loss.

He said, "I'll ride over to Harefield and see Mr Drew. I'm sure he'll do whatever's necessary in the situation."

"That would be very kind of you," Rachael said quietly. "My . . . my husband saw Mr Drew occasionally. It would be nice to think he might be laid to rest by someone he knew and admired."

George Bashford was impressed by the calmness and dignity of her manner. She was bearing up with remarkable fortitude, he thought.

"And what of your own arrangements?" he asked her. "Have you thought yet what you'll do between now and—well, until everything is over? You'll stay at the rectory, I suppose?"

"She's welcome to put up wi' us here," said Mrs Flynn at once. "It'll be lonely for her all by herself in that gloomy place."

Rachael looked across the room at Dinah. For a moment the other's bitterness showed through the tears before she turned her head away.

"Thank you. It's kind of you to offer. But I think it best I return to the village. The rectory is my home, after all . . . that is, until there's a new incumbent for the parish."

"Oh, but that'll probably not be for some time," Bashford said hastily. "Look how long they took after old Yardley died. You'll be with us for a while yet, we hope."

She gave him a faint smile and rose to her feet.

"There's nothing to keep me here any more."

She drew the shawl around her shoulders and stood facing him. For several seconds their eyes held each other's, the young farmer's full of concern, and some hurt at her words. She was still wearing his late wife's gown, the pale violet silk she had had on last night when they sat together in the garden. Somehow, that brought him comfort.

Rachael's gaze dropped and she moved past him towards Dinah, pausing when she reached her chair.

"I'm sorry . . . so sorry," she said simply. "You told me once that we didn't fit in here. You said we'd be happier back in Lewes."

"I don't remember that," Dinah answered sullenly.

"But you said it, even so. And you were right. Esmond was never really happy in this place . . ." Her voice broke a little. "And now he'll never leave it. Poor Esmond. How he would have hated to know that."

Her head drooped and George Bashford was at her side in a moment. Even in her grief her lustrous beauty remained undimmed for him, stirring him into feelings of desire as well as of protectiveness; and he had to make a conscious effort to suppress the urge to take her within his arms and still her trembling mouth with his kisses.

Rachael felt the pressure of his hand on her shoulder and turned away.

"No—no, I'm all right. It was just . . . I think I'd like to go back now."

"Of course. I'll take you if I may."

"Yes," she said; and went out through the door without another word or look for any of them.

Outside, seated in the trap in the lane, Rachael wept.

The hours had passed so cruelly since last night when she and Esmond had stood together here in the darkness. She had been so afraid of him, not knowing what would happen,

313

what he might do. It had been a nightmare; and at the time she had despaired of finding any escape from it.

When he had left after committing that act of violation upon her body, she had briefly considered death as a means of freedom. And now, indeed, death had set her free.

Just as before, the wind rustled the leaves of the trees edging the lane, and she shivered in remembrance.

"You're cold," George Bashford said at once. "Let me wrap you."

He leaned across, and she averted her face so that he would not see the tears.

"There. Is that more comfortable?"

Rachael touched the blanket covering her knees, and nodded.

For a while they proceeded in silence, the horse moving slowly, its reins slack, picking its way between the mud ruts. Up on the hill pastures work had stopped for the midday meal—the "beever"—and apart from a distant ploughman standing beside his ox team, the countryside seemed deserted.

There was a melancholy brooding about the autumn landscape, as though all nature were mourning the approaching death of the year.

Bashford flicked the reins to quicken the horse's step.

"I looked for you last night. I drove along here after you'd gone, hoping I'd find you somewhere along the way."

"Yes. We saw you go by."

"You did? Where were you, then? I thought you must've taken the path across the fields."

"No. We were close to the alehouse still. Esmond . . ." Her voice faltered. She went on hesitantly, "Esmond drew me into the hedge so that you wouldn't see us."

"Wouldn't see you? Why in Heaven not? I only wanted to know you were safe. He was in such a wild mood, I thought—well, I was afraid you might come to some harm, the way he dragged you off."

He shifted his gaze to her bruised face, and when he spoke again his tone was savage. "He had no damn right to abuse you like that."

Rachael hunched her shoulders defensively.

314

"It wouldn't have happened if I'd been open with him from the start."

"So he beat it out of you, did he? All that business about the Fordhouse?"

She made no answer.

"By God, I wish I *had* seen you last night! At least I could have spared you that. I'd have told him the facts myself."

"What good would it have done? I'd have had to face him alone in the end."

"I could've warned him off. He wouldn't have been so free with his fists if he'd known he'd have to answer to me for the hurt he caused you."

"You don't know what he was like. He would never have listened. He might have turned on you, too. I think he was a little insane. After you'd gone by, he stood in the middle of the lane and shouted after you . . . something about your treachery. I don't remember. So much has happened since."

Bashford frowned. "Treachery? What treachery? What did he imagine I knew about him to betray?"

Rachael shook her head.

He went on, "Your husband did talk a bit about himself when he came over to Spring Hill that day. It was when you were in Lewes. But then, he'd taken a drop too much ale and I couldn't understand half of what he was saying. He was plain drunk, to tell you the truth."

"That must have been it. He was never a man for drink. There were times when I wished he were."

Bashford frowned again, and fell silent, turning his thoughts over in his mind. The trap had passed the spot where the Poole sisters had found her the previous evening before he could bring himself to voice his feelings.

"I must say this—" he began firmly. Then stopped, wondering if, after all, this was the right time.

She looked at him, waiting.

He began again. "Rachael . . . don't take offence, or think I mean to cause you hurt. You've taken enough, I know. But I must say this. I think the way things have worked out—well, your husband was a sick man. I saw enough of him to guess there was something wrong, something in his mind. There was no happiness between the two of you. No warmth. In the end, I believe he'd have destroyed you. No, don't look at me like that! You know it's so. Whatever you took from him last night was only the start. A man like that, once he turns to violence, he never leaves off. He gets a taste for it. I know. I've seen it happen. And there's only so much a woman can suffer before her spirit's broken."

Moved to fresh despair by his words, Rachael bowed her head, the tears staining the violet silk with dark patches.

Eventually, in a small, choked voice, she said, "It's all so like a bad dream still. Ever since that time in Buckfield, everything has seemed so. As though nothing about me is real any more."

"And what of me?"

"You?" She turned her brimming eyes to him.

"Yes."

The trap swayed over a deep rut, throwing them together. Bashford's hand met hers upon the seat, and closed over it.

"Don't make me a part of your bad dream, Rachael. That will be forgotten in time, once your hurt's healed. I don't want you forgetting me. Ever."

Slowly, she withdrew her hand.

"You say nothing seems real any more," he persisted gently. "But I'm real enough. My feelings, they're real. You must surely know how dear you are to me—"

"No!" Her cry silenced him. "Please, don't. Not now."

"Very well. I'll change the subject. I'm sorry. I shouldn't have presumed on your grief."

"It's not that. It's . . . too soon."

At these words, dragged so reluctantly from her, George Bashford's spirit leaped. Too soon. Not yet. Was that what she was saying? Wait a while?

His face relaxed, and he smiled.

Ever since that moment he had held her in his arms to comfort her during the rainstorm, the warmth of his love had been growing. While her husband lived, his thoughts of sharing that love with her had been no more than a wishful dream. But the instant he had learned that Esmond Bates was dead, his shock had been followed by a rush of joyful amazement.

316

She was free. Free! She *could* be his!

And now she had said, not yet—it's too soon.

From this time forward there was an unspoken bond between them both, he told himself. She had made him a promise—an invitation—an assurance for the future. He would press her no further, content to wait until the period of her mourning was over.

34

"Man that is born of a woman hath but a short time to live, and is full of misery. He cometh up, and is cut down, like a flower; he fleeth as it were a shadow, and never continueth in one stay."

The Reverend Mr Drew, a tall, angular figure in billowing white surplice, moved slowly at the head of the coffin bearers. The words of the burial service were caught up on the wind and carried faintly to the man and woman standing at the side of a newly-filled grave some way off.

"In the midst of life we are in death: of whom may we seek for succour but of thee, O Lord, who for our sins art justly displeased?"

Dinah Flynn watched the elmwood coffin lowered carefully to the grass beside the hole in which it would presently lie. An hour ago, the same words had been spoken over her Frank, here where she stood, before they put him away from her into the ground. And now it was the turn of Esmond Bates.

She was glad the graves lay so far apart.

"Yet, O Lord God most holy, O Lord most mighty, O holy and most merciful Saviour, deliver us not into the bitter pains of eternal death."

Restless beside his mother, little Frankie removed his thumb from his mouth. Before Dinah could prevent him, he had scrambled up on to the mound of raw earth covering his father and half-jumped, half-slid down the other side, dragging with him the spray of evergreens.

"Oh—you little devil! You bad, wicked boy!"

At the sudden cry, Rachael Bates, beside Esmond's coffin, raised her head. Through the heavy veil covering her features she noticed for the first time that Dinah was still in St Anne's churchyard, standing with her cousin Jack Adams near the wall at the far end.

Earlier, from an upper window at the rectory, she had watched Frank Morgan being buried there in the shadow of the copse; and she remembered how she and the stallion leader once upon a time had stood there together within the concealment of those trees.

Then Effie Underwood had called up to her and she had turned away from the scene and composed herself before joining the funeral party awaiting her in the hall.

Beside her now, the undertaker's assistants took up the ends of the rope bands lying beneath Esmond's coffin and with a smooth practised movement swung it out over the yawning mouth of the grave.

"Thou knowest, Lord, the secrets of our hearts," continued Mr Drew earnestly, "shut not thy merciful ears to our prayer; but spare us, Lord most holy, O God most mighty, O holy and merciful Saviour, thou most worthy judge eternal, suffer us not, at our last hour, for any pains of death, to fall from thee."

The coffin swayed slightly from side to side as it was lowered until it came to rest at the bottom. The men stepped away, and Mr Drew made a little motion of his head towards Rachael.

She looked across the open grave, at Arthur Collins standing near George Bashford. Then she moved forward and threw down the spray of flowers she had carried during the funeral service. The white petals were strewn across the top of the lid, obscuring the brass nameplate.

Mr Drew bent towards the mound beside the grave.

"Forasmuch as it hath pleased Almighty God of his great mercy to take unto himself the soul of our dear brother here departed: we therefore commit his body to the ground; earth to earth, ashes to ashes, dust to dust—"

There was a dull thud as the first handful of earth struck the coffin.

"—in sure and certain hope of the resurrection to eternal life, through our Lord Jesus Christ, who shall change our vile body, that it may be like unto his glorious body, according to the mighty working, whereby he is able to subdue all things to himself."

George Bashford had accompanied Rachael to Stillborne's farm to identify her husband before his body and that of Frank Morgan were removed to the mortuary at East Grinstead. Dinah Flynn had already made the sombre journey, and the stallion leader's tarpaulin-shrouded corpse had been taken away and placed on the bed of the mortuary waggon.

Rachael found Esmond's covered body laid out on a hurdle in one of the farm outbuildings. The constable who conducted her to the makeshift bier lifted the covering back a little way to expose the head, its shattered cranium roughly bandaged with a piece of sack-cloth.

She had turned away.

"Yes. That is my husband."

"You formally identify the deceased as Esmond Jezrahel Bates, ma'am?"

"Yes," she said again.

The constable had written something in a notebook, and then leaned forward and covered up her late husband's misshapen face.

At the two separate inquests, verdicts of death by misadventure were returned on both men. Their remains were brought back to Weatherfield for burial on the twentieth day of September, exactly a fortnight after the violent tragedy in Stillborne's barn.

Throughout yesterday, parishioners had come to pay their final respects to their late minister, passing in single file past the open coffin in the rectory parlour.

Their numbers had surprised Rachael. Until Ralph Underwood casually remarked that it must be the manner of her husband's death, rather than the death itself, which was exciting such an exhibition of parochial piety.

Effie and Ralph had arrived on the evening before the funeral. Rachael had insisted that they spend the night in the front bedroom: she herself had never slept in it again, preferring to make do with a couch in one of the back rooms.

The Reverend Arthur Collins had elected to travel from Lewes overnight and was at the rectory only a short time before the funeral party left for the church. His wife had been unable to accompany him. She remained at the bedside of her father, Mr Kingsley, who was not expected to live out the week.

"Almighty God, with whom do live the spirits of them that depart hence in the Lord—"

On the far side of the churchyard little Frankie screamed lustily as his mother caught him by the arm and dealt him a slap across the back of the head.

Without interrupting the flow of his prayer, Mr Drew glanced towards the source of the commotion, then returned to his book of Offices.

"—and with whom the souls of the faithful after they are delivered from the burden of the flesh, are in joy and felicity—"

From a canvas roll beside the wall, Jack Adams took the wooden cross he had carved and pushed the shaft well down into the soft earth at the head of the stallion man's grave mound.

"—We give thee hearty thanks, for that it hath pleased thee to deliver this our brother out of the miseries of this sinful world; beseeching thee that it may please thee, of thy gracious goodness, shortly to accomplish the number of thine elect and to hasten thy kingdom; that we, with all those that are departed in the true faith of thy holy name, may have our perfect consummation and bliss, both in body and soul, in thy eternal and everlasting glory. Through Jesus Christ our Lord."

"Amen."

The group beside the open grave cleared their throats. As Mr Drew started on the final prayer for the burial of the

320

dead, Jack and Dinah, with little Frankie, now reduced to hiccoughing sobs, passed by a mere few yards away.

Rachael looked up, half-hoping to exchange a word or two after the service. But Dinah seemed to quicken her step on purpose, and without turning her head went on rapidly down the path.

Waiting at the lychgate was Charlotte Smith. And beside her, leaning his arm in a familiar attitude against the post at her back, stood Ralph Underwood.

"It struck me as odd. Yes, singularly odd," observed Arthur Collins.

Rachael waited until he had finished helping himself from the plate of cold meats before enquiring what.

"Why, that so few of dear Esmond's parishioners attended this morning's service."

"There's nothing to be read in that, sir." George Bashford spoke up. "Today's a work day. Most folk hereabouts will be at their employment."

Ralph Underwood held out his glass to be refilled

"But there were several women standing out in the lane—"

"Yes, and you standing with them," his wife interjected tartly.

"I was about to say, I wonder they didn't trouble to take themselves into the church? Then again, perhaps it's not done in these out of the way places?" Sipping his drink, he glanced maliciously at Bashford, standing over by the window. "A superstitious lot, the peasantry. Two funerals together, y'know. They were probably looking for a sign from On High to show 'em who'd make the third."

No one answered. Ralph had been drinking since breakfast and was growing somewhat tiresome.

There had been a brief, embarrassing scene at the lychgate between him and Jack Adams which had threatened to spoil the end of the service. How it started, Ralph refused to say. But he had made some insulting reference to Charlotte, claiming he had known her well in Lewes. Known her very well indeed. And Jack had taken umbrage.

The incident had left a sour taste in everyone's mouth and cast an even deeper gloom on the funeral feast in the rectory parlour.

Effie Underwood moved here and there about the room, picking things up and putting them down, trying to pretend that nothing had happened, striving to be her usual bright, amusing self; and only succeeding in irritating the others.

"What a pity that nice Mr Drew couldn't stay longer. Such a pleasant man. And there's so much to eat here, too. Those dear creatures in the kitchen have managed wonderfully. And what quaint names they have—Charity and Comfort! So fitting. Whatever would Rachael have done without them this past week? I wish I could borrow them both and—"

"Sit down, Effie," her husband said curtly. "And be quiet."

Arthur Collins, on a chair beside the red lacquer Chinese cabinet, coughed and adjusted his steel-rimmed spectacles.

"Even so," he resumed, as though no one else had spoken since his last observation, "it struck me as exceedingly odd that an entire parish should so notably absent itself from the funeral of its own minister. It puts me sadly in mind of Chaucer's knight—'now in his cold grave alone, without any company'."

"Mr Bates will have his company this evening," said Bashford. "They'll all be along to give him a leave-taking, don't you worry, sir."

Ralph Underwood sneered. "You think so?"

"Can you think of a reason why they shouldn't?"

"Only that the late lamented Reverend Mr Bates had a knack of making himself—shall we say, unloved? I don't suppose for a minute he'll be mourned much beyond these four walls. Or within 'em, either, come to that."

Rachael gasped. There was a sudden silence in the room.

Then she turned on him. "That was an unkind, ungracious thing to say!"

"And most unwarranted," Arthur Collins added sharply. "I think you owe Mrs Bates an apology, sir."

The ruddy-faced young man looked at them both, then lowered his eyes and gave a shrug.

"Sorry. Spoke out of turn."

He threw back his head to drain his glass and immediately made to refill it from the bottle at his elbow.

"Perhaps you'd best leave that alone," George Bashford said darkly.

"Why? Are you suggesting I'm drinking too much?"

"No."

"Good."

Deliberately, Ralph plied his glass and raised it towards the other.

Bashford looked at him coldly. "It's merely that I hate to see good wine abused. Especially my own."

Again, there was an uncomfortable silence in the room.

"Ah . . . Did I hear you say that you were returning to live in Lewes?" Mr Collins asked Rachael.

She nodded.

"Have you somewhere in mind?"

"I intend to go back to the rooms I had before . . . before my marriage. In Flood Street. In fact, I go tomorrow."

"But I thought the old shop had been bought up," Ralph Underwood put in.

Rachael answered shortly, without looking at him.

"The shop, yes. But Mr Bashford made enquiries. The rooms above are not in use. I shall rent them from the owner."

"I am relieved to find you have everything so well settled," Mr Collins said with sincerity. "My wife and I feared the sudden shock of poor, dear Esmond's death would leave you quite without direction."

"The people of the parish have been a great comfort. I've received many offers of help and support. They couldn't have been more kind."

"Mr Bashford especially," Ralph said below his breath.

She heard him.

"Yes—Mr Bashford especially! Without him I don't know what I would have done these past weeks."

"It's becoming something of a habit, isn't it? Your being rescued from awkward situations by one man or another—"

Before the rest of the company had time to react, George

Bashford was across the room and pulling him up from the couch to his feet. The two men were of much the same height, and the farmer looked the other directly in the eye as he spoke, his words controlled, but an edge of anger to his voice.

"Folk are beginning to find your behaviour tiring, Mr Underwood. If you cannot remember that this is a house of mourning and temper your tone accordingly, I suggest you take yourself straight back to Lewes. And smartly!"

Ralph shrugged off the restraining hand.

"I didn't mean anything by it," he answered sullenly. "It was only meant as a joke."

"Then it was in very poor taste, sir. This is hardly the time, nor the place, for jokes."

Effie glanced at Rachael's frozen expression.

"Oh, Ralph! How could you speak so? That was a nasty, hurtful, spiteful thing to say of Rachael. I'm thoroughly ashamed of you."

Without waiting for her husband's response, she went on, "Disregard him, do, Mr Bashford. And you, too, Rachael, dear. You take no notice, either. I don't know what's possessed him, truly I don't. Ever since he set eyes on that young woman at the church gate—"

"Beg pardon, Mrs Bates, ma'am." Charity Poole knocked at the open door. "There's a message for you."

"Who is it?"

"Jack Adams, ma'am."

"Oh? Yes . . . thank you. I'll come at once."

As soon as she had left the room, Effie Underwood voiced a question that had been nagging at the back of her mind all day.

"What I can't understand is what that horse fellow . . . Morgan . . . what he and Esmond were doing together in the first place."

"I don't think you should be asking such things, ma'am," Bashford said impatiently. "Not at this time, any way."

"But this was the same man who carried Rachael away to Buckfield, wasn't it? Ralph swears it was. Don't you, Ralph?" She turned to look at him. "Oh, well, don't answer me. I hope you're not going to sulk. You told me yesterday the man

324

killed with Esmond Bates was the very one you found at the Fordhouse with Rachael."

"But . . . this is all very disturbing." Arthur Collins looked hard at Bashford. "I had no idea—no idea at all, that this Frank Morgan was the same wretched creature responsible for that disagreeable business in the summer."

"It was the same man," the other replied tersely. "But as to the deaths being linked . . ."

Effie pursed her lips and continued, "There's a story going about—"

"If you have no objection, ma'am," Bashford interrupted shortly, "it's a subject best left in peace now. No possible good can come of raking up bits of village talk and looking to find a mystery where there's none. The facts were investigated thoroughly enough at the inquests—"

"The inquests?" Rachael came back into the room. "What were you saying?" She looked enquiringly at him.

He shook his head. "Nothing. It wasn't of importance."

"That's right, Rachael, dear. It was nothing." Effie smiled brightly. "We were only talking. Who was your messenger? Did I hear someone say Jack Adams? I hope he hasn't returned to make fresh trouble with Ralph. There's been quite enough of that!"

"No, no trouble. It was a different business. His father is the local carrier. They're coming tomorrow to load the furniture."

As she spoke, Rachael Bates moved over to where Bashford was standing by the window. She held a note out to him.

"It's from Dinah. Would you care to see it?"

"From Dinah?" he hesitated, then took the paper from her and unfolded it. "But it's addressed to you."

"I'd like you to read it, even so."

Puzzled, he looked at her and was pleased to see her smile suddenly. It was the first time in weeks that he had seen her young face lose that pinched, strained expression.

Lowering his eyes, he read the ill-formed, childlike writing.

"Dear Mrs Bates. I am sorry I treated you so ill. It werent our fault, how could I think but for grief. I couldnt let you leave with no word. Will you come back to see the baby one of

325

these days? I hope everything goes well with you. Yours. Dinah Flynn. PS Mr Bashford took the horse did you know."

He looked up again when he had read it, and returned it to Rachael. Carefully she re-folded it.

"I suppose it's the best farewell I could hope for, considering the circumstances," she said quietly. "I'm glad she's made her peace with me. It's taken a burden of guilt from my mind."

She made to turn away; then swung back to face him again, uncertain.

"George . . . Thank you for letting the Brighton Regent live. Why did you?"

He kept his voice low so that the others could not overhear his reply.

"You asked. Besides, he's a good animal. I can use him. That's made you happy?"

"Yes."

"Then my money's well spent."

35

Molly Flynn had taken the view that it would be a needless waste of time and money to close up the alehouse for Frank Morgan's burial.

What should she do? she remonstrated with Dinah. Sit here behind locked shutters while customers stood thirsty in the lane? Never turn away business. Her father, the old Captain had told her that often enough; especially towards the end when he shook so badly he could no longer hold anything steady and young Molly had taken his place in the ale-room.

It came as no surprise in the district that Mrs Flynn stayed away from the stallion man's funeral and opened her house as usual. Everyone knew how things had stood between her and Morgan.

But there were one or two disapproving murmurs that she should expect her daughter to put aside her mourning as soon as she returned from the church; and there were some customers who spoke up and said it was lacking in feeling to make the young woman work on the very day her man had been buried.

"If you don't like it, you know what you can do about it," Molly Flynn had said.

And that had been an end of the matter.

Now the customers had gone and the alehouse closed for the night. Dinah did the clearing as she did at the end of every evening, working by lamplight to put everything ready for the next day's trade.

She had been awake since before dawn, lying in the darkness of her room thinking about Frank, and then about George Bashford buying Frank's horse and giving her the money to put away for the children; and then about Rachael Bates, who had no children.

The funeral service had seemed unreal, a dream almost. When the coffin was being lowered into the ground she had looked about her, half-expecting to see Frank leaning against the wall there, watching as well. Thank God Jack had been with her, or she might have taken it into her head to go running off to Stillborne's to ask if they knew which farm he'd moved on to.

She had been glad of the work today at the alehouse. It had stopped her brooding too much, had settled her down into the routine of life again.

Sighing, she threw a cloth over the beer-pots she had just finished wiping and put ready on the counter, after rinsing them clean at the pump beside the shallow brownstone sink. There were many alehouse keepers who did no more than dip the dirty vessels into a bucket of water under the counter, but Mrs Flynn liked her things to be properly cleansed and rinsed, even though it meant extra work for them both.

Through the window, the pale light of a newly-risen harvest moon touched everything with silver.

Dinah pushed away a strand of hair with her forearm and leaned back. She felt weary, and dispirited still, and the

327

sudden thought of Frank lying so cold in his grave beneath that same moonlight reawakened the sadness of recent weeks.

Something pressed against her skirts, rousing her from her melancholy thoughts. She looked down to find the mongrel bitch beside her, alerted by the distant sound of bolts on the passage door being shot home for the night.

"Locking up time, is it, Jess?" She bent to stroke the smooth head. "Come on, then. Let's put you out."

Even then, she lingered a while longer, staring out through the window into the silvered darkness, until the dog's wet nose nudging at her hand finally stirred her to go through to the kitchen.

Her mother looked up as she came in.

"Well, you've lost him for good this time."

Dinah walked to the other end of the room without making any response, and opened the garden door.

"Did you hear me?"

"I heard you."

Wearily she turned back towards the table where the other was busy trimming and refilling the oil lamps.

"Aren't you interested at all?"

"In what, Mam? What you going on about? I'm dead tired. Can't it wait till morning?"

Mrs Flynn pushed a lamp across the table. "Here, see to this 'un." A rag followed. "John Jackson was in here tonight."

"Jackson the foreman? What brought him by?"

"He had to go to the village to collect Farmer Bashford. Seems they had a bit of a feast after the parson's funeral and Mr Bashford had to be there. Of course." She sniffed. "Staying on all hours. Right in the middle o' harvesting, an' all. Jackson weren't too pleased."

"Why? He's farm foreman. He gets paid to manage by hisself."

Her mother looked at her knowingly. "He'll *need* to manage by hisself now. Till the farm gets a new owner. There, thought that'd open your eyes! Jackson told me in his own words not half an hour since."

"Mr Bashford's leaving?"

"That's what he said. 'Right out o' the blue,' he told me

'Never gi' us so much as a word he were thinking of selling up.'"

Dinah frowned but said nothing, concentrating on trimming the lamp wick.

"Don't you fret about losing your job, though, Jackson says. They'll keep on the dairy workers whoever it is buys Spring Hill."

"I'm not worried over that. The money Mr Bashford's give us for the horse'll see us comfortable for a bit."

"Aye, he did right by us there. You and me, our Dinah, and the little 'uns. We won't go wi'out, thanks be to him."

She set to cleaning the remaining lamp.

"It's all on account of her, you know," she went on after a while, a little bitterly.

"Who?"

"That Mrs Bates at the rectory. Now her husband's gone, I reckon Farmer Bashford will be after her to marry him."

Dinah seemed undisturbed by the idea. "Not yet, surely. She's only just been widowed."

"I don't mean yet awhile. But you mark my words. She'll be Mrs George Bashford come this time next year."

Molly Flynn watched her daughter replace the tall glass chimney, waiting for some response.

Dinah remained silent.

"Well?"

"Well what, Mam?" The younger woman's voice took on an edge of impatience.

"Are you going to let him slip away out o' your grasp?"

"Oh—don't start on that again! You've been talking about me an' Mr Bashford these past months till I'm wearied of it. You play your cards right, my girl, an' he'll be after you to ved him, mark my words if he don't.'" She imitated her mother cruelly. "There was never nothing atween us to let go, can't you understand that yet?"

"He's always been good to you, always seen you was all right. Look at the stuff he let you have when our Belle was born."

"That's just his way. He'd gi' you the clothes off his back if he thought you needed them."

329

"Have it your own way, then. You wasted your chance there, my girl. A bit of encouragement and civil kindness and your feet might've been under his table by now. Instead o' throwing yourself away on that blasted Frank Morgan—"

"You stop that, d'you hear! I'll not have you saying one word against Frank. Never again!"

Dinah gripped the edge of the table and glared across it at her mother. Two red spots of anger marked her cheekbones as she displayed something of the quick Flynn temper.

The other's lips tightened.

She turned away, and after a moment or two said peevishly, "Very well. Have it as you will. From this day on I'll not mention his name again. Not in this house."

Dinah lowered her head and continued her work in silence. Outside, the strident cry of a night bird sounded from the apple trees and was answered from further off by another.

"It's all over the village, the way he's been dancing attendance on her," Molly Flynn began again at length. "Hardly a day's passed that he hasn't been up at the rectory. Just as well for her good name them Pooles are there still. And now this news that he's to sell! Jackson said he told him he's buying a stud farm across the country at Arundel."

Her daughter looked up again, the momentary flash of anger over.

"So that's what he wanted wi' Frank's horse."

"That's it, clear enough. I've been wondering to messell what it was he were up to, buying the beast like that. Now we know."

"And he's getting rid o' Spring Hill on account o' Mrs Bates leaving the district?"

"That's what they're saying."

"But it's only Lewes she's removing to. Arundel's a fair old step on from there."

"What's a step? It'd hardly be right for them to shift off to the selfsame place together. And they can't be wed afore a year's up, now can they? If you want to know what I think he's been a-doing some mighty fast work, has Mr Bashford. There's three things all fallen out nicely for him. Her a widow

330

woman. A place just far enough off to start afresh. And a good stallion none o' the local dealers would touch wi' a ten-foot pole. Come next harvest, he'll have built hisself a good trade wi' that horse. Everything sorted and settled and a home a-waiting. That's the time he'll be back in Lewes after her, you see if I'm not right."

Dinah stood her lamp to one side of the table and began folding the paper protecting the surface from oil spills.

"Well, I wish him good fortune. Her an' all. She deserves some happiness, poor woman. She had little enough being married to that husband of her'n, God knows. Mr Bashford's had a regard for her ever since she come here in the spring."

She paused, reflecting. Then gave a faint smile. "And to think it were me as first brought them together."

"*You* did?"

"Aye. Don't you recall, they'd hardly a stick o' furniture at the rectory when they first come, and I said to him as how they could mebbe buy some of his'n that he'd got stored? Him going over to see her, that's how they started."

Mrs Flynn shook her head and gave a sigh of resignation.

"Well, it's too late to be going on about it now. What's done is done. There's no use in trying to change things once fate's set our course for us."

Then another thought struck her. She brightened a little.

"Don't you worry, though, our Dinah. We'll wait to see who it is buys Spring Hill. Mebbe you'll have better luck wi' *im*."

Before leaving Weatherfield on the morning following the funeral, Rachael Bates had gone to each of the cottages in the village to bid farewell to her late husband's parishioners.

It was not a task that took long. Though showing sympathy and some regret, they seemed already to have distanced themselves from her, and few expressed the sentiment of looking forward to seeing her about the village when she returned to visit Esmond's grave.

Her few personal things were already packed for the journey in the Underwood's carriage. Comfort and Charity Poole would lock up the rectory once Jack and Priam Adams had finished crating and loading the household effects, to bring into Lewes to the rooms in Flood Street.

Now it was time to leave.

She took her last walk along the brick path between the rosemary bushes and late-blooming flowers and paused at the gate to look back at the house. She remembered the hopes she had cherished when they first came to Weatherfield; her prayers that the difficulties of her short marriage would be eased now that she and Esmond had a home of their own at last, and privacy from constant supervision.

She had hoped, and prayed, in vain. Charming though the house itself was, she had not found happiness within its walls.

She raised her eyes and glanced up at the window of the bedroom above the porch, half-obscured by the climbing rose whose heavy scent had filled the room all summer. For the rest of her life, she would never smell that scent again without remembering her husband's face on the last night she had seen him alive.

"Rachael!"

Effie Underwood's voice calling from the carriage at the edge of the green reminded her that they were waiting to depart. She turned away and crossed the lane.

"I'd like to walk by myself as far as the crossways. Would you mind? It isn't far, and I won't take long."

"Of course we don't mind. Do we, Ralph? The little walk will do you good. We'll go ahead and wait for you."

Rachael stood alone, watching the carriage and its pair of matched horses move smartly away until they had disappeared from sight on the bend beyond the village.

Then she began to follow on foot, and within a short time had left Weatherfield behind her.

The late September morning was cool and overcast, the first faint chill of coming winter in the air. At the field verges the bracken was starting to die, green fronds withering into sunset colours of yellow-orange and red.

Rachael walked steadily on. She welcomed this chance to be alone, the lane deserted, everything quiet except for the distant sounds of sheep on the hill pastures and the twitter of hedge sparrows.

332

She paused once to look back over the countryside towards the village, then went on again, slower now that the lane had grown steeper.

Someone was standing beside a field gate in the shadow of the high hedge which at this point rose on either side to form a concealing border running for a mile or so uphill to the crossways.

Seeing him there, Rachael hesitated. Then, as the figure moved forward, she recognised who it was and went on towards him, smiling.

"I couldn't stay away. I had to see you one last time before you went," George Bashford said, falling into step beside her.

"And I hoped you'd be here. Have you waited long?"

He offered his arm and she took it at once, experiencing again that warmth and security his presence seemed to bring.

"Not very long. Your friends drove by just now, and I thought for a moment you'd changed your mind about going with them when I didn't see you there in the carriage."

"I decided to walk."

"Yes. Mrs Underwood said you were coming on by yourself."

They continued along the lane without speaking for a time, content merely to be in each other's company.

Then Bashford said, "It was around here I first set eyes on you. D'you recall? The signpost had been shifted and your carrier didn't know which road to take."

"Yes, I remember."

"I'll visit you in Lewes. If I may."

"Of course. I'll be pleased to see you."

"I'm leaving the district myself, you know."

Rachael's steps faltered. She stopped, and looked up into his face, frowning a little.

"*You* . . . leaving?"

"Aye. I'm selling Spring Hill and removing to the other side the county. I've bought a farm there. It's a place called Sonningale. D'you know it at all?"

She shook her head.

"It's a pleasant situation. I hope you'll visit it." His blue eyes were suddenly very serious. "You will come, won't you."

"Yes."

She hesitated a moment; then—"But why? Why are you going? You've never spoken of selling Spring Hill before. When did you decide this?"

"Oh, recently. It was time for a change, I thought."

A farm waggon passed them, going down to Weatherfield, the driver touching his whip to his hat-brim as they stood back beneath the overhanging branches to give him passage.

When the rumble of wheels had died, George Bashford turned Rachael towards him and cupped her chin in his hand, tilting her face up to his.

Quietly, he said, "I want you to promise me something. No, don't be alarmed. I remember what you said last time, about it being too soon. I'm not going to press you. But I have to know something before you go away."

"What is it?"

She touched his fingers lightly and he released her.

"While you're alone in Lewes you'll maybe meet somebody new . . . somebody who'll welcome your acquaintance. You're a lovely woman, Rachael. There's bound to be some man wanting to court you. What I mean is. . . perhaps in time you'll feel you'd like to wed again. If so, if you do, you'll tell me first, won't you? You won't go doing anything without letting me hear of it beforehand? I want you to promise."

She nodded

"It is important," he persisted. "I'll be in Lewes every so often, whenever I can, and I'll always leave word where to find me. Just don't you go marrying anybody behind my back while I'm away."

"I won't. I promise you, I won't," she said softly.

She had no certain proof as yet. It was too early for that. But she feared that Esmond Bates's assault had left its legacy within her womb. And if that were indeed so, she would need all the loving help this man was willing to give.

Such thoughts did not flow from the cold calculation of reason: Rachael had been drawn to George Bashford from the moment of their first meeting, and the subsequent course of their friendship had served to deepen and strengthen a

334

affection for him that could flower so easily into love. Something had been awakened within her by the stallion man's pursuit; for the first time in her life she had been made aware of the power of a man's sexuality and the strength of her own womanly desires. It would be no effort to give herself in body as well as heart to a man as physically attractive as this trustworthy young farmer.

Bashford reached inside his waistcoat pocket and withdrew a small silver coin. Across its face a deep notch had been scored. He bent it neatly so that the coin broke into two exact halves. One half he replaced in his pocket, the other he put into Rachael's hand, curling her fingers tightly around it.

"Here's a token to remind you. Keep it safe, and think of me."

"I will."

He pressed her hand and smiled.

And then, reluctantly, moved away and began to walk on with her towards the crossways.

ALSO AVAILABLE FROM CORONET

DOROTHY EDEN
☐ 20001 4 Millionaire's Daughter   £1.95
☐ 33961 6 An Important Family   £1.95

JILL DOWNIE
☐ 33028 7 Turn Of The Century   £2.50

ELIZABETH LYLE
☐ 28108 1 Cassy   £1.75

MARY ANN GIBBS
☐ 26793 3 The Tulip Tree   £1.25
☐ 25101 8 Young Lady Of Fashion   £1.25

ANNA GILBERT
☐ 26683 X The Leavetaking   £1.10
☐ 28644 X Flowers For Lilian   £1.25

All these books are available at your local bookshop or newsagent, or can be ordered direct from the publisher. Just tick the titles you want and fill in the form below.

Prices and availability subject to change without notice.

CORONET BOOKS, P.O. Box 11, Falmouth, Cornwall.

Please send cheque or postal order, and allow the following for postage and packing:

U.K. – 50p for one book, plus 20p for the second book, and 14p for each additional book ordered up to a £1.68 maximum.

B.F.P.O. and EIRE – 50p for the first book, plus 20p for the second book, and 14p per copy for the next 7 books, 8p per book thereafter.

OTHER OVERSEAS CUSTOMERS – 75p for the first book, plus 21p per copy for each additional book.

Name ....

Address..

....